W9-DIM-176

The Happy Island

DARWIN
TEILHET

The
Happy Island

WILLIAM SLOANE
ASSOCIATES, INC.
Publishers • New York

Copyright, 1950, by
DARWIN TEILHET

First Printing

Typography and format designed by
LEONARD W. BLIZARD

Manufactured in the United States of America

Published simultaneously in Canada
by George J. McLeod, Ltd. Toronto

Aloha to Byron Bryant of Capistrano Camp

The Happy Island

1

Parker Mattison woke from a dream in which E. P. Tothic refused to sign the contract. For a minute or so longer Park rested on his side of the wide bed, waiting for himself to become completely awake. The dream left him feeling oppressed although he was awake enough by now to realize there was no real reason for it. He was certain E. P. would sign a contract for five years instead of merely renewing one for another year. He asked himself why he should have had such a hell of a dream.

Even with the dream beginning to fade, the uneasiness was still in his mind—a sense of anxiety and urgency that he didn't wholly like. But when you're almost through your thirty-fourth year there's reason for some anxiety. By then you need a plan to secure yourself against the future. It's necessary to know where you'll be five years hence, and crowding forty. Already he was a little too far up the ladder to get back if he was clumsy or unlucky enough to fall off. Then he opened his eyes, and thought, nuts! By now he knew his way around too well to loosen his grasp of one rung when reaching for the next one up the ladder. He had no intention of falling. Moreover he had E. P. all set for signing. The contract was as good as in the bag. Why worry about it?

He gave his head a shake to clear the cobwebs and rolled it to the right to say good morning to Laina. But he discovered Laina was not beside him in bed. He hastily lifted his head, a shadow of anxiety troubling the candid, good-tempered face. She was not in the bedroom, either. Then, relieved, he heard the gurgle of water running out of the tub in the bathroom. Laina must have got up and gone in for her bath while he was still asleep. He sat up, completely awake. He didn't like having this involuntary start of apprehension remind him that a morning might someday come when Laina would be gone for good, and not just from her side of their wide bed. From habit he looked around him because ordinarily the act of waking was agreeable in this bedroom. He still thought it the most pleasant bedroom he had ever had.

On its walls hung the excellent reproductions of Gauguin's "Horsemen on the Shore" and "Parau Api" given to him seventeen months ago by Harry Kimball. Through the large windows of the bedroom he could see south across the Pacific to the blue horizon—although recently he had begun to think of how many thousands of miles he was from everything else. To the east he had a glimpse of the pale green towers of the new Kamehameha Hotel. Then came the curving beach of white imported sand, the red and brown roofs of the old town, the white steeple of the church built by the missionaries over a hundred years ago; and beyond, the dark green rise of cliffs which swept away to the other side of the island.

Although this morning he saw all that, it didn't delight him as it once had and he was not really aware of seeing it. Despite his nakedness he felt uncomfortably warm. He decided this was going to be another very warm morning. His head moved to the right; once more he was reminded of Laina's absence. It evidently had been even warmer last night than usual, for there was still a dampish impression of her body on the linen sheet. He saw that Laina's crushed pillow was even damper from her head and her heavy hair. The linen still held the scent of her sandalwood perfume and the lingering scent brought to his mind the thought of her thick, dark red hair. He called, "Caroline?" and paused. He had not meant it to sound as if he were impatient. "Hey, Caroline?" This time his voice had an inquiring note.

"Hey, Park," Laina's fresh voice answered from behind the closed bathroom door. "In a minute."

He looked left to the electric clock purring on the bed table. It was nine o'clock. This was Monday morning, he reminded himself. He was supposed to see Harry Kimball at eleven. He had promised to attend Harry's party tonight and to take Laina with him. What else? He recalled there was another meeting with E. P. Tothic and Dick Stewart at one o'clock this afternoon. At that, he glanced more sharply at the closed bathroom door.

Park had managed carefully with Laina. She knew that whenever he had a free day he liked to paint. It did not excite her curiosity when he went off in his Buick with his box of paints and collapsible easel. And the meetings with E. P. and Stewart were few, and were never scheduled on the same day of the week. At intervals two or three whole weeks were skipped because it was not wise to allow patterns of action to form which might attract curiosity or attention. To hide successfully what you were actually doing, Park learned during the war that ended in 1945, you deliberately appeared not to be hiding. You hid behind window glass, so to speak.

That was not a paradox, although Park didn't mind having it sound like one when he first discussed it with E. P. in Washington. E. P. was then a colonel with supplies at the Pentagon and not as happy helping to win the war as he'd expected to be. Park was a first lieutenant, Marines, assigned to the M. O. branch of the Office of Strategic Services. While he was not entirely happy in Washington, he was not frustrated. That was seven years ago when Park's outfit was still being called the Cloak and Dagger outfit. There had not yet been an executive order disbanding the Office of Strategic Services because the war was really ending this time. Now it made Park laugh whenever he read the newspapers and was reminded of the C.I.A. that had been set up to replace the O.S.S. of that middle world war already receding into history.

Laina opened the bathroom door and walked gracefully across the blue linoleum floor. With each step a slim wet foot left a double imprint where the arch lifted cleanly. She said, "I thought you were still asleep."

She stooped to kiss him lightly, holding her hair away from his face.

"I just woke up. Isn't this an unusually warm morning?"

"You always ask me that. You think every morning is unusually warm."

"Isn't this one?"

She shook her head, smiling.

From the bed Park watched her seat herself on the koa-wood bench before her dressing table. She combed her dark red hair and began to brush it with long even strokes and on mornings like this when he had the time Park enjoyed watching her. He thought perhaps she enjoyed having him watch her although she had never told him she did. She was a tall slender girl of twenty-two whose skin was like amber in color and smoothness. Park had never known such skin existed until he'd met Laina and after a bath it had an even fresher glow to it.

Presently, she glanced across at him. "I waited for you last night until I fell asleep," she said, stating a fact which might interest him, nothing more. She had lost almost all of the soft kanaka accent from her speech. "Why didn't you wake me?"

"It was too late, nearly three. I had to finish that painting for Harry Kimball. I promised to give it to him today."

"May I see it?"

"If you want to. It's in the front hall."

"Park—" She hesitated. "I know I'll like it."

"Don't let it worry you."

"I do try to like them, Park. But why do you have to paint those green and red skies?"

Park stretched like a big cat until all his ribs were in outline and then eased his feet to the floor. He stood up and glanced down at Laina. The green dressing gown was casually tied around her waist by a tasseled cord, the long V opening from the waist to her throat and shoulders. When he did not answer, she raised her eyes to him, flicked a glance down at herself and back to him, calmly closing the gap.

"Why do you?" she repeated.

There was a pause before he spoke. He had to recollect her question. Even after six months there were still times when he could not quite believe all this delight in her was possible.

"Harry Kimball seems to have found a few people who don't

object to skies of that color. The son-of-a-bitch has sold every painting I've given him so far. What do you think of that?"

"You never told me."

"I didn't know. I haven't seen Harry for a month. When I called him yesterday to say 'hello,' I learned the news. He sold that Pohaku Point landscape for seventy-five dollars to some woman from Denver. Then he sold that one I did of Ilohana Cove while you were bargaining with the Hinonis for their boat. Guess how much? One hundred and fifty dollars!"

She jumped up and flung her arms around him. "It's wonderful, Park!"

It was not wonderful but he didn't tell her so. She felt very desirable and yielding. His arms tightened. A sense of urgency flowed through him as if somehow Laina and he had started racing each other with rows and rows of hurdles lifting before them. Then he felt her hands resisting against his shoulders. She gave him a direct, almost vexed look and it was as if the race had not quite started after all. He was being called back for a fresh start. He took a deep breath.

Park said, "I'll have a quick bath."

"We can't this morning, Park. Yesterday I told you I'd made an appointment at the hairdressers'. Why do you think I waited for you last night? You never listen. I have to be in the city at the hairdressers' at eleven this morning."

"We've at least an hour. What's wrong with an hour?"

"Nothing's wrong with an hour when I haven't an appointment afterwards at the hairdressers'. It's this hair of mine. Why can't I have it cut short?"

"This new clipped seal style for women's hair won't last. Let's don't start talking right now about having your hair cut."

"All right," said Laina and paused, half rebelliously, before asking, "But suppose you had hair as heavy and long as mine? I have to put it up in pincurls after every time I go to bed with you and I'm not going to the hairdressers' this morning with my hair done up." Park remained silent, and after another pause Laina offered, "If we don't have to go to Mr. Kimball's party tonight, I'll call and cancel the appointment."

Park looked at the electric clock. He had promised Harry. . . .

"You say," she said.

"Harry's giving the shindig for me. He thinks it'll help sell my paintings."

"We'd better go," Laina said instantly and Park liked her very much right then.

She might have been angry about it but she wasn't. Her hair was still as soft and her skin was still as smooth but he had the sensation that she was taking herself off the race track and was helping him to take himself off it, too. She kissed him when he wasn't expecting it, as if she were a little sorry for him and a little sorry for herself; and she stepped back. Park felt that the morning suddenly had rocked forward, beginning to go on for them both.

"We could," said Park, "get home early tonight."

She looked at him. "Let's," she said. She appeared to put it entirely out of her mind until tonight. It was more difficult for him to put it out of his mind and he delayed leaving the bedroom, watching her go briskly to one of the built-in clothes closets of monkey-pod wood. She took a clean silk slip. Frowning a moment over a decision, she finally selected a cotton print frock with no sleeves. She glanced back at Park.

"May I use your Buick to go into the city? I don't like driving across the island in that old heap of mine; it doesn't go fast enough. Last week two fools from the hotel started out after me in one of the big Cads the hotel rents to tourists. They followed me clear to the city, honking their horn and trying to make me stop."

Park's eyes became very blue.

"Why didn't you tell me?"

"I did but you never listen. I wish the tourist agency would think of something besides palm trees and hula girls for their ads. Some tourists believe everything they read."

"Look," said Park, the good-tempered expression closing back over his face again. "Take my car any time. Any time." He opened the bathroom door. He stopped. "You know something?" he said, very easily. "On mornings like this I wonder why I put up with you."

"You won't have to many more weeks," she said, as easily as he had to her. "Then see how much you miss me."

In the bathrooom he noticed how scrupulously she'd cleaned the tub for him after her bath. He turned on the cold water faucet which delivered lukewarm water into the tub. He stepped on the scales. He'd lost another quarter of a pound. Losing another quarter of a pound wasn't enough to worry about.

Last week, he remembered, when they were dancing at the hotel Laina had said she liked him looking so lean. He remembered the orchestra had been playing an old tune and some of the words of the song ran through his head. He liked that song. It seemed to fit but he didn't know why. Park whistled a few notes softly to himself.

He made them laugh and he made them cry.
Oh, he was the cockeyed mayor of Kaunakakai.

He'd weighed a hundred and sixty when Laina and he had gone dancing together last week. It was a hundred and fifty-seven and three-quarters this morning. Before leaving New York in 1948 he'd weighed a hundred and seventy-six which wasn't being fat for his height but it certainly wasn't being lean. He ate enough. He ate three meals every day. It was the climate.

"Oh, he wore a lei and he wore a smile . . ."

It ran through Park's head. He'd wear a lei and he'd wear a smile. As long as you never worried about it and never let anything get you down you were all right.

He heard Laina call to him through the door, "Hey, Park. I'll squeeze a glass of orange juice for you."

He lowered himself into the tub. Yes, he'd miss her. He'd miss her too much if he allowed her to sail alone to the mainland. He'd think of something. She imagined a mainland that didn't exist. Her wish to escape the islands for good and live on the mainland had become an obsession. He remembered that moment in the bedroom when Laina had felt so fresh and desirable against him and the need between them had begun again to be urgent. But she hadn't been angry. She'd understood and was wanting to help, clearing away the track and calling off the race. It was all right. They could get home early tonight. "Let's," she'd said.

He wished he hadn't promised to go to Harry Kimball's party tonight. "I'd like to have you meet Parker Mattison," Harry would say. "He's doing some very good stuff, very good. Very modern. I don't say it's influenced by Gauguin. Don't misunderstand me. It's not Gauguin. Parker's struck out on his own. But there is an analogy if you begin to consider it. Gauguin broke away from business, too, you know. He did his very best stuff on South Sea subjects."

Oh, hell! Park reached for the soap and had it slip out of his hands.

Laina knocked.

Park said, "Have you got my orange juice?"

She came in, looking cool in the white sleeveless dress with the small blue circus prints on it. Around the wrist of the hand carrying a tall glass of orange juice he saw she was wearing the inexpensive silver charm bracelet he had bought her last April. She wore it nearly every day and it gave him a slight sense of guilt every time he became aware she was wearing it. He had paid fifteen dollars for it at the Chinese Bazaar when he easily could have afforded ten times that amount and it irked him because he could not run the risk of arousing her suspicions by buying her the more costly presents he would like to give her.

"What service this morning," said Park. "Thank you."

She had squeezed the orange juice for him, he knew, because she was really very pleased to have him lend her his car. But she said, "Park, if you need it you don't have to give it to me today."

"Any time," Park said. "Your Chevy's good enough for me. All I'm doing today is seeing Harry Kimball and driving south toward Koko Point for a try at another landscape. I'm safe. Nobody's going to honk at me."

She looked down at his straight hairy legs in the soapy water and looked away. She said, "Don't be too certain. The beach is covered with mainland schoolteachers in for another of those three-day holiday tours of the island. You keep the hell away from the beach and young schoolteachers, Mr. Mattison." She regarded her face in the mirror. "Park—we *will* come home early tonight?"

"Yes," said Park. He placed the empty glass on the wet tile floor and reached for her wrist with the charm bracelet around it. "Some day I'll buy you one of gold."

She smiled. "I'd rather have this one, please— Oh, damn, Park!" She vigorously pulled free. "Your arm's dripping water on my skirt." The five charms tinkled faintly as she dabbed at her skirt with a hand towel.

"That was clumsy of me."

"It's all right. It won't spot."

He heard the faint tinkling again as she rubbed her skirt with the towel. He had bought the first charm for two dollars when he bought the bracelet. It was a typewritter no bigger than her thumbnail to commemorate the time before she met him when she was a secretary at the plant. The miniature pineapple was a token of their first picnic together when they had gone to Pohaku Point. The third charm was a tiny enameled can supposed to represent a can of beans. It was for their first dinner together in this house. She had never pretended she knew very much about cooking. The automobile of pewter from the Japanese novelty store on the beach was for her Chevy. The fifth charm was a tiny boat of silver. He had spent five dollars for it last month to celebrate the successful conclusion to a protracted and often furious period of bargaining with the head of a kanaka family of fisherfolk who lived on the little cove at the foot of Pua Cliff below the house. For the sum of eight dollars a month old man Hinoni had finally agreed to give Laina the use of his small sailing boat on week ends, providing she furnished the gasoline for its inboard motor and did not demand its use if the Hinonis' larger and newer boat was laid up for repairs or scraping.

Park remarked thoughtfully, "Those five little gadgets look

lost on your bracelet, at that. How would you like an easel or a paint palette or something of that sort if I can find it? You ought to have something to remind you that you're going around with a painter."

"That," she said hesitantly, "might be fun to have." She smoothed her hair before the mirror, not looking at him.

"Caroline—" he said. "Caroline, have you had a chance to see the new landscape I finished last night?"

"Only just for a minute . . . Park, please don't forget and want to stay late tonight. Harry Kimball likes to talk so much. The people he invites always expect you to know they're important."

"Well, don't let it worry you."

The direct eyes now sighted at him. "It doesn't worry me. I've had people stare at me before I met you."

"I mean my new landscape," explained Park. "I do well enough. You don't have to like what I paint."

"Park—" She hesitated. "Park, can I tell you something?"

"Sure. Why not?"

"You never listen."

"You'd be surprised about me."

"Park, I'm no brain. I never said I was a brain. But we had a class in modern art at the university. At least I didn't flunk it. I don't care how much Harry Kimball praises your paintings. I don't believe what he says. He's working you around to give you a hotfoot."

"Harry won't give me a hotfoot."

"He'll give it to anybody he has a chance to. Don't you ever read that newspaper he publishes? I don't trust him."

"Basically," said Park from the tub, "you're a royalist but you don't know it. You wish the islands were still an independent nation under their own king."

"That's not true. I want Hawaii to be the next state as much as anyone else but I don't like someone like Harry Kimball printing in nearly every issue that he's on our side for statehood even if most of us are only part white or not even white at all. It's not fair of him to claim all the old white families out here are either openly or secretly against statehood because they're afraid of being dominated by Orientals. He hates the old ka-maaina families because he isn't one of them and he's jealous—"

"Well, hey, Caroline?"

She bit at her lower lip. "I just don't trust him."

"You don't understand him. Even if he's made a good thing out of his gallery, he's still a newspaperman at heart. He likes print-ing gossip because the tourists like reading gossip. He likes to agitate. The old families living here are stuffy and he likes giving them a poke every now and then."

"Park, you know those two Gauguin reproductions Harry Kimball gave you? Ever since you hung them in the bedroom, I've looked and looked at them."

"What's wrong with them? Even if you don't like them, they're fine paintings."

"I *do* like them. I'm trying to tell you. I got used to them. But I look and look at what you do and can't get used to yours. They scare me."

Park laughed. "They can't be that bad, Laina."

"I wish you wouldn't call me 'Laina.' "

It was short for "Kealalaina"—"Caroline" in Hawaiian. He knew she disliked anything which reminded her she was hapa-haole, or of mixed blood. He wished she were not so sensitive about it.

"Caroline, I'm sorry. But I think of you as 'Laina' because it's a very pretty name for a girl I can't ever seem to have enough of."

She gave him a rather vexed look, although something starry and pleased showed in her eyes. But she was too concerned about him to allow his frankness to distract her from what she wanted to say to him this morning.

"Look at how you're spending your money, Park. You don't even have time to paint much. Why don't you go back to New York and get a regular job again?"

"Why worry about it? Am I worrying about it?"

"I just don't like seeing a nice guy get himself torn apart."

"Well, thanks," Park said. "I like to know you think I'm a nice guy."

"What did you think I thought you were?" asked Laina.

"Park, I know where you'll be in another year. You'll be flat on the beach. You'll be like other nice guys who came here to paint or write a book or do something important. You'll end by hating yourself if you stay. You know you're spending too much. You wouldn't try to pick up extra jobs if you weren't. I'm costing you too much, too. Last April you should have told me when I thought you were another mainlander with a wad of money in your pockets. I thought you were helping Mr. Kirsch as a favor. How could I guess you did his bookkeeping because you needed the money?"

Park tried to pick up the bar of soap between his feet and failed. Then he said, "Look. Let's don't get started talking about something we don't have to worry about."

"You always say that. You never want to talk about anything that bothers you. You won't even talk about letting me shear off some of this damn hair."

"Well, all right," said Park. "If you want to cut off some of your hair, go to it. If your hairdresser takes off more than an inch tell him I'm going to come into his shop and bust all his windows. Now as a personal favor would you like to wash my back before you beat it?"

"You go to hell," said Laina. "You never do listen to me."

"All right. I'll go to hell," said Park. "Before I go why don't you think about going to New York with me in December? I might have to go back there for a few weeks."

"I'm not going anywhere with you. The first of November I'm sailing alone for the mainland. Last April I told you I wanted to. I wouldn't have come to live with you if I hadn't wanted to get away from this island as quickly as I could. I didn't hide it from you. I'm going to forget you the minute I get aboard ship. The next man after you who sleeps with me will be my husband or I'm sleeping alone the rest of my life. I won't go to bed with him until he is my husband. I hope he'll be somebody who has a ranch in Oregon and raises sheep and cattle and likes kids, lots of them. If he ever suggests taking a trip to Hawaii I'll kill him."

"You've got it all worked out," said Park gently, "haven't you?"

"I had it all worked out a long time before I met you but I was interrupted." She opened the door. "Park, if you need your car I can be back around two."

"No, yours is fine for me. If you'll feel better, I'll try to paint a blue sky for you this afternoon instead of a green sky. How's that?"

"Give it up," said Laina. "Get away like I'm getting away before it's too late. We will come home early from Mr. Kimball's, won't we?"

"Yes," said Park. "The earlier the better. Look, Caroline. It takes time learning to paint. I'm not broke. I like keeping my hand in as an accountant. I can think about painting while I'm earning extra money. Half of painting is thinking of what you want to paint. Now, don't worry. Think about going to New York with me in December, will you? Who wants to live in Oregon? You won't like it there. Won't you miss me?"

The smoky gray eyes studied him.

"Yes," she said slowly. "Last April I didn't know it would be like this. You get a job in a plantation office as typist at thirty-five or forty a week. You're glad to see the last of your boss when you walk out."

"Good God!" said Park, violently.

"Good God," she said, mocking him. "Didn't I tell you in April?"

"Do you think you're punching a time clock?" Park asked. "In the bedroom a little while ago, was that what you were doing with me?"

"That's the trouble," she said. "I didn't know it would be like this. But I'm going to Oregon and never coming back. I'm going to forget you."

And then Park slid down into the bath water and he thought it was going to be all right. "Caroline," he said, as easy as he'd ever said her name, "I'd like you to do something for me today. I'd like you to buy yourself that trick new evening dress you were looking at last week."

"All right," said Laina with not much of a pause. Her face smoothed out. "I will buy it. Thank you, Park. I'll wear it tonight. You can see Harry Kimball's mob of mainlanders staring at me and at you, too. You can watch them thinking, 'I thought those native girls came cheaper.' See how you like it, Park."

She shut the door.

A little later Park heard his Buick roll over the gravel driveway and turn into Hibiscus Road which wound downward to connect with the main highway passing north and south across the narrow middle section of the island. He caught himself whistling that rather silly and cheerful tune. He stopped abruptly. But the refrain still ran through his head:

> *He made them laugh and he made them cry.*
> *Oh, he was the cockeyed mayor of Kaunakakai.*

2

After shaving, Park dressed rapidly in the bedroom which Laina had already put in order before leaving, the bed made, everything picked up. He knew Laina still did not like to leave the bedroom to the Japanese woman who came to attend to the house. He selected the gray sharkskin coat and trousers which the Chinese tailor in the city had made for him last summer, his mind considering what had to be done at the one o'clock meeting with E. P. and Dick Stewart. It was nine thirty-five; about now the company transport ought to be landing at Makakina airfield, after bringing E. P. in from Honolulu. E. P. used the regular airlines to Honolulu but it was quicker to have the company plane meet him and take him for the hour's flight to the Makakina airfield than to try to make connections with the island airline which packed the tourists back and forth.

E. P. had been on the mainland for two weeks, which was about as long as he ever remained over there before jumping back here at least for a few days before rushing off again. Last year about this time E. P. had been nearly eighteen solid days over there which was almost a record, since the war. He had returned with a new wife which had been a surprise. Park hoped E. P. wouldn't spring any really big surprise at this afternoon's meeting.

Park would give E. P. the general progress summaries. E. P. would want all the details on how the Bull Amani-Nogusi prize fight was shaping up. That was a particular and special and delicate project in which E. P. was very much interested. And Park wanted to bring up the new contract. He thought that ought to be about enough for today's meeting. E. P. would be in good spirits for he was always in good spirits upon returning to the island; but he wouldn't ask for too many details.

When Park pulled the belt tight he discovered his trousers hung slightly loose around the middle. The trousers had fitted snugly three months ago. He guessed it was the climate. Out here you never woke up hungry. You'd think you'd be hungry but you weren't. Why not begin having two breakfasts every morning, one here at the house as well as a second on the strip or, if he drove to the city, at Jake's?

In the kitchen he set the pot on the electric stove to have hot water for instant coffee, dropped two slices of bread in the toaster, and found some Kauai cheese in the refrigerator. The cheese smelled all right. While waiting for the water to boil he became restless. He started thinking about the landscape he'd completed last night. He had to give it to Harry Kimball this morning and he wanted Harry to approve of it. He passed through the warm humid air to the front hallway.

In the front hallway he stared reflectively at the greens and reds and purples of the scene he had painted from memory. The Sunday before, Laina and he had gone sailing from Ilohana Cove in her rented boat and from the sea that afternoon Park had sighted toward the red and green lines of the Pua cliff towering above the shore. He hadn't intended to stay up until three o'clock last night to finish the canvas and as he looked at it he was disappointed because he did not seem to have caught the feeling of last Sunday afternoon when looking toward the shore. Under the slanting rays of the late afternoon sun it had seemed to him he was seeing something which struggled upward from unimaginable depths and lay there panting on the horizon, blood streaking its scaly greenness.

It was not so much a visual impression but an erupting sensation of an almost physical nature which remained in his mind. After Laina and he returned tonight from Harry Kimball's party, perhaps he ought to explain to her that he was not trying to paint anything you actually saw with your eyes. It had been a mistake to tell her they were landscapes. She was being too literal. He would explain that his paintings were—well, what were they? His mind brought him up sharply as if for an instant a gulf had split open before his feet.

In 1948 he'd given three entire days to wandering around the New York Museum of Modern Art. The more he saw of the paintings hung there the more he was convinced that those boys couldn't paint either. Nobody really knew what modern art was. If a painter repeated often enough and loud enough that he was painting important modern works of art he was bound to find a few people who believed him. If he kept his head and was intelligent or lucky about it and could get other voices to join in with his he began to acquire a name for himself. Well, why not? Park had discussed it with E. P. who was staying in New York at the time to help shape up the project. E. P. had laughed. It had delighted him.

"Why not?" E. P. had said in 1948. "At least nobody can prove you aren't a painter. Once you get on the island see if you can frame an introduction to Harry Kimball. He's started an art gallery. Watch out for him, though. He's a troublemaker. He hasn't any use for some of us with a solid stake in the island. He'd pull us all down if he had the chance."

The reason Harry Kimball wasn't a solid citizen and couldn't ever be a solid citizen on any island or anywhere was because Harry was one of those men who liked to be needling solid citizens and giving them a hotfoot as often as he had a chance. It was a game with Harry.

It pleased Harry beyond measure when a wealthy mainland woman walked into his galleries with every intention of purchasing a five-dollar piece of Cantonese soapstone carving and walked out, rather breathless, after paying two or three hundred dollars for a modern koa-wood chair or ivory necklace carved like gardenia buds. Harry was pugnacious, too. If you did something no one else liked then Harry was inclined to step over to your side and give you a hand. It was a game, basically, Harry against all the solid citizens; and Park knew how it was when a man was having it basically a game.

Although it began as another detail of the job to do, because

E. P. had suggested working in with Harry, it had passed that stage. Harry had gone to bat for Park. He'd sold Park's landscapes. Without completely realizing it, now Park very much wanted Harry to like these landscapes.

But it never started as a game for Laina.

"Oh, he wore a lei and he wore a smile . . ."

Park stopped himself. When he started whistling to himself in the empty house the tune didn't seem quite as lively and carefree as he remembered it to be. In the kitchen again, Park drank two cups of instant coffee which tasted exactly like instant coffee. He inserted a slice of yellow Kauai cheese between the two slices of toast and forced himself to begin eating.

He turned on the radio. A voice said ". . . is Station HOK, at the top of your dial, the voice of the happiest island in Hawaii and the happiest place to live in all the world. Here on this happy island all of us are happy because we have work to do and time to do it and are paid well to do it. And we are happy because we have time to play and time to be with our families. And we are happy because this is a happy island for our children, with security for them and for us, good schools, good churches, good laws fair and equal for all, high and low. It is ten o'clock. Temperature this morning, eighty-seven degrees. And now, Station HOK, at the top of your dial, brings you another happy quarter hour of hillbilly fiddling and songs by our own Hawaiian hillbilly, Gus Maru—"

Park turned off the radio.

You couldn't be subtle. It was always important to remember you couldn't be subtle when you had to pound an idea or a concept into the collective mind of any large mass of people. You had to lay it on with a shovel and keep laying it on with more shovels. It was a basic principle. At the meetings Dick Stewart was always asking, "Can't we be more subtle, Mattison?" Of course, Stewart was wrong. If you said anything often enough and loud enough you could count upon at least ninety per cent of the people who heard you believing what you said. That was statistics. The Germans had done even better before and during and almost until the end of the war. The very last year of the war with Germany, Park remembered, when German nerves were badly frayed Dr. Goebbels had started pounding home, "German people are courteous people to each other." By God even then it began to take effect.

Sometimes Park got tired of hearing about the happy island. Even if he had originally suggested to E. P. that everyone living on this island must be rapidly conditioned into believing it was the happiest island of all the Hawaiian islands and a paradise on earth—even so, sometimes he got goddamn tired of hearing it said.

He finished his sandwich. He went down the back steps to the garage with the air brushing against him like tepid yellow wine, the tumbled edge of the cliff not more than a hundred feet beyond the back wall of the cottage; there was that effect of space, of emptiness, with the huge thrust of ocean pushing upward into the middle distance and slowly, so very slowly, melting out into the blue sky. Once Park had liked to sight out toward the sea.

He got into Laina's Chevy and started the engine. She hadn't bought the Chevy on the happy island. It had come with her from Honolulu, on the middle island, although originally she came from Kauai, the island to the farthest north in the archipelago. Before agreeing to live with him Laina wanted Park to know how she had happened to buy the Chevy. At sixteen when she was in high school on Kauai she became engaged to marry Ben Subie, a third-generation Japanese boy who was home on two weeks' leave before sailing off to war with the other volunteers of Japanese ancestry. Laina did not know that Ben had signed his five thousand dollars' war insurance over to her until the government notified her after Ben was killed in Italy.

After graduating from high school, instead of finding herself a job as typist in one of the Kauai plantation offices, or marrying, as she could have easily, she headed for Honolulu. She enrolled in the University of Hawaii. Five thousand dollars seemed a great deal of money to her then. She paid twelve hundred for a secondhand Chevy because she'd always wanted to own a car. It was six years old when she bought it in 1946. Even secondhand cars came high that year. By now it had the look to it of an old man who has lost all his teeth and goes around with his shirt tails hanging out.

Its brakes were not at all good so Park shoved the gear into low while driving down Hibiscus Road. He had always liked this road and still did. For one thing, you didn't have so much of that effect of space and emptiness which you had when you stood near the edge of the cliff and looked straight out over the Pacific. You had the island under your feet—or, rather, under the wheels of the Chevy. Off to the northeast you could see a volcano lifting high into the sky and a volcano always looked very solid and here to stay even if sometimes it fooled you.

As Park descended halfway down Hibiscus Road the mountains to his left sloped away rapidly and ceased screening the great pineapple fields covering the wide central valley. Then, lower, the land tilted to meet him. The view below had a greenness and lushness which reminded Park of those technicolor travelog features he used to have to sit through in New York before the war. Even the towers of the new Kamehameha Hotel had an emerald greenness which was not quite real. Once, by accident, Park got that identical shade of greenness on one of his canvases. He tried afterward to duplicate the shade but he failed. He still thought, though, he might get it again if he continued trying.

At one end of the beach was the Kamehameha Hotel, like a vast cake with turrets and towers of pistachio sugar icing, all surrounded by palms, by flowers, and by four acres of a blue-green grass so smooth and even that tourists might think the lawn was lathered and shaved twice a day. From the hotel for half a mile south curved the shining white expanse of beach. Immediately after the war this beach had been blasted out of coral rock, and smoothed and graded and filled in with barge-loads of white sand. A new four-lane highway followed along the half-mile curve of beach. Through the center ran a bridle path, lined on both sides with royal palms. At intersections were massed gardens of flowers around high graceful steel pillars. Hidden among the lights at the top of the pillars were cone-shaped loud-speakers which filled the air with soft music except for the hours of the public concerts at the pavilion. The highway suddenly narrowed half a mile south of the hotel and vanished as if embarrassed into the hot, fetid town which had been a native village when the missionaries erected their church in 1831.

On the other side of the highway had sprung up a long row of bright new shops and stores with tourist courts and smaller hotels and beach houses behind them. Kimball's Galleries was midway on the strip, not far from the new Kamehameha Cinema and the pavillion. Park ran the Chevy along the curb and stopped. He reached into the back seat for the canvas which he had packed carefully, for the oils were still wet.

Sometimes when he did not see Harry Kimball for a while he was apt to forget how much he enjoyed being with Harry. As Park entered Kimball's Galleries he wondered if he were not getting into a frame of mind where he was slightly apprehensive because he half expected people to change if he did not see them for an interval. Even if he had not seen Harry for a month he had telephoned him yesterday. And Harry had sounded very cordial, asking to have more paintings as quickly as possible. A hundred and fifty dollars was a sizable pot of money, too, for someone to pay for any painting. Harry was very good at selling, though. It made Park wonder uneasily if he had improved as much as all that or if Harry might not merely have found another gullible mainland woman. It would be Harry's idea of a hell of a joke. It would be even more of a joke for Harry if privately he believed Park's paintings were as rotten as Park indifferently had assumed them to be.

Park remembered Laina's warning this morning. As he approached the receptionist's desk, the canvas under his arm, despite himself he felt a faint tightening of anxiety.

But the Chinese-Hawaiian girl at the reception desk said Mr. Kimball was not in. She had tawny-colored hair and when she smiled there was something about her which reminded him a little of Laina. Mr. Kimball had been unexpectedly called to the printers. He had left word, if Mr. Mattison came, that he was sorry and he would see Mr. Mattison tonight.

"Well, fine," said Park. "Can I leave this for him? It's another canvas I've done."

The girl said she would give it to Mr. Kimball this afternoon when he returned. When she smiled she did have something about her that put him in mind of Laina although she did not have Laina's looks.

Now that Harry was not in, Park was disappointed. He had counted on having a quick lunch with him before driving to Koko Point for his meeting with E. P. Tothic and Dick Stewart. He remembered he had promised himself to eat more regularly than he had been eating, and he stopped in at one of the small drug stores on a side street for a counter lunch instead of going to the Grass Shack drug store which was usually crowded with tourists at this time.

He had two glasses of milk and an egg sandwich but it was a mistake to have ordered the egg sandwich because it tasted greasy. When he got up from the stool, a small but distinctly uncomfortable sensation ran up his throat from the pit of his stomach as if he had swallowed a very thin ribbon of brass. He stopped at the prescription desk and said he wanted something to settle his stomach. The man behind the desk was an old man, a white man, a "haole" the word was if you were a tourist and were collecting a few to prove you had been here longer than those who came in on yesterday's plane from Honolulu. He had that yellowness which somehow haoles acquired after they lost that rich distinctive tan of the first five or six months and had lived here a decade or more.

"What's wrong with your stomach? I can't give you something unless I know what's wrong with it, can I?"

The old man looked like a nice old gent but he looked tired and he did not look very successful and he should, Park thought, spray his place more regularly unless he liked having so many flies.

"It might be the egg sandwich."

"That might be, too," said the old man. "I don't get fresh eggs like I used to get 'em. Since the Grass Shack and the hotel and all the new places have been built, all the good eggs go there."

Park looked at his watch. E. P. always expected you to be on the dot for one of his meetings.

"I can give you some antacid pills. Those Japs working at the Grass Shack would charge you five dollars and tell you the pills'd cure your stomach and hives, too, if you got hives. I say if a man's stomach goes wrong he ought to see a doctor."

Park had no intention of seeing a doctor. He felt fine. He was losing a little weight but he knew why. It was the climate and not eating enough. Besides, if he went to a doctor there was always the possibility of E. P. hearing of it. When E. P. paid big money to a man he expected that man to stay well and earn his fees.

Park said, "I'll have a try at your antacid pills."

"My brother-in-law's a doctor. He don't live more than two blocks from here. I could give you his name."

Park said he would drop in again if ever he felt like seeing a doctor, stopped long enough at the counter to swallow one of the pills with a glass of water, looked again at his watch, and walked into the yellow shimmer of sunlight toward Laina's Chevy.

It was an easy run south from the glitter of the strip, over the Niuniu Cliff Road, fifteen miles to Koko Point where E. P. had established himself since the war in the old Tothic summer house. On the way, after thinking about it, Park pulled the bottle of pills from his pocket and tossed it out of the car. While he was concerned about the meeting, he felt very strong and fit, otherwise. He had no particular taste at all in his mouth. You could begin imagining something was wrong with you, he thought, and before you knew it you were taking time off to see doctors. He could see Laina giving him one of those direct inquiring looks, too, if she ever saw him swallowing pills. When you got to be forty, or forty-five and fifty, it was time to start taking pills and realizing you were beginning to get along. He still had time ahead of him before that.

He turned off onto the Koko Point private road, following around the curve, until presently he saw the old brown shingled roof among the silver-green hau trees with the tall coconut palms in the background. He stopped Laina's disreputable heap behind E. P.'s unobtrusive 1948 Pontiac sedan. Ahead of the sedan Park noticed Dick Stewart's new Cadillac convertible. It was a nice job. It must have cost close to six thousand dollars, Park estimated.

Stewart was a dumb bastard for spending so much more every year than he earned. One of these days Stewart ought to think about asking E. P. for a contract, a lifetime contract at that, even if the company executives weren't ever supposed to think of contracts for themselves. The workers had a union contract and it came up for renegotiation the first of December, which was one reason Park had to do something in a hurry about Bull Amani, the president of the federated island unions. At least the workers had a certain permanence and continuity guaranteed, but for some reason the top brass of management never thought of trying to grab contracts for themselves. Perhaps, Park thought, the top brass believed contracts were undignified.

He got out of the Chevy and walked around the corner of the house and E. P. was up there, waiting, on the wide cool veranda. "It's good to see you, Park," cawed E. P., and ran down to meet him, returning with him to the veranda—the "lanai" it was really called out here. E. P. was forty-six and there was nothing of a boy about him in appearance until his sallow shoe-box head became illuminated, all of it, not merely the face, with the delight only a boy can have when welcoming one of the other boys in the gang.

"How are you anyway?" asked the cheerful voice. "We don't see enough of each other, Park. Can't we do something about it?"

"We're seeing about the maximum of each other, E. P.," Park said. "Much more and it wouldn't be safe."

E. P. seemed to scrutinize him a moment longer than necessary. "You're looking very fit. Our climate must agree with you."

"It's a fine climate," said Park.

"A man can't do a bang-up job unless he keeps fit."

"Well, I seem to manage to keep fit so far."

"I want you to keep managing to keep fit," said E. P. "You'll find in this climate it won't hurt to take a month off every year or so. If a man keeps fit and runs his work right, he can take a month off."

"I've got that in mind, too, E. P."

"You get a month in New York and look around," E. P. said. "We'll see a few shows together. I'll manage to get back when you're there. It'll be like old times."

"I thought of taking time out in December."

"That's a good month," E. P. said. "I'll meet you in New York in December. We'll go to a show together. Now, how have you been, otherwise?"

"I've been thinking about the new contract," Park said.

"Put it in the contract," E. P. said. "Fix it for you to take a month off. Give Meaker and Kirsch a month off, too, if possible. I don't want you boys to get stale."

"We won't get stale," Park said. "I'd like to talk to you about the contract if you've got time."

"It's a detail today, Park. Let it go for later."

"I was thinking you might not be here when it comes up for signing next month."

"If I'm not, I'll have someone available to go over it with you and sign it. Now don't worry about it."

"I'm not worrying about it, E. P. Stewart's O.K. I don't mind going over details with him when you aren't available but I'd like very much to take up the contract with you direct. I've been thinking we ought to have a five-year deal, E. P., not year to year."

And then there was a moment when E. P. didn't reply and Park wondered if all the continuity and permanence were going to smash right here, now.

He'd thought of Dick Stewart as being a dumb bastard for spending more than he earned as if every year more money was certain to come in. By God, thought Park, I'm a dumber bastard; and he felt a flow of agony.

Park had charged twenty-five thousand for his services the first year; thirty-five thousand, the second. After giving Sally a lump settlement of twenty thousand, paying her Reno expenses, paying taxes, and paying Laina's and his expenses here, Park had about eight thousand dollars in the bank to show for two years of excruciatingly difficult work. Park knew Stewart received a salary of seventy-five thousand a year as vice-president in charge of industrial and public relations. In the five-year contract Park planned to ask for a large enough budget to pay himself seventy-five thousand every year for five years. At the end of the time he hoped to have a quarter of a million dollar nest egg.

He waited for E. P. to say something and felt sweat spring out on his forehead. All E. P. had to do right now was say, "No. I don't like to have a boy ask for too much. I'm terminating the whole project." Goodbye, Laina. Goodbye, everything. When you were nearly thirty-five and fell off the ladder you seldom if ever got up there again.

Park heard E. P. saying, "Yes, we've a big investment in your project. I don't see why some of us shouldn't consider protecting it for longer than a year at a time. You've passed the experimental stage. But leave that for later. Come on inside. I've a surprise for you."

"Goddamn it, E. P., you didn't get married again?"

E. P. was still laughing when Park and he entered the long old-fashioned living room. All Park's faculties became instantly alert and wary for he saw a new man, someone he didn't know, waiting there along with Dick Stewart.

Stewart said dully, "Hello, Mattison," and it looked to Park as if perhaps Stewart had been surprised by the new man, too.

E. P. said, "Park, I want you to meet Buddy Morton. Don't call him Wilfred or he won't like you and I want you two boys to start liking each other. Buddy, this is Park Mattison."

"How do you do, Mr. Morton," Park said.

Mr. Morton smiled shyly. He was the only one there dressed in a business suit and it was one of those hard-finished English herringbone worsteds which helped to add to the picture of the new boy which Park was hastily trying to assemble in his mind. Park was willing to bet Mr. Morton's double-breasted business suit had been tailored by a London tailor. He decided Mr. Morton wasn't more than his own age, perhaps a year or so younger, although it was always hard to estimate the age of these small, neat, frail-looking men with thin, rather shy faces and thin, neatly trimmed mouse-colored hair.

Mr. Morton was still silent and still smiling shyly while E. P. explained about him. Buddy had joined the outfit last year, as comptroller for the sales department in Los Angeles. Buddy had flown out with E. P. last night to stay here permanently. Buddy did such a bang-up job in Los Angeles that he was going to be jumped to vice-president and general manager of the outfit or some such title, E. P. hadn't decided precisely yet. It was a detail to come later.

E. P. looked around and noticed Dick Stewart standing there. He said kindly, "Dickie's been doing such a bang-up job in his department we're giving him a boost, too. He's being promoted to a very necessary and diplomatic assignment. Some of us have decided we should have a serious look at the competition we're receiving from Mexican pineapples. Dickie's going to be the boy to investigate what they're doing in Mexico and tell us whether to start lobbying in Washington against Mexican grown and canned pineapple. Meanwhile," he added, as if it were another detail, "Buddy can put Dickie's department under his wing."

There it was.

Park saw the Chinese whose name was Billy coming across the worn grass mats with a wide tray upon which were bottles, glasses, a syphon, and a miniature silver tub filled with ice cubes. Park still felt the sense of shock. The new boy was in. Dick Stewart was no longer one of the boys whether he knew it yet or not.

"Congratulations, Mr. Stewart," Park said. "This is a surprise to me."

Stewart lurched a little. "Even if a fellow likes to know he's appreciated and comes up for promotion, I've been explaining to Pip that after a fellow's been in charge of a department like I have and has made a team out of it—"

"Bourbon, Dickie?" asked E. P., still kindly. "Here you are. What the doctor ordered for you, Dickie. You haven't looked too fit these past few days."

It seemed to Park that something like apprehension passed over the man's ruddy face. But Stewart said stoutly, "I don't see how you can say that. I've been working hard but I've been keeping myself fit. A fellow like me knows how to take care of himself."

Without knowing exactly why, Park began to feel sorry for Dick Stewart. He was glad he had thrown away those goddamn antacid pills. E. P. sent the Chinese into the kitchen. He said for everyone to sit down and get acquainted with each other. Park had Scotch. "Not too much," Park said. E. P. said Park always said that; E. P. was still in that fine high mood of his which came to him when he surprised some of his boys. Mr. Morton said he would have Scotch, too, please; and not too much for him, either. Stewart had a second bourbon.

"Not too much soda this time, Pip."

"Coming up, Dickie."

During the war E. P. 's sister had taken a suite at the Shoreham for a few weeks. Ruth Tothic was the first person whom Park had heard calling E. P. "Pip," which evidently was a nickname from boyhood. After coming to the island Park discovered Dick Stewart was also one of the small intimate group who said "Pip" when they spoke to the boss. It was a small thing and not important but Park hoped when the five-year contract was signed that possibly E. P. would ask him to say "Pip" too as an indication all the doors were opened.

E. P. measured a half-jigger of pear brandy for himself. Until Park met E. P. he hadn't known pear brandy existed. It was made in England from a particular variety of pear and was called perry brandy. Strangely enough, it wasn't at all expensive. Not half as expensive as the thirty-year-old Scotch and seven-year-old bourbon E. P. served his boys.

E. P. tipped back in his chair and looked at Park and looked at Mr. Morton and said, "Park, you know how I operate. I leave the details for later. On the plane coming over I told Buddy we had a surprise for him out here. I told him I had a boy I wanted him to meet and get down to cases with as soon as possible. My thought this afternoon is for us to forget your progress reports and any details, Park. My thought is for me to try roughly to sketch out to Buddy how we are set to hold this island in the right frame of mind. Then I thought you might briefly—"

"Pip—" said Stewart from the sofa as if it were still just between E. P. and himself, "Pip, I don't want you to think I don't appreciate being promoted. Almost any other time I'd give my right arm to have the chance of going to Mexico and doing a bang-up job for you down there. But I know my wife doesn't like Mexico. We happened to take a trip there before the war. I just happened to think after I've built up such a swell team of fellows in my department, like Mattison here, it just occurred to me even if it's such a swell chance for me it wouldn't be fair exactly to them if I—"

"Dickie," said E. P., as kindly as ever, "I thought it was all decided."

Park looked across at Mr. Morton. It seemed to him that Mr. Morton wasn't very robust to play on E. P.'s strong first team. It seemed to him that Mr. Morton looked sorry for Dick Stewart and it surprised Park. Usually a new boy wasn't at all sorry to be grabbing an old boy's position. Park was beginning to think he couldn't have asked for anyone better than Mr. Morton to come along right now when the new contract was to be signed but he didn't think Mr. Morton was apt to last very long in the gang. Mr. Morton smiled shyly at Park and held out a flat silver case filled with denicotinized cigarettes.

"Not right now, thanks, Mr. Morton."

Mr. Morton showed he wanted to come more than halfway. "Everyone calls me 'Buddy,' Park. You might as well start in now and save time."

Park decided he was going to like this new boy. He hoped the new boy would last at least until the contract was signed. Then even if the new boy was chopped off and E. P. brought someone else in, whoever else came in couldn't louse up anything but details for five years.

3

Park remembered once E. P. had said if you wanted to give a man a quick picture of what was being done it was a mistake to rush it at first and try to shove the picture against the man's nose. Even if you did not have much time, you had the man step back a little. You let him see the frame as well as the picture. Afterwards you could begin rushing it. And Park thought it was exactly what E. P. was doing now with Buddy Morton.

First, E. P. had Buddy step back to see the frame. The Tothic Estate, Ltd., was an entailed estate which had managed during the past hundred years to buy up most of the productive land on this island after the original Tothic, who arrived as a trader in the old days, received extensive grants from King Kamehameha III. In 1910, E. P.'s father, Enders Prentice Tothic, Sr., had foreseen a day coming when Hawaiian sugar could not be grown and shipped three thousand miles to a market to compete successfully with mainland beet sugar or Louisiana sugar. The island existed on a one-crop economy and it depended on the price the mainland paid for sugar whether everyone was lean or fat.

That was why Pater, as E. P. called his father, gambled ten million dollars on the future of pineapple. He established Paradise Products, Ltd., made himself the head of the new company, and turned the island upside down during a few furious years while ripping up sugar-cane fields, planting pineapple, and rebuilding the old Tothic raw sugar refinery into a canning plant. It was during the first world war, E. P. explained to Buddy, while stationed in New York as a captain of supplies, that he realized Pater Tothic was missing a bang-up sales bet. Originally, the pineapple packed on the island was simply shipped to brokers on the mainland who wholesaled it under a variety of trade labels.

In 1919, E. P. persuaded his father to change all that. A mainland sales and marketing organization was established as a subsidiary of Paradise Products, Ltd., E. P. was put in as president of Paradise Sales and Distributing Company, and he told Buddy, "If I do say so, I made a bang-up going concern out of it. I started advertising the Paradise brand of pineapple. We've a trade name and reputation worth millions, with warehouses throughout the country, an experienced sales outfit, and since the war we're successfully expanding into other tropical fruits under our labels, both canned and quick-frozen."

But back in 1910 when Pater Tothic organized Paradise Products, Ltd., to grow and can island pineapple, no one could have foreseen that the abnormal amount of water required for the highly mechanized production of pineapple, as well as sugar on the single remaining sugar-cane plantation at Iki, would gradually lower water tables until a shortage might be anticipated to curtail production. A few years before the last war, old Pater Tothic engaged a firm of ground-water geologists to survey the island. For a few minutes Park listened to E. P. telling Buddy about deposits of ground water stored in what were called dike complexes of the Niuniu and Pua ranges. Park had heard E. P. discuss the water supply before. Evidently out here in the middle of the Pacific additional water was found by boring or tunneling for it, just as deposits of oil were discovered on the mainland.

To keep the details for later, E. P. was telling Buddy, the ground-water experts estimated in 1939 that by 1960 the water tables of the island would be drained so dangerously low that the island's huge pumping and irrigation systems would bring forth brackish water. They had recommended tunnels into the Niuniu and Pua ranges to obtain new sources of water.

However, E. P.'s father decided not to go along with the geologists' recommendations to tunnel into the ranges for more water. He decided to turn the island upside down as he had done before, back in 1910, and to build a six-mile beach, with luxury hotels and a fashionable shopping district, to attract tourist money and to grow tourist dollars if the island could no longer grow pineapple and sugar dollars in security. E. P. said he thought his father was influenced in making this decision by his father's being afraid Hawaii would soon be admitted as the forty-ninth state.

Because there were far more island-born of Japanese descent than of any other race, old Pater Tothic feared that those of Japanese blood would take control and establish a communistic-socialistic government as soon as the Hawaiian archipelago became a state. Pater Tothic decided to make this island a Nassau of the Pacific, and gradually to get out of pineapple and sugar cane and so doing to force the unneeded Japanese and Filipino workers and their families by economic pressures either to other islands or to ship them to the mainland on pineapple barges where they could be American citizens and vote as they damned pleased.

E. P. smiled as if he knew this was the fantastic scheme of an old man and both Buddy and Park could smile, too, if they liked. Park glanced at Buddy. The new boy was not smiling at all but was listening seriously and soberly. E. P. was saying the war had interrupted his father's plans. However, at the close of the war, in 1945, Pater Tothic took out a bond issue of twenty-five millions, and with that and half that amount of capital from the Tothic Estate he had started constructing a six-mile beach on the Halepule side.

In 1947 the old man had a stroke and E. P. was brought back from the mainland. Pater Tothic signed over legal control of the estate to his son; and E. P. found himself in charge, appointing himself president of Paradise Products, Ltd. He held up his thin brown hand, explaining, "This is all between us here. This information I'm giving you is just for the gang here, Buddy."

"Fair enough," said Buddy.

E. P. was smiling again. Although his father had been alarmed about the lack of water, you could see that E. P. was not in the least alarmed. E. P. had lived long enough on the mainland to know you could trust the recommendations of bang-up ground-water experts. He stopped work on the beach after a mile of beach and highway had been constructed, along with much of the shopping district and the single hotel. He started digging in June, 1947, for new water and by early 1948 the geologists' recommendations proved to be correct. E. P. was not worried about water failing the island. Instead, E. P. had expanded production to meet the demand for Paradise fruit created by the big subsidiary Paradise Sales and Distributing Company on the mainland. The problem was not sales; that was not the problem at all, although E. P. admitted there were a few soft spots in the mainland sales organization which needed ironing out as soon as he could find time, again, to get on the tails of those boys over there. He hoped very soon to have the company firm enough financially to buy land in Mexico to start producing pineapples there, nearer the market. No, everything considered, the mainland sales organization was doing a bang-up job. It was taking business away from the Honolulu packing companies and hurting the independents on the other islands.

Park knew all this and sat back in his chair and found himself wishing he were with Laina and as soon as he realized what he was wishing he had a slight sense of shock to know how his mind was straying. He leaned forward. He wanted that five-year contract from E. P. Afterward, when he had the contract, Park could allow his mind to stray toward Laina when E. P. gave a general picture with its frame in one of these meetings. He perceived E. P. had finished giving Buddy the frame of the picture. E. P. spoke of the situation here.

"My father took out that twenty-five million issue in 1945 and it comes due next year. We depleted our capital by building the beach and the hotel and it cost us money when I used more capital to get us water and build new pumping plants. But we were not dangerously pressed, Buddy. I think you can see when I took control in 1947 my decision was wise. I had in mind the danger to us of labor unrest and unreasonable demands and the next year I brought the M. O. task force here to help us teach labor how to behave itself. But we were caught by the big strike last year which tied up business all over the archipelago. That strike last year cost this island, alone, more than fifty million dollars, if you include pay losses to small merchants as well as major losses to Paradise Products. Even a quickie strike could amount to three or four millions before you could say your prayers, Buddy."

Buddy smiled faintly. "I guess I'd better not say very long prayers."

"The Tothics have been here since 1846," E. P. said, "and we mean to hold this island. If we don't have another strike, we'll pay off the bond issue when it comes due next year. If we should have a second ruinous strike, we'd be forced to sell our mainland distributing company to one of the big Honolulu factors. That would put us out of business as far as being tropical fruit canners goes. The Honolulu packing corporations consider our island a marginal pineapple producer, anyway. Most of the Honolulu corporations are thinking of all of Hawaii as marginal both for pineapple and sugar cane and are thinking of Mexico or the Philippines as future producing bases."

"Whew," said Buddy. "I knew it was serious but I didn't know it was quite that bad."

"We'd end up in the hotel or tourist business on a reduced scale," E. P. said and it made Park sit up because until now Park had not quite realized it was that serious, either. If Paradise Products had to sell its mainland distributing subsidiary to pay off the bond issue next year, and the cannery were closed down by the big Honolulu interests, what, Park thought with a tightening of anxiety, happened to all his plans for five sweet years? You didn't need an M. O. task force on the island if you had only tourists here and no appreciable number of sugar and pineapple workers who needed to be taught how to behave themselves.

"But it's not going to be that serious, Buddy," E. P. said.

He was convinced he had first-rate insurance for building up a fat surplus which would allow the bond issue to be paid off when it came due and allow an even greater expansion of the company than in the past. The island's population was being taught how to behave itself. That was what Parker Mattison was brought here to do.

Today's population consisted, in the main, of second- and third-generation descendants of Japanese and Filipinos, with a sprinkling of Koreans and Chinese, imported originally to work in the cane fields. The first generation had a docile frame of mind. The thought of striking would have terrified the field hands. They worked hard, did what they were told to do, believed conditions were much better for them here than anywhere else; and all in all everyone on the island had a happy life in those days.

"We want to get back to that happy life," E. P. told Buddy. "Our people have lost their docile frame of mind. They're rebellious and all the islands of Hawaii will become marginal producers of pineapple and cane if that frame of mind isn't stopped. Park and his gang are succeeding on this island in establishing a docile frame of mind and eventually there's no reason why we can't expand to other islands or possibly to Mexico with the same program."

Park did not listen so intently while E. P. told Buddy of meeting Park in Washington during the last war. Two or three times Park glanced to his left at Dick Stewart sitting at the far end of the couch, staring into space. Park did not believe Stewart was listening to anything. E. P. said it had interested him greatly to find Park was one of the Office of Strategic Services men. During the war the O. S. S. boys had had the task of combating enemy frames of mind. It was psychological warfare. Task forces for Morale Operations were established in all parts of the world. Park, E. P. told Buddy, had been section chief of M. O. E., which was Morale Operations for the Far East.

After the war, E. P. said, the notion still stuck in his head that this island needed a task force for Morale Operations to change the population's rebellious frame of mind back to the old docile happier frame. When Pater Tothic had his stroke and E. P. had the problem of production as well as mainland sales dumped into his lap he thought of Park whom he had been using since the war on the mainland. In 1948, E. P. and Park went to Maine together during the month of August. By the end of the month they had drawn a blueprint for an island M. O. task force with an intelligence section and a combat section.

"An M. O. task force of any size at all, Buddy," E. P. explained, "has to have ears and eyes and a brain and it has to have fists. You'll agree to that concept, won't you?"

"I'm new here," Buddy said. "If you told me that volcano we circled this morning was made of green cheese, I'd have to agree with you at least until somebody proved you were wrong."

E. P. bent his sallow oblong head to one side like a boxer riding a quick punch. He gave Park a glance and laughed. He liked to have his boys come back at him. It pleased Park, too, to have Buddy Morton reveal a little spunk. Park hoped Buddy could last at least through October.

Then E. P. began explaining how Park had engaged Dr. Lewis Kirsch to head the intelligence section of the M. O. task force out here. Lew Kirsch was one of the best psychological statisticians in the field and had worked for Park before the war. Lew Kirsch arrived in October, 1948, six months before Park came. Park stayed in New York to tie up securely all the strings at that end. Kirsch ostensibly came to the island on a research assignment from the Pan-Pacific Sociological Institute. It was a real institute, E. P. said. It was small and almost moribund but it existed, and it now received a grant of twenty-five hundred dollars every year to prevent it from folding up before Kirsch finished his report.

Kirsch rented three office rooms in the old Priest Building. He had a staff of twenty girls who did the interviewing and three secretaries. Buddy could walk in any day. Everything was in the open. Kirsch ran frequent public-opinion polls to collect data and material for his exhaustive sociological investigations. At the same time he was glad to run surveys for the local newspapers, broadcasting stations, or merchants for really very low fees. If the local Ford dealer wished to find out why more people preferred Chevrolets than Fords, Dr. Kirsch was pleased to have the chance to help and the charge was hardly ever more than fifty or a hundred dollars. The local merchants were delighted with Dr. Kirsch and he spoke frequently at the Chamber of Commerce, Kiwanis, and Rotary Club Meetings . . .

"Just a minute," Buddy said. "If I say anything wrong, tell me. But I lost all my belief in public-opinion polls when I lost a thousand bucks betting on Dewey in 1948."

Park thought this was about where he came in. He looked at E. P. for a signal and got one. He said, "Buddy, I've been waiting for that."

Buddy smiled. "I hate losing money when I bet."

"I won five hundred dollars by betting fifty dollars on Truman, Buddy. A month before the election Lew Kirsch wrote me to bet on Truman. I was too chickenhearted to bet more than fifty dollars. Lew stuck his head out. A week before the election he went on record with both the two dailies that the national polls were out of line. He thought Truman might have slightly better than an even chance. Furthermore, Buddy, Lew's polls here have more intensive samples. Our interviewers are trained to obtain an analytical pattern—"

"Just skip all details, Park," asked E. P.

"I get too interested, myself," Park said. "Sorry. Buddy, we have two sorts of intelligence, white—or open—and black which comes from underground or concealed—"

"That's detail, Park," said E. P.

"No, wait," Buddy said. "This interests me. For example, Park, what's one source of black intelligence?"

"During the war the best sources of black intelligence came from French and Belgian whorehouses. On the island here we've lined up about seven houses we can trust. Mind you, neither Kirsch nor Meaker nor myself lets our hands show—"

"Let's leave all details for later," E. P. said. "All right, Lieutenant?"

"Yes, sir, Colonel." Park remembered to smile back.

Buddy said in a peculiar voice, "I didn't know red-light districts were allowed on the island."

E. P. said, "Don't worry about details, Buddy. Have another?" He held out the bottle of Scotch. Buddy shook his head. He offered it to Park who held up his glass to show it was half full. Park didn't really care much for Scotch. What he really liked were chocolate ice cream sodas although Laina was the only person on the island to whom he'd confessed that fact.

Dick Stewart lurched forward on the couch. "Pip, I know I'm not being subtle about it but it just happened to occur to me—"

"Here, Dickie," said E. P. kindly. "Just what the doctor ordered." He poured bourbon into Stewart's empty glass. "You didn't think I was going to forget you, Dickie?"

It seemed to Park that Dick Stewart had beeen forgotten by everyone in the room. He saw Buddy's head also turn toward Stewart.

"Pip—" said Stewart rather thickly.

"Just what the doctor ordered, Dickie. Drink it up. Let's keep moving, Park."

Park said to Buddy Morton, "That about takes care of Lew Kirsch's part of the task force. The second section is our combat section under Byron Meaker. Meaker actually engages with the enemy, Buddy. He—"

"Just a minute. What enemy? This island's part of the United States, isn't it? Aren't all the people here legal citizens? Just who is the enemy?"

Park wanted Buddy Morton to hang on at least until the end of this month. Park hoped Buddy would hang on after the end of the month because he looked like a nice guy. Buddy was not the type to louse up anybody. But Park's contract came up for renewal the first of November and, although Park didn't like to think of E. P. deliberately having the M. O. contract come up one month before Paradise Products met on December first for wage renegotiations with the unions, that was how it was.

Park wanted to give Buddy a warning for Christ's sake to remember they were not holding Episcopalian services at present. He got to his feet.

"Buddy," he said, "I'll tell you who the enemy is. Anyone on this island is our enemy, by God, who doesn't get in line with thinking the way E. P. decides the line's going to be." Park sat down.

Perhaps there was an instant of dead silence before Buddy said, "Fair enough. I asked for it and got it."

"Well, you're still new here."

E. P. laughed delightedly. "Tell Buddy about Meaker and the combat section."

"By Meaker's about our age, Buddy," Park said and paused a moment to give Buddy a chance to say what his age was. But Buddy didn't pick it up. Park continued, "He was one of the youngest city editors in Cleveland before the war, got sent to Hawaii as a public relations officer in 1942, started learning Japanese, and our outfit in Washington got hold of him. He worked with me for a year. When E. P. and I first started discussing this project, I thought of By Meaker right away. He came to the island in December, 1948, and also had to establish himself openly. He's done O.K. for himself, too. He established a one-man advertising and publicity office and hustled himself enough regular jobs to be convincing. He runs publicity for the local tourist bureau, the chamber of commerce, and the mayor pays him a retainer of twenty-five bucks a month."

"The hell he does!" E. P. said. "I didn't know that. You never told me that before, Park."

"It's a detail, Colonel," Park said. "I was leaving that for later."

Even Buddy laughed. E. P. was in fine spirits this afternoon. Dick Stewart jerked up his big handsome head to see what they were all having so much fun about.

"We've got both white and black action in By Meaker's section," Park explained before Dick Stewart tried to take the floor. "Think of it this way, Buddy. Both Kirsch and Meaker are in the open all the time. They have no visible connection with the plant or plantations. Last year we needed a more co-operative mayor. Kirsch's opinion polls kept us informed in one direction. Meaker took over the publicity for Tony Flavola who owns one of the city's big grocery stores. We got Flavola in as mayor and neither Flavola nor anyone else knows it was because it was planned that way—" His face held a derisive look. "I don't say I'm using very original expressions."

Buddy said, "You're being very helpful, Park. Pour it on."

"Let me see. Meaker has supervision of all advertising and publicity issued openly, white or otherwise—black—on the island, by the packing plant and the three Tothic plantations. Our hand doesn't show. The employees don't know about us and it would be damn near a catastrophe if they did. But we've got Howie Wright tipped away in Mr. Stewart's department who used to work with me in Washington during the war. I'll tell you about him later. Howie is part Japanese. He heads the plant's local advertising and publicity and channels on through to Meaker.

"One of the first things we discovered was that all the Tothic interests were spending forty thousand a year buying advertising space in the island newspapers and radio. Well, forty thousand dollars is quite a sizable fist to start off against newspapers and radio on this island. We've got two newspapers in the city. We did have three but last year we managed to kill off the Japanese language bi-weekly—"

"Let's leave—"

"Yes, sir, Colonel." Park didn't forget to smile.

"Proceed according to plan, Lieutenant." E. P. smiled back.

Buddy looked at them both. "What's this Colonel-Lieutenant deal between you two?"

"Why, Buddy," said E. P. "Have you forgotten there was a war? Park and I were in the war together."

It made Park wonder what Buddy did during the war because Buddy's lips clenched together. Evidently Buddy hadn't worn a uniform or marched against the enemy.

"That leaves two newspapers in the city," Park said hastily. "We've a little weekly scandal sheet published on the strip by Harry Kimball. We had our I. S. girls make a reader check and found Harry's sheet was read by fewer than six hundred people, most of them tourists. I like Harry Kimball personally but he's a barking dog. Don't worry about him. O. K. Three newspapers. We've two small broadcasting stations. One has an outstanding loan with the First National and the Tothic Estate

· 40 ·

controls the bank. So *we're* in control there. The second station is a ten-watter, on daytime only. Last year we gave Meaker four thousand dollars from our contingency fund to buy a controlling interest. We've applied to increase the power to fifty thousand watts."

Buddy swallowed. "Did you say *fifty thousand*—"

"Fifty thousand," said Park. "When you want something, why not ask big? We've hired one of the best Washington lobbyists to help push it through. We probably won't get fifty thousand watts. We'll get at least ten thousand watts which is enough to cover all the Hawaiian islands if E. P. decides one of these days it's not enough to have political control of merely this island."

E. P. said, "Some of us like to look beyond our noses, Buddy."

"That about covers all white combat action except for the *Happy Island News*. I told you we had Howard Wright in Mr. Stewart's department. Howie is editor of the *Happy Island News* which Meaker and I got underway through Howie as soon as I arrived here a year and a half ago. It's issued once a week for the employees of the packing plant and plantations and their families. It's a company house organ, yes; but I doubt if you've ever seen a house organ like ours. It looks like a New York tabloid. We run Japanese and Filipino inserts inside. It's white combat and black, too. It has a lot of misdirection. For one thing we slam hell out of E. P. and the top brass in every issue—"

"In a nice way," E. P. said.

"In a nice way, Colonel," smiled Park. "If any employee has a beef we not only run it but whoop and holler. Furthermore, it has a circulation of twenty-two thousand."

"God Almighty!" said Buddy.

"There are eighteen movie houses on the island. If they don't run the films we want them to run we turn on the heat with the newspapers and the broadcasting stations. Our fist keeps building up. Seventeen of the movie houses, including those on the plantations, stay in line. We've had trouble with one owned by a tough little gent at the south of the island but we—"

"That's another detail," E. P. said rather sharply.

"O. K.," Park said. "That about does it, Buddy, as far as white combat M. O. We don't use black pressures unless it's absolutely necessary."

Buddy swallowed. "May I ask a question?"

"Ask anything. E. P.'s given you the ticket. Anything."

"This tough little gent you said owns a movie which won't— stay in line? Are you planning to use those black combat tactics on him?"

"Buddy," E. P. said, "let's leave the details."

Buddy paused a moment. Then he said, "I had no idea. I had no idea at all."

Park said gently, "We have to be careful with terror tactics, Buddy. Usually we keep away from anything too rough. It can cut two ways."

Buddy said, "Whew!" and took a long breath. He smiled sheepishly at E. P. "I thought from what you hinted while we were over the Pacific last night, you had brought in a dozen or so strikebreakers."

"We try to prevent strikes from happening," Park said. "We try to prevent trouble. We try to make any strike harder to happen by conditioning everyone here into believing this is the happy island." Park's crisply pleasant voice changed slightly. "How fortunate you are to live on this happy island. It has the best working conditions in the world. Here, you're as good as your boss. Every day over your radio you're reminded how happy this island is. At work in the plant or in the fields you hear music and songs and now and then a few pleasant words from our loudspeaker towers to remind you this is the favored land. Or, go to the movies. See for yourself. You'll see news-reel shots of the outside world which show you the terror and misery and wretchedness away from this happy island. We have," Park explained, the warm persuasive quality fading from his voice, "standing orders with the two biggest newsreel serv-ices to airmail us rush all shots of accidents and catastrophies of any kind taking place on the mainland. If you can read, it's in your newspapers. Most of the island population doesn't much like to read. For them we have the *Happy Island News* with comic strips and photographs and words of one syllable. Well, yes, I suppose we scare the hell out of them now and then. Why not? The rest of the world *is* a rotten insecure place to live in compared to what some of us—" he flicked a quick one at E. P. "—think this island can be. As long as there are no more strikes. 'Go to work every day and do your job and you and your family will be happy' is what we want to get over."

E. P. said, "Amen. Boys, we'll have drinks on that."

Dick Stewart had gone to sleep. His big handsome head was not as handsome as it used to be lying at an awkward angle on the arm of the sofa. E. P. said, "Poor Dickie," and adjusted the head to a more comfortable position. Then the three of them had drinks and it was nearly four o'clock.

They walked out on the veranda which Park had to remember to call a lanai. The acres of cool mowed grass ran down to the white brick wall with the blue-green sea on beyond. Park still believed it was the most beautiful view in the world.

Buddy said, "You haven't explained where you come in." The air was warm and humid but it had a fragrance to it and Buddy's face got a little color back into it.

"I think I explain easy enough," said Park. "I connect through to E. P., as I'm doing today. For example, Kirsch has completed another opinion poll which ordinarily I'd give a quick report on this afternoon. This is headquarters. Staff decisions are reached here with E. P. and Mr. Stewart—or you, now, replacing Mr. Stewart. I liaison down from top brass. Howie Wright, the fourth boy with us—the editor of the *Happy Island News*—he liaisons upward from the employees. His job is the tough one. Wright, Kirsch, Meaker, and myself are the only four on our side who know we have an M. O. task force. E. P., Mr. Stewart, and now you, Buddy, you're the only three on your side. I connect through to Kirsch because, as I told you, I used to be a C.P.A. I spend two to three days a week, openly, presumably working as Kirsch's bookkeeper." Park hesitated. It was unreasonable to be embarrassed but he was, slightly. "My excuse for being here—" He saw E. P. grinning. "Hell. I paint pictures."

E. P. laughed.

Buddy protested, "Even if I am new here—"

"It's not a joke," E. P. said. "Harry Kimball believes Park is a second Paul Gauguin. Harry actually has sold all of Park's paintings."

Park said, "There are some advantages, Buddy. A painter is like a postman. If you take a paint box and easel along with you, nobody's going to ask what you're doing."

Buddy said, "It's slightly cockeyed but it makes sense."

Park thought of that old tune which had started going through his head earlier this morning.

E. P. was asking, "Does that wind up everything, Park? You can give Buddy details later and you can show him how the task force actually gets down to specific problems."

"Do you want a report on how the prize fight is shaping up?" said Park.

"What prize fight?" Buddy asked E. P.

"We're shaping around to get rid of a hot chestnut with our local Federation of Independent Unions. I can explain that to you later." E. P. asked Park, "Is everything under control?"

"I think so, E. P."

E. P. gave him a sharp, questioning look.

Park said, "Bull Amani wanted to back out early this week. He's tied in again now so he can't back out."

"I'm counting on you, Park. Don't let me down."

Then E. P. looked at his watch and Park began wondering if Laina had returned from the city by now. He hoped she hadn't asked the hairdresser to cut off any of her hair. He heard E. P. telling Buddy they could call it a day. Would Buddy wake up Dickie Stewart? E. P. was having dinner with Dickie and Cecelia Stewart tonight but he'd drive Buddy to the Kamehameha Hotel to say hello again to Buddy's wife and kids and be sure they realized they hadn't been entirely forgotten.

Buddy shook hands with Park. "You've been very helpful to a newcomer. Thank you, Park. If you're not doing anything before dinner, why don't you have a cocktail with Mrs. Morton and myself at the Kamehameha? I'd like to hear more of the actual operations."

E. P. laid his hand on Buddy's shoulder. "You don't see any-thing of Park outside of this house except where it's safe. You heard him say Howie Wright had the tough job of being an undercover man at the plant? What do you think might happen to Park, here, some dark night if any of our local labor leaders learned he was working for us? Have you thought of that?"

Evidently Buddy had not thought of that until this moment. Park did not like to think of it, either, because when you went into an undercover job you were paid not to be found out. You could plan for everything else. You could constantly plan to insure you would not be found out, but if once you were found out it became a contingency beyond any planning. About all you could hope for was time to run for it and that was not really any sort of a plan about which you ever spoke, even privately to yourself. Park became even more embarrassed and told Buddy, "E. P. likes to be dramatic. I won't be found out."

"I hope not for all of us concerned," Buddy said and it seemed to Park that Buddy had said it rather oddly. He watched Buddy go into the house.

E. P. was saying that Buddy was a very smart sweet boy. He hoped Buddy and Park would get along together. He didn't want anything to prevent the two from being a bang-up team.

"I can't think of anything," Park said.

"I can't spend as much time on the island as I've been spending since Pater had his stroke, Park. We've got water and our new pumping plant and the tourists are bringing us a good secondary revenue from the beach. Now I plan to be on the mainland for longer intervals than before, to jack up our sales company over there into making next year a bang-up sales year. We'll need every cent we can scrape together by the first quarter next year to meet our bond issue in March. I'm counting on Buddy to be my chief of staff here to watch production and I'm counting on you and your boys to get that troublemaker, Amani, out of the picture and to go on the long-range program of establishing a docile frame of mind to prevent future troublemakers from getting into the picture."

"We'll need another twelve months at least," Park said, "before we'll have a docile frame established that firmly. We're getting there but it takes time."

"Yes, but I think you're past the experimental stage."

"I know we are. That's why," Park said, "I'd like to propose a five-year contract when our project's up for signing again the first of the month."

"Don't forget. You promised to get the right boy in as president of the unions and Amani out, while you were establishing a docile frame of mind."

Park had a feeling the floor had slightly tilted under him.

"Look, E. P.," he said. "You aren't making it a condition we get Bull Amani out if we're to have a five-year contract?"

E. P. placed his brown hand on Park's shoulder. "You were going to have Amani out by August and the right boy in. Now, it's October."

"Goddamn it, E. P. You know how we have to work. We can't work direct. We'll get Amani next Tuesday night."

"You know how I operate. Just get the right boy in as president of the unions, and I'll sign a five-year contract for your gang. If Bull Amani's off the island or out of the picture Tuesday, and the right boy's taken over the unions, I'll sign the contract before I leave for Los Angeles. How's that?"

Park had a gust of resentment against E. P. Dick Stewart had loused it up over a year ago with Bull Amani. It was Stewart's mistake. It was not fair of E. P. to lay down a condition which made the five-year contract contingent upon saving Paradise Products from a new strike because of Stewart's error. Immediately, Park realized he was not being fair to E. P. Everything would go if there was a second strike following the big one last year which had crippled the company financially.

"I couldn't ask for better, E. P.," he said.

The thin brown hand gave Park's shoulder an affectionate shake. "I know I can count on you. Now, between us and the gatepost, Dickie Stewart didn't work out. He wasn't what the doctor ordered. I have a hunch Buddy Morton's going to be what I needed. Make a friend of him. Don't allow anything to interfere with making a friend of him. That's an order, Lieutenant."

"It'll be an easy order to follow, Colonel—"

Park did not have time to smile back because Buddy had come to the door, calling anxiously, "Pip, can you come here, please?"

Park was surprised, hearing Buddy call the boss "Pip." It meant somehow that Buddy had got himself admitted to the inner circle and Park wondered when all that had happened. Park could not believe in a year's time Buddy had become familiar enough to call E. P. by his intimate nickname. For all of being an old shoe and one of the gang, E. P. was a slow man to select intimate personal friends.

"Pip—" Buddy was asking more urgently, "how do we get a doctor in a hurry? Dick Stewart won't wake up. His face has turned a peculiar color and he seems to have trouble breathing!"

4

It was almost seven when he returned. When he glanced into the bedroom he saw Laina had already laid out his white linen jacket, white linen trousers, a fresh shirt, a yellow cotton tie, white silk socks, and white knitted cotton shorts on the bed. It wasn't late because Harry Kimball wouldn't expect them until between eight-thirty and nine but there wasn't too much time, either.

Laina said, "How did it go?"

Park showed her the empty white frame of canvas.

"I'm sorry," she said.

He thought she was, too. She believed he had been all afternoon on one of the points of land trying to paint and he hadn't been able to paint and it was what he wished her to believe. She could be sympathetic but he didn't want her to feel sorry for him.

He began to strip for his bath while Laina sat before her mirror, preparing to cream her face. She had wrapped one of those long silk scarves around her head, probably to protect her hair while she took her bath. He could not see what she had done with her hair and instead of telling him he realized she was waiting for him to ask. When he unloosened his belt his gray sharkskin trousers fell straight down to his ankles. For a moment he stopped thinking mixed thoughts about Laina's hair and Dick Stewart and the new boy and the five-year contract and was thinking only that tomorrow he would have to remember to eat more heartily than he had today.

He heard Laina ask, "What will Mrs. Okomura think if you always scatter your clothes around the bedroom?"

Mrs. Okomura was the Japanese woman who attended to the house and Park did not really care what she thought.

"By now," he said, "I expect she realizes we do about what every other couple does in bed as well as sleep in it."

He saw Laina's face stiffen as she stooped to pick up his trousers. He should not have said that and he knew it. She picked up his coat from the bed and his silver pencil fell from a pocket to the floor and she said crossly, "I never saw anyone so untidy," and placed the pencil on the bedstand and hung the sharkskin coat and trousers on their proper hangers for them to air. "Don't you know everything molds in this climate, Park?" She turned, relenting a little. "Did Mr. Kimball like the landscape you gave to him this morning?"

"Harry wasn't in. Listen, Caroline. Don't worry about my paintings. They're abstractions. I had a good day today even if I didn't do any actual painting." He reached into one of the monkey-pod wood cabinets for a clean towel. "Did that goddamn hairdresser cut off much of your hair?"

"I was ashamed of myself for being so rotten to you this morning. I decided if you want my hair long, I'll leave it long until we say goodbye to each other for good. Look."

He looked while she unwound the scarf from the shining hair. He didn't think this was precisely the right time to persuade her to stop thinking about leaving for the mainland by herself in November.

"My God," Park said.

"Don't you like it?"

"I believe I do when it's brushed up like that. But it makes you look like hands off, beware, don't touch me, mister."

"At least those mainlanders at Mr. Kimball's party tonight won't decide I've just stepped out of a grass skirt."

He stepped behind her and kissed the back of her smooth neck.

"Let's see the dress you bought."

Laina hesitated. "Park—I decided not to buy a new one."

"Listen, didn't I tell you I wasn't broke?"

"I'll wear my lace dress. You liked it and I wore it only once before when we went dancing at the hotel last week. Remember?"

Park remembered. It had been a lovely evening. That old tune the orchestra had played for the next-to-the-last dance somehow continued on in his head. In the bathtub he whistled the notes to himself. He felt much better than he had this morning when taking a bath and even the water almost felt cool. All the rancor he had had against Dick Stewart vanished. He hoped the poor bastard would pull out of it all right at the hospital and not die. It was a tough way to die, being unconscious, not even knowing you might die, unable to make a fight for yourself.

When Park emerged dripping from the bathroom he discovered Laina had not made very much progress toward dressing for the party. Evidently she had been thoroughly displeased with her first try at making up her face for she was creaming it a second time.

Park said, amused, "It always looks good to me without paint."

She wiped off the cream and Park could hear the faint airy rustle of her green silk dressing gown against her bare legs as she swung around to face him.

"Will you tell me something if I ask?"

"Sure. Anything."

"It's serious to me. Park—do I look like a mainland girl now with this hairdo? If you'd met me for the first time on the mainland, would you have guessed I had Chinese and Hawaiian blood in me?"

The small curved face was anxiously regarding him. Without makeup, the face had a bare look to it like the curve of a sea shell which Park recalled picking up on the beach a few Sundays ago and holding to the sunlight. All the beauty in it had been from the warm coloring and the regularity of the surfaces. Instead of being the dark redness of her hair, her eyebrows and eyelashes were of such a pale brown they were almost invisible against Laina's fine amber-colored skin. He knew one of her grandfathers had been a Scottish sea captain. After her anxious question, he was even more reminded of it tonight for it seemed to him that he was seeing the fresh shiny face of a Scottish girl. The mocking mouth, the uptilted nose, and the smoky gray eyes had nothing exotic or mysterious or foreign about them.

"Please, Park," asked Laina.

"Right now without makeup on you're my girl anywhere. Your eyes have no more of a slant than mine. But when you're slicked up to be taken out for the evening you become something very special. I think darkening your eyebrows and lashes and smearing that stuff on your eyelids does it. I can't believe then it's still my girl who sometimes braids her hair into pigtails and rolls up her kimona sleeves to wash my back when I'm having my morning bath." He dropped the towel on the floor and scruffed his feet on it. "Is that an answer or not?"

She went to him. "You *are* nice, Park."

He felt the weight lifting from this afternoon. The prize fight next week would finish off Bull Amani as bully boy of the new local Federation of Independent Unions on the island. The thousands of field workers and packing-plant employees would be so sick for having bet their savings on the island's local champion and having lost that the Bull would be lucky to get away from the island before some excited Filipino field hand stuck a shiv through him. Charley Wong, the tame goat, would be the F. I. U.'s next top man.

While they were driving down Hibiscus Road toward the strip of twinkling lights curving with the curve of Halepule Beach, Laina switched on the radio. It was too late to receive more than the tail end of the eight o'clock news broadcast from station HOK. Park felt his nerves give an infinitesimal jerk when that voice suddenly began shattering into the darkness of the Buick's interior:

". . . afternoon, while inspecting sites for the new low-rent villages soon to be erected for field workers on this happy island, Mr. Stewart unexpectedly collapsed. He was promptly rushed to the Tothic Memorial Public Hospital where he revived enough to insist he was entitled to exactly the same generous treatment given to any other island worker, no more, no less. He was placed in one of the double rooms with Fred Kokala in the bed next to him. Fred has a broken leg and helps in the machinery room at Iki Plantation.

"All the thousands of Paradise Products' employees who know Mr. Stewart in person, and look upon him as a friend, will be relieved by Dr. Thomas Austen's statement. Dr. Austen says Mr. Stewart has simply been working fourteen and fifteen hours a day for too long and now must take a long rest. Mr. Stewart also has issued a statement asking station HOK at the top of your dial to say, quote, tell everyone I'll be in bang-up condition by next week and right there at my ringside seat watching my good friend Bull Amani prove he could be the world's heavyweight champion if he were not more interested in championing the worthy interests of union labor on our happy island, unquote. Mr. Stewart has requested all his friends who are planning to send flowers—"

Park snapped off the radio. While he was very pleased because Howie Wright, liaisoning through Byron Meaker, had done such a fast job of it with the newspapers and broadcasting stations, Park didn't think it was necessary to listen to all the lies and misrepresentations potted up in a hurry to hide the truth of how and where Dick Stewart had collapsed. As editor of the *Happy Island News*, Howie Wright could appear openly as an employee without being afraid to show his hand. It still gave Park satisfaction to recall how surprised Buddy Morton had been to discover the efficiency with which even a minor emergency was promptly shifted behind scenes.

He turned south into the cross-island highway which ran toward the strip and Halepule Beach and became aware of a fragrant sandalwood-scented inner core of darkness filling the Buick's interior. With his right hand he reached to take Laina's left. Then he realized he had shut off the radio, forgetting how much Laina liked to listen to it.

"Why didn't you stop me?" he asked, and reached down to turn it on again.

She took his hand away from the knob.

"I can listen to the radio when you aren't with me," she said, and folded his hand between hers. "Was it an awfully tough day?"

"It was a good day," Park said.

"I try to like your paintings," Laina said. "I think about them. Couldn't you paint today because of what I told you this morning?"

"Just don't think about my paintings," Park said.

A mile farther, he made a left-hand turn at an intersection, around one of the tall graceful towers from which music and, from time to time, recorded announcements issued into the bright night air. He ran the Buick in front of the single French restaurant on the strip. The others were Hawaiian restaurants which featured roast pig luaus; and Chinese or South Sea restaurants where you could have roast pig luaus for the asking, sometimes for a dollar less.

When Park helped her out of the car he had that feeling of pride and pleasure which he always had when he saw her slicked up to appear among the mainlanders on the strip at night. Her face had become striking with the dark slashes of eyebrows, the suggestion of glistening blue shadows over the eyelids, the darkened fringe of eyelashes, and the mouth so vividly red. Even her nose somehow seemed to have lost its comic tilt.

A crowd of noisy tourists emerged from "L'On Y Mange Bien." Park heard the sudden break in the voices. He saw Laina's chin thrust upward with an air of defiance and knew they were all staring at her. She turned. She occupied herself by looking at the new poster advertising the fight next week between Bull Amani and Tiger Nogusi. The billboard hid the vacant beach lot between "L'On Y Mange Bien" and a new drug store.

Park wondered what Laina would say if he told her how he'd nearly failed to persuade Doc Fields to advertise the fight with huge posters. Doc said he'd been running weekly fight shows for sixteen years. He'd never had to spend over fifty dollars before on advertising. It was a detail of course; one of a great many which somehow had to be coordinated and attended to day after day or week after week. Park hadn't failed to persuade Doc to buy posters and space but it had been necessary to have Howie Wright put heat on the printers of the *Happy Island News* to get the posters printed at cost. Before Park was finished with this single detail, this one complicated as most of them were by the constant necessity of not showing his hand, his head had been suffering from that bursting sensation which was recurring a little too frequently to ignore much longer.

Park slipped his arm inside Laina's. She was friendly and very casual as if possibly they hadn't known each other very long and were on their second or third date with each other and only beginning to get acquainted. He saw Laina reading the announcement and he read it, himself, trying to pretend an interest he did not have in an announcement he had asked By Meaker to prepare for Doc Fields:

Under the Management of Walter "Doc" Fields
Tuesday, October 24, Paradise Sporting Club
BULL AMANI VS. TIGER NOGUSI

Doc Fields, Park recalled, had protested because it was too short but By Meaker had said you wanted something short and something big so it could be read a mile away by five-year-olds. By Meaker hadn't said the thousands of Filipino plantation hands couldn't read any better than five-year-olds. Park supposed it was what By had been thinking.

"Ready?" he asked Laina. "I'm hungry."

"I don't believe it," Laina said. "Let's hurry and eat before you stop being hungry."

She always had an appetite like a horse. Park never had understood how she could eat so much food without having it show. He ordered lamb stew, a green salad, and a glass of milk. Half an hour later he sat back and watched her finish a big steak from the island of Hawaii, railroad potatoes, fresh island string beans covered with soya sauce, salad, and a side order of rice and curry. He still didn't understand how she did it. She sighed. She wiped her mouth with the napkin. She opened her purse and brought out her lipstick.

Park said, "How about a double order of ice cream with fresh bananas?"

"Well—" She put down her lipstick. Then she looked at him. Then she laughed. She picked up the lipstick. "You're awful."

"Go on, if you're still hungry."

"I'll last." She peered at her face in the little mirror inside the flap of the French red leather purse Park had given her on her twenty-second birthday. "Park, you didn't forget to ask Doc Fields for tickets to the fight, did you?"

"There'll be a hell of a mob at that fight."

"Can't we go?"

"I don't give a hang about going, Caroline."

"Everyone I know except you likes prize fights. Even when I was a kid in Kauai, Ben Subie took me to the fights every Friday night."

"Let's decide later. I can always get a pair of good tickets from Doc if you really want to go."

"If you don't want to—" she said dubiously, her voice trailing away. She finished with her mouth.

"We can decide later."

"Park," she said suddenly, "I was thinking about you and me at the hairdressers' today. I know we rough around with each other sometimes and argue, but these last few weeks I'd like it to be nice every minute. Until I say goodbye to you, I want to do anything you want to do."

Unexpectedly he had something well up into him. For an instant he nearly forgot the restaurant was packed with people, mostly tourists, who might think it interesting and very romantic if they saw him take Laina into his arms and kiss her hard on the mouth, and who might stare at Laina more than they had been staring. Park sat where he was and the unexpected welling inside him subsided. It wasn't the time, here, to explain to Laina that she was going to be with him next November and quite likely for the next five years and she did not have to think of saying goodbye to anyone in a few weeks.

Park said, "I'll ask Doc for a pair of tickets tomorrow. How's that? Are you still my girl now?"

"You know I'm still your girl."

He looked at his watch. "We'd better shove. We'll say 'hello' to Harry and leave early. All right?"

"Park—" Her voice dropped. "If I told you how you could make a lot of money quick, would you be angry?"

"Hey," said Park. "Am I that tough to get along with?"

"No, you're not tough to get along with. I never said that. But after the movie today—"

"What movie?"

"I saw a movie after I finished at the hairdressers'. It was a rotten movie, too," she said, aggrieved as she thought of it. "I don't know why we have so many awful ones lately. After the movie I ran into Hattie Subie. We had a soda together. I know you don't like her, Park. But Hattie and Herby Subie did take me in when I was broke."

"I haven't anything against the Subies. I don't even know them."

"Park, I did mean it when I told you I wanted everything to be nice every minute these last few weeks. I won't see Hattie again until I sail."

"Hell. See her whenever you like. Anytime."

Park was aware that Laina believed it annoyed him to have her see Hattie or Herby Subie because it renewed old memories of her life before she had met him. At first Park had thought nothing of it when she told him about Ben. It was only after two or three months that gradually it became unbearable for Park to think of anyone, even a dead boy, having been with Laina before him. "He was going away," Park still remembered Laina saying unhappily. "He didn't expect to be killed. He expected to return when the war was over. He said 'aloha' instead of 'goodbye.' I wish I'd stayed with him every night those two weeks instead of only the last two nights." Park wished she hadn't told him.

There was also another and much more valid reason why Park didn't want Laina to see much of the Subies. Herby Subie had been secretary of the local I. L. W. U. branch. When Laina's insurance money ran out in Honolulu and she could not continue a fourth year at the University, Herby had got her a job as secretary in the Paradise Products' packing plant down here. That was before the island was struck along with all the other islands last summer. Laina walked out with the other employees and saw her savings melt.

After the field workers, plant employees, and longshoremen finally pulled free of the I. L. W. U. and organized the Federated Independent Unions for this island alone under Bull Amani and old Charley Wong, president and vice-president, it was little meek Herby Subie who had been voted by unanimous acclamation into the secretary's chair. Herby hadn't even moved from his old office in the hiring hall. Only the "I. L. W. U." part of the sign on his door had been changed to "F. I. U."—nothing else had changed for Herby. Park had no real grievance against Herby, except the unreasonable one for his being the brother of that dead boy who had loved Laina. However, he did not wish to attract the attention of any of the local leaders of the F. I. U. He knew it was best on general principles to have as little to do as possible with the Herby Subies even if they were Laina's oldest friends on the island.

"What did Hattie Subie have to say for herself?" Park asked. "Didn't I read in the newspapers the unions' contracts come up for renegotiation in a month or so? Will Hattie and those girls at the plant have enough brains this time to ask for forty cents more an hour or strike? You certainly used to get paid lousy dough when you were at the cannery."

"Oh, Park," said Laina disgustedly. "You're as unreasonable as Bull Amani, trying to talk all those hotheads in the plantation and longshoremen unions into believing they should have forty cents more an hour. It would do you good to meet Hattie and Herby someday and have them explain why a good union shouldn't try to wreck a company by asking for too much money. Herby wants to see the company build new plantation camps and sewers and get better schools like the company keeps promising. But just because Herby went to the University, the workers think he's some sort of a nut. Mr. Wong's nice, but he's too easygoing to listen to Herby. And Bull Amani shouts and roars about forty cents an hour. Good night!"

Park was perfectly satisfied to have the island workers believe little Herby Subie was some sort of a nut, good enough to keep union books, but not very practical. The housing program which Paradise Products had been promising since before the war would cost much more than even Bull Amani's impossible wage demands. Long ago the money accumulated for a housing program had gone into building Halepule Beach and when E. P. had curtailed work at the beach, the rest of it had gone into constructing tunnels for water into the Niuniu and Pua ranges. The housing program would have to exist on paper and in promises made through the loud-speaker towers dotting the island until the bonds were paid off next year and the company got back its financial wind.

Park said good-naturedly, "O. K. What did Hattie have to say?"

"I'm not supposed to tell anyone. But I don't see why I can't tell you. After all!" said Laina, again smiling. She did trust him. Very much. "Hattie says she and Herby are betting two hundred dollars that Bull Amani wins next week. Hattie says it's a terrible secret. Herby heard it from a friend of his in Honolulu. The reason Tiger Nogusi stays in Honolulu to train in private is because he's got consumption. Bull Amani's certain to knock him out in the first round." She asked Park anxiously, "Have you heard that? Has Doc Fields told you?"

"Doc hasn't told me, Caroline."

That much was true. A month ago, without Doc Fields knowing anything about it, Byron Meaker had flown to Honolulu to plant the rumor from that end about the Tiger having consumption. It was better to have the whispered word spread to this island from Honolulu. It was more believable. It increased the betting fever. Park and By Meaker hoped every field worker and plant employee and longshoreman in the F. I. U. would bet and keep on betting that Bull Amani would win.

"No, Doc hasn't told me, Caroline."

"That means he doesn't know, Park! Herby Subie is probably the only one who knows on this island. Just think! I'm going to draw a thousand dollars from my savings. Hattie says

Jake Kutu, in the makakina district, is still offering nearly even odds on Bull Amani. If I won a thousand dollars it would mean I'd have over four thousand by November when I sail instead of three. You ought to bet all the money you can spare. Aren't you happy I told you? It shows I haven't been punching a clock with you for all these months. And it *hasn't* been tough with you. After I've said goodbye, I don't want you ever to think I thought it was tough with you. I will miss you, I'm afraid."

"Caroline—"

Park's lips tightened. If she bet a thousand dollars she would lose it, for Tiger Nogusi was going to win. It was completely in the bag. Doc Fields had crossed up Bull Amani. Doc Fields and Jake Kutu, the island's principal betting commissioner, had rigged it between themselves. Doc Fields believed he had thought of the scheme himself. Park wanted Doc Fields to continue believing it because Park didn't want his hand to show at all in the fight next week.

Park knew that Bull Amani was going to be smashed into a bloody piece of mutton before being dragged out of that ring. Bull Amani would abruptly cease being the idol and hero of all these islanders who were so nuts about prize fights. It was in the bag. E. P. Tothic wanted Bull Amani chased off the island and that was exactly what was going to happen and no one's hand was going to show. It had been a very delicate and precise piece of shaping which Park had undertaken nearly seven months ago. It couldn't fail. And if Laina were persuaded to bet more than a thousand dollars, Park was thinking rapidly, she would lose every dollar of it. Well, go on. Tell her to bet her whole wad. If she lost all her money she couldn't sail November for the mainland. She'd have to stay.

"Caroline—" He tried a second time.

Yes, it was one way to hold her here. Last April he had at last persuaded her to quit her job at the plant. From the secretarial salary she frugally had saved eight to ten dollars a week for the fund to take her to the mainland. Park agreed to deposit seventy-five dollars every week to her account in the First National Bank and she agreed to live with him for the next half-year. At first she tried to give what she thought she was being paid to give. Park was patient, and he enjoyed her discovery that nothing was demanded of her. She quit believing she had to punch a time clock. Presently she began to give him of herself because it became the one gift she had which she could freely give or withhold. Yes, Park was thinking, let her lose every dollar she'd saved. It was a means of holding her. . . . His shame at how close he was to using it made him speak harshly.

"Caroline, don't be such a fool."

When her eyes opened very wide Park noticed they did have a slight tilt at the outer corners toward the smooth temples.

"Has Doc Fields told you something? Good Lord! Tell me! The Subies can't afford to lose two hundred dollars on a fixed fight."

"Listen—"

Belatedly he saw the gulf open. He'd done exactly what no man working underground for an M. O. task force ever should do. During the war it was a principle he had constantly repeated to the young intelligence agents selected to be dropped into France and later into Germany: Never show your hand and particularly never show it to a girl behind enemy lines whom you find you're beginning to like.

"Listen, Caroline. It's your money. Go ahead. Bet on Bull Amani."

She was staring oddly at him as he spoke.

"All right, Park. I won't tell Hattie."

"There's nothing to tell."

"But I'll feel like hell if Hattie and Herby lose their money and you knew the fight was fixed and couldn't let me warn them in time."

"Let's forget the fight." Park came around to her side of the table and held her chair for her. "If we're too late at Harry's shindig we won't be able to get away early. Or don't you want to go home early?"

"I won't tell Hattie," said Laina loyally. "I still want to go home early. I'm still your girl until we say goodbye."

5

Harry's shindigs were given upstairs in the long room above the galleries which had a balcony facing east. Because Harry Kimball did not like the sea as well as he did the land, he had his balcony facing east with a view of the cliffs and vast fields slanting away from the cliffs and great shadowy peaks looming up under a real tropical moon.

At Harry's shindigs there were always interesting people from the mainland. Harry was always there, each time a little larger than Park seemed to remember from the time before. Hortense Dorens was usually there. She was Mrs. William Taylor Dorens, Park knew that much about her, the widow of Admiral Dorens. He had been told she was still in the New York social register. She lived in a little beach house of her own near the hotel and entertained a great deal.

While Park did not believe that Hortense Dorens and Harry Kimball necessarily slept together, he did believe that Hortense probably acted as Harry's shill in a polished and discreet manner. He thought there were probably Harry Kimballs and Hortense Dorenses at Miami and on the Riviera and all the fashionable beaches of the world. They managed to do all right for themselves among the solid citizens. When you got to know them it was impossible not to admire their cool brass.

After Laina had begun living with Park, the two had gone only twice to Harry's shindigs even though Park previously had enjoyed them. It wasn't because Harry Kimball lacked tact. He liked Laina and Park. He always asked them to come. It wasn't that Harry had changed but somehow, each time Park got caught within Harry's mob of guests, Park had the fantastic notion he had lost Laina forever. It was as though the laughing girl with the dark red hair was a stranger who would never return with him to a small house high up where you heard a Hawaiian wind blowing at night. And Laina had admitted to Park that it scared her to be at Harry Kimball's; she also found herself lost among strangers. When she looked for Park, he would be talking to mainland girls whom Laina thought always appeared so sure of themselves.

So they had ceased going to Harry's until now again, tonight, they entered the tiny courtyard where three Filipino boys were strumming Hawaiian ukuleles. Guests whom Park didn't know were ascending the wide teakwood stairs. The colored lanterns were swaying gently from the long balcony. Someone behind Park said, "Not Mattison? Good evening, Miss McKenzie."

It was the artist Phil Parsons who had lived here at least ten years. He did very good water colors and dry-point etchings which Harry Kimball sold. He told anyone who listened that Mattison did not know the first principles of painting and was always surprised because Park was so good-natured about it. Parsons halted on the teak stairs and said, "I don't talk behind people's backs, Mattison. I saw that latest painting of yours this afternoon and I told Harry Kimball if possible I think it's even worse than anything you've done before."

"Well, don't let it worry you. I'm still in there, trying my best, Phil."

Park would have continued upstairs but Laina halted.

"Mr. Parsons, I'm no brain. I never said I was. But let me tell *you* something, Mr. Parsons—"

"Hey, Laina," said Park.

"You're jealous of Park. Park's paintings have things exploding in them. I bet they scare you. I bet you look and look at them like sometimes I do and at first they look cockeyed and next they start scaring you because it's like the world in them has started to blow up. That's why you don't like Park's paintings!"

Park was laughing. When he looked back he saw Phil Parsons wasn't. Parsons had a puzzled and surprised look on that lined face of a craftsman.

Somebody said, "Hello, stranger," and Park didn't know who he was, either. The crowd at Harry's was in a constant state of flux. In two months' time everyone here might be new to meet. Park stood on his toes, sighting around for Harry Kimball. He felt Laina's arm holding his tightly against the soft curve of her body. He felt her breathe in deeply. She had stuck up for him against Parsons. She'd stunned Parsons. When he glanced at her she smiled back at him.

"I didn't mean to get so mad," she whispered. "But, good night, Park! Mr. Parsons isn't so wonderful."

"Let's have a drink on us," Park said.

Girls dressed in blue and yellow and red kimona jackets and short skirts passed obligingly among the guests with glasses in their hands. For the most part they were the girls who helped attend shop downstairs in the daytime. A few were haole or white girls. One looked pure Chinese. Another had the thickset figure of a fourth-generation Japanese with all the shutters closed over the flat face.

But the tall one Harry must have placed to guard the huge cut-glass bowl of punch had tawny hair almost as long as Laina's when hers was down and a lively intelligent face. Under her pure white kimona she had the same pointed thrusts of breast, and below the skirt the beautiful long legs which ran true in all the Chinese-Hawaiian girls Park had seen. It made him think almost a new race was being developed where it was the rule and not the exception for the women to be something quite spectacular. At first he did not recognize her in the white kimona. She was the new receptionist whom he had seen this morning in Kimball's Galleries. When Laina and the tawny-haired girl saw each other they regarded each other curiously for an instant and then smiled as two sisters might smile. The girl held out two cups of punch.

"Good evening," Park said. "I didn't know you at first."

The punch was very good; it was strong, cold, and tangy from fresh pineapple juice and champagne and island brandy.

Laina let Park lead her into one of the little alcoves where for a moment or so they could stand very close together with no one likely to know.

"Harry seems to have his whole staff of girls up here working for him tonight."

"Was that very pretty yellow-haired girl one of them?"

"She's his receptionist. One of these days Harry'll find that place of his unionized and he'll have to pay time and a half when he uses his staff to serve drinks." Park looked out from the alcove. "We won't have to stay very long."

"If you're sure we're going home early I might start to get a little high."

He turned his head to her. "Not too high?"

Laina was smiling. "Just high enough. . . ."

By the time Harry located them he had a small swarthy man in tow on one side and a blonde girl on the other. At second glance Park decided the girl was about thirty and saw the color of her short curly hair was that moonglow color which Laina had said the beauty salon at the new Kamehameha Hotel was trying to sell all the mainland women this month. Sometimes it surprised Park to discover all over again how tactful Harry Kimball could be when he wished. When Harry began explaining who everyone was, he said Miss Caroline McKenzie was one of the McKenzies of Kauai. It was true. Laina was a McKenzie from Kauai. But Harry said she was as if the McKenzie family owned about all of the island.

Both the swarthy-faced man and the blonde girl appeared impressed. Harry was introducing Park. "Mr. Brolly, this is Parker Mattison. I've told you about Park. And this—" Harry's booming died away as he turned to the blonde girl. Evidently he'd forgotten her name.

The blonde girl hastily said she was Janet Tolliver from Chicago—Mrs. Charles G., really, if anyone wanted to be silly formal about it. Park wondered if Mrs. Charles G. knew a girl could get tight more quickly in this climate than a girl could in Chicago.

As if everyone should know who Edith Peters was, the blonde

girl from Chicago was saying Edith Peters had asked her to look up Hortense Dorens at Halepule Beach and wasn't Hortense really just awfully sweet? Hortense had asked Janet to be sure to come to Mr. Kimball's tonight and so here Janet was. Wasn't it just a lovely evening? But Janet did not know what had become of Hortense. She hoped Hortense wasn't lost. Janet really felt lost even if it was being such a lovely evening.

The swarthy man asked Laina, "How long have they been having girls like you out here, Miss McKenzie?"

For a moment Laina regarded the swarthy man. "I expect about as often as they have boys out here. It happens all the time."

"What do you know?" said the swarthy man. "She speaks lines, too."

Park stepped forward one step but Harry's thick hard hand closed warningly around Park's wrist. Harry said, "You may not know who Mr. Brolly is, Park."

The blonde girl from Chicago said, "Oh, Mr. Brolly! I just love all your pictures."

Park didn't think he was going to like Mr. Brolly very much even if he knew who Mr. Brolly was.

"Harry," Park asked pleasantly, "if you invite too many of us picture painters aren't you afraid of lowering the tone of your shindigs? I saw Phil Parsons sneaking in a little while ago, too."

Laina forgot she was among mainlanders. The Hawaiians were a race to whom laughter came easily and the Chinese had a strong sense of humor. Laina did not have enough of the Scot in her to prevent her from being greatly amused.

"Park," she said, laughing, "wake up! Mr. Brolly is a big Hollywood star, aren't you, Mr. Brolly? I used to go to all of his gangster pictures when I was a kid in Kauai."

The blonde girl appeared slightly staggered. The swarthy man stared at Laina with even more admiration. "What do you know?" he said softly.

Harry Kimball explained quickly, "Cyril, I wanted you to meet Park. That painting I showed you this afternoon is only one example of Park's stuff. Don't misunderstand me, Cyril. I won't say Park is influenced by Gauguin. There is an analogy there, though."

"Why all the sales talk, Harry?" said Park. "Laina, suppose we have ourselves another drink?"

"Don't get Park wrong, Cyril," Harry said. "We take him as he is."

"Mr. Brolly," said Park, beginning to enjoy this a little, "don't get Harry wrong either. We also try to take him as he is, along with our volcanoes and other impressive scenic attractions."

"I started collecting modern art before anyone ever heard of Eddie Robinson's collection," Mr. Brolly said. "Or the collections those other punks started to muscle in on the publicity. I might even buy that painting of yours Harry wants to sell me providing you can keep your trap shut long enough not to talk me out of it."

The blonde girl was regarding Park with interest. "Honey," she said, "what kind of things do you paint?"

Once Harry Kimball had claimed he'd played fullback for Pennsy U in 1915 before patriotically enlisting and being sent here to help guard Hawaii against a Hun invasion. Park had never believed Harry because before that Harry had once claimed he'd been a deep-sea diver and had also claimed he'd been the youngest professor of Sanskrit at Chi U. However, tonight Harry carried the ball very well for old Pennsy U. He hauled Park after him in a line plunge. He planted Park off in the alcove behind the table where the Chinese-Hawaiian girl was serving the guests punch and he said, "Don't misunderstand me, Park, but *are* you crazy? Cyril Brolly liked that painting you brought in this morning."

"Look, Harry. Don't give me a hotfoot in front of Laina again." Park had a recurrence of that feeling of panic about Laina which he'd had the other two times he had taken her to Harry's. Suppose this time he did lose her for good? He tried to see where that movie bastard had taken her.

Harry grabbed at his arm. "Who's giving you a hotfoot?"

"All right," said Park. "Let's save the sales talk for the customers. That painting I left for you this morning wasn't any good."

"Who said it wasn't any good?"

"Phil Parsons just told me so. Laina doesn't like it."

"My boy, you never used to be so sensitive about your work. Phil Parsons is a traditionalist. You can't expect him to like it. I admire Laina greatly but I don't admire her judgment of paintings. That last painting of yours is the best thing you've done. You should have more faith in your talent."

Park had faith enough in himself but not as an artist because he knew why he had started painting and why he had to continue. He had been doing all right, too, until he had started wondering if perhaps he did have an unsuspected talent. When you felt yourself wanting to believe your own M. O. it was dangerous. He looked up distrustfully at Harry.

"You thought it was all right?"

"My boy, I told you. I think it's the best you've done yet. Now, who's been saying I'm giving you a hotfoot?"

"Look, Harry, everyone knows how you are. Laina doesn't think my paintings are any good. She didn't want me to come tonight because she has the idea you're working me around to give me a hotfoot with my painting. Have fun," said Park. "But next time just don't give me anything in front of Laina."

"My boy, *have* you been drinking?"

"I've had one glass of your punch. Where's Laina?"

"Park—" Harry clamped his thick hands solidly on Park's shoulders. "Listen to me a minute. You've allowed Laina to disturb you. She's a smart girl. *All* Chinese-Hawaiian come smart and she's got enough Scottish blood in her to be even smarter. It's the appearance of more and more girls like her, and men of mixed bloods as well as girls, which gives me hope for Hawaii when it becomes a state. It encourages me to continue my little crusade against the old haole traditions which would like to have the islands still marked off in caste lines as they used to be. *Don't* misunderstand me about Laina. But she *doesn't* know what she's talking about if she doesn't like your paintings."

"Let's leave these details for later," said Park, pulling away from Harry. Because he had promised to take Laina home early she had decided it was safe for her to have three cups of Harry's punch. While three cups of pineapple juice and champagne and brandy punch might not hit you at once so you could feel it as three cups of bourbon or Scotch might, Park knew that Harry's punch was insidious. Park did not like to think of Laina somewhere off with that movie bastard as the punch began to lift her gently a little higher and a little higher. "Where," he asked, "did that movie character take Laina?"

"She's a smart girl. She's taken him on the balcony with at least twenty other people there to prevent little Cyril from trying to embarrass her. Now listen to me. I'm not yet certain I'm going to allow Cyril Brolly to buy that new painting of yours. If I've got a hotfoot for you tonight, it's one you'll like. You've got something in those cockeyed paintings of yours. I don't know what it is but it's something. Perhaps I took you on nearly a year and a half ago as a hotfoot for some of these solid citizens swarming in from the mainland. Now it's stopped being that. I want more paintings out of you. I want to give you a big show next February. I don't know how much you've got left from your savings. Don't misunderstand me," Harry said, "but a girl like Laina doesn't come cheap. I want you to stop working as a bookkeeper for those second-rate merchants in the city. I'm going to invest in you."

"You're going to what?"

"I'll gamble two hundred and fifty dollars a month on you for the next year to keep you going. Those last two paintings of yours brought in a total of two hundred and twenty-five dollars. I think I sold them much too cheaply, but at least there's ninety dollars waiting for you in my office when you need it. I think we can bring in very much more, my boy, if you'll do as I say. I'll require at least one painting a month from you and, I hope, two, instead of the one every two or three months you've been bringing in. I'll have a show for you. I'll back you. Now, say something."

Instead of feeling grateful, Park was annoyed. Unreasonably, he had a second wave of greater annoyance because he knew he ought to feel gratitude and could not. He had to continue as bookkeeper for Kirsch and Doc Fields. Suddenly, without the least expecting it, he found himself on a limb with Harry Kimball trying to saw it off. Park tried to discourage the offer by deliberately being unreasonable about it.

"Harry, I wouldn't want you to misunderstand, either. There are times like this when I don't trust you worth a damn. Your idea of a very funny hotfoot would be for me to quit my part-time jobs and go on your bounty. Suppose after a month of it you changed your mind? No, thanks."

Harry said earnestly, "My boy, *you* mustn't misunderstand me. I like you better than any other young man I've met around here in a long time. I wish we were the same age and we could go off from this island on an adventure of our own. But I've been here too long and you must permit me to have my adventure with you in my way. . . ." For an instant the granite-colored eyes in that vast moon face did not seem as merry as they usually did. "I can make money with you. If you don't like receiving a subsidy, I shouldn't object to paying you a lump sum—say, three thousand or so—on account. Most dealers get thirty per cent. I should want a straight fifty-fifty split until our accounts were square. Cyril Brolly's interested in you. He'll buy. But I've another prospect coming to meet you tonight. Hortense is bringing her over now."

"Bringing whom over?"

"Mrs. Morton."

"Who?" said Park.

"Mrs. Wilfred Morton. She flew in this morning with her husband. Buddy Morton doesn't count; he's one of Junior Tothic's latest bright boys—but the Morton woman *is* somebody. Hortense Dorens got very excited about Mrs. Morton, Park. You can thank Hortense for being on the job. That family has lumber money which makes little Cyril's movie money look like four cents. Her family endowed the Seattle Museum of Modern Art, for one thing. If Hortense is right, I think Mrs. Morton will be our baby. She inherited all the family money. *She* was the only child," Harry said. "Now say something more about a hotfoot."

"Mrs. Morton is coming—here, tonight?"

"Hortense is camping over at the hotel now, waiting to fetch the little lady into my parlor. Don't misunderstand me when I say it, but who knows better than I how to sell a rich mainland woman *anything* salable in romantic Hawaii?"

It was a double hotfoot. In his mind Park had a picture of himself jumping agitatedly from one foot to the other while the soles of his braided leather Hawaiian sandals burst into flames. It was a picture with enough truth to it to give him ironic amusement. Thinking it a great favor, Harry had offered to subsidize Park for six months at the rate of two hundred and fifty a month. Now Harry was bringing Buddy Morton's wife to the shindig in the expectation of selling her one of Park's paintings.

Park did not have to refuse or accept the subsidy at this moment. He could take time to think how to evade Harry's generosity without having a refusal arouse Harry's suspicions. But the problem of what to do about Buddy Morton's wife was immediate. Park decided to go along with it. He thought it might be one thing more to help clinch the contract if Buddy's wife could be talked into buying a painting by Parker Mattison. It would be rather dramatic evidence to Buddy that M. O. was a real force. It could shape almost anyone's frame of mind, even Buddy's wife, exactly as you wished a frame of mind to be shaped. It would bring, Park was quickly thinking, the facts directly home to Buddy.

"Harry," he said, "sell Mrs. Morton that painting I gave you and you still can keep sixty per cent."

"I'm going to start being an honest dealer with you, my boy. Fifty per cent is enough. I'll ask a thousand from Mrs. Morton. When little Cyril Brolly hears she's paid a thousand, we ought to get fifteen hundred from him for your next—"

"Harry!"

It was Hortense Dorens, wearing one of her most fantastic hats. She was very small and had blue-white hair and, Park decided every time he saw her, twenty or twenty-five years ago she must have had every eligible officer in the Navy trailing after her. She was quite breathless from hurrying upstairs so fast.

She explained that Mrs. Morton was here, now, downstairs. Hortense had asked Cherry Sumosati to show Mrs. Morton the lovely Chinese carvings in the Chinese room before bringing her upstairs. Hortense wanted a few minutes to be certain Harry and Park were ready. Mrs. Morton had had to come alone because her husband had been called back to the hospital. Hortense thought poor dear Dickie Stewart probably was dying.

"Dying—" said Park before he thought.

He clamped his teeth together. He was not supposed to know Dick Stewart. He couldn't ask questions. He wished he hadn't eaten so much highly seasoned lamb stew at that French restaurant tonight because he could feel it move inside his stomach. He no longer was wryly amused by the chance offered to humbug Buddy Morton's wife. Buddy might not like having his wife humbugged; he might not like having the facts brought home to him so directly. The contract was too close to being in the bag to risk arousing Buddy's resentment. Park began wishing he hadn't come to Harry's shindig tonight. He began wishing he knew where Laina was right now. He wanted to go to the balcony and get her away from that movie bastard and leave early as the two of them had planned instead of remaining here to have Buddy's wife look him over.

He saw Hortense's little bird eyes were examining him. She was asking, "Please be charming to Mrs. Morton, Parker. I've seen how charming you can be when you care enough to try."

"Roughly," Park asked, "how much money has Mrs. Morton got?"

"Roughly," said the widow of Admiral Dorens spitefully, "about fifty-three millions in her own name. Is that enough for you to try to be charming to her tonight?"

"Park knows what to do," Harry said. "Bring her up, Hortense. Mrs. Morton doesn't have to get *too* interested in Chinese carvings tonight. We don't want that, do we?"

Hortense said, "Stay right here, you two, so we can talk," and darted away through the mob.

Harry told Park, "Don't misunderstand me, but let me do the talking."

"O. K.," said Park, sighting once more toward the balcony. "Don't worry about Laina either."

"I'm not worrying about her."

"She's a smart girl," said Harry. "All those Chinese-Hawaiians are smart and she's got enough Scot in her to be extra smart even if she doesn't know a good painting when she sees one."

Park looked sharply at Harry to see if that was another hot-foot. Harry's big moon face seemed dead-serious.

"Just so we don't drag it out with this Morton woman," Park said. "I want to leave early. I've got to work tomorrow in the city. We'll talk about that subsidy of yours later this week. It might be something to consider but I don't want to drop my jobs unless I'm certain I'll have money coming in for longer than six months. . . ."

He saw Harry was not listening.

Harry swung his bulk around toward the wide entrance which opened into the upstairs hallway beyond. Then Park caught a glimpse of Hortense escorting a young woman with her through the mob. Park saw the young woman before she saw him and for an instant stared incredulously. The young woman advancing at Hortense's side had fair, brown, crinkly hair and large blue eyes and she was dressed very simply for someone who had fifty-three million dollars in her own name. At her side she was holding a large straw hat, now slightly crushed, which mainland women usually bought at the beach shops upon arriving.

At first Park's mind refused to believe it could be her: Ellen Morton—Buddy's wife? *Buddy Morton's wife?* That spring evening in Washington of 1945 when everyone knew the war was going to end soon, Ruth Tothic had introduced him to an Ellen Morgan, not Morton, Park was certain. No, by God, this could not be Ellen Morgan, the Ellen who had called him "Captain" as if she had forgotten his name and did not wish to be told again what it was.

Hortense and the slight young woman disappeared in the crowd. Now they appeared again. It was the same Ellen. She was almost exactly as he remembered her. The crinkly brown hair looked neat and trim and perhaps it was cut a little shorter than she had worn it during the war, when it had been a soft feathery bob, but it wasn't shingled. In five years she had scarcely changed, except that the tautness around her mouth was gone. He remembered how under each eye there had been a little fold of flesh which gave her eyes the appearance of bunching up, ready for laughter. They were still the same banjo eyes, the same shade of deep blue. He even remembered when they had discovered that their eyes were of the identical shade of blue.

Now here she was. She looked up at Harry and glanced casually at Park and at Harry again. Park hoped she wouldn't recognize him. "Ellen, my dear," he heard Hortense saying, "may I introduce you to two of my dearest friends? This is Harry Kimball. He's not actually as huge as he seems to be in that horrid blue mandarin coat. Mrs. Morton."

"Aloha, Mrs. Morton," said Harry's booming voice. "Aloha is the word we have out here to greet friends. Aloha to our little shindig, tonight."

"Thank you for inviting me, Mr. Kimball."

Hortense said, "This is Parker Mattison. Harry and I have so wished for you to meet Parker. He is doing such modern— simply *such* modern painting."

"I like modern paintings very much," Ellen said, facing Park, smiling. "Mr. Mattison?"

By God she hadn't recognized him!

"Parker Mattison," said Hortense. "Harry and I hope to have everyone know the name of Parker Mattison in a few years."

The large blue eyes were staring at him, with something surprised and unbelieving forming in them. Park heard Harry's booming voice. Harry did not want Mrs. Morton to misunderstand him. He was not saying there was an analogy between Paul Gauguin and Parker Mattison. He had not meant to bring up the subject of painting tonight because he had these little shindigs every so often as a way to relax and forget he had galleries downstairs. However, as long as he had mentioned it, he did have a new Parker Mattison downstairs which was the best piece of stuff he had seen for a long time. In its way it was as good as a Gauguin; it was every bit as good as a Gauguin.

The booming voice gave Ellen an opportunity to recover from the shock of recognizing Park. He saw that she remembered him. After five years she had not forgotten him either. For an instant she hadn't believed it could be him. *Buddy's wife!* It was excruciating. He could imagine her faltering or making a fool of herself or bursting into hysterical tears but it was only in his imagination. After Harry's booming voice ceased she regarded her watch and said evenly, "I am afraid I can stay only a few minutes. My husband was called unexpectedly to the hospital. I expect I ought to go back to the hotel in case he should try to phone me."

"How is poor Dickie Stewart?" Hortense asked.

"I'm afraid I can't say," Ellen said. "It has been quite bewildering. My husband and I arrived only this morning. My husband dumped the children and me at the hotel and had to rush off with Mr. Tothic. He came in for dinner and before we could finish was called away. I didn't even have a chance to ask him what to do about looking for a house."

"I know of several houses along the beach, my dear," Hortense said. "Good houses are very scarce but I know of one which might be the one you're looking for."

"It would be kind of you, Mrs. Dorens."

" 'Hortense,' my dear. We mustn't be so formal with each other out here, Ellen."

Harry boomed, "Hortense, why don't you show Mrs. Morton the Stewart place? Cecily won't be able to keep that establishment if Dickie—I heard it on the radio. Dickie is going to take a long vacation on the mainland if he recovers."

"I'm afraid I must run." Ellen gave her hand to Harry.

"Aloha again to you, Mrs. Morton," boomed Harry, patting her hand. "Aloha is also the word we have out here to say 'come again' as well as to say 'greetings' to our friends, new and old. Aloha, aloha to you, Ellen."

Perhaps it was Harry's booming voice that flustered her. Park was waiting for her to turn to him. She did. Park said, "Aloha, Mrs. Morton," and tried to pick it up from Harry to make a joke of it and ease it off for her as much as possible.

She even stuck out her hand in that boarding-school manner he remembered and said, "So pleased to meet you—" It would have been all right had she stopped there. But her mind tricked her. Her mind must have been thinking of that night five years ago when she had called him "Captain," because she now said, "So pleased to meet you, Captain—"

Park had that same instant of agony he knew she was having. At least she was quick. She tried to cover her slip. "Captain Jones," she said. It was as though he could see her mind whirl and gasp and attempt to hold steady. "Captain Jones, yes, he did tell me I would find such interesting modern work at Kimball's Galleries. I believe he mentioned your name—Mr. Mattison." Her face had drained dead-white. Neither Harry nor Hortense seemed to have noticed that faltering transition from the first mention of "Captain," the stricken pause, the second "Captain Jones," and the more assured tone when she said it the third time, and continued, hauling herself up from the gulf.

He remembered to release her hand. He saw her fair brown hair was damp at the temples. He imagined his temples were even damper. "It's nice to know," he heard himself saying, "that Captain Jones likes my paintings." His voice sounded shakier than hers had. After her single slip she'd covered for herself better than he was doing.

"I must go now," she told Harry again. "I'm sorry my husband couldn't come. He was unexpectedly called to the hospital. You see, we only landed this morning."

She was beginning to repeat herself.

Then she tried to smile. It was a wretched smile.

"My dear," Hortense Dorens was saying, "it's such a hot evening, isn't it?"

It seemed to Park that Ellen Morton fled, although she merely walked very fast. Hortense darted after her to accompany her to the hotel. Park wanted to wipe the sweat off his face and didn't, aware Harry was staring at him.

"Who's Captain Jones?" Harry asked.

Park said, "I don't know all the names of the mainlanders you've been showing my paintings to this last year or so."

"Captain Jones?" Harry said thoughtfully. "I'll ask Hortense. She'll know. Whoever he is, he's done you and me a favor. We're going to do all right with that Morton woman, my boy. You had the right attitude toward her, a little too shy perhaps, but it didn't hurt. These wealthy women like them shy. What do you think of her?"

Park didn't know what to think. In his mind he saw E. P. and himself on the lanai of the old summer house this afternoon. Again he heard E. P. say, "Don't allow anything to interfere with making a friend of Buddy, will you? That's an order, Lieutenant." E. P. expected you to carry out his orders. If it came to a showdown between Buddy and Park with E. P., Park didn't know which one would be the stronger. At all costs he did not want to risk a showdown, and if there had to be one he didn't want it until after E. P. had signed the contract.

With a five-year contract Park would be safe even if Buddy Morton tried to have him removed. In a showdown, Buddy would have to go if anyone had to go. Park could not believe Ellen had told her husband; she would have had too much pride. This afternoon at E. P.'s place, Buddy Morton had gone more than halfway to be friends. No, Buddy could not know. Not many minutes ago it had amused Park to think of Buddy's wife buying one of his paintings because it would, he'd believed, help bring the facts directly home to Buddy. Now Park did not want anything of the facts brought home to Buddy. Buddy—Park thought, stupefied—Ellen's husband. It meant Buddy was the husband who had been away three years during the war as a civilian economics adviser stationed in England. And Park had stayed an entire night with Ellen during the last spring Buddy was in England.

As from a long distance off he heard the blonde girl from Chicago cry, "Oh, there you two are!"

Harry was not pleased to see her because he wanted to discuss Mrs. Morton with Park, although he was very polite. Park knew the blonde girl wasn't really a tart when she said, "Hello, honey. It's a lovely lovely evening, isn't is? Have you seen the so-cute little garden below?"

She wasn't really a tart but by now she had had enough of Harry's punch not to care if she was behaving like one. Park was almost sorry for her but he did not have the slightest need for a strange girl from Chicago. He wanted to get the hell out. He sighted again toward the balcony and still couldn't see Laina and wondered if she and that movie bastard were down in the little garden. He shouldn't have come here tonight. He had never expected to see Ellen again in his life.

Park heard the blonde girl who really must have been quite high saying loudly to Harry, "If Mr. Cyril Brolly just happens to ask for me will you tell him I just had to get back to the hotel and I'm sorry but I don't think after all that Charles G., if he were here, would want me to go alone with somebody from Hollywood in that private boat trip around the island tomorrow? Just tell Mr. Brolly he probably can ask that big tall red-headed girl to go with him instead of little me. And thank you so much, Mr. Kimball. It has been just such a lovely lovely evening."

6

From her side of the Buick Laina said, "You don't know how glad I was to see you."

"Is a movie star that tough?"

"No," said Laina, "but I wanted to get home early. What happened to you?"

"I got stuck."

"Not with that blonde girl?"

"What blonde girl?"

"That blonde girl from Chicago," said Laina.

Park laughed. "The one who had most of her hair clipped off?" he asked.

"Good night," she said but she didn't say it too indignantly, "her hair wasn't clipped that short. You know that."

"It's how you'd like yours?"

"No, not *that* much," Laina said. "No. But she was pretty."

"She had a lovely lovely evening," Park said.

He was trying to decide what to do about discovering Ellen was Buddy Morton's wife. The more he thought of it, the more he was convinced the best thing to do was to let it ride and to do nothing at all. He thought Ellen would want to let it ride, too. There ought to be no reason for alarm. It was unfortunate she was on the island. At least neither of them would be caught by surprise if they should happen to meet another time, but Park meant to avoid further meetings with her if he could.

"Did your movie star have a lovely lovely evening?" Park asked, as an afterthought.

"Park, he's an old man. I'll bet he's an easy fifty-five. I didn't mean to push him so hard. Even if I am a half-head taller than he is, I didn't think I was *that* strong. Now," she said regretfully, "he probably won't buy your painting."

"Good."

"He told me he was going to offer Mr. Kimball five hundred dollars. That was before he tried to kiss me and I pushed him into Mr. Kimball's poinsettias. Five hundred dollars! I should have let him kiss me."

"Like hell you should. Let me sell my own paintings."

"He looked funny when he fell into the poinsettias." She giggled at the recollection. "If you want to know, I wasn't really very tight."

Before Park could get down to the garden, Cyril Brolly had tried to kiss Laina. Park had been worried about what might happen with Laina taken off somewhere by that movie bastard. It gave him an emotion of more than merely masculine pride to know that, instead of allowing herself to be fondled, Laina had shoved the little bastard into Harry Kimball's flower garden. It seemed to him of a sudden that all the years had been much emptier than he had known before he found Laina. He slid an arm around her shoulders, feeling her respond and move closer.

"Suppose I'd never met you?"

"Oh, Park! Suppose we never knew each other at all?"

"How would you like one of those little silver bottles to hang on that bracelet? Don't we need something for you to remember when you pushed a movie star in the face?"

"Park, I pushed him in the stomach. And I didn't get very high on Mr. Kimball's punch. I just feel comfortable and happy right now." She sighed, resting her head on his shoulder. "Yes, I'd like a silver bottle. Please."

As he drove toward the turnoff to Hibiscus Road, he knew he should have been amused by what had happened. Most men who saw Laina probably wanted to kiss her. After all, he was thinking, you kissed women who were almost strangers to you when you greeted them and they kissed you back. A kiss meant nothing at all any more. Still, Park did not like to think of Cyril Brolly trying to kiss Laina. It made his left hand clench tightly around the steering wheel when he thought of that little man grabbing at Laina and trying to press his mouth to hers. Park didn't know what he would have done had he arrived in time in the garden. Possibly he might have laughed at Cyril Brolly. He hoped he could have let the incident ride. On the other hand, he might have beaten the hell out of little Cyril. It was a curious thing, he was thinking. You did not like having another man try to share anything of your girl with you. You didn't like to have any son-of-a-bitch try for your girl.

Another thought came to Park. If you married your girl and had children together and a son-of-a-bitch tried for her, really tried for her, not merely for a kiss in a garden, it would be an act of shattering wickedness against you and everything you cherished. Park tried to prevent his thoughts from constantly returning to Buddy and Ellen Morton. Buddy did not know. Ellen would not have been such a little damn fool as to tell him.

The traffic light turned red. Park stopped the Buick at the intersection, Laina promptly raising her head from his shoulder. He withdrew his right arm. He wished she were not so self-conscious, ready to imagine the instant the Buick stopped that tourists driving alongside in rented cars would look through the Buick's windows and see a haole in there with his arm around a kanaka girl.

To his left, one of the graceful steel towers lifted from a traffic island in the highway. As the light stayed red for the duration of its eighty-five seconds, the music which had been coming from the loudspeaker at the top of the steel tower faded. Park heard a whirring sound and next a voice broadcast from the loudspeaker twenty feet above the car:

"A thirty-second interruption of happy island music for an important announcement to all the guests of happy island. Welcome, malihinis! Double welcome, kamaainas! In the old romantic Hawaiian days the romantic Hawaiians called newcomers 'malihinis.' You newcomers here are the 'malihinis.' If you have vacationed more than once at Halepule Beach, you can join the kamaaina club. When you are a kamaaina it means you are an old-timer, one of us. Now malihinis and kamaainas, if you have not yet got your free malihini buttons or the genuine carved coconut rings given free to all kamaainas, go to the tourist bureau office on the strip—the authentic grass shack next to the Kamehameha Cinema. Go for your free malihini button or free carved kamaaina coconut ring which you can proudly wear to show you belong to the brotherhood of the happy island. Also you will receive a free illustrated booklet. This booklet explains why every one of the hundred thousand men and women and children on this island is so happy. Here we pay high wages to our workers. Plans for beautiful model villages at low rents are already being drawn up by skilled architects—"

Park stuck his head through the open window. For a bursting moment before the light turned green he felt like shouting to that mechanical voice for God's sake to shut up. Surprised at himself, he pulled his head inside the car and stepped on the gas. Only last week he had gone over the new announcements before they were recorded to be interspersed with musical recordings which were played eighteen hours a day through the system of loudspeaker towers erected on the strip and rapidly being erected at strategic intervals in all the sugar-cane and pineapple fields. He had approved Byron Meaker's and Howie Wright's announcements. Every one of the M. O. had been very pleased with himself last week. Now he had caught himself thrusting his head through the car window on the verge of shouting back at what amounted—if not actually his own—at least to expressions of ideas he had originally suggested.

He turned left into Hibiscus Road and after five or ten minutes the road began to climb. The moon was shining. Far out at sea were the lights of two ships, probably pineapple barges being towed by an invisible tug. He slowed the Buick and ran slowly around one of the wide curves of the road. He did not know what it was about moonlight, mountains, ocean, and a tropical night. He did not think the tourist bureau knew either, but it was something that struck you even if you thought you had seen it so often you were immune to it. Perhaps it was having a girl like Laina with you, Park thought.

Laina said, "Look, Park."

"I am," said Park.

"Isn't it beautiful?"

"They're probably two pineapple barges."

"Pineapple barges don't have so many lights. One's the coastal steamer on its way to Hilo, I'd guess. And the other's a tramp ship. Do you remember that poem?"

"What poem?"

"Don't you remember? 'Ships passing in the night.' It always makes me sad somehow."

Park started the Buick up the grade.

"Ships that pass in the night, and speaking to each other in passing," Park said. "Is that the one?"

"Yes," said Laina, surprised. "That's the one. How does the rest go?"

"I've forgotten."

For a time neither spoke. The motor thrummed steadily and through the tilt of the windshield Park saw the sweep of night stars at the turns. Laina moved in the scented darkness and made herself comfortable with her head fitting into the hollow of his shoulder, her legs curled up on the seat.

"It makes me feel sad and lonely, Park. I can't help it."

Park felt her stir close to him. He thought he knew how Laina felt. He felt the same way a little. It *was* a sad feeling, but somehow a good one, better than it should be. That was the part of it the tourist bureau didn't know about. Laina and the warm night sky were different from the things the loudspeakers said about the island. Maybe it was just that Laina was different and she made the other things different, too.

Laina was very different from Ellen Morton. He wished he didn't have to think about Ellen for this little while, and about Buddy, and E. P. But you had to, even at a time like this, if you were operating an M. O. Still, he wished he could try to forget about Ellen and about what her being Buddy's wife could do to the M. O. if he didn't handle her right. Damn it, with Laina right here.

Ellen was different from Laina but if he thought back hard Park knew he would remember that once, for a long instant, he had felt something of the same way about her. Not quite the same, but something like it. Besides, now that he was remembering, it seemed to him that in the past five years he must have changed a little himself. He remembered the morning had been one of those soft spring mornings that Washington sometimes had. President Roosevelt had died the week before. No one expected the war to last much longer. People at the O. S. S. were beginning to think about their old jobs and about getting out and nailing them down before the rest of the horde swept in.

It was a morning, a day, and it became an evening with nostalgia in it. That morning in the spring of 1945, Park had received a letter from Bill Finnhaven, of Hertz and Finnhaven, public and industrial relations, with offices in New York and Boston. Bill Finnhaven was Park's second cousin and during the depression had helped Park through his last years at Harvard. In 1937 Bill had taken Park into the firm as an accountant. Now Bill's letter said Park's job as general business manager of the firm was still waiting. How soon did Park expect to get back to New York?

Park was writing a reply to Bill when Colonel E. P. Tothic telephoned from the Pentagon. He and Park had planned to go to Green's Hotel that night for dinner. Now E. P. was explaining something else had come up. Park was hoping as soon as the war ended that he could pull the Paradise Products Company, Ltd., into the firm of Hertz and Finnhaven as a new account. He was careful not to indicate annoyance over the telephone.

However, E. P. wanted Park to come along. E. P. said his sister was in town and his sister had a girl friend who had arrived this morning. A second man was required. At that time E. P. was between marriages and he seemed to believe because Park was unmarried that Park at a moment's notice could be a second man. He never asked if Park had other plans. Perhaps that was because Park was eager to adjust his plans to meet those that E. P. made.

"Well, thank you, E. P.," Park said. "What time do you want me to be at the Shoreham?"

As Park drove higher and higher on Hibiscus Road with Laina, he remembered he hadn't even asked who the second woman was. He hadn't been interested then. He remembered, too, how warm and beautiful the evening had been when he got out of the cab and walked into the lobby of the Shoreham. It was one of those evenings when it seemed as if everyone had decided to celebrate and to enjoy himself because nothing like this, tonight, was going to last much longer. An era was passing.

Most men of E. P.'s importance would have waited upstairs or in the ballroom, expecting Park to seek him, but E. P. did not do it that way with the boys he liked. He was waiting patiently in the lobby near the flower stand. Park saw E. P. had an air about him of celebrating, too. E. P. was in the summer uniform which had been tailored by the best tailor in Washington.

"There you are, Lieutenant!" E. P. had said, his delight upon seeing Park lighting up his whole head, not only his face. "How are you anyway? I don't think we see enough of each other, do you, Lieutenant?"

Park had been promoted to captain five months ago. E. P. still called him "Lieutenant" as if it had become a special form of salutation between them. It was something special binding them together which E. P. wanted. Park believed he understood.

"I've got a real girl for you tonight," E. P. said, taking Park's arm in that friendly fashion and guiding him around a cluster of Navy officers and their girls.

As they continued down the long crowded hall to the main ballroom, Park politely said he was looking forward to meeting Miss Tothic. E. P.'s cawing voice altered slightly. E. P. had not been referring to his sister although Ruthie was a real girl, too. E. P. knew he was lucky to have a sister as able as she was. She had come to visit him for a month to bring him up to date on everything happening on the island. Yes, Ruthie had a sound business head on her. She was very good at sizing up people. Both E. P. and his father had high respect for Ruthie's business judgment.

When speaking of his sister's business acumen E. P. was smiling, Park noticed, but it was as if momentarily E. P.'s mind had gone elsewhere and had forgotten a smile was still on the face. Park's heart beat faster. By God, E. P. was showing him off to his sister tonight. Park had the sudden conviction if he received the sister's approval that the Paradise Products' account was well on its way to being signed by the firm of Hertz and Finnhaven.

Immediately E. P. returned to his other manner, the courtly easy manner of an older man toward a younger who was a friend. E. P. was referring to Ruthie's friend, Ellen, although Ellen was really dragging her tail tonight. It was fortunate Ruthie was here to cheer her up. This morning Ellen had flown into Washington, expecting to meet her husband. An hour after registering at the Shoreham a cable had arrived from England, delayed thirty hours in transmission. It had been very tough on Ellen. E. P. blamed the Army's inefficiency.

Park did not look forward to a very enjoyable evening with a woman who was dragging her tail after heartbreaking news. But E. P. laughed his sudden joyous laugh. Ellen's husband wasn't a soldier, nothing like that. Ellen's husband hadn't had to get into a uniform. He was a civilian on the board of economic control for the American forces in E. T. O. He lived at the Claridge Hotel in London which weren't very difficult quarters even with a war on. No, the boy simply hadn't been able to get here to meet his wife.

As Park entered the ballroom with E. P. he still believed this was going to be a duty evening. E. P. had leased a suite on the tenth floor of the Shoreham which couldn't have been very difficult quarters for him, either, even with a war on. Consequently he was well known here and even with the gay mob crowding into the ballroom this spring evening, Park saw that E. P. had obtained one of the best tables. The table was not too far from the orchestra or too near. E. P. would have said it was exactly all right. It was O. K.

Park saw two young women waiting at the table with that indefinable look young women often have when waiting for someone to arrive who is a stranger to them. Even before being presented, Park decided he could tell which one was which. The one to the right with smooth black hair had something of E. P.'s oblong face, like the entrance into a dark cathedral, although her face was deeply tanned and not so sallow as E. P.'s had become in Washington. It was an ugly attractive face for a woman. She was even smaller than E. P. and dressed beautifully.

Park decided Ruth Tothic must be between thirty and thirty-five, older than he'd anticipated. That year Park was only twenty-nine. The other young woman seemed much younger, twenty-five or twenty-six at the most. Although she also was dressed beautifully, in an evening gown Park suspected had been bought to be worn tonight for the first evening with her husband after so many years, she looked much too thin and tense. The first thing about her which caught his attention was her eyes. They were a deep blue, very large, and at the same time appeared to be bunched up slightly as if laughter were close to the surface.

But the slight face had no laughter in it. She shouldn't have tried that bright orange lipstick tonight. The bright color on her mouth merely made the taut pale skin of her face look paler. The freckles stood out on her face like flecks of brown paint. As he came to the table, Park was wondering if perhaps that shade of lipstick was a shade her husband had liked three years ago. It was going to be a duty evening all right, substituting for a missing husband with a wife who was feeling sorry for herself. At least the wife wasn't as unattractive as Park had imagined. He liked those blue banjo-eyes of hers. They were banjo-eyes. That was exactly what they were.

E. P. waved his hand at Park. He said the girls would find Lieutenant Mattison a real boy. Real boys who were O. K. were hard to find these days in Washington.

Sharp black eyes inspected Park briefly, head to foot, as if he were merely the latest of a great number of O. K. boys whom Ruth's brother had casually presented to her. It seemed to Park he must have passed the inspection, for Ruth Tothic ceased being altogether indifferent. She said, "Mrs. Morgan, Ellen Morgan, Lieutenant." At least when Park tried to remember back through the corridor of time to that springtime evening in Washington, he still thought it was what Ruth had said.

The dinner had been very dull for Park. E. P. and his sister were talking about people whom Park had never heard of and frequently using island words such as malihini or pau or hooma-limali and laughing. Ellen sat there and scarcely ate. It seemed to Park she didn't even know where she was. He had a feeling that if he suddenly spoke to her she might jump and run. The orchestra played at least a dozen numbers.

Ruth broke off her conversation with her brother to look at Ellen. She asked Park bluntly, "Don't you like to dance, Lieutenant?" almost as if she were someone up there in the top brass and had the right to give orders.

Park knew E. P. did not care to dance. He had not known whether he was expected to ask Miss Tothic or Mrs. Morgan—as he thought of Ellen's name then—to dance. He was sitting there, thinking what a hell of a duty evening this was going to be.

"Ellen," said Ruth, still brisk about it, "you won't help yourself by behaving like a whipped dog. Snap out of it, darling. You used to like to dance."

"I'm afraid I'm very much out of practice," Ellen said. However she glanced at Park.

Park saw tears in the blue banjo-eyes.

When she stood to accompany him to the dance floor, he could not tell whether she had pretty legs because that was the year girls were wearing such long evening dresses, even if they still wore the short skirts during the day. She was very thin. He was surprised at her thinness when they began to dance. At first she held herself stiffly away from him. He hoped Hertz and Finnhaven would give him a full partnership in the firm if he brought in the Paradise Products account. Because he did not care in the slightest what this slight girl thought or cared of him, he deliberately found the line of her legs with his and held her more closely in order for them to dance as if they had been on a dance floor before. She did not draw away. He began to have the notion that the legs pressing his might be very pretty legs under the long skirt.

Then something rather surprising began to happen. Perhaps it was the gay lilt of the music that caused it as much as anything else. Even when Park thought of it afterward, he was never able to describe it exactly. It was as if the slight little body dancing so primly against him began to change and he felt it change. He did not know why it stirred such a response in him. Ellen started speaking about her husband. Her husband had diabetes. He couldn't enlist. When the chance had come early in the war for him to do something, he had jumped at it. Neither of them had known he would spend three long years in England.

And while she was speaking to Park about her absent husband, as nearly as Park afterward could put it to himself, it seemed as if her body was trying to wed itself with his and challenging him to do something about it. Or it was as if she didn't know she was dancing with Park and thought she might be dancing tonight with a man who had been away from her for three years.

During a pause Park said, "I'm not sure I heard Miss Tothic say your name correctly. When I meet a good dancer I like to know her name."

"It doesn't really matter, Lieutenant," said Ellen, "does it?"

"It's Captain," Park said. "But that doesn't matter either."

"I'm so sorry, Captain."

"I can't call you Captain," Park said. "I do like dancing with you."

"Won't 'Ellen' do for this evening?" and she was smiling slightly, herself. He decided she would be a great deal of fun if she could forget her husband.

The music had started again.

"I'm Ellen with whom you had to endure a dreadful dull evening a week after President Roosevelt died. You're the captain who danced so nicely with me the night I was in Washington when my husband couldn't meet me."

"Thank you, Ellen," Park said. "If you're going to be here a few days I wish I could show you around a little to prove I didn't have a dull evening. Or do you know your way around in Washington?"

"I don't know my way around here at all," she said while they were dancing together. "I'm flying home on the nine-twenty plane tomorrow."

After the orchestra finished playing the Star Spangled Banner, E. P. said why not come up to his suite for a nightcap? Ruth had the suite next to his. Ellen was somewhere a few floors below. Park was the only one who had any distance to go home. Park said he thought a nightcap sounded all right. Ellen had hesitated, but Ruth said, "Don't be an idiot. Good Lord, Ellen! You'll go back home and have a nervous breakdown if you don't cheer up. How would your husband like that?"

Up in E. P.'s room Ellen said brandy please but not too much please. After her second glass of brandy the blue banjo-eyes began to have a sparkle in them. She said she hadn't had so much to drink for she didn't know how long and immediately tears once more filled her eyes. Park knew she was thinking of the long empty weeks and months since her husband had gone to England.

E. P. said he'd picked up a Brahms arrangement he thought the girls might like to hear. Park knew how E. P. could be when he sat down at a piano to play Brahms. E. P. was good as an amateur, but he never knew when to quit. His sister finally broke it up by saying that Ellen had to catch an early plane tomorrow. Ruth said for E. P. to give Ellen one more brandy to be sure she slept soundly tonight. Ruth offered to go into the hall with Park where he could show her which one of the officers' caps hanging in the closet was his. In the dimly lighted entrance hall of the suite she said, "Pip has at least a dozen caps. I don't see why a man needs so many caps to fight a war, do you? Is this yours, Lieutenant?"

It was his. She'd known which one was his. From the front room Park heard Ellen's soft laughter. She had ceased protesting because E. P. had filled her glass too full of brandy. Ruth Tothic rested her hand on Park's sleeve. She glanced toward the door into the front room and closed it with a slippered foot. Once again tonight Park felt his heart begin to beat faster.

"Lieutenant—I should say 'Captain,' oughtn't I?"

"I hope it'll be plain 'Mister' in a few months," Park said, smiling.

"Pip tells me he has a great deal of confidence in you."

"He's the most brilliant man I know," said Park simply and meant it. "I hope he has confidence in me."

Evidently he could not have said anything better than that to E. P.'s sister.

"I feel something of the same way about Pip that you do, even if he is my brother. But Pip says you're a nice boy. I'm not so sure about that, Captain. I'm not so sure you're as nice a boy as Pip thinks. I think you might be a very likable young man who could find his way around almost anywhere, which is more important than merely being nice. I think I should be inclined to tell Pip I would trust you in almost anything he asked you to put your hand to. If I did, would it please you?"

"Very much," Park said, promptly.

"Now I wonder if I could ask a favor of you, Captain?"

"Ask me anything," Park said.

"I happen to be very fond of Ellen and very worried about her tonight. Wars are harder on wives than a man might think. It would be a kindness to Ellen if you didn't merely dump her off at her door. It wouldn't hurt her to be startled by having a strange man try to kiss her. It would do her worlds of good. She'll never see you again. You'll never see her" She thrust out a firm brown hand. "Good night, Captain. I'll tell Pip if he gives the account to your firm, he'll have to stipulate that you visit our island at least once every year. I might even be able to show you around out there. Who can tell?"

Nobody could tell very far ahead about anything though. Park never saw her again because two weeks later she died at Johns Hopkins after an operation for cancer of the brain. Before dying Ruth Tothic evidently had kept her word to Park. He became a full partner for bringing the Paradise Products account into Hertz and Finnhaven. When Park resigned, the firm lost the account.

But that night Park expected to see Ruth Tothic again. He still remembered how very much alive he felt as he went down with Ellen Morton in the elevator to Ellen's floor. He was thinking tomorrow he would write Bill Finnhaven and say the account was as good as in the bag. When he glanced at Ellen at his side, it seemed to him she appeared very much alive. Although she'd had three snifter glasses of brandy, she was not high. She was not high but she was not dragging her tail anymore either. Her freckled face lifted to smile at him. He smiled down at her. It was as though they did not need to say anything to each other to tell each other they both felt very pleased with the evening.

When they got out on the sixth floor Ellen said, "It's ridiculous of Ruth to think you have to see me to my door. I can find my way."

"You're a stranger here," said Park. "Have you forgotten? You don't know your way around here at all."

At her door she halted and gave him her key. He had quite forgotten Ruth Tothic when he unlocked Ellen's door. He would never know what Ruth Tothic had had in mind for tonight, between Ellen and himself, because after he had opened Ellen's door he had no mind for anything at all except his desire for Ellen. Standing there before him, holding out her hand for her key, she had become very beautiful. She was saying something breathlessly, but Park kissed her and the soft sweet voice stopped abruptly. He picked her up and carried her into her room.

After returning to the house, Laina said she thought she had that poem in a book. All the schoolbooks she had brought with her from Honolulu were in the study at the far end of the house where Park had installed the telephone even though Laina had protested, saying it was more convenient to have the telephone in the bedroom. She pulled the big brown buckram-bound book from the shelf and Park saw how smooth and shining the dark red hair was when she bent under the study light.

"Here," she said. "This is it, Park."

Park slipped his arm around Laina's waist and she asked him to read it aloud and he did, but he felt self-conscious doing it. He got as far as:

Ships that pass in the night, and speak each other in passing,
Only a signal shown and a distant voice in the darkness;
So on the ocean of life we pass and speak one another,
Only a look and a voice; then darkness again and—

"Nuts," Park said. "Nuts." He closed the book.

"Please, Park. Go on. It's beautiful."

It wasn't beautiful. At the far end of a long corridor in his mind a picture became agonizingly clear. He saw Ellen Morton as she'd been early that morning in her room at the Shoreham. She had been lying so quietly in bed next to him that he thought she was asleep. She had lifted to look down at him in the faint morning light. In her soft hurt voice she had said things that Laina's poem made him remember now. It had been a deeply moving and poignant experience for Park. He had lost something which he had had that morning so long ago because the poem didn't strike him as poignant or moving. It was a humbug. It had tricked him. It had tricked Ellen, too.

"It's not much after eleven," Laina said. "We didn't get home early but it isn't too late. I'll get undressed."

"All right," Park said. He said it absently.

She walked out. He heard the bedroom door slam. Not long after he heard the bathroom door slam.

He felt that bursting sensation in his head again. Suppose Ellen had told Buddy of that night at the Shoreham? No, she couldn't have. Buddy had been friendly this afternoon. Let it ride. Don't think about it. The worst thing he could do would be to alarm her by attempting to see her. Let it go.

The telephone rang. He had to get back into himself for whatever was wanted on the telephone. He stepped to the study door and locked it. He picked up the telephone. It was Doc Fields' rasping voice speaking from the city. Doc sounded a little drunk. Doc said he'd been trying to reach Park since early in the evening.

"I just got back. What's the trouble?"

"I had dinner with Bull Amani and Herby Subie. The Bull says he ain't going to go on with the fight."

Park whistled softly through his teeth.

"That's right. He's throwing it up. I got to make an announcement tomorrow. I thought maybe you could come in early tomorrow and help me—"

"Doc," asked Park, "where are you?"

"At my hotel. I could see you around eight in the morning if that ain't—"

"I'll see you tonight," Park said. "I'll be at your place in forty minutes."

"Park—"

Park hung up on the wheezing voice. He rang through to Byron Meaker's. "Can you talk?"

"Sure, sure," said By's voice. "Millie's loaded herself with sleeping pills. She can't sleep in this climate unless she takes on a load."

"Listen, this is trouble. Bull Amani wants to pull out of the fight. We haven't too much time to stop him. If that fight doesn't go on next week, we kiss a five-year contract goodbye."

"Where do you want me to meet you?"

"I'll be in front of the John Oliver Building in thirty-five minutes."

"You've got a thirty-two mile drive, papa."

"You'll be there?" Park said.

"I'll be waiting. Watch that bad stretch of road through Hono."

Park hung up. He removed a cigar from a half-filled box of Belinda-Belindas, stuck it in his mouth and lit it. He drew in slowly. He gave himself a long moment. He turned off the study lights. He was through the front door on his way to the Buick before he remembered Laina.

When he opened the door the bathroom smelled of sandalwood and Laina had nothing on at all and was brushing her teeth. He gave himself another long moment to enjoy looking at her bending over the basin. She put down the toothbrush, smiled up at him, and was glad he enjoyed looking at her like this.

She rinsed her mouth, straightened up, and said, "Someday I'm going to learn to smoke your cigars. I like their smell, Park."

"Listen," said Park. "Doc telephoned."

"Doc Fields?"

"He's drunk. I'd better go in and see what's wrong."

"Oh, no!"

"I'm sorry, Caroline."

"You're too easy with people. Why do you have to run when somebody like Doc Fields snaps a whip? I wish I had let Mr. Brolly kiss me! Then maybe he'd have bought your painting. We could have had five hundred dollars so you wouldn't have to jump when somebody like Doc Fields snaps a whip. Oh, Park, I could bawl. Please stay here with me!"

Park was careful when he hit the bad stretch of road going through the Hono district. He dropped down to fifty-five miles for the four and a half miles until the Buick lurched back on the concrete highway again.

7

During the big strike of the summer and early fall of 1949, Park had driven three times into the city after midnight and all three times he had found something stimulating in the careening rush through a soft tropical night. Tonight, he drove well and he drove fast but it was no longer any fun to go rushing forth on an emergency job.

As he came in on Young Street he saw Byron Meaker's long-legged shadow thrown across the deserted sidewalk by the misty yellow light from the lamp post in front of the John Oliver Building. By threw away his cigarette stub. A four-bell alarm at this hour of the night was no longer anything of an event for him either; it was merely a vexing and sometimes hazardous break in their M. O. plan which had to be repaired as quickly as possible. He climbed into the Buick, asking conversationally, "How was the stretch of road through the Hono section?"

Park said, "Rough."

By lit another cigarette. He didn't ask where they were going because he knew as well as Park that they first had to learn from Doc Fields what had changed Bull Amani's frame of mind. On the way to Doc Fields' hotel, Park gave By a general picture of the meeting this afternoon with E. P., Buddy Morton, and Dick Stewart. Park said he thought the new boy was a good choice. Buddy ought to work out all right.

"Buddy?" said By, pleased. "That fast?"

"It's what he asked to be called."

"It's a change from Stewart, anyway. How that bastard loused us up!"

"Buddy isn't the type to louse anybody up."

Park had thought it through carefully in his own mind and was convinced a girl of Ellen Morton's background and breeding would do nothing of her own accord to louse anyone up—her husband, her family, herself, or Park. She would count on Park's discretion exactly as she would expect him to count on hers. Let it ride, then.

Doc Fields' hotel was not one of the worst in the city but it was not one of the best. It was seven blocks south of the John Oliver Building and on the edge of the crowded slums of the makakina district. Clouds covered the stars and it was very dark when Park stopped the Buick in front of the old wooden hotel with a great crazy roof thrust over a long veranda. The bougainvillaea vines had creepers as big around as tree trunks and in the darkness they seemed to Park to be huge rustling snakes wound around and around the old hotel. Park hoped it would rain soon, it was very hot. He could smell the odors from the docks and every now and then the wind brought the gluey sweetish smell of pineapples from the other side of the harbor. The cannery was on a twenty-four-hour working schedule during the season.

It was even hotter and stickier in Doc's corner bedroom. The windows were open but the rusted screens were thickly matted with fluttering brown moths. The air in the room was stale and thick, and when Park tried to breathe he seemed to be breathing in something of that mothiness which was crawling over the screens. He saw Doc was not drunk. Doc was a pudgy kindly man with a squint in one eye and although he was not yet drunk, the squint was more noticeable and Park thought one side of the red face looked as if it had become partially detached from the other. Doc had lost hope. Fellas, it was no use. He was cleaned. The Bull had run out.

"Look here, Doc. We can't do anything to help unless we know why the Bull won't fight."

Doc thought it was because somehow the Bull had got the

notion he might not win the fight after all. Doc didn't know how the Bull had got such a notion.

Park said, "You promised Bull Amani the Tiger would dive the fourth round. Don't tell me the Bull thinks you'd lie to him? Everyone knows you're a square shooter."

"Fellas, he won't listen to reason. He's run out on me."

"Sure, sure," said By, taking the ball. "Tomorrow he'll run back to you."

"No chance, fellas. I'm done for. I'm cleaned."

Through eyes smarting with sweat and fatigue, Park watched By Meaker carry the ball for the home team. By's head was framed by the rusty square of brownish rustling screen. His mouth had a V-curve to it, like a clown's smile, the long upper lip folding over long sharp teeth.

By said, "The Bull's going to run back to papa sometime tomorrow, Doc. You get set for him. You get a convincer. You need a convincer. How about a postdated check? How would that be for a convincer? Why don't you write a check and have it postdated? A third party you and the Bull both trust holds it. If you doublecross the Bull he gets your ten thousand bucks."

"Christ A'mighty!"

"You aren't going to doublecross him, are you?" asked By, bending that wise sad clown's face of his toward Doc. "If you *were* planning a switch on the son-of-a-bitch, you'd be smart enough to fly the coop after the fight anyway. You wouldn't give a goddamn about any check you gave to anyone."

"Fellas," said Doc, "I'm an honest man," and poured himself another drink. "For sixteen years I been running square fights. I'll write a convincer for the Bull if you can scare him into seeing me."

It was beginning to rain when By and Park had finished with Doc and came out of the hotel into the night. Park threw the stub of his cigar into the gutter and slipped under the wheel. He told By, "That was a good job on Doc. Thanks."

"Sure, sure. I want that five-year contract as much as you do, remember."

Because the elevator stopped running at midnight they had to climb seven flights of stairs to By's offices. They were both drenched with sweat when By unlocked the door with "Byron B. Meaker, Publicity & Advertising for Paradise Tourist Bureau, BYQ Radio Station, Flavola Supermarket, New Kamehameha Hotel, John Oliver Office Building," etc., neatly lettered on the stippled opaque pane of glass. Park decided it looked most convincing. By never let his hand show but he liked to see his name on an office door.

Park stretched out in one of the red leather chairs which helped make By's private office so comfortable. By opened a fresh pack of cigarettes, offered one to Park, and said he was sorry he didn't have a good cigar. Park shook his head. He had stopped smoking cigarettes. They were supposed to be bad for your appetite. Sometimes people gained ten or fifteen pounds after quitting cigarettes.

Park said, "We've got to go after Bull Amani. If he rats the fight, we kiss a five-year contract goodbye."

"I don't see it quite that way."

"How do you see it?"

"By ratting the fight the Bull has discredited himself with all the labor elements, hasn't he? Those Filipino hotheads in the cane and pineapple fields decide Bull Amani isn't their bully boy any more. When Bull and old Charley Wong run against each other for president of the island's federated unions in November, Bull's going to lose. Charley Wong gets elected according to schedule. Charley knows he's got to cool down the plantation hotheads in a hurry, with no more talk of a big wage increase or a strike. We've got Charley under our thumb. Wage negotiations with the unions won't come up until the first of December, after the union elections. When Bull rats the fight, he's finished anyway. What more does E. P. expect? We get our five-year M. O. contract signed in gold ink."

"Well, it sounds pretty," Park said.

"You don't see it that way?"

"Lew Kirsch doesn't see it that way. He's going by his last survey of labor attitudes and frames of mind. We've got fifteen thousand plantation workers, mostly of Filipino ancestry, and they're all as green as grass about union affairs. They're hotheads. So are the longshoremen. They'll follow Bull Amani and out-vote the cannery workers as long as Bull's president. Lew says the hothead faction won't believe Bull Amani isn't the top bully boy of the island until most of them actually see him get smashed in a fight. There you are. It's unreasonable. It's illogical. It's a frame of mind. We're beat unless we get Amani into a ring. Otherwise Bull gets elected head of the F. I. U. a second year. Old Charley Wong loses. We lose."

"*We* didn't louse it up last year with Amani," said By.

"Look, By," said Park. "Dick Stewart's through. He's paid off for last year. Now we've got a new boy. He's a nice guy but I'd hate to give him excuses if we don't finish off Bull Amani."

By lit a cigarette. "I'm with you. Let's see what we've got."

The island had two broadcasting stations. It had two daily newspapers. Park thought of them all as guns which now could be trained upon Bull Amani. However, the island had some-thing else of which Park was very proud—the seventy-four loud-speaker towers. While he had not actually thought of their use—he had borrowed from the Italian Dopolavora techniques of before the war—he was responsible for convincing E. P. of their worth. Almost the entire island now could be sprayed with sound and words.

With the exception of one motion-picture house on Iki Point which was still causing trouble, all the picture houses on the island had loudspeaker towers. Both By and Park thought they should throw in the entire network against Bull Amani as soon as it became morning. The whole island would resound with the Bull's cowardice and disloyalty. In mountain and in valley his name would bray forth, searching him out. The first radio news broadcast would not go on until six o'clock this morning. By Meaker had about three hours to prepare releases for the news-papers, radio stations, and loudspeaker network. Through the day, he would have to sit at his desk, synchronizing the impulses, pushing harder and harder, hoping the words would build up and build up until presently a frame of mind had been established on the island which would drive Bull Amani into Doc's office.

An M. O. attack on one or a thousand or a million minds, Park thought, was essentially simple. In its core was a small pebble of your own endeavors. The trick, if it was a trick, was knowing how to kick that pebble loose for it to begin rolling and accumulating mass to itself until at last it went roaring and screaming like an avalanche. You let something loose. It was not quite as simple as pointing a gun at a man's brain, but it was almost as simple. If it really worked, instead of having a hole in the man's brain and no man at all, usually you had both the man and his brain engaged within the great general frame of mind. Even a year ago Park had found something exciting in launching a new M. O. attack but his eyes hurt and he was tired and he was thinking of the tough day ahead and there was none of the excitement or thrill he used to have when turning the wolves loose because a man's brain had hared off somewhere into the wrong space. He looked at his watch. Ten minutes after three, Tuesday morning. Laina would have been asleep for the last three hours.

By said, "I guess we've covered everything. I'll get cracking. Do you want me to dial Lew Kirsch for you?"

"In a minute. Have we missed anything?"

"What about Bull Amani's daughter?"

"Well, what about her?"

"She's fourteen. That's old enough in this climate. I can use Danny to steer her into Mama Pikea's for a drink. The kid's ripe and our hands won't have to show. The Bull likes his kid. He'd go crazy if anything happened to her."

After a short silence, Park said, "Save her for last. We'll use her if we have to but let's use what we've got first. Call Lew."

By's mouth became a V, his long teeth very white in the light from the desk.

"You'll pull in all Lew's interviewers to start a whisper campaign against the Bull?"

Park said, "We want that five-year contract, don't we?"

By dialed a number. Presently he said into the telephone, "Lew? It's another tough night. Start making hot black coffee because papa's coming over."

It was still very dark driving through the deserted streets and it was raining much harder when Park turned into Seashore Boulevard and after he got out of the car the white hibiscus was very fragrant in the dark rain as Park walked into the courtyard of the Seashore Apartment Hotel. He looked up to the top floor and saw Lew had his lights on. Probably coffee was being readied on the electric stove, because Lew knew how it was to have to work around the clock on a tough night shading into a tougher day.

It used to give them all a kick, too, Park was thinking. He pressed Lew's button. The door buzzed instantly. The Seashore Apartment Hotel had an automatic elevator. Park didn't have to climb more flights of stairs. What all of them wanted now was that five-year contract because that gave them five years of security. Nobody could louse you up when you had a five-year contract. Goddamn Dick Stewart for that grandstand play he'd tried last year, hoping to impress E. P. He'd loused it up with Bull Amani so it was still loused up.

Park wondered if Stewart had returned to consciousness during this long night in the hospital. Did Dick Stewart realize what was happening to him because he had loused it up for everybody concerned last year? Was he awake? Park hoped when his own time came at least he'd be awake, with all of him conscious and making the best fight he could of it. The elevator stopped. The double doors slid open and Lew Kirsch said in his warm husky voice, "I have coffee, hot and black."

It was after four-thirty in the morning when Lew Kirsch and Park completed the dozen sentences which Lew's staff of interviewers would have to memorize within another five and a half hours. The sentences had to be made short and each one had to have a meaning easily translated into Japanese or Chinese or Filipino by Lew's interviewers. Afterward, Park lay down on Lew's couch, falling instantly to sleep.

Lew woke him at six-thirty and gave him more black coffee. Park had a quick shower, another cup of black coffee, and it was seven o'clock. Park did not expect Doc Fields to get drunk this early in the day but he didn't want Doc even to start along the way until after Bull Amani was located and harried into Doc's offices.

Park meant to wait it out with Doc as long as they had to wait it out. Doc and he had breakfast at Jake's. Jake Kutu was the Chinaman who would take any bet you wanted to make and give you odds almost as good as you could get on the mainland.

Park recalled meeting a Phil Cleary at one of Harry Kimball's shindigs last year. Mr. Cleary had visited Halepule before the war when it was not as famous a beach as it was now. He had driven across the island into the city to lay a bet on Sea Biscuit with the Chinaman. For some reason he sailed back to the mainland without collecting. Then last fall he walked back into Jake's and for a gag said, "Jake, I'm Phil Cleary. You owe me some money," never expecting Jake to remember, but Jake did and paid Cleary. Jake was one of the island's institutions. He owned the ramshackle wooden building which not only housed his restaurant and cigar stand but the enormous Paradise Auditorium and Doc Fields' offices and the dingy gymnasium upstairs.

After breakfast Park stopped at the cigar stand, Doc waiting. At the other end he saw a dozen Filipino plantation hands shouting angrily at Jake Kutu in Igaroo or whatever language these particular Flips used. One was waving a folded copy of this morning's paper at Jake. Park could see the first two words of the headline: "BULL AMANI . . ." He knew the rest. He had already read the morning's paper. By Meaker hadn't lost time since last night. Park assumed the excited Flips had heard the six o'clock radio broadcast and had rushed in from the near-by plantation to try to call off their bets with Jake Kutu. Park hoped a mob of them would be in the city before noon.

Jake broke away from the Flips. He came grinning like a grinning Buddha shaped of moist yellow clay. He reached for the special box of Belinda-Belinda Fancy Tales on the shelf under the cash register. Park dropped a dollar on the counter. Jake had the match lit. Park bent forward to complete the pleasant ceremony and allowed himself a long moment to relish the Havana tobacco. It had been a tough night. It would probably be a tough day. He hadn't had much sleep. He didn't expect much more until Bull Amani walked in. By Meaker and Lew Kirsch had to do the work, he told himself; all he had to do was wait it out with Doc Fields.

Because he was established in Jake's mind as someone who could not afford dollar cigars, he had to remember to say to Jake, "Never smoke a cheap cigar, Jake. If you can pay only a dollar a week for cigars buy one good one instead of twenty cheap cigars. Isn't that right?"

Jake nodded and grinned although Park knew Jake smoked only the two-for-a-nickel cigars which came by the gross from the Philippines. Sometimes Park got tired of having to remember never to show his hand, even in the smallest of details. He puffed slowly on his cigar, the rain sweeping in from outside. He had looked forward to a good cigar this morning but it didn't have the suave taste it ought to have had.

Doc Fields wheezed, "I don't want to miss the next broadcast, kid."

This morning Doc was full of hope. He really believed the Bull might walk in any minute. He wrote a check and postdated it for two days after the fight. "Kid, that'll do it," Doc said. "Mr. Meaker is a smart man."

"All we have to do is wait," Park said.

"Have you heard this one?" Doc asked.

"If I have, I'll tell you."

"You stop me, if you have," Doc said. " 'A woman with a past don't need to worry about the future because a well-managed past will take care of her future.' Howzat?"

"That's good, Doc."

Doc opened a drawer in his desk and brought out two dirty paper cups and a bottle of island brandy.

Park said, "Not this early for me, Doc." He looked at his watch. "Let's hear how the nine o'clock broadcast sounds."

Doc turned on the radio.

It sounded authoritative over the air, coming from both stations, HOK as well as BYQ. Park switched from one station to another which confused Doc, but Park liked what he heard.

Both news broadcasters spoke of the blow to island pride if Bull Amani suddenly tried to walk out of the fight. They refused to believe the Bull would quit. Each one hoped to have the Bull located very soon. They promised their listeners to have the Bull speak on a special broadcast. Station HOK's announcer said it was one of those false rumors most likely started by fight gamblers in Honolulu. The Honolulu gamblers wanted to change odds enough for them to hedge their own bets on Tiger Nogusi. Station BYQ followed a different line of reasoning. Its announcer referred vaguely to Bull Amani's rivals in the F. I. U., the local Federation of Independent Unions. It was a scheme, this announcer suggested, to discredit the Bull with his thousands of loyal supporters who planned to vote him in again as president for another year of the F. I. U.

Park switched off the radio.

"Those longshoremen aren't going to like to think the Bull has turned yellow, Doc. There won't be many ships loaded in the harbor today."

Doc was at the window, staring down into the street.

"Christ A'mighty, look at this. I bet a thousand plantation Flips've collected around Jake's, wanting their bets called off. Maybe the Bull won't walk in like Mr. Meaker said? Kid, if the Bull don't come in, I'm whipped. I'm licked. I could tie a rock around my neck and jump off the dock."

"Listen," Park said, "all we got to do is wait. Don't worry."

If he fell asleep in Doc's rickety cane chair, Park expected Doc would let him sleep. Park expected Doc would start pouring himself slugs of island brandy. The strain was building up in Doc and while Doc wasn't a lush, on a day like this, Park knew he might get stinking. And Doc couldn't get stinking. Doc had to wait and be ready with a convincer when the Bull walked in.

Doc said, "Have you heard this one, kid?"

Park said, "You tell me," and listened to Doc. The morning heaved along. It was nearly ten o'clock. Laina ought to be waking up. In a few more minutes Park thought he might telephone her. He decided not to. He couldn't very well telephone her from Doc's office. He was stuck here. He ought to telephone through to E. P. on the private connection but he couldn't do that, either. He was stuck here with Doc, waiting it out until the Bull cracked.

He heard Doc again ask, "Say, have you heard this one, kid?"

"Let's have it, Doc," Park said, sitting up more erectly. It was beginning to be a very tough day.

At 1:15 P.M., or close to it, the telephone rang on Doc's desk. Park picked up the receiver and it startled him to hear Laina's voice. Fortunately, Doc had gone down to Jake's to get sandwiches. It startled Park and it alarmed him. He couldn't have Laina calling anywhere to ask for him.

"I worried about you driving so far last night," her fresh direct voice said.

"Well, I'll explain to Mr. Fields you worried about me."

"Oh, Park. I'm sorry. I *was* worried, though. I won't call you again."

He said more pleasantly, "We're sitting it out. Nobody's enjoying it."

"Is the fight off? I've been listening to the radio. Did you know last night that the Bull would rat like this? Is that why you said for me not to bet?"

Park hung up on her . . .

He didn't know how she would take it and half-expected to hear the phone ring. He waited. It didn't ring. Laina didn't call back; and, in addition to all his anxiety, he began to worry about Laina.

Doc must have had a few drinks downstairs because his red face had a dislocated baffled look to it when he arrived with sandwiches. Park ate half of one sandwich. He wasn't hungry. Doc and he listened to the radio. The announcers became more virulent. Where was Bull Amani? Why didn't Bull Amani step forward and explain himself? The police had broken up a small riot early this afternoon in front of the Paradise Auditorium but more demonstrations against Bull Amani were anticipated.

Park thought of Lew Kirsch's staff of girls trudging through the rain into the makakina section of the city where the longshoremen lived with their families and relatives. Laina might have been one of those girls. Lew paid his interviewers twenty dollars a day and last March Laina had gone to the offices to apply for a position and Park had first seen her then.

In his mind he now could see someone very much like Laina climbing the rickety steps of one of the dark crowded slum dwellings in the lower makakina. Her survey questions were only an excuse to introduce herself into the family. It would be a Hawaiian longshoreman's family and she would be speaking in Hawaiian and by now she had been trained in the neighborly, gossipy approach.

"*People say Mr. Amani's gone crazy,*" would be one of the sentences she had memorized to translate afterward and leave with a family.

"*People say Mr. Amani's friends have been trying to hide it until after the next F. I. U. election. He's a raving maniac. That's why he won't fight.*"

"Kid, you ain't falling asleep?"

Park jerked up his head.

Doc was sweating this afternoon. He didn't have as much hope as he had had this morning. "Kid, suppose the Bull don't come in?"

"All we have to do is wait."

"Kid, I can't take any more waiting. My insides are crawling. The Bull won't come."

Doc's red face got even more dislocated and he muttered to himself and presently he slumped down in his chair and shut his eyes a minute or so and opened them again. Then he opened a drawer and Park thought Doc was reaching for another bottle of island brandy and had an instant of complete astonishment when he saw Doc had a shiny little revolver in his hand. Doc said, "So long, kid," and lifted the revolver, his face working, the red skin shiny with sweat.

Park exclaimed, "Doc!" and jumped and batted Doc's hand to one side, twisting the revolver loose. Doc struggled and gave up struggling and sagged in his chair like an old sack. Park looked at the revolver and saw it was loaded and stuck it in his pocket. He heard a roaring through the window where a mob of Flips were collecting around Jake's. He opened drawers in Doc's desk until he found the one having the bottle in it and he poured a slug, a big one.

"Here, Doc."

Doc got it down his gullet and shivered and all his face seemed to split apart and come together in fragments. He looked up half-ashamed, half-defiantly, at Park. "Sixteen years on this rotten island. The Bull won't come. I'm busted. You should have let me do it, kid."

Park got back to his chair, still with that sense of amazement. Doc actually had tried to kill himself? Park could not believe it. Doc wouldn't have really pulled a trigger on himself. It must have been an act.

"Stop worrying, Doc."

"Kid, you still think the Bull might walk in?"

"I know he will."

"Kid, maybe I better tell you why the Bull ain't walking in."

"All we have to do is wait."

"That's what you think. You know this spring I figure a match between the Bull and a reg'lar pro makes a cleanup?" Doc's eyes swiveled across at Park. "Christ A'mighty, wasn't it you who give me the idea when first you started working here?"

"You must be thinking of somebody else."

"No, I guess it wasn't you. But you did give me an idea later. You know how I talked with the Bull. You remember. He likes the idea. He sees it gives him prestige. If he can say he licked a reg'lar pro, alla rest of his life he's the bully boy of the island. But I have to guarantee to pick a boy who'll dive. So I guarantee to pick a right boy—but, kid, it ain't all I do."

Park did not want Doc to continue with these confidences. It was awkward for Park. The less Doc believed Park knew the less danger Park would have later of a hand showing.

"Doc, it's none of my business how you arranged it with Bull Amani. I don't give a damn. I've bet two hundred on the Bull to win and I'm not going to open my yap that the fight's been fixed."

"Kid, don't you get it? The Bull *ain't gonna win* and maybe he's learned he won't," said Doc, and it was too late to shut him off. Doc was splitting at the seams. All Park could do was listen and hope if Doc got it out of his system he'd glue himself back together again. "The Tiger won't make no dive, kid," Doc was saying in a kind of wild frenzy, leaning forward on the shabby desk, beating ineffectually at the desk with both hands. "That's the payoff. Don't you remember? You give me the idea. It was . . ."

"I didn't give you the idea," Park said, but it was like trying to stop a torrent with a straw.

". . . just after I sign the Bull and you started laughing. Remember? You said suppose I go downstairs and talk to Jake Kutu? Suppose I tell Jake I got a double switch and nobody but him and me knows the Bull ain't gonna win? Everybody on the island bets on the Bull to win. Who cleans up? Jake and me can clean up. Sure, I know, kid. You were horsing it. You didn't mean nothing. But I keep thinking about it. Sixteen years I run square fights, never a fix. So now I fix a fight for the Bull. Why not fix it a good fix while I'm doing it, a reg'lar double fix? Then I clean up and get off this stinking island and go to New York. Kid, it's what I done with Jake Kutu. Only me and Jake know. But maybe Jake's squealed on me to the Bull? Maybe that's why the Bull won't walk in."

"Doc," said Park calmly, "Jake has too much invested to open his yap. Suppose he hears you've yapped to me? We both might get our throats cut. Leave me out."

Doc said he had the shakes. He was an old man. He was fifty-five. He took the bottle of island brandy and poured it into the basin. He washed his face at the spigot in the dingy gymnasium. Sure, kid. He guessed he'd had too much to drink. He'd be all right. Give him time. Christ A'mighty! He sure had the shakes. For a minute he'd wanted to blow a hole in his head. Thanks, kid.

Park waited it out in the wicker chair. He could smell the smells of old sweat and urine and leather and rotting wood seeping from the gymnasium. Doc had moods. If he wasn't down at the bottom he was on top of the world. His hope returned. He promised Park he'd convince the Bull. If the Bull walked in, Doc would convince him. Doc had that check. Mr. Meaker had been smart to think of a postdated check. Doc wished he hadn't poured the brandy into the basin. Park turned on the radio. The announcers were working on Bull Amani.

"All we have to do is wait," Park said.

"Have you heard this one?" Doc asked. "There was an Irishman, see?"

"People say he's crazy . . ."

"People say they wish they'd voted for Mr. Charley Wong and not Bull Amani last year . . ."

It was the snowball principle, Park thought. You started with a small pebble but you had to start where the pebble could accumulate a mass very rapidly. At first Park couldn't understand what the announcer on the three o'clock newscast from HOK was talking about. The announcer was describing the five minutes of silence. Evidently the announcer was speaking directly from the cannery. In a muted and reverent voice he was describing the five minutes of silence. Belatedly, Park understood what the announcer was talking about.

That poor goddamn bastard!

At four o'clock the Bull hadn't walked in. "I'll be back in half an hour, Doc," Park promised. "I'd stay sober, too. The Bull can come in, anytime."

"Kid, you still think he'll walk in?"

"He has to," Park said. "He has *got* to come in, Doc."

Park did not think he was running out from a tough day. All he needed was a short breather. He stuck his hand in his coat pocket, feeling Doc's revolver there. The Bull *had* to walk in. In half an hour Park would be back to wait it out with Doc. He drove the Buick through heavy fragrant rain toward the John Oliver Building.

What was By Meaker doing? Couldn't more pressure be thrown on the Bull? Park realized he should have checked through before now with E. P. E. P. would ask questions; E. P. was easy as an old shoe but he didn't like his boys to have failures. It was hot and sticky inside the Buick. The rain hit hard against the windshield.

Elsie Flavola, the mayor's daughter, ceased typing when Park entered and began the slow process of heaving her three hundred pounds off the chair. Park knew all about Elsie Flavola because he made it a point to know a great deal about everyone whom By and Lew Kirsch employed. But Elsie knew very little about Mr. Mattison, and what she knew had been carefully and inconspicuously organized for her. Mr. Mattison painted landscapes on the other side of the island. When he ran low on money he had the gumption to get himself jobs. She knew Mr. Meaker had wanted to assist Mr. Mattison. Three or four times he had asked Mr. Mattison to prepare a drawing or an advertising layout. But Mr. Mattison had not quite worked out. Mr. Meaker had told Elsie that Mr. Mattison was going to get somewhere someday as a fine landscape painter but he wasn't a commercial artist.

"Mr. Mattison," Elsie said. "You can't go in now. Mr. Meaker's—"

Park walked in and dropped into one of the red leather chairs. Startled, By Meaker wheeled around behind his shiny koa wood desk, hastily cupping a hand over the telephone. He glanced hard at Park. He nodded to Elsie that it was all right. He spoke into the telephone, "Danny? I'll call you back in a minute," and hung up. He looked again at Park.

Park said very softly, "Shut that goddamn door."

Without a word By shut and locked the door. He grimaced sympathetically at Park.

Park said, "We've had two small riots down in the makakina. The Flips are sore. They want the Chinaman to call off all bets. Why doesn't the Bull crack? Where's he hiding?"

"Howie Wright located him about half an hour ago at Herby Subie's place. If you want to know how I look at it, I think Subie's the smart boy. He doesn't know what's wrong but he's seen the betting odds hold and he's gotten the wind up."

"Doc Fields is splitting at the seams. We can't wait much longer."

"I've been thinking the same thing."

Having made up his mind, Park didn't hesitate.

He said, "Get going on the Bull's daughter but by God don't let your hand show in it."

By's long upper lip seemed to grow longer. "I had Danny on the phone when you walked in and scared the Bejesus out of Elsie."

Park asked, "If there's a kickback, can that pimp pin anything on you?"

"Not how I'm doing it," By said, sitting behind his desk again. He dialed a number. He looked across at Park. "Danny's a photographer. I buy photos from him to run in the tourist folders."

"We're in a nice business," Park said.

"Some of our best undercover agents were pimps and madams and sporting girls during the war. I like it better this way. We get paid more."

Park felt his head fall forward and gave it a shake and stood up. He'd be asleep if he had another minute in that easy chair. He blinked his eyes. They smarted. His wet shirt chafed his arm-pits. He stared through the rain-blurred window toward streets seven stories down. He heard By's light voice speaking into the phone.

Park looked at his watch. It was six minutes before five. He tuned in to station HOK on By's big radio. He turned the Hawaiian music louder to drown By's voice. In six minutes the news broadcast would start. He wondered if Herby Subie had a radio in his house. Two loudspeaker towers had been erected on the waterfront. Even if Bull Amani didn't listen to the radio, he couldn't escape the great bleating voices sprayed from the towers. And Lew Kirsch's girls must have started whirlpools of talk and gossip all around that neighborhood by now.

Suddenly the music ceased. A rich deep kanaka voice said from the radio, "We break in for a special news flash of great interest to everyone on this happy island . . ."

Park didn't need any particular intuition to know what that news flash was going to be. When a tough day began to fold it usually folded very quickly. Park had seen it happen before. It used to be exciting but it wasn't any longer, even at the end. What you had done was to call the cards again but it took a hell of a lot out of you while you were waiting. That rich radio voice was speaking excitedly as Park turned his head toward By.

Park said, "By, our baby's come home."

". . . now gathered in Doc Fields' offices in the Paradise Building," the voice was saying. "Mr. Amani has been shocked and astonished by the false rumors and lies which have so mysteriously sprung up about him all over the island today. Bull Amani has asked station HOK, at the top of your dial, to tell all his loyal friends on the docks, in the sugar-cane fields, in the pineapple fields, and in the big cannery, that he will be in the ring next week. He promises to K. O. Tiger Nogusi by the fourth round, if not sooner. Mr. Herby Subie, the popular secretary of the F. I. U., has just telephoned your news announcer directly from the offices of Doc Fields—"

Park switched off the radio. He had almost forgotten that all you had to do was wait after you turned the dogs loose.

He told By, "We won't need the Bull's kid. Forget her. We're in."

8

In 1931 when the depression so severely struck Mt. Morris, Illinois, a number of high-school teachers including Park's father were reduced to half pay. Park had needed an automobile desperately then. He could get a country route for one of the Chicago dailies and clear from fifty to a hundred dollars a month by driving the twenty- to thirty-mile route every morning before high-school classes. It took him six months to assemble an automobile for himself from the engine of an old Hupmobile he had found in the town dump heap, a 1922 Maxwell chassis, and old wheels, tires, and parts which the local garage gave him in return for his duties as night watchman. Park still remembered, when at last the machine was assembled, that long moment after he had cranked it and it ran. It served his purpose for the next three years. With the money he earned and saved, he entered Harvard in the fall of 1934.

Park gave himself a long moment after turning off the radio. He looked across the room and saw By's face grinning triumphantly back at him. A machine had been built during these past two years. It was small. It was only a scale model, Park thought, but within another year even this scale model could bend the hundred thousand people of this island into a continuously docile frame of mind. For those individuals who deviated, the machine could send out its lines of force and strike them down as Bull Amani had been struck down this afternoon.

He heard By's reedy voice saying triumphantly, "Mattison and Meaker, Morale Operations, Incorporated, with offices in the biggest building in New York. I wish we had the dough now instead of having to wait five more years to save enough of a stake for a national service."

"We're doing enough here," Park said absently. "Five years won't seem long."

He was thinking of having a steak dinner tonight with Laina if he could stay awake that long. But before driving to the Halepule side of the island to pick up Laina for dinner, he had to get through to Doc Fields. Next, he must report in to E. P. It was something like having to remember to lock all the doors in one house before leaving for another and more pleasant house in the country.

"Sure, sure," By said. "We're doing fine. I've got no complaints."

Park raised his head. He stopped thinking of Laina, of a steak dinner, and of first locking up one house before going to another. By's voice sounded strained. He was forgetting that this also had been a tough day for By.

"Let's have it. Don't hold back on me."

"It's being on an island. Once we get to the mainland, we'll have more space to work in and the odds won't pile up so much against us."

"It's this drastic stuff that pulls down our odds. Next year, when E. P. pays off the bond issue, we can begin to coast. We'll have the right boy in to run the union. We can concentrate on long-range white M. O."

"You're not married but I've got to think of Millie. What happens if we do tip our hand?"

Park knew what happened if you tipped your hand while you were applying black M. O. You got it in the neck.

He said, "We're paid not to."

"If anything ever does go wrong, I'd have to get Millie out of here in a hurry. I wouldn't like to count on E. P. standing by us if we made a mistake and tipped our hand."

"We couldn't count on him. He'd have to drop us and I'd tell him he'd have to."

"Don't get me wrong. I'm not thinking of myself. I like this job."

"Look. I know how you feel about Millie—" Park stepped to By and gave him an affectionate shake and as he did so he was reminded of how E. P. often gave him an affectionate shake. But Park was not as demonstrative as E. P. was inclined to be; and Park did not think he got quite into his gesture all that E. P. usually managed to convey in his. He stepped back and said very seriously, "If ever we find we're running into anything that looks like real danger, I'm willing to decide right now to get Millie off the island in a hurry. By God, I'll ship Laina out with her."

"We could have everything crash fast if our hand got tipped off to the wrong people. I get down to the Makakina airfield every so often. Station BYQ's thinking of broadcasting a daily program from the field at the time the tourists leave on the afternoon run for Honolulu. It wouldn't louse anything if I managed to make friends with one of the boys operating a charter service, would it?"

Park thought for a moment.

"If we got into a really tight situation, we wouldn't want the girls to go to Makakina field. If you wanted to grab somebody on the run, where would you first think of looking on an island like this?"

"You're right. I'd go to the Makakina airfield."

"Let's do it this way. As soon as the contract's signed, you do some scouting for someone who has a good safe airplane to rent at one of the smaller airfields at Iki or Pohaku. Make friends with the guy. In an emergency, you can rush Millie and Laina—"

"Just a minute," said By. "I still don't want you to get me wrong. I'll put Millie and Laina on a plane but Mrs. Meaker's boy isn't leaving for any place until you do. I never had it better than working with you."

Park felt embarrassed by By's declaration of loyalty.

"Nuts, this is only the beginning. We'll have it better than this before we're through. We've both been under a strain. What we need is a breather as soon as we can find one." He took the telephone. "Let's get Doc Fields and start locking up."

Doc's voice sounded blurred over the telephone.

"Kid, this is the happiest day of my life. Kid, will you tell Mr. Meaker he can have his choice of any of the best seats for the fight I've got left? That goes for you, too. . . ."

After having tucked away Doc Fields for the day, Park was in a hurry to report in to E. P. and head for the other side of the island. But By detained him a minute longer. By said that might be an idea, getting a breather for a few days. Why not have the week end after the fight for themselves? By's wife had been asking to be taken to the Mountain House on the island of Hawaii where there was cold weather and sometimes you could see snow at ten thousand feet above sea level. Millie didn't know anything about Park except that he was a painter who lived on the Halepule side of the island. By had married her after the war. Why didn't Park fly with Laina to the Mountain House for the same week end? By suggested. The two couples could happen to meet. By did not see how it would show their hand to the two girls.

"Let's do that," said Park and opened the door.

What By needed was a week end with Millie, Park thought. It would give By a chance to recover his perspective and to realize your best possible security was not in planning for an emergency exit but in planning continuously and relentlessly never to allow your hand to show.

The rain had ended when Park crossed the street from the John Oliver Building. He was thinking of how pleased E. P. would be to hear that Bull Amani had cracked. The air was very fresh. Park heard the mynah birds cawing at him from the copper cornices of the Chinese Bazaar and they reminded him of E. P.'s cheerful caw.

Park liked going into the Chinese Bazaar. It was always crowded and you could go in and out and no one ever thought anything of it. Inside, he made his way without haste down one aisle and another, from the smell of dried bulbs and ginger candy to the smell of gardenia flowers and sandalwood. He remembered last night when he had driven home from Harry's with Laina, and he paused a few minutes at the third counter from the silk counter. Although the Chinese Bazaar did not have as expensive jewelry as you could buy at Kimball's Galleries or the other fashionable stores at Halepule Beach, it had a greater variety of everything.

Five minutes later, Park stepped inside one of the telephone booths under the stairs and dialed E. P.'s unlisted number.

In his private office E. P. had two phones. One phone was hooked in with his secretary's phone and the switchboard on the first floor of the cannery. The second phone had a direct line. The procedure was simple but secure. During the war French underground agents had used similar procedures. You dialed. The second telephone buzzed softly at E. P.'s desk. If E. P. was there he picked up the telephone. He said, "One, two, three, four——" and on to ten and waited. It was to identify his voice. Park did the same to identify his voice. No names were ever given and Park always called from a public phone booth. It was impossible to trace the source of calls from public phone booths. At present Park considered these telephone procedures as dry runs or practice runs. He didn't think E. P.'s lines were tapped. However, a time might come when the lines would be tapped. Sooner or later the enemy got around to trying to do to you what you were doing to him and for the past eighteen months all lines feeding into the F. I. U. meeting and hiring halls had been tapped with a twenty-four hour wire-tape recording of all calls. Four of Lew Kirsch's highest-paid girls were on that job . . .

Expecting E. P.'s caw, it surprised Park to hear another voice say, "Morton speaking. Hello. Hello?"

Park could identify Buddy's voice. He broke procedures. "This is Park. Where's E. P.? I'm reporting in to him."

"Park," Buddy said, "have you heard about Dick Stewart? It was this afternoon. He died in the hospital. I've been hoping you'd get in touch with me. Where have you been?"

Park hesitated for a moment. "Buddy," he said, "where's E. P.?"

"He flew to Honolulu at three o'clock this afternoon," said Buddy with an odd note in his voice. "He's flying tonight to Los Angeles. Something came up."

"What about Stewart's funeral?"

"It's on Thursday, but E. P. can't be here. The funeral's on my shoulders," said Buddy, the odd note beginning to have a meaning for Park.

The news of E. P.'s sudden departure surprised Park but it did not surprise him greatly. Evidently Buddy had not yet discovered that sometimes E. P. would haul tail for a week or so when a situation became hot.

"He asked me to have you arrange for Howie Wright to run something in the *Happy Island News*. Frankly, I don't know what E. P. means, Park."

Park did. No one must have the mistaken notion that E. P. had flown to the mainland to avoid Stewart's funeral. If E. P. had flown off it was because of a real emergency. There ought to be a long statement in the Wednesday issue of the *Happy Island News*. Here, E. P. would write with deep emotion of his good friend, Richard Stewart. In the last paragraph it would be best for E. P. to mention his unexpected departure. He would be sorry he couldn't be here for the funeral. "I know Dickie Stewart would tell me, 'If you are needed in Los Angeles, you go. Paradise Products and its employees must always come first. They have always come first with me, above any personal obligations. I want them to come first with you even if I am no longer here . . .' " Something, Park thought, like that. He'd call By Meaker. By could get through to Howie. Howie Wright was good at writing things like that for E. P. He could write it and sign it with E. P.'s name and have it run as an editorial on the front page of the *News*.

Park explained what E. P. expected in the *Happy Island News*. There was a pause. "Frankly, Park, my head seems to be spinning. I want to know about this fight. Where can I meet you? Where is it safe for me to meet you?"

Park would not have chosen to meet Buddy at the end of a tough day. When you had slept with another man's wife, even if it was more than five years ago, it required a certain mental adjustment before facing the husband. Park would have preferred to wait. However, Buddy was insistent.

On the way to Halepule Beach, a Studebaker trailed the Buick for nearly twenty miles. Park first noticed the Studebaker when slowing down for the rough section of Hono Road. It was not deliberately following him, he realized, because it continued around the wide curve toward the old town when Park wheeled

· 117 ·

right into the Outrigger Club's driveway. But for the last ten of those twenty miles he had almost convinced himself that the Studebaker was trailing him. It was a gray Studebaker. The late afternoon sunshine had slanted against its windshield, the light reflecting so brilliantly that it was impossible for Park to see the driver in his rear-view mirror.

He gave the Buick to one of the attendants at the club and strolled through the camellia gardens toward the beach and the long wooden pier at the south where he was to meet Buddy Morton. He looked at his watch. It was ten minutes after six. You never did know in a business like this if something might not inadvertently tip your hand. It could happen by accident. It was one of the hazards against which you always had to be on guard. Park did not think anyone had deliberately followed him. However, tomorrow he would ask Lew to look into it. By tomorrow night Lew could have a list of all gray Studebakers on the island and the names of the owners. It could be a practice test.

The air was rosy colored and very clear after the rain. The rows of cabanas on the beach had about emptied. A few surf-board enthusiasts were coasting in on slow oily green combers. Park walked around a woman lying on a grass mat, a dark-skinned beach boy rubbing her white back with scented coconut oil. The woman was resting on her stomach and wore a yellow French-style pair of ruffled diapers and nothing more. To one side of her was the crumpled wet wad of discarded yellow halter. Park saw the beach boy's dark hands pressing down around the woman's ribs and going under her and up again and under her again. The woman lay there face down with the brown curly hair circled by her white arms and after Park had passed on it seemed to him he still could see her, lying there so quietly, scarcely breathing.

He wondered what these mainland women thought the beach boys were. Did they think of the beach boys as something like animals, not quite human? Was that why the women would fly to the island and lie on a rosy beach at dusk and pay the beach boys ten dollars an hour to massage and knead away a resentment against the days of living? Perhaps that was it.

· 118 ·

He found himself wondering how Ellen Morton would like it on the island after she had been here six months or a year. Park had seen other young mainland women gradually change. Would Ellen some day lie on the beach at twilight and have scented coconut oil rubbed into her skin? Park remembered her small soft breasts. It was very early in the morning but there had been enough light through her window at the Shoreham for him to see her quite distinctly when she sat up in bed, the sheet and blanket falling away. Afterwards, he remembered lifting his eyes toward her face. She'd had a shocked expression, the great blue eyes staring down along herself to him. Then he had ceased looking upon the beautiful white meadow to the curve of throat and rise of head. A momentary regret or even a sorrow for her had vanished as his heart took up a more violent beating. He hadn't remembered having a momentary regret or sorrow for her until now. It had been a long time ago.

Park waited at the far end of the pier. It was safe enough here, he decided. He saw the two remaining fishermen wrapping lines around their poles, preparing to leave. He stuck his hands in his pockets and sauntered toward them, the wind ruffling his hair.

"What luck, gentlemen?" he asked, polite, never pushing too hard.

The fishing here wasn't half as good as you got back home in Minnesota, they said. That was where to go to fish. Park's blue eyes were friendly and sympathetic but he did not reply. The two men threw their traps across their shoulders and called, self-consciously, "Aloha," as if they only had learned the word today; and they passed by the small slight figure of Buddy Morton. Buddy was still wearing mainland clothes, a lightweight gabardine this time, the expensive sheen already dimmed by the heat and Buddy's sweating.

Park said impulsively, "For God's sake, take off your coat before you melt."

"I keep forgetting." Buddy smiled shyly. He pulled off his coat. "Is it always this hot?"

"This," Park said, "has been one of our cooler days."

It made him think he had been here for a long time. He could go to one of the grass shack tourist offices and ask for his kamaaina coconut souvenir ring. He sat at the end of the pier and dangled his legs and Buddy sat beside him, smaller and thinner than Park, and dangled his legs, too. Park noticed how the rosy dusk seemed to curve and fold along Buddy's good line of jaw and high-bridged nose. Buddy looked back at him through the rosy twilight as if he enjoyed being here with Park and sitting here together and not saying anything. Park thought what a nice guy Buddy was.

Presently Buddy admitted he had to talk to somebody. E. P. had told him he could trust Park. He and his wife used to tell each other everything but now Buddy couldn't even talk things over with his wife. E. P. said Buddy was not to discuss business affairs with Ellen or anyone except the three or four officers in the company and possibly Park Mattison. So here he was, Buddy said. Good Lord, what a day! He had to blow off to somebody.

Park wondered how Ellen Morton was at listening when Buddy told her everything. He wondered how Buddy would take it if Buddy ever discovered his wife did not tell him quite everything.

"Let's have it," said Park, still good-naturedly.

After E. P. pulled out in the afternoon Buddy had been left alone in the big private office. He was supposed to be in charge while E. P. was away. Buddy was a banker. He didn't know the first thing about running a packing plant. He supposed everyone in the plant knew he didn't know, too. By now everyone must have learned he was the great-nephew of old Mr. Tothic. He would have been pegged as a relative brought in and given the sugar bowl. Perhaps that was why E. P. had asked him in. He hoped not; he didn't believe in nepotism. But there it was. His grandmother had been the sister of E. P.'s father. Buddy's side of the family still held a minority interest in the Tothic Estate which controlled Paradise Products Corporation and the plantations.

Buddy paused, giving Park a long look. "Didn't E. P. tell you about me?"

Park had not been told. It interested him to discover Buddy

was in the family. It explained why Buddy so familiarly had called E. P. "Pip," yesterday. Evidently Buddy did not know that E. P. was always very casual with introductions exactly as Buddy did not know that E. P. often hauled tail for a week or so when a situation became too intense. E. P. called it by another name. E. P. would say, "Let them stew in their juices for a time." After Thursday, when Dick Stewart was laid to rest, Dick was going to be given a good long time to stew in his juices. A god-damn good long time.

Park said, "I haven't had a chance to talk with E. P. about you or about much of anything. Having him haul tail so soon caught me a little by surprise."

"It caught me more than a little," Buddy said with that odd tone back in his voice. "For example, do you know anything about tin cans?"

"I know Paradise Products is the third largest user of cans in Hawaii."

"I used to be a banker, a finance man. Park, I didn't even know we used that many tin cans. Tomorrow I have to be in Honolulu at nine in the morning to talk with the people of the National Can Company about tin cans. Good Lord!" He dangled his legs. He looked at Park. "What about this fight? Can you tell me? How does a prize fight fit into the operations of the Paradise Products Corporation?"

Park could tell him.

Buddy remembered the big strike last year, didn't he? All the islands were struck. At that time the I. L. W. U. controlled all workers in this island. The I. L. W. U. had the longshoremen. The field workers and plant employees were affiliated. Bull Amani was head man of the longshoremen and had helped or-ganize the field workers. Old Charley Wong had organized the plant employees. The M. O. task force—Park admitted, telling it straight—had not been here long enough last year to have had as much weight as he wished. However, Lew Kirsch's research staff was active. Through the surveys both E. P. and Dick Stewart had been able to watch a decline in labor's enthusiasm for the strike. By July, last year, it became evident that old

Charley Wong would pull the cannery union away from the I. L. W. U. if Bull Amani would join him with the longshoremen and field workers.

"Just a minute, Park. If your group hadn't been driving wedges, would this island have split away from the big national union to form its own independents?"

"We may have oiled the bearings a little. Early in August we learned Bull Amani had decided to throw in with Charley Wong. Kirsch took a quick straw vote. The longshoremen were in favor. After that, all we had to do was wait a few weeks."

Park wanted to explain about Dick Stewart without rancor. Stewart was dead. He had died at 2:41 this afternoon in the Ruth Tothic Memorial Hospital. He would never louse up anything again.

"Fair enough, but what happened?" asked Buddy.

"Instead of trusting our surveys and waiting, Mr. Stewart rushed into a private dicker with Bull Amani. He gave Bull Amani ten thousand dollars of company money to promise to pull the longshoremen from the I. L. W. U. and in that way break the strike."

Buddy's voice had a swift sharpness. "Good Lord! That was stupid of Stewart. You didn't approve, did you?"

"Hell, no. Stewart plunged into it without telling E. P. until it was done. It's a short-range policy, any time, for a company to bribe a labor leader directly, one hand to another. And it had consequences. It kept lousing us up. Suppose the rank-and-file members heard Amani had been bribed by a company man? I expect the Flips would try to kill Amani but I'm not concerned about what would happen to him. We'd have a kickback against E. P. and all the favorable attitudes we've been building up. You can see how Stewart got us in a hole. Bull Amani likes the taste of money. He wants more. Remember, these aren't mainland unions. The president of the F. I. U. is a dictator, and the labor council has very little to say. As a result, Bull Amani has us by the short hairs unless we get rid of him. He's been agitating for a forty-cent-an-hour overall increase. He knows it's way out of line and E. P. can't grant one-third that much. But last month Amani asked Stewart for fifteen thousand dollars—"

"Fifteen thousand!"

"That's right. If he doesn't get it he'll continue to agitate for an impossible wage increase. In December wage renegotiations come up, with Bull Amani threatening to call the whole island on another strike unless the company takes care of him, personally, with fifteen thousand in bribe money."

"It's blackmail," Buddy said. "If you give in once, you'll be expected to give in more and more."

"That's exactly why we've got to get rid of Amani as fast as possible. Fortunately, for us, Charley Wong's the next most popular leader. Kirsch's straw polls show that Herby Subie's a low third in popularity, a very low third. He's a Kauai man and he had a year or so at the University of Hawaii. Because he's always trying to persuade the Flips to improve their diets and to dig proper sewers for their shacks, he's counted as something of a nut. By getting rid of Amani, old Charley Wong's certain of being made acting president in time for wage negotiations. He'll be elected officially when the unions have their annual meeting next year. Wong's a right boy. He'll have the prestige to cool down rank-and-file members. He'll refuse to call a strike. He'll show Amani's demands were unreasonable."

"What of Herby Subie's hopes for a housing program?" asked Buddy. "Hasn't Paradise Products been promising that for ten years?"

Park wondered if Buddy hadn't been here long enough to realize what side he was on. He said, "Look. Don't worry about Subie. The Flips and longshoremen think he's a screwball. I hope to God they continue to think so. Wong's our boy. Wong will stall off talk about new camps and sewers until E. P. pays off the bond issue and we all can begin to breathe again."

"My God," said Buddy. "Is Wong one of your spies or something? Is that how you're so sure of him?"

Park's voice hardened. He knew there were certain details concerning the operation of the M. O. project which even E. P.

didn't care to know about. He said, "When we came here two years ago we started checking back on Wong and all other labor leaders. We can control Wong."

"You could send him to prison for something you've found he's done?"

"Something like that. Just take my word. Once Wong is in, our troubles will be over. All we need is to have the right boy in."

There was another long silence with the surf rolling in over the sand. Park was prepared to suggest they call it a day when Buddy spoke, this time very quietly and thoughtfully.

"Park, I'm not squeamish but all of this has been a shock to me. I won't sleep tonight for thinking about this M. O. force we control."

This was an attitude toward M. O. which Park had not expected from Buddy.

Park asked, "How else can we do it? Right now, we're completely loused up unless we use M. O. In the past, management has tried everything else and lost."

It was true, too. When you looked at it, nothing used in the past had been more than a temporary palliative. It was a form of warfare; and labor always had a hundred times or a thousand times more men than management had. Basically, labor would always have more sheer force than management.

"It frightens me stiff," was all Buddy said.

"If we don't get Bull Amani out before December and the right boy in," Park said, "we'll have another strike on our hands."

Buddy contemplated Park through the twilight. Finally he asked, "I'm wondering if the end ever justifies the means, though?"

That was a damned peculiar question for Buddy to ask! "Bull Amani was loused up for us last year, Buddy. It wasn't our mistake."

"I don't say it's your mistake. Was it entirely Stewart's mistake? In his way wasn't he attempting to follow the same policy Pip ordered you to follow? I grant you you're using much more ingenuity than Stewart did. What I'm trying to say is that Paradise Products has forgotten certain moral obligations to the people on this island. Haven't we a moral dilemma on our hands?"

Park felt his stomach muscles cramp. A moral dilemma? If Park had inherited Buddy's wealth and position he thought he might be able to consider abstract problems of morality. He wondered why it was that the second and third generations of wealthy families often became heated about their moral obligations? Why didn't they give up their wealth? Why didn't they try starting from scratch and find out how well they liked it? Had the founders of family fortunes been so warm about moral obligations?

He heard Buddy saying earnestly, "It seems to me both great-uncle Enders and Pip should have thought first of the promises made to the people here. It seems to me the development at the beach and the tunnels for new water might have waited. I know I don't set policies for the company. But Pip's policies make me wonder." Buddy's voice came clearly and distinctly. "I shouldn't care to work very long for a concern which had to lie or to threaten its employees or the public."

Did E. P. know Buddy had these ideas? Park doubted it. All successful business establishments lied. Did Buddy consider advertising, for example, an expression of the truth? Had Buddy ever been under a foreman on an assembly line or a salesman on the road under a sales manager who was under someone above him, all applying the prod? A business corporation was not concerned with the truth or what was good or what was fair. Its sole concern was to stay in business and pay dividends.

Listening to Buddy, Park felt the same frustration and dismay which he recalled from the war. The Office of Strategic Services had offered ideas for psychological warfare which the high brass in the Chiefs of Staffs had declined. Evidently the high brass believed that you did not do certain things even in a war. A hundred years ago the same sort of mind had argued for wooden ships instead of iron. And here was Buddy speaking of moral dilemmas and moral obligations because his mind was incapable of realizing that M. O. was merely a new and better fighting tool.

When Buddy finished, Park did not rush in. He wanted to

decide in his own mind exactly how to say it. He stood and he waited for Buddy to stand.

"Buddy, I'd hoped you and I were going to make a go of it, together."

"I've had the same hope. I believe we are, too. Personally, I'd like to see you inside the company, not acting as a consultant or an agent for us. If I'm right and we are facing a moral dilemma, I should like to see at least the hurtful phases of M. O. completely eliminated. But company decisions are out of your hands and mine. This morning Pip told me he wanted to go over the financial details of a new contract with you. I think you should know I've decided to inform Pip I'm not competent to judge the financial details of a contract which has been drawn up to carry out policies of his with which I'm not in agreement. I think you should deal directly with Pip."

"Whatever you like," said Park.

He had expected to have a showdown with Buddy. He had been mistaken. He saw Buddy's concerned friendly face through that rosy dim light and he wished he could tell Buddy to forget moral obligations and moral dilemmas or cousin Pip wouldn't keep him very long on this island. Even if Buddy's side of the family had a minority interest in Paradise Products and Buddy was connected to E. P. by blood, E. P. wasn't that sentimental. Stewart and E. P. had gone to college together. This afternoon Stewart had died and he had merely loused up a labor leader a year ago. Stewart hadn't had a frame of mind unreconciled to the frame of mind the boss expected.

Buddy was saying, "If anyone ought to stick his neck out to persuade cousin Pip to change company policies, I certainly should be the first before expecting it of anyone else. Isn't that a fair statement?"

If you wanted to run headlong into E. P., and trouble, it was a fair statement. But Park said gravely, "It's your neck, Buddy."

"I'll try to take care of it, thanks. You see, I know Pip, too."

Park doubted if Buddy really knew E. P. but he had nothing more to say. Park realized Buddy was not going to louse up the details of the contract. His anxiety had been needless; Buddy was very fair. It exasperated Park to know Ellen was Buddy's wife, because he found his liking for Buddy increasing. Park remembered E. P. had said to allow nothing to interfere with making a friend of Buddy. That was an order, Lieutenant.

E. P. ought to be very pleased because it had been a successful day after all. Bull Amani had been harried into Doc's office. Dick Stewart was dead. And Buddy was really very fair and wanting to be a friend.

Buddy glanced at his thin expensive watch. He said he had promised to have dinner at the hotel with his family. Buddy and Park walked across the darkening curve of the beach, the pavilions of the Outrigger Club all in shadow like galleons under sail. Buddy said, "I knew there was something else. I nearly forgot. I hear my wife met you last night at a party Mr. Kimball gave?"

It seemed to Park that his heart skipped a beat. "There was quite a mob at Harry's last night. Wasn't Mrs. Morton that attractive tall blonde girl? Yes, I did meet her briefly."

Buddy chuckled. "You're thinking of Mrs. Tolliver. She flew across the Pacific with us. Ellen's small, with brown hair."

"Oh," said Park. He did it fairly well, he thought.

"Don't apologize. I shan't give you away. Ellen doesn't shine much in a crowd and you have to know her to appreciate her. But she was impressed by you—rather, she was impressed by your painting. I was to look you up this afternoon. Mr. Kimball showed her your painting this morning. She was very excited about it when she telephoned me this noon."

When Park pulled his hands from his pockets, his hands were so adhesive with moisture that they pulled out the cloth linings, too. He pushed at the linings, shoving them in.

"I'll ask Harry Kimball not to stick her too much, Buddy."

"It's not that. I'm afraid *you're* stuck. You see Ellen's father founded the Museum of Modern Art in Seattle. That," said Buddy, dryly, "was probably a tax deal, but Ellen takes it quite seriously. After his death she became chairman of the board of trustees. Either you're a better painter than you realize or

Harry Kimball ought to be selling pineapples for us instead of paintings because Ellen's convinced you've great natural talent. She thinks you're more of a find than a young Mexican muralist she helped last year. She asked me to get in touch with Mr. Mattison and gave me the address Mr. Kimball had given her. You see, she thinks I should discuss money arrangements with her discoveries."

What the hell was Ellen up to, Park asked himself.

He said, "Money arrangements, Buddy?"

"Brace yourself. She wants to write to the museum and have them offer you a four-thousand dollar scholarship to go to Paris and study painting. She's certain she could get the scholarship for you in time for you to leave by Christmas."

Park was startled. He had never anticipated such a move from Ellen. He was aware of Buddy's bright expectant gaze. Buddy had a great sense of humor. It was funny. It was even funnier than Buddy knew. Very funny. Buddy stopped laughing.

"I warned you to brace yourself," said Buddy. "I'm sorry but you don't know how you looked, Park. I couldn't help laughing."

"Did you kill her idea?"

"Good Lord, you don't know Ellen. To show you how the island is corrupting me, I shall tell her I didn't have time to ring you at the address she gave me. I shall keep clear of it. This is your show. You see her yourself."

"Look, Buddy—"

Park wished you could wipe out the past. It had never occurred to him that Ellen would act to get him off the island, away from her. It was damned rash of her. She must have acted on impulse. She ought to have known enough to let it ride . . .

"Look, Buddy," he repeated. "I can't go to her."

"Yes, you can. Kimball knows she wants to offer you a scholarship. Do it through Mr. Kimball, as a favor to me. I dislike having to lie to Ellen any more than necessary."

"All right."

"You'll see her?"

"I'll see her."

"Fair enough. I wish you luck. Remember, she'll tell me everything. I'm going to look forward to hearing how well you came out with her. Don't hurt her feelings if you can help it, Park," asked Buddy, laughing no longer. "She likes to help people with talent. I don't much enjoy having this happen to Ellen, you know."

"I imagine you wouldn't. I'll be careful," Park promised. "I'll be as careful as I can."

Park had that same bursting sensation in his head as he drove his Buick along the highway, the graceful towers spraying soft music into the air. He turned left on Hibiscus Road. It seemed to him if only he could hang on through this week and next that finally he would enter that long cool stretch of land where even the trees lowered their branches to save you the exertion of reaching very high to pick off the sugar plums. He didn't know what he would say to Ellen tomorrow when he sought her out. "We used to tell each other everything," Buddy had said. Didn't Buddy know that no one really told anyone everything? He was sorry for Ellen and Buddy. He was sorry for himself and Laina and for the hundred thousand people of this island and for all the other people in the world who hoped to find the sugar-plum trees someday.

When he turned into the driveway the Buick's headlights flared over an automobile in the driveway. It was not Laina's Chevy. It was a large black Cadillac sedan. All the lights were on in the house. Park heard the tinkle of music from the portable phonograph which Laina had brought with her from Honolulu. Laina came through the fragrant dusk to him and whispered hastily, "We have guests, Park. Be nice to them. They have a surprise for you. I'm so happy." He was so exhausted he was incapable of thinking who the guests might be, what the surprise was, or why Laina was so happy.

9

Laina led Park into the front room where he saw Cyril Brolly with the blonde girl from Chicago. Sometimes it was an advantage to be close to total exhaustion. Park simply stopped walking. He was almost past feeling surprise at anything. He did not know why an elderly movie actor with a blonde girl in tow had decided to call upon Laina and him and he didn't much care. Quite obviously, Mr. Brolly had stayed on to see him. Evidently the purpose of the call was as much to see him as to see Laina.

If you saw a girl and were attracted to her and wanted to try for her there were many procedures much less complicated than calling with a girl of your own upon the other girl and her lover. No, Park didn't believe Brolly was trying for Laina that way. It was something else. Perhaps he wanted to show off his conquest of the blonde girl after such a crashing failure with Laina at Harry's shindig.

Park noticed Laina was not wearing any makeup; she looked as fresh as apple blossoms, the dark red hair coiled in thick braids on top of her small head. She was wearing another of her print dresses, showing beautiful bare shoulders and the long beautiful bare legs below the crisp skirt. She slipped her arm through his as they entered, which was unusual, for ordinarily Laina was wary about Park and herself in the presence of others. As they entered there was that instant. Then Park understood. He admired her for it. She paused almost defiantly. All right, she was living with him. Let them think what they liked.

He saw the movie actor was wearing one of the Outrigger Club blazers, fawn-colored slacks and socks, and leather sandals. The blonde girl was also wearing a print dress; although hers was probably much more expensive than Liana's it was not cotton and consequently did not look as crisp. The blonde girl had not yet learned what to wear in a hot humid climate. Both of them were holding glasses filled with ice and, at least, liquid. Park wondered what Laina had found to give them. There was no whisky or brandy in the house. Park felt Laina's arm tremble slightly. By God it was like being newly married. She wanted him to make a good impression. At the same time she hoped he would be proud of her because she knew how to receive guests graciously.

"Well," said Park, "this is a pleasant surprise."

Laina explained rapidly, "Mr. Brolly asked to see you, Park. I thought you'd be home an hour ago."

"I'm sorry I was late."

"Cyril and I just barged in," said the blonde girl. She regarded Park with lifted eyebrows. "Darling, you haven't already forgotten my name?"

Evidently she called anyone "darling," or perhaps it was because she was with Cyril Brolly. Everyone from Hollywood called everyone else "darling" and it meant nothing at all. It was Mrs. Charles G. Tolliver, from Chicago. She had flown across the Pacific with Ellen and Buddy Morton. Consequently, at least she would be acquainted with them. What was her first name? Park remembered it was Janet.

"Hello, Janet. Welcome. The same to you, Mr. Brolly."

"Make it 'Cyril,' old man. I want to be a simple ordinary person out here. I want to forget Hollywood, old man. Just take me for myself, will you?"

"Whatever you say, Cyril. That's not lemonade Caroline's given you two to drink?"

"Park, it's all we had in the house."

"Darling," the blonde girl assured Laina, "I loved having you pick fresh lemons from your trees to make lemonade for us."

Mr. Brolly held up his half-filled glass and tinkled the ice cubes, his swarthy frog's face asking to be taken for itself today.

"Lemonade. I'm drinking it. It's my second glass. What do you know, old man?"

"You're lucky," said Park. "Laina and I usually drink milk. We live a wild life up here on the cliff."

Cyril Brolly finished his glass of lemonade with a flourish. He stepped in front of the open south window. Below him was the tiny garden dimly revealed by the light shining down from the living room. On beyond was the whitewashed brick wall with the iron gate which had rusted fast. Beyond the wall was the night, all the stars now visible; and that great space was out there, too, where the cliff fell away a thousand and more feet to the dark rocks below. Evidently Mr. Brolly was not oppressed by so much space.

He was making a speech, Park realized. All his life Mr. Brolly had longed for a simple idyllic existence where he would be taken just for himself. He wished to leave the strain and bustle of Hollywood because those punks in Hollywood had too many false values. They didn't understand real art or genius or why a man needed to be taken only for himself. The deep voice trembled. It had a note of expert pathos in it. Mr. Brolly envied Park Mattison. Yes, he did. He envied Park and Caroline because they were living an idyllic existence. They could always be themselves.

Mr. Brolly ceased speaking. Park decided the speech was ended. He wondered if he was supposed to applaud. He saw Mr. Brolly and the blonde girl exchanging glances. They were looking at Laina and smiling at her and she was smiling back. Now all three of them were regarding Park with an air of expectancy as if they were sharing a secret. They waited for Park to ask them. He saw that he was supposed to be curious. He was too tired to be very curious about anything.

"Well, well," he said. "What have we now?"

"Park," cried Laina, "Mr. Brolly's bought your painting. Cyril's bought your painting. It's why we've all been waiting for you."

Now what was he supposed to say? Well, well, think of that. Harry Kimball had nicked this little frog-faced actor for a square yard of canvas with oil paint splashed on it. The more you saw of someone else's racket, the more you saw it was also mostly M. O. It was the same everywhere. This little gent was supposed to receive six thousand dollars a week from his studio. Probably he actually got a third of that which was still a good salary. The motion-picture business was lousy with M. O., but very few of the boys in Hollywood knew they were dealing in it. They thought it was publicity. Perhaps they thought it was art.

"Well, Cyril. I feel honored. I don't know what to say."

Mr. Brolly also was honored. He had paid one thousand dollars, cash, this afternoon to prove what he thought of Park's talent. He had been in Kimball's Galleries. That wealthy Morton woman had come in with Harry Kimball and an artist named Phil Parsons was with them. But Mr. Brolly had said, firmly, "Mrs. Morton, I've heard of your museum in Seattle. I have a small collection but I am proud of it. I know you can buy any picture you wish, because after all I'm only a ham. I'm only a ham picture actor even if I am a star. But I have a feeling for this Mattison. If I buy this Mattison I can take it to Hollywood and do something with it there for Mattison's future."

Mr. Brolly had learned if you asked people to take you as you were, a simple ordinary person who appreciated good art, not a cinema star, usually people were inclined to do the right thing every time. Mrs. Morton could buy him out a hundred to one because he had not had a father in the lumber business. He had come up from nothing. He wasn't ashamed of it, either. But he did have a good modern collection in Hollywood, much better than Eddie Robinson's. So Mrs. Morton had agreed not to bid against Mr. Cyril Brolly. She would ask Mr. Kimball to let her be the first to see Mr. Mattison's next painting.

"I seem to be getting up in the world," said Park, giving Laina a malicious glance. Perhaps after this his paintings wouldn't worry her so much. She looked back at him indignantly as if still ready to argue about them. Then her eyes sparkled. That rich Hawaiian delight in a joke, even when it was on herself, made her expression merry. It pleased her to be so wrong about Park's paintings.

Mr. Brolly missed the glance and look between Laina and Park, still considering himself the center of the stage in the role of a famous person congratulating a new protégé. There was more good news, Park, old man. Mr. Brolly asked if Park knew exactly who Mrs. Morton was? She ran the Museum of Modern Art in Seattle. It was filthy with money, old man. Mr. Brolly owned two paintings by that young Mexican surrealist whom the museum had sent to Paris a year or so ago. And Mr. Brolly had been in the Kimball Galleries when Mrs. Morton was informing Harry Kimball she believed Mr. Mattison deserved a fellowship. She had asked her husband this noon to get in touch with Mr. Mattison and explain to him that he could have one of the four-thousand-dollar Paris fellowships.

"Paris!" exclaimed Laina. "Park, aren't you excited?"

"Old man, this is a great day for you. Have you heard from Mr. Morton?"

"Who?" asked Park, thinking the cat was out of the bag. He hadn't got to Ellen Morton in time.

"Mr. Morton, her husband. He'll phone you, old man."

"Park's been working for that fight promoter most of last night and today," Laina said to explain why Park appeared so stupid about the good news. ". . . Park, I told them how you have to work to earn expenses. Now you won't have to work like that."

"Let me get my breath," said Park. "I'm bushed."

"Darling!" exclaimed the blonde girl to Mr. Brolly. "It's almost like a movie, isn't it, finding a poor artist and being the first to inform him he'll be famous? I'm just thrilled to death."

Everything seemed to have been said. All the cats had jumped out of the bag. There was a long silence and Park wished that Brolly and the blonde girl would go. He was relieved when he saw the blonde girl glance at the platinum watch strapped around her pink sunburnt wrist. He heard Mr. Brolly cordially inviting him to stop off in Hollywood on his way to Paris when that scholarship came through.

The frog-like face turned to Laina. "Darling, you'll be with him, won't you? He wouldn't leave someone like you behind. I'll want both of you as my guests."

It seemed to Park that the blonde girl's eyes turned from brown to yellow and back to brown.

She said a little too loudly, "Cyril, darling, I know we'll all have such a lovely time together in Hollywood, just the four of us."

Laina said nothing at all. Park was careful not to glance at her. He wondered about Mr. Charles G., in Chicago, and if the blonde girl believed an affair on Halepule Beach with an elderly movie actor would continue as the great passionate episode of her life. Evidently she had concluded it would.

With exactly the right note of skepticism, Park said, "Well, I'll have to see that fellowship money before I believe in it enough to plan on it."

Now they just had to go, the blonde girl was saying. But before they departed, what about the fight next week? Park again steadied himself. He looked hard at Laina. She was defiant. Damn her for a vixen. She knew he didn't want to take her to the fight. He saw her jaw set obstinately when Mr. Brolly explained that this afternoon he had purchased four tickets to the Amani-Nogusi fight. He let himself listen to Mr. Brolly. He gathered Laina and he were expected to accompany Mrs. Tolliver and Mr. Brolly. Apparently Laina and he were to feel flattered. They had become protégés of the famous Cyril Brolly. Mr. Brolly was enjoying himself.

"Fifth row from the ring," said Mr. Brolly. "It was the best I could get from the speculators. I was listening to the radio all morning. Caroline told us that you keep accounts for the local fight promoter. You ought to have the dope on the fight for us —what do you think of this Amani pug? Should I lay dough on him, old man? I used to see Tiger Nogusi at the Legion matches in Hollywood. Tiger's fair, nothing extra. He was a novelty because you don't see many Hawaiian-Japanese fighters, but he was game, old man. He'd mix it up in any fight, old man."

The bursting sensation increased for Park. He didn't want to take Laina to the fight because he knew there would be a riot. It was link after link in a chain and he had not foreseen there would be so many small links to hold together. His thoughts raced while he said he didn't know any more than anyone else.

All he did was keep the accounts of ticket sales and balance the books. Doc Fields was a very close-mouthed gent.

Park mentally balanced one risk against another. He saw Laina was eager to have him accept Mr. Brolly's invitation. It had not been easy for her today. She had even phoned him at Doc's office. He hoped she would agree to fly with him to Mountain House. If he made an issue of the fight, he could not tell what Laina would do. It would be awkward if she said to hell with him; she was going, anyway. Later he would have to explain somehow why he was refusing the scholarship. Laina and Ellen and Buddy Morton and E. P. and Dick Stewart's death and Bull Amani wanting another bribe and the five-year contract—he had not foreseen all the links. If he hit Doc for four ringside seats and there was a riot he still ought to be able to get Laina safely underneath the elevated ring to the trap door which opened to the basement below.

As Hortense Dorens had observed, Park could be most charming when he wished. He thanked Mr. Brolly. "Look, suppose you turn in your tickets? Give me a chance to repay your kindness. Part of my deal working for Doc Fields is to get a few choice tickets and I expect I can get four ringside seats for us, free. How about it, old man?"

For a space next morning they lay there, and he listened to the rain against the windows. Even when it rained it was never really cool in this climate. No wonder your books began rotting away in a few months unless you wiped them regularly. He was flat on his back and she was resting quietly on her side, one arm under her, the other flung across his chest. His right arm was thrust through the warm hole where her neck bridged across from her shoulders to her head which was comfortably contained in the hollow of his shoulder. Her thick hair lay in heavy tangled folds on the linen.

He rolled over on his arm until his cheek touched her forehead. He asked, "All right?"

Her eyes remained shut. For answer she contentedly moved her head up and down within the depression of his shoulder.

He liked lying here in bed with Laina against him while rain poured greenly over the windows. He drew his hand through her hair. Her eyes slowly opened, looking up to him.

"Park . . ."

"Yes?"

"I've been thinking while waiting for you to wake up again."

"Look. I wasn't asleep."

"I've saved three thousand dollars. I'd pay my own way. You'd know I'd be taking you for yourself and not for money any longer. If you want me to, I've decided I'll go to Paris with you."

"Paris?"

"Wake up. Have you forgotten?"

He had forgotten that Ellen Morton hoped to pack him off the island and out of sight by her money and influence. Last night Cyril Brolly had told Laina about the four-thousand-dollar fellowship. The cat was out of the bag before Park had been able to get to Ellen and ask her to hang on and let everything ride. Park wished Laina had not mentioned Paris this morning. It reminded him of what he must do as quickly as possible. He rolled his head to the left, sighting at the electric clock. By now Buddy would be in Honolulu, leaving Ellen alone at the Kamehameha Hotel; it was thirty-two minutes after nine.

He told Laina, "Hell, I did forget."

It was a few minutes after ten by the big clock above the reception desk in the lobby of the Kamehameha Hotel. By this time of morning most of the hotel's guests had come down for breakfast in the great glass-enclosed lanai south of the lobby. In their gold jackets and white cotton pants, barefooted Filipino boys had hauled from the greenhouse tubs of potted guavas, young banana trees, and towering white ginger. The bottle-green pointed leaves of the blue allamanda vine twined across the gingerbread ceiling. A greenness and freshness was in the lobby, with the clear sweet fragrance of ginger flowers like a major theme through the other softer odors of allamanda and carnation and guavas in bloom.

Park halted at the cigar counter. The pretty Chinese girl

opened the box of Belinda-Belindas to which he pointed. He dropped a dollar on the glass counter. He was in a savage mood. The Havana tobacco had lost its taste. He stepped into one of the phone booths and asked for Mrs. Wilfred Morton. As he waited there was a thump in his ears. It angered him to feel such anxiety. "She doesn't answer," said a voice into his ear. "Who is calling, please?" He hung up.

He was relieved. He did not wish to see her or to talk with her. It had been long ago. She was someone else now, not that slight girl with the freckled face and the blue banjo eyes who remained at the end of a corridor in his memory. She was Mrs. Wilfred Morton. She had fifty-three million dollars. She had loused him up by going into a panic. He would rather have Laina and everything else he would have at the end of five years than any number of Mrs. Wilfred Mortons. "We tell each other everything," Buddy had said. Park didn't think he ever wanted Laina to tell him everything. He wished Laina had not told him she had given herself twice to that Japanese boy who was now dead.

He dialed Lew Kirsch's number and heard Lew's warm husky voice. He asked Lew to locate all the owners of gray Studebakers. No, it wasn't anything to worry about. It was a dry run, that was all. Lew asked if it was any particular gray Studebaker? Park tried to remember. Yesterday afternoon the sun had been shining against that gray Studebaker. But the license number? In his mind he seemed to see the license plate and it had been covered with a dusty film, the numbers hidden as if it had been sprayed with oil. Again he felt a tug of anxiety. But that Hono stretch was covered with road oil. No, that explained it. No one had deliberately spilled oil on the license plate to prevent him from seeing the number.

"Make it a dry run, Lew. Nothing to worry about. Any news from Meaker?"

"He's arranging some publicity pictures of the fighters with Doc Fields."

"Howie Wright?"

"He hasn't called."

"I'll check in later."

He left the phone booth. He passed along the arcade and looked into the great flowering lanai from one of the open spaces. The lanai was closed in by glass to prevent the sea breezes from blowing salt spray in on the mainlanders. At the far end of the lanai, Park saw a brown-haired young woman seated at a table with two young boys and an elderly nurse. He decided one boy was possibly ten and the other was four or five. He guessed they were half-through breakfast. At least two hundred other guests were eating breakfast and he did not want to walk through the lanai with all eyes staring when he spoke to Ellen and asked her why in hell she hadn't let it ride?

He went to the newsstand. It was ten-thirty by the big clock near the gilt stairway. He bought a copy of the morning *Daily Sentinel* and noticed that this week's issue of Harry Kimball's scandal sheet, *The Weekly Advocate*, was displayed. He bought that, too.

He found a big cane chair near the arcade and sat down, smoking his cigar, hearing the voices of the Filipino boys on the other side of two tubs of banana trees. Somtimes when you were in the hotel, and the tourists were not near-by, it was like being in a strange land for all you heard were the Filipino boys talking their queer language; or perhaps the Chinese girl at the cigar stand would slip over to the desk, and then you heard her and the Chinese clerk clacking softly together.

He saw the morning *Sentinal* had two headlines. One said that Bull Amani was going to fight. The other announced the death of Richard Stewart, yesterday afternoon. Amani and Stewart shared pictures on the front page. The inside page had a long statement signed by Enders P. Tothic, Junior, president of Paradise Products Corporation, Ltd. In one thousand words E. P. said he was sorry Dickie Stewart was dead. In the last paragraph he said it was unfortunate that an emergency had called him to Los Angeles but he knew his old friend would understand and would want him to go. Howie Wright hadn't lost time. It was all there. When the five-year contract was signed, Park expected Howie would ask for a stiff raise. Howie deserved a boost. Howie was deeper in the big slot machine than anyone else, even Park.

He leafed through the pages. The sixth was a full-page advertisement for the Flavola Super-Market: "A New Shipment of Fresh California Vegetables—Just Arrived!" Because almost all the available land on the island was given over to sugar cane and pineapple, which were really more valuable, vegetables were imported from the mainland and the beef was imported from one of the big ranches on the island of Hawaii. If you needed vitamins, you could get them at any of the drug stores for only ten per cent more than you paid on the mainland.

Opposite the full-page ad was a small paragraph buried in the seventh page which Park did not miss. He read it twice. As a news item it was unimportant. Last night the Sam Akinako movie house at Iki had burned down. No one was hurt; it happened after the last performance. The police were investigating. The Akinako movie house was one of the few non-union houses on the island. It was thought that union projectionists had set the fire because Sam Akinako, the owner, had refused to engage a union projectionist.

Byron Meaker would also expect a raise after the contract was signed. Park did not like to be drastic because you risked having it cut two ways but that tough little son-of-a-bitch, Sam Akinako, had asked for it. Union projectionists! Park reminded himself to ask By Meaker how he had managed it but changed his mind. He didn't want to know. Let it ride.

Harry Kimball's scandal sheet varied little from week to week. God knows how Harry got all the gossip concerning the tourists; probably most of it came from Hortense Dorens. Three pages were crammed with gossip. Four pages were cramed with another one of Harry's long and virulent attacks on the old white families of missionary and trading stock. "Stuffed Shirts and Deadheads," Harry had headlined this week's editorial. "It's an open secret," Park read, "that one reason Hawaii has not yet been admitted to the union of states is because many of the old kamaaina families of Hawaii cannot make up their minds what they want, as lords of the islands. On one hand, much of their huge income still comes from their inherited investment in island sugar. They know if Hawaii is admitted as the forty-ninth state that island sugar will no longer be discriminated against and subject to unfair restrictions. On the other hand, the large majority of kamaaina families are desperately afraid the American-born descendants of Oriental immigrants, and particularly of Japanese immigrants, will form political *huis* to gain political ascendency and control of Hawaii as soon as the islands become admitted as a state. As a consequence of this wavering and indecision on the part of the great families who for generations have mulcted Hawaii . . ."

Nuts!

Park wondered why Harry was so bitter against the old white families. He knew Harry had come to the archipelago after the first war. For a man who liked to talk about himself, Harry was remarkably reticent about what he had done before establishing his fashionable store on the beach. Park had heard that Harry had started a small weekly in Honolulu years ago and Park gathered—from whom he forgot—that Harry failed, came to this island, once again attempted a newspaper, and failed a second time before going into the curios and notions business for tourists. Harry had always liked giving someone else a hotfoot. Park thought one of these days he might ask Harry what he had against the old families to see how Harry took such a question. Park stuck the scandal sheet in his coat pocket and wiped sweat from his forehead. It was going to be another warm day. He stood up and looked at the big clock. He threw his cigar into one of the sand-filled glazed Chinese pots, and strolled again into the fragrant humid arcade.

Suddenly his blood began pounding in his ears. Ellen had passed through one of the glass doors. He could see her looking up to the sky. It had stopped raining, and the light breeze blew her hair and pressed her yellow linen skirt against her legs. She returned. She smiled down at her two boys. Some of the other mainlanders were watching the pretty picture of the young mother and her two sons. Yes, the boys could go on the beach. Be careful. The nurse nodded. Park wondered how it would be to have a couple of lively kids. He almost envied Buddy for those two boys.

Ellen waited, the nurse leading the two boys through the door. Park saw the older boy go running along the bright white beach. Ellen stood there a moment. She turned. What will I say to her? There was something stubborn in his mind, like a block. He wanted to turn, to go, to let it ride. He couldn't.

She was going toward the right. He'd missed her. He'd wait and telephone and see her in her room. She came into the lobby and he saw her stop at the newsstand and buy several magazines. She had a bright yellow ribbon in her brown crinkly hair this morning. She glanced toward the elevator. Park stepped between the potted trees. She came around by the cigar stand, rather small, and still, Park thought, very slight. She did not see him and passed farther along the arcade toward the flight of winding stairs which led to the balcony.

Park stepped in front of her and said politely, "Mrs. Morton—"

She turned. She had that half-smile of inquiry which people who were really very nice but really very wealthy reserved for servants and casual encounters and then she saw it was Park. She was startled.

He said quietly, "Mattison, Mrs. Morton. Park Mattison. Mrs. Dorens introduced us at Mr. Kimball's party."

"Oh, yes. Of course. How do you do, Mr. Mattison."

"I hope you don't mind my stopping you like this. I wonder if I could see you for a minute, please?"

At the end of the arcade, on one side of the gardens, was a formal maze composed of paths which wound through high clipped hedges of frangipani, all the flowers from pale pink to the color of ripe cherries. Here were white iron benches and you could sit on one of them and your head would be hidden by the line of hedges and you could still look toward the hotel and see the head of anyone approaching.

It was as though they both knew in advance where they were going because Ellen and Park walked through the arcade and turned left at the same time into the high hedges instead of continuing into the colorful garden. He waited for her to sit on one of the benches and when he sat he was careful not to sit too close to her. They were both very polite and reserved. Neither wished to press the other. He noticed she smoothed the linen skirt over her knees. She probably didn't know she had done it. She waited for him to speak.

He said, "I don't believe I can accept your fellowship, Mrs. Morton."

"I'm very sorry if you can't. I was impressed by your painting. The museum likes to encourage painters with talent."

"I like it out here."

"If you found the first year in Paris profitable, often the museum renews its fellowships for another year, Mr. Mattison."

"It's very kind of you. But I live in a small house up on the Pua Cliff and I'm happy with things as they are, Mrs. Morton."

She removed a pack of cigarettes from her white braided leather bag. She took a cigarette, tapping it on the back of one hand. The blue eyes were staring at a lizard on the path. Park struck a match. He noticed her fingers trembled when she placed the cigarette in her mouth and lifted her face to him to light it for her. It gave him an indescribable emotion to realize she was terrified of him. My God, she need not be. He had no wish in the world to break into her life.

He said quickly, "Ellen, look. Stop thinking you have to buy me off. If you don't louse me up, I won't louse you up." Then he lit her cigarette and threw the match on the gravel.

"Thank you," she said in a very small voice. She might have been thanking him for lighting her cigarette.

He looked at his watch. Because she had been brought up with the knowledge that someday she would inherit a great fortune, he assumed she must have been constantly warned of the dangers of unscrupulous men attempting to prey on her. Evidently she had expected him to try to blackmail her. He felt a resentment toward her and at the same time rather pitied her.

"Well . . ." he said, smiling.

She stood. There was a silence. She glanced at the sky. "Will it rain again today, do you think?"

"Probably. We often have more than one rain during the day in this season, Mrs. Morton."

She still hesitated. He decided she was trying to bring it back to a normal area of a casual encounter with a person to whom she had been recently introduced. He did not want her to misunderstand. He thought she should realize he was established here and had good reasons for not wanting to go to Paris other than not wanting to be bought out.

He explained, "This happy island has almost become a second home for me. I paint. I have everything I need."

She regarded him. Then she said, "I know Mrs. Tolliver. We flew across the Pacific with her. Last night she mentioned going to see you with Mr. Brolly. It is Mr. Brolly, isn't it?"

"Yes, Mr. Brolly. He bought a picture of mine. Caroline and I enjoyed seeing Mrs. Tolliver and Mr. Brolly again."

He mentioned Caroline's name deliberately. Ellen should know that there was nothing he needed or asked for except to be left undisturbed.

Ellen said, "Mrs. Tolliver mentioned she had met the most extraordinarily beautiful girl at your place." Impulsively she extended her hand to him. "Thank you for speaking to me this morning. I am sorry—if the offer of a fellowship disconcerted you. Please let me arrange to have the offer withdrawn without its embarrassing you."

"Well, thank you, Mrs. Morton . . ." He released the small hand.

She waited a moment longer Her blue eyes were still troubled. "You do have talent," she said hesitantly. "Your painting is primitive, obviously done without formal training—but it has tremendous vigor. I shouldn't like to have you think I would be willing to—to deceive the trustees of the museum by recommending anyone for a fellowship who didn't deserve it."

She walked away and he watched her go. He saw her vanish around the end of a hedge, the yellow ribbon very bright in the crinkly brown hair. It had been much easier than he had expected. Still, he wished she had not tried to have him think that she believed in his paintings. "You do have talent," she had said.

Why hadn't she let it ride? Presumably, she ought to know a little about paintings and artists; she wasn't like the foolish women from the mainland who were so easily humbugged by

Harry Kimball's sales talk. People with too much money believed they owned all the world and some of them became righteous about it, like Ellen and her husband. Duty! Moral obligations! Christ! She knew he couldn't paint. Why hadn't she ignored his fraud or told him it was daubing and laughed at him for pretending to be something he wasn't? He would have thought more of her if she hadn't given in so easily.

As he walked across the bright green lawn of the hotel grounds he recalled that day and that night so long ago when there had been something of a nostalgia in the air. He felt that same bittersweetness this morning as if he were going into a new realm. It was too late to go back. He stopped. He looked at one of the posters advertising the Amani-Nogusi fight.

He was sorry for Ellen and Buddy and there was a touch of contempt for them in his feeling which he wished were not there. They were both filled with the same vague righteous yearnings but when the chips were down you could push them over quickly enough. Park had pushed Ellen over with no trouble at all this morning. E. P. would push Buddy over if Buddy was fool enough to risk sticking out his neck as he had promised to do last night on the pier. Crack the whip and they jumped. They had been brought up on cushions and while they had good hearts and were filled with good wishes, threaten to disturb their cushions and they become weak as water. Still, Park found himself wishing that Ellen had not been qiute so obviously terrified by him this morning.

10

In the ring it was the sixth round of the semifinals. Park did not care whether the flashy young Filipino or the Negro middleweight was leading because the next fight was the important fight tonight. He heard the roar increase when the Filipino struck hard with a left. The crowd wanted the Filipino to win.

Park was surprised at the passionate intentness of Laina's expression under the white smoky glare beating down from the banks of lights over the ring. She had insisted upon wearing her bracelet tonight because she was so pleased with the miniature silver bottle. He thought it looked tawdry and commonplace around her wrist, but he was proud to see how neat and self-contained she appeared in her tailored linen suit of pale green with a silk scarf of the same color wrapped tightly around her head to protect her hair. She had done much better for herself, Park thought, than Janet Tolliver had, who was at Laina's left and screaming enthusiastically at the fighters. The blonde girl from Chicago had not yet learned how you dressed for this climate. Instead of covering herself for protection from the dust and swarms of insects, her bright shingled head was completely exposed. And she was wearing one of those low-cut silvery evening dresses which left her arms and shoulders bare. Tomorrow the blonde girl's skin would be covered with tiny red bites.

He heard the hard thud of gloves. The crowd surged. He felt Laina's arm rub his as she leaned forward, wholly absorbed. He envied her. He wished he could lose himself even for a minute as she had lost herself into the crowd-feeling while the two men furiously battered each other in the ring. He had an iciness in his head and he felt removed into another dimension.

Doc Fields must have managed to pack eight thousand lunatics into the auditorium tonight. If a riot started some people were going to be hurt. Quietly Park touched his coat pocket. Doc Fields' short-muzzled .32 police-model revolver fitted snugly in Park's hip pocket. After accompanying Laina to the Buick tonight, Park had asked her to wait while he returned to the house for a cigar. He removed Doc's revolver from the army foot locker where he had hidden it. He was not at all certain what impelled him to slip it into his pocket. Had he come alone he would have come unarmed.

He sighted coolly and critically at the men in the ring and decided the Negro was being very cute, allowing the Filipino to expend himself in this round; but he didn't give a damn about who won. He was close enough to one of the boarded sides of the ring to reach out with his foot and touch the wood with the toe of his shoe. A few yards from him a square opening had been cut through the boards. He took advantage of the tumult to observe carefully where Laina and he sat in relation to the placing of the other seats around the ring.

The head and shoulders of a radio technician thrust from an opening cut like a small door at the bottom section of one side of the ring. Across the aisle from Park were newspapermen and tables lined up in a row for their use. On the nearest table was a microphone into which the *Pacific Morning Chronicle's* sports editor was speaking breathlessly, his eyes glued upon the two fighters. A cable ran from the microphone down to the technician with headphones clamped to his ears and along his body and into the dark space under the flooring of the ring. A trap door was there, Park knew, because the radio cable dropped to a portable monitoring station in the basement.

If there was a riot, Laina was agile and quick enough to crawl through the opening and skin down the ladder like a fireman. But Park didn't know about the blonde girl.

The bell clanged. The crowd booed the Negro as he returned to his corner. Laina seized Park's hand. "I get so excited at fights!"

Mr. Brolly spit out a frayed stub of chewed cigar and turned to speak to the blonde girl. A woman in the row behind leaned forward and asked Mr. Brolly to autograph another program. Park pulled out his watch. It was ten minutes to ten. Bull Amani and Tiger Nogusi ought to go on in another quarter-hour. Laina pulled her hand free and turned in her chair, kneeling on the seat in order to see more of the crowd behind her.

He watched her for a moment or so. She was completely absorbed. He had never tried to analyze why he resented it each time Laina spoke of wanting to cut her hair short. Now, as he regarded her almost impersonally, he saw how the pale green turban protecting and hiding her hair shaped her head and gave it an appearance of nudity which was new to him. Suddenly he became intensely aware of the pressure of her hand on his shoulder as she braced herself. It was as though she had become aware of his gaze, and of him. He saw her head turn, her face questioning him. Then her hand felt down for his and squeezed it. She didn't need to speak. All his thoughts seemed to flow forward in time until he had returned with her to their house on the cliff. Her lips were bright as she smiled down at him. Then she looked away, toward the crowd behind her.

Her excitement pleased him. Despite his anxiety there was something like anticipation at the back of his mind, and it began to glow warmly in all the iciness. He had not realized how sexually stimulating it could be to take a girl with you to see men smashing at each other in the ring. Something sardonic passed through his mind. He expected Mr. Brolly and all the men with girls were experiencing that same glow of anticipation, if not actually thinking about it, feeling a stir and an emotion while watching their girls with sidelong glances.

"Park," he heard Laina ask, "isn't that Mr. Kimball? Look!"

She pointed. Six or seven rows back an enormous grinning moon face lifted. Harry waved. With him was the tawny-haired

Chinese-Hawaiian girl whom Park remembered from the shindig last week. He had seen her again this morning when he was having a cup of coffee with Harry. She had come for Harry to inform him Mrs. Stewart was waiting at the galleries. Park wondered what Mrs. Stewart had wanted of Harry Kimball.

He waved good-naturedly to the huge art dealer and sat down, Laina tugging impatiently at his arm. The ring was being cleared. The bell clanged. The seventh round was coming up and Laina hugged his arm.

"The Filipino boy's going to win, isn't he?"

Park looked at her and her eyes were shining.

"Well, he might," said Park, smiling.

Park didn't really believe the Filipino would win but you never could tell who was going to win a fight until the referee counted ten.

He wished Harry Kimball were not here tonight. He knew it was unreasonable of him but when he saw Harry he felt as if Harry were still on his tail. Until this morning he had not seen Harry since the night of the shindig. For the past four days he had known that Harry was the owner of a gray Studebaker.

It hadn't taken Lew Kirsch long to run through his big I. B. machines his file of cards listing automobile owners. That much was easy. Within less than an hour Lew had a complete list of all Studebakers on the island—and Harry Kimball's name was among the owners. However, Lew never classified ownership of cars by their colors. It took his staff almost forty-eight hours before the list could be reduced to twelve gray Studebakers with the names of their owners.

Seven of the Studebakers were owned by the Hammakuri Taxi Company. Three of the Studebakers were old models, recently painted. They were owned by three separate gangs of Flip plantation workers who pooled their money for cars as well as for the blonded hapa-haole girls from the houses in the Makakina district. The two remaining Studebakers were 1950 models, one purchased three months ago by the manager of the Flavola Super-Market. The other had been purchased less than a week before by the Harry Kimball Galleries.

Whenever Park thought about it, it was like having looked at a mountain from one aspect for many months and suddenly having gone part way around the mountain and looking up again and discovering it was not at all what it seemed to be when you saw it from the front. Park was not certain that Harry was all he appeared to be from the front—someone who made a good thing out of the Kimball Galleries, had shindigs two or three times a month, and liked to publish a little weekly scandal sheet which no one took very seriously except the tourists who came and went from the island . . .

"Oh, Christ!" cried Laina angrily, sitting back in her seat.

Park peered through the hot glare and saw the Negro triumphantly clapping his hands over his head; he still didn't care who had won this fight. He was still thinking about Harry Kimball.

For several days Park had been occupied in Lew Kirsch's office, on the details of the new contract; he had decided not to face his growing uneasiness about Harry until after he got from under the present load. A new frame-of-mind survey was underway to be completed before the F. I. U. elections next January. By the end of the week E. P. had returned to the island from Los Angeles and there had been another meeting at Koko Point where Park had failed to give a full report.

Park's thoughts dovetailed into his recollections of the meeting with E. P. It was the first time since being employed by E. P. that he had not provided a full report. Park had not said Harry Kimball might have tailed him. Park had not wished to alarm E. P. unnecessarily a few days before the five-year contract was to be signed. He did not believe any automobile since then had tried to tail him. It was only for that one time; and it still could be a coincidence, nothing really to be concerned about.

After Park had finished analyzing the trends appearing in the new survey, he remembered, E. P. had cawed cheerfully, "Let's leave all details for later. You boys are making bang-up progress. *I'm* satisfied we're on the right track, Lieutenant."

"Thank you, Colonel."

"We've got to make it a policy to see more of each other, too.

But I have to call it short today. Buddy and I still have company business to hash over. Nothing concerning your job, though. By the way, what about my fight tickets?" The sallow face turned briefly toward Buddy. "Don't tell me Buddy forgot to ask you?"

Park promptly absolved Buddy who had not forgotten. But you could probably count upon a hell of a riot. It might be wiser for E. P. to stay home and listen to the fight on his radio. Park knew with any big organization there were always court politics and usually a favorite at court. He preferred to hold himself a little in the rear, allowing someone like Dick Stewart to be court favorite. However, at that meeting, E. P. and Buddy were no longer quite the same as before Stewart's death.

"All right, Lieutenant," E. P. had said. "Whatever you say, Lieutenant. You're the boy. *I* know how to follow an expert's orders, even if others don't."

It was something like that throughout the meeting—Buddy silent, his thin face expressionless. Park didn't want to be promoted court favorite over Buddy. You got up there at the peak, next to E. P., his top boy. After that you had nowhere else to go except over the peak and down. Buddy was a damn fool if he had tried to talk to E. P. about moral dilemmas.

Yesterday Park had completed the draft of the new contract. This morning he had planned to sleep late. Recently, however, Laina was up at eight o'clock and getting his bath ready for him. She hated cooking but she was trying to learn to prepare breakfast for him, to get him to eat more.

"Good night! I can do that much for you. You've lost another pound, haven't you?"

She didn't prepare very good breakfasts because she could not really cook. She was much better in bed, Park told her, and she slapped his face. She watched him leave, believing he was going to paint today. He drove to Halepule Beach where he saw a new gray Studebaker parked in front of the Kimball Galleries. He decided to have a try at Harry and quit delaying it any longer. When Park entered "L'On Y Mange Bien," it was about nine o'clock. He knew Harry often came in between nine and nine-thirty for a cup of coffee. Park ordered ham and eggs and coffee. The coffee had too much chicory in it and didn't taste much better than the instant coffee Laina made for him mornings. He really wasn't hungry and was studying the plate of ham and eggs when Harry appeared.

Harry asked, "How's Laina taking it?"

Harry was referring to the fellowship offered by Mrs. Morton before she cabled the museum and discovered there were no more fellowships available this year. It was frightfully embarrassing for her but Mr. Mattison had been so remarkably decent about it, she had told Harry . . .

Park said Laina was still sore because the offer had been withdrawn. However, he'd warned her that people with wealth sometimes made promises they couldn't keep. Harry sat down, ordering a pot of black Kona coffee. To forget their disappointment, Laina and Park were leaving this coming week end for Mountain House on the island of Hawaii. He hoped to try a landscape with snow in it for a change.

"Don't misunderstand me," Harry said, "but I'm pleased you didn't leave for Paris this year. We'll have a show for you in February." He drank his coffee and filled the cup again. He drank it boiling hot. "I'm not through with you yet, my boy."

"I'm counting on you, too, Harry."

Park was patient. He would give Harry enough time to mention the gray Studebaker if Harry were of a mind to do so.

"You can count on me, my boy. You can."

"For five hundred and ninety dollars," Park said. "You owe me ninety from the other two paintings and you haven't paid me for the last one you sold to Brolly."

"It's four hundred and fifty for the last one, you know."

"I thought Brolly paid you a thousand?"

"We can't leave out expenses, can we?"

Then Park laughed . . .

"Harry, I won't argue with you."

"I'm preparing a little brochure about you for your show, my boy. It costs money," Harry explained. "I need autobiographical details, too. You were born in Mt. Morris, Illinois. Your father taught commercial classes. You worked your way through Harvard, you told me?"

"I had a second cousin who helped me was what I told you."

"It sounds better to say you worked your way by yourself. You became an accountant. What was the firm?" Harry removed a pencil from his pocket.

"Hertz and Finnhaven, management consultants. I told you all that, once."

Another principle when you went underground in enemy territory was never to lie concerning facts which someone could easily verify. You told the truth, but you did not have to tell all the truth.

Park had never told Harry that he brought the Paradise Products account to Hertz and Finnhaven. He hadn't said who brought it into the firm. Instead, he had said only that Hertz and Finnhaven handled the account. He had not hesitated to inform Harry that he had often seen Mr. Tothic when Mr. Tothic was in the New York offices of Hertz and Finnhaven. Park admitted that having the Paradise account in the firm must have started him thinking of these happy islands in the Pacific.

In the restaurant that morning he made it clear to Harry that he had remembered these favored isles after the compulsion in him to paint became so strong that he sold his junior partnership in the firm. Park admitted that he had even hoped Mr. Tothic might remember him. Perhaps he might be able to paint well enough to sell a few paintings as illustrations in the national advertising for Paradise canned pineapple, guava, papaya, mango, all their canned products. But Park's hopes, he told Harry wryly, had not worked out.

Mr. Tothic was always too occupied to see a painter. That much was a lie; but it was a lie Park didn't believe Harry could track down. He remarked candidly, waiting for Harry to finish the coffee, "It might be I'm not good enough to paint pictures for ads."

"You're going at it the wrong way, my boy. Let me sell your paintings for you. Pip Tothic isn't your man, anyway. What does he know about buying art?"

" 'Pip'?"

Park had not had to pretend surprise.

."Didn't you know, my boy? It used to be 'Poipay' when he was a boy. You don't know what 'Poipay' means in Hawaiian, do you? It's Hawaiian for 'shut up tightly.' He was a nervous little bastard, I've heard, and if he couldn't have his own way he'd throw fits and puke all over himself. His Hawaiian nurse would call out 'Poipay! Poipay!' and the beach kids picked it up."

Harry laughed. He had a boisterous laugh. Park had not known; and he did not believe it. Once he had liked Harry but he was no longer very certain either of liking Harry or of trusting him.

"Pip's life as a kid must have been made miserable by those kanaka beach kids until his sister got old enough to do something." Harry's little eyes looked at Park and something reflective and somber came into them. "You never knew Ruthie," said Harry, finishing his coffee. He stuck his pad of notes into his pocket, and began the process of lifting up his bulk from his chair. "Ruthie shortened the nickname to 'Pip' and everyone forgot what it meant. That was like her. She died during the war. She had more brains than Pip ever had and enough courage for ten of him. But she died. She died."

Park said, "You knew her?"

Harry's little eyes seemed to contract.

"Yes, my boy. I knew her. I know everyone of importance." He called for both checks and in something of another tone he rumbled at Park, "Expenses, my boy. We'll put that down as expenses."

Park recalled the malicious thought that had come to his mind on that morning in the hotel while he was waiting for Ellen Morton. He asked pleasantly, "What's set you so much against the old white families of the islands? Did you try to make a play for Ruth Tothic when you were younger?"

Harry stood still. Park could not tell whether he had touched him at all. Harry said, "My boy, I wouldn't have had a chance with Ruthie. Don't you know I'm a carpetbagger? Haven't you learned by now that all of us haoles who weren't born here of the right families are nothing more than carpetbaggers or, at the most, hired hands to run the plantations and attend to the business interests of the haole lords and their ladies?"

Park laughed.

"Don't laugh at me, my boy. I know what I'm talking about."

Together they had walked to the sidewalk and there was the new gray Studebaker still in front of Harry's galleries. Before Park could ask if he had bought a new car, Harry nudged Park in the ribs and said, "How do you like it?" Last week he had followed Park's Buick from the city in the new Studebaker. Evidently that afternoon Park was too preoccupied to notice. Harry had driven the Studebaker after Park to the Outrigger Club. He had seen Park go toward the pier and started to go after Park but stopped when Park met Buddy Morton on the pier.

"I knew he wanted to talk to you about that fellowship Mrs. Morton was offering," Harry said, regarding Park.

Park thought of all the trouble he had caused Lew Kirsch's staff in locating the owners of gray Studebakers on the island. Everything was explained. Harry saw him that day by chance and followed. But Park was not quite so relieved about Harry as he should have been.

"I wish you'd joined us, Harry. I needed your advice."

"You did well enough, evidently." Harry lowered his head at Park, the creased bags of flesh under his eyes filling out. "Don't misunderstand me, but ever since we met Mrs. Morton I've been puzzled.

"About what?"

"Either you or I startled her that night when Hortense introduced us. Now, *don't* misunderstand me, my boy. I often startle people. But I've asked myself if you mightn't have met her before? Hortense Dorens doesn't know of any Captain Jones who ever visited the galleries."

"Where would I have met her without knowing who she was?"

"I'm often mistaken, my boy," said Harry. "I was merely puzzled."

Then that tawny-haired Chinese-Hawaiian girl approached Harry to say in her sweet kanaka voice "Excu' me, Mr. Kimba' . . ." Mrs. Stewart was waiting for Mr. Kimball in the galleries. Harry had not said why Mrs. Stewart was waiting. Perhaps

· 155 ·

Harry did not know but at the time Park wondered. He was still wondering. Afterwards, he began to wonder about Harry's explanation of following after him in the gray Studebaker. It seemed to him that possibly Harry had told some of the truth but not all of it. Time had elapsed on the pier, Park recalled, before Buddy arrived. Where had Harry been? Harry must have hidden himself in the camellia gardens, watching. You never actually knew who was going to win a fight until the fight had ended because often the man you were fighting was more than he seemed to be.

Park did not have a very clear memory of those two and a half rounds of the fight between Bull Amani and Tiger Nogusi. There was the sound, the constant sound. Each time you thought it had reached such a pitch of intensity it could not increase; but it did. He was aware of Laina's nails digging into his flesh. There were several insane moments when somehow he also was standing on his feet beside her. It was as if only the two of them existed within a great roaring whiteness.

After the first round, while Bull Amani's seconds were desperately patching at that enormous mound of flesh, Park was surprised to see a man he did not know come down the aisle and wriggle around past the newspapermen to where Doc Fields was sitting. Doc wriggled into the aisle. Park looked up at that beefy disjointed old face, and Doc squinted back down at Park. For a minute Park thought Doc wanted to say something to him. Then Doc and the man hastily pushed toward the rear of the auditorium. Park wondered if someone had fainted or had died from the excitement. After the bell sounded the second round, he forgot Doc's leaving.

Tiger Nogusi had weighed in at 192. He was thirty-two or three, getting along in years, but not too old for Bull Amani who had weighed in at 216 and was thirty-five although his age was given as thirty-one on the program notes. Bull Amani was a vain man. Park watched Tiger Nogusi up there and he did not think that tall lean man with the hideously pockmarked yellowish face could ever have been vain.

You still couldn't hear yourself speak after that second round. Park didn't know whether or not Bull Amani would try to get himself off the stool to continue into a third round. But there were at least four thousand Flips here tonight from the plantations. They were a solid mass in the balcony and along the rear downstairs of the auditorium. By now they must have realized the money they had bet on Bull Amani was lost and their voices had a shrill violence above the steady roaring growl. A broken pop bottle came flying down, crashing into the ring; Park saw Bull Amani jerk and look back and upward out of the single eye still open. The Bull was afraid.

Park felt Laina's hands tugging at his sleeve to attract his attention. She was trying to ask him a question. She placed her cheek against his, her lips moving against his ear. He could not hear her question. Laina's eyes looked despairingly at Park.

For Park there was a sense of unreality to that third round. It was like watching an act. A hulking comedian marked grotesquely by red paint was turning the fight into a farce. The slim yellow man was assisting by playing it straight. Bull Amani had been bully boy of the island for so long that the rising torrent of jeers and catcalls and howls from those thousands here tonight must have been as stunning to him as the dim realization that the fight was not going to end as he had believed it would. He had commanded his longshoremen by his fists. He had beaten them. He had taken their women. He was the bully boy. Now he was running away from a man smaller than he was.

Park saw the lean yellow man dart in again and knock down clumsy arms. Christ! Bull Amani sprawled heavily on the canvas. Park saw the dripping head lift stupidly, one eye staring unbelievingly out of the red mask. The Tiger stepped lightly away and waited. The air seemed to shake with violence. Why the hell didn't they throw in a towel? Park saw the two longshoremen who were acting as the Bull's handlers. One must be pure Hawaiian and was very big. They were both standing at a far corner, their arms on the canvas; they were watching the Bull and to Park there was something terrifying in their faces. They were waiting. Now the Bull saw them waiting for him to stand up and take more of it. The Hawaiian's mouth twisted. His head jerked. He spat tobacco juice at the Bull.

"Tiger! Tiger!"

It was one enormous roaring voice from all of the thousands of voices. It should have made Park feel triumphant to hear everyone in the mob yelling for Tiger to go in and finish the Bull. It was what Park wanted. After tonight, E. P. would sign the contract. In the aisle three Japanese policemen were fighting with an enraged Flip. A knife flashed and fell not far from Park. He kicked it under his seat.

Instantly he became detached from the noise because he knew what was coming. Up there in the ring that hulking comedian slowly climbed to his feet. Laina sprang to her feet, pulling at Park's arm. The Tiger circled Bull Amani, his left arm flashing and flashing; Amani turned blindly and clawed for the ropes. He was climbing over them when one of the longshoremen rose from the other side in all the bright light and knocked him back into the ring. It was not funny. Somehow the ring was filling with other shapes. A dozen little Flips managed to fight through the police and were piling into the ring to Park's right. A chair crashed. Then a jagged pop bottle spun crazily in the glare. Doc was a goddamned fool to allow pop to be sold tonight.

Park had a glimpse of the blonde girl's stricken face as men rushed between her and Mr. Brolly, climbing to the ring. They were like ants crawling over a mound of earth with the Tiger standing sardonically to one side. Park shoved Laina toward the passage. He was shouting at her and she did not hear him but when she saw the opening she knew where to go to escape the tumult. She crawled inside. One of the radio men tried to follow. Park didn't remember hitting anyone. All he saw was a man pitch backward against the table, a microphone clattering, another face there against blackness still trying to speak calmly and in orderly sequence to the radio audience. Park whirled and grabbed the blonde girl.

She screamed when a nail caught her skirt. She continued screaming as she frantically descended, the silly skirt pulled up around her. She nearly fell down the ladder but Park caught her. He saw Mr. Brolly's feet step insecurely one after the other on the top rungs. He hadn't known Mr. Brolly was that close behind them. The basement had a moist sweaty smell. Even down here Park could hear the huge roaring from above when more Flips charged the ring. He saw Laina waiting to one side in the long dim corridor. The man at the monitoring table dazedly stood up.

"This way, quick," Park said to Laina.

He took her hand. He looked once behind him and saw the blonde girl and Mr. Brolly running after them. Dust filled the corridor from the pounding and confusion above. At the end of the corridor Park knew a door opened to cement stairs leading to a side alley. The door was covered with sheet iron. It was not locked but the hinges had rusted. Park tugged at it. A single electric light bulb dangling from the ceiling poured a blue radiance upon Laina. She tried to help him. Her eyes were very bright. Mr. Brolly pressed forward.

"Can't we get out of here, old man? Janet's not feeling well."

The blonde girl moaned and clutched at Mr. Brolly.

Park stiffened, looking past Laina. Behind her, wooden steps lifted into blue obscurity, turned at a right angle, and vanished upward to the first and second floors, giving passage up and down to the section of the building behind the auditorium. Park saw grotesque shadows fling outward along the concrete walls a second or so in advance of the five men. In that instant Park had the fantastic hallucination of seeing himself standing on a blue beach, Laina at his side. And a tidal wave was surging forward. It was terrifying. Park saw a small man and four huge men come toward them. The small man was in the lead. He was thrust forcibly toward Park by the violence flowing down the wooden steps.

"Herby!" cried Laina.

Momentarily, Park felt as if the tidal wave had frozen before roaring over him and the blue beach. The four Hawaiian stevedores silently ringed them all, the little man teetered on his toes. It was Herby Subie, Laina was exclaiming. Herby had shiny black hair brushed straight back from a bisque-colored forehead which projected over the rest of his face and, Park noticed, one eye was cocked inward and the man's hands fluttered agitatedly like brown moths. He was wearing a pink tie and green shirt and white cotton coat and trousers and he was clean, intensely clean; the top of his head came no higher than Park's chin.

What, Laina asked, was Herby doing in the basement? Was he trying to get away from those maniacs upstairs, too? She introduced him. Herby Subie. Mr. Brolly—Mrs. Tolliver. And Park Mattison. This was Park, Herby. She did not say so but it was warm in her voice: Please like each other, both of you. Please.

Herby did not trouble to introduce the stevedores. He ignored the movie actor and the blonde girl. Hello, Mr. Mattison. Yes, he had seen Mr. Mattison in Doc Fields' office. Park could not remember having noticed Herby there. Perhaps it had been in the crowd that gathered in Doc's front office when the fighters weighed in. Park had been totaling ticket sales on the adding machine in the rear office, swearing to himself because Doc hadn't told him in time for Park to think of an excuse to slip away. Perhaps it had been then. So this was Herby Subie?

"Will you help me open this door, Mr. Subie? It's stuck."

"I hastened for you, Mr. Mattison, when I saw you leave upstairs. Doc wants you a minute."

"Does he?" Park said mildly.

Park ceased trying to open the door. It was too late to attempt to run for it. Again he had the sensation of standing upon a deserted blue beach, a tidal wave pouring higher and higher. The stevedores' silence was ominous. Park stopped thinking of himself and thought of Laina.

"If Doc needs me, sure. We won't need to keep Laina and our guests, will we?"

Herby told one of the Hawaiians to open the iron door and the Hawaiian opened the door. It was like that, very quick. And it was slightly humiliating when someone else opened a door by pulling at it with one hand. The Hawaiian placed himself in the opening. The surly face was not quite human.

Park tried again. "What's Doc want?"

· 160 ·

"Business," Herby answered.

It was surprising to hear such a deep voice from such a reedy little chest . . .

"Herby," protested Laina, "can't Park take me home?"

Mr. Mattison might be detained for a half-hour or so; Herby was not very specific. Herby offered to send Mike with Laina and her two guests to get them to their car and to ride with them to the Halepule side. Mike would take care of them. Evidently Mike was the stevedore waiting at the entrance. Mr. Brolly rolled his eyes but did not speak. The blonde girl sagged against his shoulder. It was really a dreadful evening for her. Park felt Laina's hand touch his sleeve.

"Laina—" Park told her. "I'm still on Doc's payroll. I'll be along later." He spoke to Mr. Brolly. "Sorry about this, old man. We get excited about our fights out here. I ought to have warned you. I'd better see what Doc wants."

"It's O. K., Laina," Herby's deep voice said. "We don't need Mr. Mattison too long. We get him back to you."

Herby was being very kind to her. She believed him, Park saw, although it provoked her because Doc Fields was always asking for Park at the worst hours. But she couldn't do anything about it until Park quit working for a fight promoter.

She made a despairing face at Park. "I'll wait up for you."

The Hawaiian grunted and ponderously climbed to the alley, Laina and Mr. Brolly on either side of the blonde girl. Before the iron door closed Park had a glimpse of Laina's face as she looked back. Half of it was revealed by the blue light, the other half was in shadow. She made another despairing grimace.

"Upstairs, please, Mr. Mattison."

Park inclined his head as if he were still listening. Herby's face was bisque-colored, flat, expressionless, the forehead like a partially open drawer which did not belong there. But something in Herby's voice reminded Park of so many voices of enlisted men he had heard during the war. They were respectful but not too respectful and had a coolness and a racy quality. Particularly with the veterans brought to Washington by the O.S.S. from the first campaigns in Africa and Italy, it had seemed to Park as if

Brooklyn and Illinois and Texas and all the divergencies of voices all over the country had become fused into something new. Now that quality sounded in Herby's voice. It was not a Japanese speaking from that Japanese face. Park was willing to bet Herby must have fought in the Italian campaign where so many Japanese-American volunters from Hawaii had given such proof of loyalty.

"Up where?"

"Doc's office, Mr. Mattison."

You never knew how a fight really would end, Park thought. He was being paid to use his head and not a gun to extricate himself from hazards he had to chance in a line of work little different from the line of work followed by a professional soldier of fortune. One and the other hired his skills and he took a professional pride in doing his best as long as he was paid. Park did not know what had gone wrong with his plans. In a split second he had to decide whether to chance it with Herby or to tear everything open. When you pulled a gun on someone you irrevocably committed yourself. As he hesitated, Park understood at last how much alone he was, not only here in a basement corridor but wherever he went. It came to him that Laina was the only person who cared enough to wait up for him and to grieve if he did not return to her.

11

W ell, let's see what Doc wants now," said Park.
He decided to follow along with it as far as he could.
He recalled By Meaker worrying about what would
happen if one of them tipped his hand. Park had always known
if ever his hand was tipped, it would happen too suddenly to
have an emergency exit planned in advance. You had to take it
and try either to ride it through or to run. They did not attempt
to search him and that, at least, was a hopeful sign.

Herby and Park climbed the stairs and the stevedores stumped
heavily behind them. Park still heard the shrilling from hundreds
of Flips who must by now have massed densely around the ring
in the auditorium. He wondered if Bull Amani had got away.
Doc's office door was open, the lights on, but Doc was not there.
Herby stepped aside for Park to enter, ordering the stevedores to
wait in the hall. Park pressed a hand to his forehead. Where was
Doc? Had they killed him?

Beyond the front office was a door opening through the parti-
tion to the long narrow office where Park worked. Near the iron
safe was a third door into the dingy gymnasium, now unlighted.
Before Park could enter his office one of the massive stevedores
came around from the refuse-littered hallway, bulking large
within the gymnasium door. The stevedore closed the door.
Well, they weren't missing much tonight. It looked as if a hot
spot were developing fast.

"Where's Doc?"

"I misled you," said Herby apologetically. "Doc isn't here. Laina . . ."

The deep voice trailed off, leaving the rest unsaid. Laina had been in the basement corridor with her guests. It had been quicker and easier to say that Doc was waiting for Mr. Mattison. Herby's hands writhed.

"Open Doc's safe, please."

"Is this a stickup?"

"No, no. But Doc ran out on us."

"Well, get him back. I can't open Doc's safe without his permission."

"He's not coming back. He took off from the Makakina airport in a private amphibian for Honolulu, probably to catch one of the early morning freighter flights to San Francisco."

"A square shooter like Doc, running off?" said Park, but he heard the hollow ring in his own voice. He was convinced that Herby was telling the truth.

"So will you open the safe, Mr. Mattison? I wish to see if the money is there. Doc promised Tiger Nogusi five thousand after the fight."

Herby knew about that? There was a surprise for you . . .

Park asked, "Just whom are you dealing for? I thought Bull Amani was your boy?"

"That shark's filth?" Herby spat to one side. "Bull betrayed us."

"If two men are in a ring, what do you expect? One usually loses."

"Bull betrayed the workers by giving us all shame to see how shameful he was in the fight tonight." Herby's features became convulsed. "And the fight was fixed."

"Who told you that?"

"Willi did."

"Willi—"

" 'Tiger,' you call him. Tiger told me the fight was fixed."

It was an effort for Park to say coolly, "If that's true, I expect you must have made a pocketful of money. Congratulations."

"If I'd known in time do you think I'm such filth to keep it to myself? Let me explain. Willi Nogusi was born at Iki, here, this island. His father was a convert—a Mormon—preached here —moved to Kauai to preach there. Could I guess Tiger Nogusi was the same little Willi Nogusi I used to know? You remember when they came to weigh in?"

Park nodded.

"Bull—that shark's filth!" Herby spat a second time. "He asked me to come with him to meet the newspapermen. Willi was here. He'd flown in from Honolulu. And he recognized me, because I didn't know him. He'd grown big. Tonight, to please him, I drove with him from the hotel to the auditorium before the fight. He asked me who I was betting on. I told him I'd heard he was sick. I'd bet two hundred dollars on Bull Amani. He asked me, 'Do I look sick?' "

Park said, "If you can prove the fight was fixed, all bets can be called off."

The hands were like birds caught in a net . . .

"But it was a fix for all of us to believe Bull would win easily so we'd bet on him. The fight was fixed back again. Can we complain? Can we protest? Can anyone protest because one fighter goes into a ring and does his best to beat another fighter? There is nothing. And Bull—our symbol—how many thousands of F. I. U. members were there tonight, seeing his disgrace?"

Park sat on the edge of the desk. Perhaps it was not going to be the hot spot he had thought it would be. He clasped a knee between his hands.

"But why open Doc's safe?"

"Is the money there?"

"Tiger's five grand?"

"Yes."

"So what? It's not your money."

"Mr. Mattison . . ." Herby's cocked eye appeared to whirl wildly. He bent down his head. When he looked up he appeared to grow several inches taller. The bisque-colored face with its ridiculous forehead was composed and grave and his deep voice had something in it like guns firing. "Mr. Mattison, if the money

· 165 ·

is there, close the safe. It is all I ask. Tiger will be up here as soon as he dresses. I'll tell Tiger he must give the five thousand to the F. I. U. as a contribution."

It was fantastic. Park wanted to laugh but he didn't.

"Listen," he said. "He won't give you the money."

"I will try to talk to him," said Herby. "Please open the safe."

Park got off the desk. His anxiety for himself was no longer as great. The fight was fixed but it was a double fix. It was fixed to be legitimate. Nobody could squeal. Park hadn't realized it was quite that secure. It made him feel good. Tiger had yapped, sure, at the last minute; but it was still secure. The rug had been pulled from under the F. I. U. boys. All this fanatical little gent could hope for now was to argue Tiger into giving five thousand dollars to the island workers. Well, nuts.

Park kneeled in front of the safe. He doubted very much if Doc had left five grand loose. When he opened the safe it was empty except for a manila folder and an envelope on the top shelf. Park became quite rigid for that instant when he saw his name written in Doc's scrawl on the envelope. It was a short note from Doc:

> Kid—I'm getting out tonight but I don't want anybody to say Doc Fields blew after sixteen years of running square fights without paying his bills.
>
> Most of the bills I've taken care of. The Bull got all he had coming before the fight. I paid the Tiger's training expenses while he was in Honolulu. In the manila folder is his signed receipt for the thousand I paid him to make the fight. So that takes care of the two boys.
>
> I'm leaving you a power of attorney and a thousand to my account in the First Nat'l. I don't know anybody but you, kid, I trust to pay the rest of the bills which probably will come in. They won't amount to much— a printing bill, whatever Mr. Meaker charges on publicity, janitor service, you know, odds and ends. I want my record left good.
>
> I owe you a hundred bucks for this month, After you

pay off the bills there ought to be two or three hundred still in the kitty. You take it as a bonus. You been a good kid, Park. If ever you get to New York, look me up, Doc Fields. I'll be in the phone book, no fooling . . ,

Silently Park handed the note to Herby. He opened the manila folder and dumped a dozen bills on the desk. He picked up a receipt. It was for one thousand dollars, value received, tenth of September, signed "William Brown Nogusi," the signature large, as if written by a child. He became aware of a pounding at the door of Doc's outer office. He glanced at Herby who was still scowling over Doc's note. Herby went into the outer office and opened the hall door and for a second or so Park was by himself. He brushed the flies away from his face and looked through the door.

A tall man in a worn checked suit was there with Herby. He looked bigger in the checked suit than Park remembered him in the ring. It was Tiger Nogusi. He was Japanese and he was Hawaiian and probably had haole blood in him as well, for he was a big rangy man with a pale yellowish face which had not recently been in much sunlight. His thin brownish hair was still wet from his hasty shower. With all that, there was something else. Tiger gave the impression of hurling himself forward even when he paused before Herby Subie.

Herby said, "Wait, Willi—"

Herby reeled as if propelled by an invisible spring. A chair toppled over. Next, the hand opened. It took Park by the loose shoulder of his coat. Park was lifted up and set back on his feet, the impact driving up through his spine.

"You—" said Tiger. "Where's my dough?"

"Easy," said Park. "What dough?"

"My dough. Doc tole me you worked for him. You son-of-a-bitch. You helped Doc screw me!"

"Willi!" cried Herby. "Don't! He's a friend . . ."

Then Tiger hit Park. The room flew apart. The dazzling light receded and became the electric bulb again and Park managed to turn his head. He saw table legs and another chair which was tipped over on the floor, the checkered pants legs of the Tiger, Herby's cotton trousers which were like two white stalks growing up from the floor, and then Park put his hand to his stomach and thought he would vomit. He didn't. He reached for one corner of the desk. He got to a knee and one foot. He thrust his hand into his pocket. He grasped the revolver, a sickness writhing in his belly. He stood on both feet, legs trembling.

"All right," Park said through his teeth, "you son-of-a-bitch, yourself."

Gradually the room drew together for Park. He got air into his lungs. He curled his finger on the trigger. With an effort which brought drops of sweat to his forehead, he hauled his hand empty from his pocket.

"You lolo!" said Herby bitterly to the Tiger.

Tiger asked, "How I know he ain't in this deal with Doc? Dint Doc say he had a smart boy working here for him?"

"Look," said Park, "if I was in the deal would I be here now—"

"Keep your trap shut," said Tiger. "And don't call me no son-of-a-bitch again."

"Look, you son-of-a-bitch, why not use that dumb head of yours?"

Tiger stepped toward Park but this time Herby was there between them. With that gunfire sound in his voice he said to the Tiger, "You're the son-of-a-bitch and you know it. You let them pretend you were sick. Would you like me to yell for Jake and Kiule and Tom in the hall? They could work you over good, couldn't they? You carried a union card before you joined the Navy and got taught how to use your fists. You lolo bastard!"

Park saw Tiger shift uneasily on his feet. Tiger looked at Park as if somehow Tiger and not Park was on the spot and Tiger was realizing he had made a mistake about Park. He said, "Herby, Doc tole me I could come here and git a quick cleanup. I been away so many years I forgot so many people was still around I used to know. Honest."

Bitterly, Herby said, "If that dough was here in the safe I was going to make you turn it over to us. I wish I could decide about you. Are you filth like Amani or can you see what you've done to your friends and people on this island?"

Park said, "Listen, Herby. The Tiger was finagled into this, like we all were. Hell, I lost dough on the Bull. But the Tiger got screwed, didn't he?" Park wanted to get the thing ended for him to get the hell out. He saw the Tiger was giving him a sheepish uneasy grin, as if by some unimaginable shifting the two had joined together against the reedy ridiculous little Japanese. Park offered to draw a check on Doc's account for at least a ticket back to the mainland if the Tiger was broke.

"I ain't that broke, Mr. Mattison, but I take that offer kindly. Doc tole me he had a smart boy he trusted to keep his books. You'd think he'd think enough of his fighter like me and his own boy to take care of 'em, wouldn't you? It's what happens when you git on a dam' island like this. You and me both have been screwed. So's Herby been. So's ever'body, I guess, 'cept Doc. I got off this island and Kauai, too, oncet. I'll git off again. I'm through being screwed by these islands where nobody's any good but these dam' haoles."

"Hey," said Park, feeling better, much better. "Are you trying to hurt my feelings?"

The Tiger said, "I ain't including you in these dam' island haoles. You're more like them mainland haoles who come to my bar at Reno and say, 'H'areya, Willi?' like I was as good as them. You ought to see my bar in Reno."

Herby's hands fluttered more wildly. He promised he would manage with Willi Nogusi. They had caused Mr. Mattison enough trouble tonight.

"Nuts, I've got a month's salary and a bonus," Park said. "Why should I complain? That was a nice fight, Mr. Nogusi, even if you cost me money I'd bet. I'll take you up on it and have you buy me a drink if ever I get to Reno." He looked again at Herby. "Are those Flips still trying to wreck the joint or do you think I'd have a chance to catch a cab by now?"

The next morning, Wednesday, Park decided not to delay until the weekend before flying Laina to Hawaii. He told her to pack and be ready to leave at noon while he drove down to Halepule Beach and got tickets on the 12:20 plane and saw Harry Kimball. He'd explain to Harry he wanted to try painting at least one picture of snow on Hawaiian volcanoes.

"Park, should we go?"

He continued lying to her because he did not have the time this morning or the patience to maneuver her with the care he usually took. He said he'd seen Mr. Meaker who'd handled the publicity for the fight. Mr. Meaker had friends in Honolulu who directed the big national advertising campaign for all the islands in mainland magazines and they were looking for an artist to buy work from out here. Park thought he might have a chance if he could prove his painting was not restricted to the one island. It was a thin lie and he knew it but Laina believed him.

"I'll hurry," she said. "Yes, I do want to go."

At a drug store in Halepule, Park first tried to get through to the plant by the private connection and no one replied, neither E. P. nor Buddy. Next, he rang E. P.'s residence at Koko Point.

"I've been hoping you'd phone," said E. P., very warmly. "We never do see enough of each other any more, do we, Lieutenant? I've felt a little under the weather since getting back from Los Angeles. I might have picked up a flu bug on the mainland but that fight last night cheered me and seeing you will be the best medicine a doctor could order . . ."

When Park walked in he found E. P. had set up a desk and chair on the veranda which you had to remember was called a lanai and the morning sunshine was very bright. E. P. looked slightly yellowish. But Park had not forgotten how E. P. was about himself. Despite his distrust of anyone around him who showed symptoms of being anything other than fit and prepared to do a bang-up job every minute, if E. P. felt at all indisposed he was likely to call in a doctor or to demand a consultation of doctors at the clinic in the Ruth Tothic Memorial Hospital. It was a foible of E. P.'s, but it was nothing to resent. There were so many other more pleasant aspects of E. P., his graciousness, his delight in seeing you, his lack of side, his willingness to experiment with new techniques and to pay for them, that Park knew few clients could compare with him. Despite his slight yellowish color, E. P. was in a fine mood this morning as he listened to Park report the developments after the fight. Last night the police rescued Bull Amani from the enraged Flips, secretly rushing him to the Kalinua docks at the south end of the island where he was put aboard a tramp steamer for Australia. This morning, Park had heard from both By Meaker and Howie Wright. Yes, everything was very much under control. Old Charley Wong was scheduled to step in as acting president of the F. I. U. until the elections next year. Howie Wright had had breakfast early this morning with Charley.

"Pass the word to that boy, Wong, he'll get a ten-cent-an-hour wage increase and no more," E. P. said grimly. "Even that much will add close to four million dollars to our operating budget next year."

"Howie told him not to expect more than seven or eight cents. Wong will cooperate with us."

E. P.'s face turned yellow and bleak. "That boy had better cooperate with us."

Then the bleakness vanished and his long face no longer looked yellow at all. He smiled and Park smiled back. They both knew Charley Wong had to cooperate, although it gave Park a slightly sick feeling when he recalled what Lew Kirsch's probing had uncovered about Wong. He tried to tell himself that Wong had changed by now and had become a kindly harmless old party with a wife and young children of his own. Yes, everything was under control this morning. The wrong boy was out; the right boy at last was on his way in.

E. P. praised Park. "I give you my congratulations. You haven't forgotten any details at all."

"No, I've even brought along the new contract," said Park.

E. P. smiled that smile which illuminated his entire head. He said he expected Park might bring along the new contract. If it was agreeable to Park, though, E. P. would rather stew over the contract tomorrow or the next day. He did not quite feel himself for serious work today. He could see Park Saturday or Monday and sign the contract then after they had agreed on all the details.

"Whatever you say," Park said. "You've been working too

hard. A day or so of doing nothing in the sun ought to be good for you."

"We've all been working too hard. You're beginning to look peaked, yourself."

Park grinned. He said he was thinking of taking a few days off to fly to Hawaii. E. P. paused a moment. He was very much a gentleman and there was a code about such things. Also, in a sense, he was Park's colonel. And there was a code for a colonel to follow as well toward a splendid subordinate.

"I hear she's a striking young lady, Lieutenant. Even if it's rather early in the day, would you grant an older friend the privilege of a drink with you in her honor?"

It was done exactly right. Thus Park was informed he had his colonel's full approbation for a short leave of absence. Park had never seen E. P. quite so mellow, drinking a glass of perry brandy before lunch. But it was a morning to celebrate.

"You're not charging me too much in your new contract?"

"Seventy-five thousand for myself, E. P."

"You're a viper, Lieutenant," said E. P., but he was still smiling. "Yi! Yi! Little did I think I vould cherish a viper!" E. P. fancied he was very good at Jewish impersonations. Often he could ease off a tense meeting by telling a really funny Jewish story, all in dialect, too, real Jewish dialect. Park felt very pleased, listening to E. P. A one-day total stop-work would cost the island about three times the yearly fee Park was asking for the next five years.

E. P. walked to the Buick with Park, halting there, laying an affectionate hand on Park's shoulder. "You've earned a leave of absence. Enjoy yourself. I want you to enjoy yourself with that young lady."

"I expect to," Park said. "You've been working harder than any of us. Can't Buddy take over long enough for you to have a week of loafing? If you picked up a flu bug in Los Angeles you'd better shake it off."

"That boy isn't ready yet to take anything over," said E. P., his face becoming long and sallow. "I've got to do some talking to that boy . . ." Then he smiled and asked, "Why not call me

'Pip'? All my friends do," as if he sincerely believed all his friends did call him that.

"Well, for one thing you never asked me."

"Ruthie began calling me 'Pip' years ago, I never knew why. You remember my sister Ruthie, don't you? Call me 'Pip.' I'm asking you to now, Lieutenant."

For years Park had looked forward to being admitted to the intimate circle. When at last E. P. asked him to use the name "Pip" he found it stuck in his throat. E. P. would not request his friends to call him "Pip" if that nickname had the meaning Harry Kimball claimed it had. But, still, it stuck in Park's throat. He drove the Buick back along the cliff toward Halepule Beach, deciding as soon as he returned from the island of Hawaii that he was going to ask Lew Kirsch to start probing into Harry's past to learn why Harry was so virulent against the old white families of the islands and particularly, Park now had gradually realized, against Pip Tothic. It was about time, Park thought. He still wondered what Dick Stewart's widow had wanted of the art dealer and publisher of the local weekly scandal sheet. He didn't think he liked having Dick Stewart's widow seeing Harry Kimball.

12

After an uneventful flight across the 220 miles of open sea the two-motored transport picked up the northeastern coast-line of the island of Hawaii. It turned inland, thrumming north of Mauna Kea at an altitude of eight thousand feet. The snow-covered cone of the volcano lifted another six thousand feet above the flight level of the transport.

Laina pressed her face to the window. The view was incredible. Off beyond the snowy slopes of Mauna Kea was the white peak of Mauna Loa in a cloudless blue sky. And when Laina pressed her left cheek to the window and sighted back toward the tail, almost directly east, she could see a third peak, that of Pua Hualalai. This one was only some eight thousand feet high and consequently little thought of on the island of Hawaii. The flight was her first long airplane trip. It was the second time she had been off the ground in an airplane.

"When I was sixteen and in my last year at Kauai High," she said, "Ben Subie saved up and bought me a ride in an airplane as a surprise. It was for fifteen minutes."

"Fifteen minutes? Think of that."

The gray eyes opened. "Go to hell," she said suddenly, and turned her face from him.

Park crossed his legs. "Caroline?"

She made no answer.

He was a son-of-a-bitch. He didn't know why having her talk about Ben Subie got under his skin. Yes, he knew why, but he didn't like to think that he knew. Fifteen minutes in an airplane! Park was paying her fare for a flight to Hawaii but there was nothing generous or disinterested in what he was doing in comparison with that fifteen-minute flight she received six years ago from a boy who was now dead. By God, he wished he could think of something to surprise and please her as much as that kid had by buying her fifteen minutes on an airplane.

"Look, Caroline. Would you like me to open the rear door and jump out for you?"

She turned her head and said soberly, "Park, if you'd known Ben, you'd have liked him."

"Perhaps," Park said. "But not if you were around at the same time."

"Good night!" said Laina. But presently she laughed. Then she pressed his hand and, determined to miss nothing, eagerly turned to the round window.

It was good to be alive this afternoon and flying with Laina over to Hawaii. It almost frightened him to realize how greatly he was enjoying this flight. He kept forgetting that she had seen so little of the world in her twenty-two years—the island of Kauai, three years in Honolulu, and the happy island. No wonder she was like a child seeing so many new marvels.

They arrived at the Hilo airport a few minutes after two in the afternoon. By radio-telephone Park had arranged to have Mountain House send a private limousine to meet them. The road up Mauna Loa passed through forests of giant fern trees, upward over the ancient lava flows, higher, still higher, until the air became clear and wonderfully cool.

"Park," she said excitedly, "I can feel it clear down to the bottom of my lungs!"

It was very good to be alive. Park had never seen Laina so completely happy and he didn't think he had ever been so completely happy himself.

He was glad he'd decided not to wait until the week end. Their room was on the second floor of the annex to Mountain House. Byron and Milly Meaker would not arrive until Friday. It gave Park two days to be alone with Laina among complete strangers.

He was on a pinnacle, knowing E. P. would sign the contract. E. P. never failed to keep a promise.

It was as if Park could sight behind him, downward, seeing the town of Mt. Morris, all of his boyhood. Before his thirty-fifth birthday he would be earning seventy-five thousand a year. By the time he was forty, if he were careful and invested wisely, he ought to have a nest-egg of at least a quarter of a million. When he was forty Laina would still be under thirty. And this was only the first pinnacle. He had five years in which no one could louse him up while he prepared for even greater pinnacles ahead. Park was very glad he had taken Laina to Mountain House before By and Milly Meaker arrived. Her delight to be here intensified his. In turn, his delight was like wine for her.

After dinner they went for a walk and for a time thought they were lost when the cold fog swept around them. When they returned to their room, Laina's nose, her cheeks, and even her blunt little chin were red; and she said her fingers were tingling. She exclaimed with pleasure when Park turned on the old-fashioned radiator. Steam clanked through the pipes. She had never before been in a dwelling heated by a real furnace. For the first time in her life she undressed in front of a steam radiator.

"Park, I'm so happy I could die!"

"Listen. Put something on or you'll freeze."

"The radiator's getting warmer."

Park folded his hands under his head and watched her go to the window after she turned off the lights. She raised the shade and the moonlight shimmered eerily down through the cold thin fog pressing against the window pane.

"It's so beautiful."

She lifted her corner of the covers and slipped in beside Park.

"Hey!"

Her legs were like ice.

She warmed her legs. Presently she said thoughtfully, "All we needed was to get away from the island. Can't we keep on? Do we have to go back? I have three thousand dollars. You must have some money in the bank, haven't you? We don't need that fellowship. It's crazy of me to think so but I've a feeling we've just managed to escape from something terrible happening to us. Park—*can't* we?"

She lifted to look down at him through the darkness. Cold air flowed along his body. Park had forgotten how cold it was when you were up so high.

"Let's talk about it tomorrow, Caroline."

"Will you, really?"

"We'll make plans. It's why we came here."

"Park, you don't know how frightened I was after that riot, when Herby Subie stopped us in the corridor. Gosh, didn't he look grim?"

"I told you about it. Doc blew. Someone had to tie up the loose strings and I was the fall guy. You shouldn't have been so scared."

"I was scared. I thought Doc had talked you into some scheme and Herby had found out and was after you. The only reason I left you was to be outside so I could help you. If you hadn't come home when you did, I'd have telephoned Hattie."

Although he knew Laina had not gone away that night to desert him, it moved him unexpectedly to have her say why she had gone. He tried to make it sound lighthearted.

"There's my girl."

She protested, "You needn't say it that way. I really could have done something. In Kauai, Herby carried a card. He quit when the war came but the reason he went into war work instead of volunteering with Ben was that he was afraid the government would find—" Park heard her voice abruptly stop.

He held himself relaxed beside her as if he had not just heard her say that Herby Subie had once carried a card. He knew what that meant. You could carry a union card, too, but when someone said you were carrying a card it didn't always mean that you carried a union card. Park could feel Laina's heart beat more rapidly.

"Herby's a Red?" he said, finally.

"Oh, Park," she said. "I shouldn't have told you. Herby isn't a Red any more. I know he isn't. Ben told me he wasn't and Ben wouldn't have lied to me. Herby changed his mind about the

Reds during the war. He decided he wanted nothing to do with them but he was afraid the Army might discover he'd once signed a card, so he never joined up. My God, Hattie and Herby treated me like their own sister when I came here. The only reason in the world I'd have threatened Herby was if he'd tried to hurt you that night."

"Well, he didn't try to hurt me that night. He was a nice little gent who got sucked into betting money on Bull Amani like the rest of us."

"Park, you didn't tell me you'd bet money on Bull Amani."

"Well, I didn't bet much."

"How much?"

"Look, Caroline. Can't we forget that fight?"

"Yes, Park," she said meekly.

"It was only a few dollars."

"Good night! I don't care how much you bet. I'm just sore because Doc Fields cheated everybody. Even you. And you did so much for him, too." She paused. "You won't say anything? About Herby, I mean?"

"It's nothing to me what Herby was. Forget you told me. Why don't we stop thinking about Herby and the fight?"

But Park could not stop thinking about Herby after Laina had become silent. You tried, he thought, to stay under cover but a day always came regardless of how careful you were, when you got your hand tipped. Take Herby, for example. If what Laina said was true, Herby had turned away from the communists—but there it was. He could still find himself nailed because he had confided in a younger brother who was now dead. It was like a needle buried deep in Park's flesh, pricking at him again, as he thought of the intimacy which once existed between Laina and that dead Japanese boy who had confided his brother's secret to her.

Park lay there with dark thoughts running through his head. He felt isolated from Laina until she moved, sitting up, liking the cold air on her skin.

"Park—I'll unbraid my hair if you want it loose before we go to sleep?"

Sleazy fog was thick at the windows next morning. At breakfast they heard a waiter tell the woman at the next table that the weather at sea level was not much better than up here. According to the weather report over the radio, all the valleys as well as the city of Hilo were blanketed by wet fog.

At lunchtime Laina said she felt funny.

Park asked, "You're not coming down with a cold?"

She was furious at herself. Park said the only way to lick a cold was to get to bed. He packed her into bed, ordered hot lemonade and whiskey for her, and gave her three aspirins.

About two o'clock in the afternoon she fell asleep. He went down to the lobby to buy a cigar, planning to smoke it in the lobby. They had fifty-cent Corona-Coronas which were good enough. He was lighting his cigar when the manager found him. They had a long-distance radio-telephone call for Mr. Mattison.

It was By Meaker. The connection was bad. By's voice came and went. Sometimes By had to repeat. He was trying to explain what that bitch had done. What bitch? Dick Stewart's wife—Cecelia Stewart—she had torn off all the wrappings. At noon today Harry Kimball had issued a surprise edition of his scandal sheet with her whole story in it. The island was like a hornet's nest.

"Hold it, By. How safe is it to talk over these radio-telephones? Can't anyone with a short-wave receiving set tune in on us?"

"No, I checked. These things are scrambled at both ends."

"All right. Now who spilled what? Say it slow."

"That bastard spilled it to his wife."

"What bastard? Listen, By, we've got a lousy connection. Say everything again. Say it slow."

By said everything was loused up like it had never been loused before. Before he died, that bastard Dick Stewart had spilled to his wife. She went to Harry Kimball. Mrs. Stewart told Harry that E. P. Tothic asked her husband to bribe Bull Amani with ten thousand dollars to call off the strike last year. She claimed E. P. fired her goddamn Dickie after her goddamn Dickie did what he'd been told to do. She claimed her goddamn Dickie was

· 179 ·

fired so E. P. could install one of his relatives. Harry Kimball printed everything Mrs. Stewart told him. It was all over the islands. It had caught them with their pants down. For the last half-hour By had been continuously on the telephone before getting through to Park. E. P. was wild. He was asking why Park chose this particular time to be absent from his post of duty?

"Park?"

"I'm still listening," Park said.

"I thought you had hung up on me."

"I was thinking," Park said.

He was thinking at least Laina and he were on this island, miles away from the happy island. He was thinking that Laina would be pleased they were sailing in a hurry to the mainland and she would not ask him why he suddenly decided to go. His luck had not quite run out. He was thinking that much but he couldn't think any further because his stomach was turning itself inside out.

He said, "O. K., let me have it. How much did Mrs. Stewart spill about us for Kimball to print?"

There was a silence from the other end and the air waves sounded like faint faraway and slightly hysterical laughter and then By's voice came on again. It was not quite that bad, papa, but it was bad enough. This time it was only E. P. who had tipped his hand. Buddy Morton had gone to talk to Mrs. Stewart. It was E. P. who was caught with his pants clear down over his ankles. E. P. had been lying. Dick happened to be one of those pack-rat types who kept private records of all money received and disbursed, and Dick's widow had found her husband's account book for last year. In it Dick had noted that he had received ten thousand dollars in August, 1949, from "Pip," and, also, that two days later he had paid it to Bull Amani in return for Bull's agreement to break last year's big strike. Mrs. Stewart had found her husband's account book and it was enough for her to pin E. P. and go to Harry Kimball, but she knew no more than that. The M. O. project was still in the clear. At least that bastard, Stewart, had not loused them up from his grave that far.

Park's stomach began to untie itself. He was startled, but he was careful not to let it show when he began speaking to By. This was trouble, and it was embarrassing for E. P. to be caught with his pants down, but it was not really big trouble. It was a setback, but it could be handled. Stewart's widow hoped to hurt E. P. by claiming he had asked her husband to bribe Amani. It was all because E. P. had hared off to Los Angeles instead of remaining for Stewart's funeral.

"Listen," said Park, "it's nothing to us whether E. P. lied. He's paying us to protect him and we can, if everybody keeps his head. The Stewart blast is a side issue. You and Howie Wright have enough pull to prevent it from going into the newspapers or over the radio. Tell E. P. to stay holed up at Koko Point until we can take the heat off him. Have Buddy continue to say 'no comment.'"

"We'll have labor riots here if we don't do anything more than—"

"Listen, give the unions something else to think about. Get through to Howie Wright in a hurry. If we use our heads we'll turn the Stewart blast into an advantage for us. Have Howie ask old Charley Wong to propose an emergency general meeting of all union members for Saturday morning at the Paradise Auditorium. Instead of waiting until next January for them to elect Wong as regular president, have a meeting called Saturday to repudiate Amani and elect a new slate. Wong hasn't any opposition unless Herby Subie thinks—"

"No," said By's voice. "I've talked with Howie. Wong's got little Herby packed on ice. The Flips and longshoremen think little Herby's too much of an idealist to suit their taste."

"O. K. We'll have the right boy elected officially right now. E. P. ought to give us a bonus for that. Next week, Lew Kirsch's staff can start whispers and rumors against Kimball's scandal sheet. All the Japs and Flips know, anyway, that Kimball has a phobia about them. We'll plant the idea that Kimball's trying to incite trouble between the unions and E. P. in order to close down the plantations and cannery. We'll shift the heat from E. P. to Kimball. Meanwhile, get Howie going on a mass meeting

Saturday. I'll have to call you back to tell you what time I'll get there today. I've got to see about plane schedules . . ."

When Park stepped from the phone booth he saw the great bare expanse of windows in the lobby blurred by the thick mist thrusting against them from outside. Although he had told By that it was nothing to them whether or not E. P. had lied to them, it was much more to Park than he wanted it to be. He decided E. P. had been harder pressed last year by the big strike than anyone had guessed. Then he thought of the seventy-five thousand a year he would receive every year for five years when E. P. signed that contract; and he thought grimly of the hole E. P. had got himself into by trusting that bastard Dick Stewart last year. More than ever, E. P. was going to need professionals. As long as your client paid you, why worry about whether he had lied by saying it was Stewart who had loused them up?

Park went to the desk to ask the manager how soon the next airliner departed from Hilo and learned all airplanes on the island were grounded. It would be impossible for Mr. Mattison to leave today, but perhaps sometime tomorrow the fog would clear, although at this time of year the weather was most unpredictable. It might be two or three days. A steamship departed twice a week. Mr. Mattison could reserve accomodations if he wished on the steamship leaving Sunday. Park shivered. He was safe. He was in the clear. Only E. P. had tipped his hand. Still, Park had been up very high. He realized he had forgotten how cold it could get when you were up so high.

13

On Thursday evening and much too frequently during Friday the manager of the hotel assured Park the island of Hawaii was having its worst weather in fifty years. Laina remained in bed—not because her cold was worse, but because Park deliberately persuaded her she must. He urgently required Laina out of the way while he did everything possible from the telephone booth in the lobby to maintain communication with By Meaker and at the same time to extricate himself from the weather trap holding him here.

"Oh, Park," said Laina Thursday night. "If you think it's best, I will stay in bed. I'm so mad at myself. It's silly to have a cot brought in. I'm not that sick. Honest."

He was still awake late Thursday night when he heard her whisper unhappily, "Park, are you asleep?" through the darkness separating them. He did not answer. The darkness was cold, a brittleness in it. He could smell the faint scent of her sandalwood diffusing into the cold darkness and he thought of her lying there not an arm's length away from him, so warmly and snugly under the blankets.

He had warned her a cold might have serious after-effects if you exerted yourself when you were unaccustomed to a high altitude. She believed him because she had no reason not to believe him. The scent of her sandalwood seemed to touch lightly his forehead and hair. He forced himself to remain quiet until he heard her soft even breathing. It served him right, he told himself silently, to be stuck here on the cot. He had earned it. If he expected to frighten her into staying in bed he had to go the whole distance.

Friday night Park spoke for the fifth time to By from the booth in the lobby. Although the airliners were not scheduled to leave until noon tomorrow, Park had arranged to hire a private plane which was taking off at seven tomorrow morning from Hilo, providing the weather forecast held. For God's sake, By asked, get here tomorrow morning. Thursday evening the labor council had voted on old Wong's suggestion. Tomorrow at ten in the morning the F. I. U. was holding its big emergency meeting in the Paradise Auditorium to elect new officers and to repudiate Bull Amani's betrayal.

"E. P.," said By's voice, "wants you here in time for the meeting."

"I'll do what I can. No new developments?"

"The island's still boiling but you were smart to have Wong call that meeting. There's more talk about the big meeting tomorrow now than anything else."

"Is anybody running against Wong?"

"Herby Subie'd be the only man available, but he's announced that he's running for reelection as secretary. Buddy's going to Koko Point to be with E. P. during the election. I'll pick you up at the airport and drive you over."

"I ought to arrive between nine and ten, tomorrow. Take everything easy. With Wong elected, he can act as brake on the hotheads."

"For God's sake, don't delay over there any longer. It's tough here, papa."

Usually By managed to give an impression of a slightly frivolous attitude when the going got very tough, but Friday night Park noticed By's voice did not sound at all frivolous. It sounded tired and strained as if By's tail had been chewed to a ragged stump.

That night Park explained to Laina that Mr. Meaker had been telephoning him. She remembered those friends Mr. Meaker had in Honolulu who directed the general tourist advertising for all the islands? Well, they were meeting with Mr. Meaker tomorrow. Mr. Meaker wanted Park there even if Park had not yet had time to prove he could paint other islands. It was a big chance to meet with these men and find exactly what they wanted. Consequently, he was flying out early tomorrow. He had chartered a small plane. Because the weather might still be rough tomorrow, he wanted Laina to take the steamship Sunday night.

"Oh, Park," wailed Laina. "I like flying. Let me go with you."

He was thinking of the big meeting tomorrow morning when the right boy would be voted in and he was still thinking that it was E. P. who had loused them all up, not really Dick Stewart, and he was not as patient with Laina as he usually was.

"It costs money to charter a special plane. I'd have to pay double to take you. You do as I say."

The hotel manager had recommended Fred Kalk to fly Park to the island. You could not go wrong, the manager said, when you chartered Fred Kalk to fly you in his amphibian. Somehow, though, Park had gone wrong. Everything was still off the beam and in the soup Saturday morning. Instead of leaving Hilo by seven, the tower did not clear Fred Kalk's amphibian until nearly eleven, an hour after the F. I. U. convention convened on the other island.

Park telephoned a last time to By. They were shoving off in ten minutes. By promised to be at the Makakina airfield at one o'clock, waiting for Park to land. At present, he was sitting in his office, receiving reports from Howie Wright who was covering the meeting at the auditorium. Nothing much had happened so far. Herby Subie had to present the annual secretary's report to the members. By didn't believe the elections would be called for another half-hour or perhaps an hour, depending on how long Herby spoke.

Whenever Park was away from anyone for very long he tended to become apprehensive upon returning. It was as if he feared that people with whom he had to deal would change unfavorably toward him during his absence. Possibly it was because he had a professional awareness of how short peoples' memories could be. As soon as Park was in the air this apprehension struck him almost with panic. He wanted to arrive and find everything the same as it used to be with E. P. and now he was no longer as certain about E. P. He recalled Laina's passionate cry that first night in Mountain House, "All we needed was to get away from the island. Can't we keep on? Do we have to go back?" He had an impulse to tell Fred to turn back before it was too late.

He saw Fred look at him anxiously. Perhaps Fred thought his passenger was going to be sick. Fred shouted, "It's certainly rough soup, isn't it, Mr. Mattison?"

Park nodded. It was rough soup. He had to stop thinking of E. P. having been the one who loused them up instead of Stewart. He decided not to tell E. P. that he knew. He would wait and see whether E. P. denied Mrs. Stewart's charges or admitted their truth. Park didn't want to embarrass E. P., but still, he wished E. P. had not shoved the blame on Stewart. Something in Park crumbled slightly and it made him want to turn around and examine E. P. more closely and that was always a mistake with a client. To have good relations with a client you needed to like him, to have him as a friend as well. It was better that way. You wanted him to stay the same always.

He was, Park decided, making too much of a small thing. E. P. had been hard-pressed last year. That was all. It did not mean he had changed. He was returning to the same boss and the same crowd. A thought passed through his mind. He must not think of them as belonging to a crowd. He must think of them as all being in the same gang. He remembered E. P. often liked to say, "We've got a bang-up gang of boys together to do a bang-up job this time." And E. P. was a bang-up boss. E. P. would know as well as any of them that the M. O. project was not at fault for what had happened in the past few days. No one could have foreseen that Dick Stewart's widow would rush to Harry Kimball with information damaging to E. P.

She had kicked off a hell of an avalanche, too. Park did not believe he could have done any better than the boys, even if the weather had cleared sufficiently for him to leave Hilo before now. He was reminded of the German break-through during the dreadful December of 1944 when the weather prevented American and British air support. It was, he told himself, an apt analogy. By January, 1945, the situation had been contained. Well, with old Wong elected, at last having the right boy officially in, the situation on the island ought to improve noticeably in a few days. The rumors and whispers would shift the heat away from E. P., too. It was a break-through, he would say to E. P. It was not really the catastrophe it appeared to be on Thursday.

Park looked at his watch. It was twenty-six minutes after eleven. Both stations HOK and BYQ usually had short newscasts every fifteen or thirty minutes during the morning hours. He shouted to Fred Kalk, asking if Fred could bring in station HOK on the amphibian's receiving set. For a few minutes through the earphones Park listened to a rebroadcast from the mainland, then at eleven-thirty the ten-minute news broadcast came on. Park listened to the announcer and as he listened he had the feeling you have when you are in your bathtub and the water starts draining away and you seem to be draining down the drain along with all the water.

Instead of delivering a long dull annual business report, Herby Subie gave an hour's passionate speech, condemning Bull Amani's betrayal with bitterness and violence. The radio announcer quoted excerpts from Mr. Subie's speech. The announcer appeared to be enjoying the sensation. Park wondered violently why the hell By or someone didn't stop the goddamn announcer? What were they all doing while this catastrophe was splitting them at the seams? Herby Subie said he had nothing personal against Mr. Wong but he did not believe this was the time to elect Mr. Wong president of the F. I. U.

Park could see it all. Herby had implied that Charley Wong had too much of a reputation for being able to see the company's side of an argument during union negotiations. Herby announced this was a time which required a fighter and who had proved himself a better fighter than Willi Nogusi? Willi Nogusi had been born on this island. He had worked in the cane fields. By defeating Bull Amani he was the new hero of the island. He had lived here and he knew the shameful conditions of plantation camps and of the rotting wooden sewers and the lack of adequate schools and of the promises made for ten years by Paradise Products. In the December negotiations Willi Nogusi could champion a demand for a fair wage increase, not the ridiculous and unreasonable demands asked for by Bull Amani. He could demand from Mr. Tothic that the company begin the housing program this year, along with granting reasonable wage increases. Either that, or Willi Nogusi could lead the biggest strike this island had ever seen.

". . . Mr. Nogusi," the announcer's voice was saying, "was elected a half-hour ago by a three-to-one vote against Mr. Wong. Afterward, the convention voted unanimously to support Mr. Nogusi and Mr. Subie and the labor council . . ." and then the voice stopped abruptly, a second voice came on immediately, saying station HOK was now bringing you recorded chamber music from the station's studio. Evidently someone, perhaps By Meaker, had at last done something to that goddamn announcer. Park sat strapped in his small uncomfortable seat, and wondered if this was how you felt when you knew you didn't have much longer to live. He thought of how he had been on the pinnacle back there on the volcano with Laina. He thought of the months during which he had planned to throw Bull Amani out. He thought of going three or four times a week to Doc Fields' office and of listening to Doc and urging Doc not to postpone the fight past August even if it was the picking season and he remembered how he felt when Doc delayed the fight until October, with more months of waiting, of smelling stale sweat in Doc's office. He thought of all he had done. He thought of all By Meaker and Kirsch and Howie and everyone else had done to make certain no one ever could louse them up again. The wrong boy had been kicked out. Instead of the right boy getting in, now two wrong boys were in.

He had time to decide what to do and what to say to E. P. because the weather closed in and Fred Kalk had to go on instruments. For fifteen or twenty minutes Fred got completely off the beam and didn't know where they were, but Park was not really aware of the buffeting the amphibian was taking six thousand feet above the unseen Pacific.

The M. O. task force had not been here long enough to establish a docile frame of mind to hold against the emotional storm resulting from Mrs. Stewart's blast at E. P. in Kimball's scandal sheet. The M. O. network could hamper Subie and Nogusi and stir dissension in the ranks but it needed another year or two years to be strike-proof. This was Saturday, the twenty-eighth of October. The wage renegotiations were scheduled to begin the first of December. There was very little time—thirty-three days. Park thought of all his hopes for a dazzling future, seventy-five thousand dollars every year for five years until he had a nest-egg large enough to keep him securely at the top of the ladder. He had failed to get the right boy in. He had no squawk coming if E. P. refused to sign the contract; Park had known the conditions. Then he thought of what might be done in thirty-three days to get Nogusi and Subie out of the picture and to get the right boy in; he had been horsed around all he was going to be.

He was not quitting. All he needed was one more final spurt. He thought of what you did in a war if you needed to get two wrong boys out of the picture. In a war you did not wait until all other measures had failed. You used drastic measures. Well, this was also a war, but Park tried to look at it dispassionately. He could go ahead and use all other measures first. He had thirty-three days. He could give himself twenty days to try everything else and still have a safe margin if all else failed. Then if he had to, by God, he would permanently eliminate those two jokers from the picture. There it was. He wondered why he did not feel more relieved after finally reaching a decision which was certain to give him five sweet years on the happy island.

When the twin-motored amphibian landed that afternoon at the Makakina airfield, Park felt shaky as he placed his feet on solid ground although he had wanted to appear calm when By Meaker arrived to greet him. He glanced around, surprised that By had not yet arrived. He frowned at his watch. It was six minutes after two. Park had told By he would arrive at one but because of the soupy weather they were a good hour late.

The amphibian had halted in front of a row of private hangars, away from the airport building and Park had never been at this end before. From this end the airport was unfamiliar. The sun was shining brightly although there were puddles in the macadam runways from the recent rains. Park decided he must have forgotten how warm and humid it could be when you were not high on the slope of an island volcano. He decided he also had forgotten how it was when you returned to a place even if you had not been absent many days.

At a distance of a third of a mile to the north, the airport building looked rather shrunken and insignificant against the metallic greens of recently sprayed pineapple fields in the background. The yellow sunlight had a harsh glare which hurt his eyes as he looked about for By. The airport seemed deserted. A puff of wind rolled a cloud of red dust over the long south-north strip.

Fred jumped stiffly down from the amphibian's cabin. He dropped Park's two pigskin bags to the macadam which gave off a faint steamy smell of asphalt and drying rain water.

Fred asked, "Isn't anyone meeting you, Mr. Mattison?"

"I thought so," Park said. "I'll wait a minute longer."

The wind had fallen again. Through a gap in the purple mountain toward Halepule side Park saw a glimpse of the sea. He had not known you could feel so lonely and lost all of a sudden in the middle of an island airport. It hit him unexpectedly. He thought of how different it had been last Wednesday when Laina and he had left on the regular scheduled flight to Hilo.

A cheerful noisy crowd always gathered to see one of the big two-motored transports go soaring into the magnificent sky of real Hawaiian blue. Flags fluttered from the airport building whose four outside walls of plaster were covered with colorful murals of the old romantic Hawaii. You did not notice that the torrential rains had already washed off large portions of the mural on the windward side of the building. From the loudspeakers came the sad sentimental melodies of "Fare Thee Well" and "Aloha, Oe." A man from the tourist office was there with baskets of fresh carnation leis. Two hapa-haole girls appeared, dressed in celophane grass skirts and not much else. And both were delighted to pose while you used up the last of the color film in your camera.

Although Park knew it was M. O. for departing and arriving tourists, it had become something more than a contrived piece. He remembered Laina had felt it, too. She was wearing the pale green tailored suit which gave her such an air of being someone whose picture you had seen beautifully reproduced in one of the color pages of *Town and Country* or *Harper's Bazaar*. A warm breeze ruffled the trim linen skirt. As she turned to Park she lifted a hand to clutch at one of those wide straw hats which usually only mainland women bought at the beach stores. Most of the men in the crowd swung their cameras away from the two girls in cellophane skirts to snap pictures of Laina for it was one of those moments when she looked her best. Park saw tears in her eyes. She had said angrily, "Christ, I'm going to cry. . . ."

That Wednesday noon it was like the last act of a successful New York production, the stage filled with charming people having a high time for themselves. Although you knew it was make-believe, still you were reluctant to leave your seat when the curtain fell. You wanted to see it all over again. Park thought it must have been something like that last Wednesday. But whatever it was, it was not here today. The stage was empty. Park had returned to the same seat but the show was gone. He was not seeing it all over again.

He picked up his suitcases. Evidently By had not waited it out. He saw Fred looking at him. He wondered why it was embarrassing for two strangers to break away from each other. after being together a short period. You never knew exactly what to say.

"Any time you're ever in Hilo, you can always reach me at the airport. If I'm not there, they'll certainly get in touch with me for you." Fred raised a hand in a gesture. "Happy landings. Parker."

It was the first time Fred called Park by his first name and Fred appeared unsure of himself when he did it.

"Well, I'll certainly look you up if ever I'm in Hilo. Happy landings to you, Fred." Park lifted his hand.

He thought he probably sounded unsure of himself too. He knew he certainly did not feel as sure of himself as he had assumed he would after he landed. As he walked toward the airport building the distance seemed to increase instead of diminish. The sun was hot. The two bags dragged at his arms. His left arm began to ache when he was halfway to the building. Why hadn't By waited? Park's apprehensions returned. By would have a good reason for not waiting.

As he lugged his bags into the empty passenger hall of the building, he heard the clacking of the teletype recorder from the C.A.A. weather room beyond the door at his right. He decided to telephone By's office, then place a call through to Koko Point, and next try to find a cab. He walked toward the telephone booth and saw someone inside, telephoning. It was Byron Meaker. Park rapped on the glass.

By hung up and stepped out of the booth and at first glance it did not seem to Park that By had changed. By looked thin but he always looked thin. He was wearing brown and white sport shoes, handsome nylon tweed-checked slacks, and his colored beach shirt was extremely gay. He looked as if he was either on his way to or returning from the beach. He was not carrying a coat. He grabbed Park's hand and pumped it. He was very happy to see Park. He said the tower had received the amphibian's signal when it came around for a landing. Instead of losing time, By put a call through to Buddy at Koko Point. Although they were alone in the hall, By lowered his voice.

"You heard the news?"

Park nodded.

"Nogusi president, and a vote to strike—"

"I heard it," said Park. "Let's get going."

By picked up Park's two bags. His Plymouth was hidden on the other side of the airport building. On this side a kanaka was mowing a lawn which was turning yellow from the drift of metallic spray carried in by the wind from a nearby pineapple field. Two Flips in pearl-gray suits had driven a rented Ford to the taxi strip on the side. No airliners were due for hours, and with nothing better to do they were watching the kanaka mowing the lawn. By glanced at the Flips and refrained from saying anything more about the catastrophe this morning. He opened the luggage compartment, shoving in Park's bags. As he closed the compartment he asked conversationally how Laina was?

Park said she was taking the steamship Sunday night. The weather was too thick for her to risk flying across today. He paused, implying that it had not been too thick for him to risk getting here, but By did not pick it up with any approving comment. By slid glumly under the wheel.

Park got in beside By and perhaps because he was thinking about Laina, abruptly he said he had lied to her—as if he had never lied to her before. He said he had told her he had to get here today because he had a big chance to sell some paintings.

By casually said, "I wish Millie was that dumb," and drove the Plymouth away from the airport.

It stung Park unreasonably. But he clamped his teeth shut. This was not the time to slam back at By against Millie. He asked, "How is Millie?"

By looked at him hard and Park had the uncomfortable feeling of having asked the wrong question. He said, "Millie's still in the hospital. I told you yesterday morning on the telephone."

Park remembered. Thursday night Millie had taken too much luminol.

"Is she better?"

"She'll live," By said laconically and crossed the highway on the green light, turning left around a high steel tower to go toward Halepule Beach and Koko Point. By had much more than Millie on his mind. "Do we start packing?" he asked. "We've lost that contract. E. P. can't meet that housing demand. If those jokers pull a strike on him in December, Paradise Products is finished." He started swearing softly and tonelessly at E. P. and Park held off to give By time to get it out of his system. By liked it here, too. By didn't like the idea of giving up the dazzling dream of five sweet years until they accumulated a large enough nest-egg to open offices of Mattison and Meaker,

Morale Operations, in New York, with the big utilities as likely clients; there were organizations that ought to pay big money at the drop of a hat for the kind of services offered by an M. O. national task force.

"That rotten lousy son-of-a-bitch," By said. "*He's* sick. He's there at Koko Point, and he thinks he's sick. That's fine. That's wonderful. He doesn't have contagious germs. He's pure. But if one of us shows up at a meeting with so much as a cold, what happens? That's different. We aren't keeping very fit, are we? He might catch our germs. So he's at Koko Point, but he's not too sick to blame us. *He* loused it up. He had Stewart bribe Amani. But does he say so? Admit it? No, by Jesus. So we're all loused up. So I go back to Ohio to hunt for a rotten newspaper job!"

Park waited for By to blow off all the steam before saying in a composed and reasonable tone, "Look. It might not be that bad."

"We're stuck," said By. "We got thirty-three days."

"O. K.," said Park, "but I don't think we're stuck."

"Instead of getting one wrong boy out," By said, "now we've got to get two wrong boys out. In thirty-three days."

"Look," said Park. "Let's assume for a minute we might get those two jokers out. Even if we do, we've got to cool down the rank-and-file members, haven't we?"

"Sure, sure," said By. "But what use—"

"Listen a minute," said Park. "Let's use everything we've got, starting tomorrow on an anxiety compaign to scare the rank and file about what'll happen when their jobs go. Pile it on over the towers, the radio, newspapers, movie houses, the works."

By gave him a quick look. "That can be managed, papa."

"We've still got Wong," said Park. "We've got Wong and a small faction supporting Wong. That's a start."

"It's a start, but not much of a start."

"Let's keep our heads," said Park. "I want you to get Lew Kirsch off to Kauai tonight. Have him charter a plane. He can't lose time."

"Kauai?" By didn't sound quite as dragged as he had. "Where Herby Subie came from?"

"Herby used to carry a party card," said Park. "I want Kirsch to start digging and keep digging until he gets proof."

After passing the rough section of road at the Hono plantation, By increased the Plymouth's speed. Now the Plymouth faltered and slowed down and then Park heard By ask, "You're sure?"

"If Lew digs he'll get proof."

By stepped on the foot pedal again. "You got it from Laina?"

"Keep her out of this," said Park brusquely.

They came into the long curving four-lane highway with the ocean so close, blue and sparkling. It didn't seem possible that there was soupy weather on the other side of the island.

Park said, hesitantly, "She thinks a lot of those damned Subies, By. I don't want her to think . . ." He knew precisely what he did not want her to think—that it was he who had sicked the dogs on Herby Subie, But he didn't know exactly how to explain it to By.

By's long upper lip looked shiny in the sunlight through the windshield but it was slowly tucking in and down as his mouth curved. "Sure, I'll get Kirsch started."

"There's Nogusi," Park said. "We can get to him. I'm positive we can get to him if we have time. I don't know how much time it'll take."

He told By about the night in Doc Fields' office after the fight when Willi Nogusi came for money which was not in Doc's safe. Willi needed money; he owned a half-interest in a Reno bar and he was hoping to buy the other half. Park would not forget how savagely Willi had cursed the island. Willi had said he had got away from it once before and he would do it again. Park had had the impression that night that Herby Subie had Willi under his thumb and was starting to make Willi march. It had been brilliant tactics this morning for Herby Subie to retain control of the F. I. U. through a front man, the new hero of the island, but it might not be very good strategy.

By said, "I can sick Danny on Willi without tipping our hand if you think it's worth it.

"Right now, everything's worth a try."

"You know Mama Pikea's on the beach?"

"Only what you've told me."

"It's exclusive, supposed to be only for haoles. I suppose Danny could arrange to get Nogusi fixed there with a girl. Mixed bloods aren't usually allowed. It would keep out the rest of Nogusi's crowd so we'd have a chance to work something. You remember the degenerate moral charges we managed to plant on that Swede bastard in '43 who was broadcasting for the Germans from Stockholm? Why not try the same thing on Nogusi?"

"Anything," Park said. "But make it fast."

"Sure," said By although he did not sound very sure at all. "I'll manage somehow. At least I can get Danny to wangle Nogusi into Mama Pikea's. I'll manage somehow," he repeated. He glanced at Park. He had driven the Plymouth through the old town and was now driving along the winding cliff road. "Thirty-three days, papa. I don't think we've got enough time."

Park wished he had stopped at Halepule Beach to have at least a sandwich. It might have helped the gnawing pains in his stomach.

"Look," he said, "I'm filled up with being horsed by those two jokers. I had six weeks' training during the war for one of those Jedburgh teams we were dropping into the French underground. O. K. I can still goofer a car to have it look like an accident. We'll try everything first and if there isn't any other way, we'll take those two jokers completely out." He regarded By. "I want five sweet years here, don't you?"

By turned into the private Koko Point road, driving slowly.

"Don't get me wrong, papa," he said. "But you're not married. I've got to think of Millie."

Park lifted his hands from his knees. Gently, he laid them back upon his knees. He did not know Millie very well. As he remembered she had a button nose and very black eyes and she was small and plump and By was in love with her.

"Well, I think you should think of Millie."

"I just want an escape plan."

"We'll do it this way. We don't need two for a goofer job. You work on the escape plan."

By stopped the Plymouth.

"To hell with that," he said. "One guy can't chop off those

· 196 ·

two jokers without help and you know it. If that son-of-a-bitch, E. P., hadn't loused us all up like this, you and I wouldn't have to sweat out our guts planning a chop-off job, either. We go out on the limb, not E. P. I want an escape plan if we get shoved off the limb into thin air. What's wrong with asking for an escape plan?"

If you get shoved off the limb, Park thought, you didn't need to plan where you were going. You dropped. What you had to plan was to avoid being shoved off the limb when you planned to take care of two jokers.

"Let's don't kid ourselves," Park said. "How far can you run in the middle of the Pacific?"

"If we chop off those two jokers," By said stubbornly, "we'll have Flip riots. If we have bad riots this island could be too hot for haole wahinis. I'd want to get Millie off the island."

"Hell. Did you scout around Iki or Pohaku to see if you could find a good safe plane to rent at short notice from one of the small fields?"

By whistled. He said sheepishly, "If you want to know, I forgot. What with E. P. and Millie in the hospital, I forgot."

"That's the best I can think of."

"It's good enough for me. That takes care of Millie. It's all I want. I'll go along with you. I've done a little checking on Nogusi. He's living with the Subies. He and Subie drive to the labor hall every morning in Subie's ashcan model Oldsmobile. That car's probably parked all day on one of the lots near the hall. I'll lay a time-sheet for us on it. We can flip a coin to see whether I goofer and you spot for me or you do the job and I stand watch. But we'll try everything first, won't we?"

"Everything," Park said. "I just want those two jokers out."

"That's my dish, too."

Park was still thinking of Millie. He wondered if By thought she was beautiful. Perhaps if you were in love with Millie you would think she was beautiful. Perhaps that was all that was necessary—to be in love, and as long as you were in love the girl remained beautiful even if she had a button nose and let herself get plump.

"Look, By. What's so wrong with a newspaper job in Ohio?"

By turned his head to Park. "For one thing, Millie hated it. She's forgotten how much she hated it but I haven't. For another thing, I don't like being paid in peanuts any more. I like big dough as much as you do."

"I'm not so sure I'm any goddamned good for you."

"Papa, I've never had it better."

"Don't ever tell me I never laid it on the table for you."

"You lay it down and I pick it up. 'Mattison and Meaker—' That's us, every time, isn't it?"

"We'll try everything else first," Park said.

When By halted his Plymouth behind a company Dodge from the cannery, Park saw Buddy sitting on the wooden middle step of the high old-fashioned veranda—"lanai" it was called here, Park reminded himself. And E. P., he must remember, was to be addressed as "Pip."

Buddy raised his head. For an instant the sensitive face remained closed and impervious as if the Plymouth's arrival had caught him when his thoughts were far away. He walked slowly down the steps and waited there and Park decided Buddy looked about the same as ever. He looked tired and he looked thin, and Park wondered if E. P. had been pushing the new boy around today.

Buddy said he had been worrying about Park these past two hours. In another half-hour he would have ordered an air search. He did not offer to shake hands but Buddy was never much at shaking hands and that did not bother Park, although it bothered him slightly to know Buddy had been concerned about his safety. It was easy to like someone who thought enough of you to order an air search on his own responsibility. But Park did not wish to like Buddy too much or to analyze the reasons why not, either.

Buddy did not forget that By Meaker was also here. He asked if Mrs. Meaker were any better today? Yes, By said, much better, thanks; and appeared pleased that Buddy had remembered to ask. They were walking up the steps to the wide lanai, Buddy between them. It seemed to Park that all three of them were avoiding any mention of E. P. Nothing would be quite the same for any one of them since they had learned it was E. P. and not Dick Stewart who really loused it up. Buddy was saying earnestly to By that you had to watch it if anyone in your family began taking too many sleeping tablets. Buddy remembered when he had returned from England in the summer of 1945. His wife was taking far too many tablets for her own good. He had been compelled to be very strict with her.

By said from now on he was going to be very strict with Millie. It gave Park an unexpected twinge to learn that Ellen Morton had been taking too many sleeping tablets that summer after the spring of 1945, and Buddy had been compelled to be strict. Instead of opening the door immediately, Buddy hesitated as if there were still something more to be said.

Park said, "How's E. P. taking the bad news?"

"I don't really know how E. P. feels about anything," Buddy answered with that odd tone in his voice which Park had heard once or twice before. "You'll have to decide for yourself. If you're asking me how I'm taking it, I haven't quite decided. I don't like it, I know that."

Park did not understand what Buddy didn't like. He didn't have time to think of what it might be because Buddy had been here long enough to dislike quite a few things. Park also noticed Buddy said "E. P.," not "Pip," but that was something to be considered later.

Billy, the Chinese butler, announced that Mr. Tothic was ready to receive them. It was the first time Park had ever been inside E. P.'s bedroom. He had no time to think about Buddy. You never really knew after you had been away if everything would still be the same when you returned. . . .

It was not until later when he harked back to this meeting with E. P. that the bedroom took shape in his memory and details and impressions crowded into the vacant places of his mind. He recalled that the darkened room had that sickroom smell. It was probably the smell of eucalyptus vapor steaming from the electric vaporizer on a small teakwood table at the foot of E. P.'s bed. His attention was briefly distracted by the sound of a piano softly playing. He jerked his head in surprise to see who was playing a piano in here. The music was coming from one of those new combined wire-tape and radio machines which was pushed between a huge teakwood bureau and a big window whose worn red velvet drapes were drawn tightly against the explosion of sunlight from outside. The costly machine struck Park as being incongruous in this old-fashioned bedroom.

It was later, too, that he realized why he had a sense of shock when he first saw E. P. lying there under a single sheet on that iron bed. It was a boy's bed in which E. P. lay at a slight angle to fit in comfortably. It must have been the bed E. P. had had ever since he was a boy. Park recalled, beyond the small unshaven man in that boy's bed, the quaint blurred figures of children in dress of the early 1900's trooping across the wallpaper, playing in an English countryside. And he saw all the old nicked teakwood furniture; he heard the soft liquid piano notes of someone playing over and over again Debussy's "Suite Bergamasque" on the wire-tape recorder which evidently had been adjusted to repeat. Somehow, too, he had a vision come back to him. It was of Buddy deep in thought on those worn steps, flooded with sunlight, while E. P. lay in that darkened room where nothing very much had changed since he was a boy.

Only E. P., Park now saw, coming to the bed, had changed. The spider's web of wrinkles which always showed more when E. P. was tired had etched deeper into the sallow unshaven face. Looking down, Park had the impression of a cathedral doorway beginning to crumble, with gray weeds growing rank about the entrance; and it was an effort to rid himself of so improbable an association. Park waited for E. P. to take the ball.

14

It was not a long meeting. E. P. took the ball, saying he wasn't quite himself yet and wanted to keep this meeting short. He did not ask about Park's flight nor did he ask any of them to sit down. The meeting began without the playful preliminary tossing of the ball with which E. P. often beguiled his boys into the right spirits.

Park promised, "I'll keep details to a minimum, Pip, until you're back in the saddle."

"I keep myself fit. I consider it a duty to Paradise Products and to this island to keep myself fit and because I've kept myself fit, I'll be over this flu bug and in the saddle by Monday. We can hold this meeting today to brass tacks. You heard what those boys did to us this morning at their labor meeting?"

"Pip, I'll admit at first it gave me a jolt—"

E. P. interrupted Park. "Can't we keep the ball rolling faster by keeping everything on a staff level at this meeting, Lieutenant?"

It made Park feel like a subordinate who pressed too eagerly upon his friendship with a commanding officer.

"Yes, Colonel. Sorry."

"I think you've let me down, Lieutenant. For all your work the past six months, what have you accomplished? It looks to me as if you've merely kicked the devil through one door and he's come back through a second. I can't see any basic thing to choose from between that boy, Amani, and this new boy,

Nogusi. It looks to me as if we simply shuffled around to get another wrong boy in."

Sometimes you had to know when to take it and to listen and Park thought this was one of those times. E. P. neither mentioned Mrs. Stewart's charges which had set off the labor explosion this morning, nor attempted to repudiate them. He ignored her as you would ignore a vile thing which had spit at you in passing. He spoke solely of the election this morning of a prize fighter instead of a safe man and of the resolution passed to press for the housing program. He said it meant a strike because the company could not pay out millions now for a housing program without running into financial disaster. It looked to E. P. as if the project to establish a docile frame of mind had run aground. He was sorry but it looked that way to him, and after fifteen minutes of summing it up for Park, E. P. was still sorry but it looked that way to him.

Park listened and he remembered the five-year contract which was still unsigned and once again he heard Laina's passionate cry ring through his mind. He glanced at Buddy whose expression in the shadows was unreadable. He heard E. P. finally saying, "You know how I operate. If I've misjudged you, simply tell me. I don't like thinking you haven't measured up in this emergency. You take the ball."

Park took the ball and as he spoke he heard the pleasant crisp sound of his own voice and it seemed to him something inside himself was jeering. He could almost see a row of clients in the shadows to whom he had spoken in the past, giving them the soothing syrup before presenting a plan. Always there was trouble. You always had to be ready with a plan, not only good enough to cope with the new trouble, but good enough to persuade the client to keep you on the job.

Park asked E. P. to remember that the most recent survey by Lew Kirsch's staff indicated a favorable frame of mind toward island high brass. But even this was too recently established to be solidly rooted. Mrs. Stewart's blast went off like dynamite to cause a violent break-through back to a less satisfactory attitude. When you had a break-through you needed to contain it. They had until December first when wage negotiations began. That gave them thirty-three days. If thirty-three days were not sufficient, they would make more time for themselves.

First, Byron Meaker and Park were determined to throw in all M. O. pressures available to frighten the workers from their rebellious attitudes, the newspapers, the radio, the towers, the movie houses, rumors, whispers—the complete ticket this time. E. P. was sitting up, listening so attentively that the sheet fell around his lap. He lifted it to cover the graying bristle on his chest with an oddly prim gesture which embarrassed Park enough to throw him off his stride.

"Go on," said E. P. encouragingly. "I'm glad to see you're finally sparking."

Park went on . . . there was that five-year contract, seventy-five thousand dollars a year, dangling before him if he went on fast enough to grasp it. Secondly, he said, they planned to use Howie Wright to liaison directly with the Wong faction to block the hotheads from precipitate action. Wong still had the influence to stir dissension in the labor council meetings. Third, it was necessary to discredit Subie and Nogusi with the unions to have them replaced as quickly as possible by Wong.

"What about Subie? I want to hear how you propose to get that maniac out."

"Herby Subie," Park said, "carried a communist party card. We're sending a man to Kauai tonight to get background material to smear Subie as fast as we can. We—"

"Just a minute, Park," said Buddy from the foot of the bed.

Park glanced at Buddy. He had almost forgotten Buddy was in the bedroom.

Buddy said, "How do you know Herby Subie's a Red now?"

With something waspish in his voice, E. P. said, "How Park knows Subie's a Red is a detail, Buddy. If Park says Subie's a Red, I'm satisfied. At least Park has started to spark. Go on, Lieutenant."

Park felt uncomfortable about going on with Buddy in the bedroom. He wished Buddy were not here. "Nogusi's still an unknown quantity but I think Herby Subie made a hell of a mistake to use him this morning to capture the unions." He explained how he had met Nogusi after the fight in Doc Fields' office and he repeated what Nogusi had said. He hesitated, before revealing By's and his plan to have Nogusi admitted into Mama Pikea's. He glanced at Buddy in the shadows and saw a stiffness on his face. He wished he had one-tenth of the money Buddy had. If he had, he wouldn't have to be here in this dim boy's bedroom where everything appeared to be the same as it always had been, with Buddy there, looking stiffly at him and no doubt thinking righteous and moral thoughts. Park paused. He felt it in his legs and he wanted to lean against the wall and rest but he stayed where he was, waiting for E. P. to make up his mind. Here it was, now, one way or another. Goodbye five sweet years.

E. P. said, "That program's all well and good, Lieutenant, but it's not definite."

Park knew it was not; he didn't want to make it too definite with Buddy in the room. You could not tell what a boy like Buddy was thinking. Almost from the day of his arrival, Buddy had indicated opposition to the M. O. program. Somebody ought to take Buddy in hand and push him, push him hard, to teach him he didn't belong in this league.

E. P. was saying waspishly, "You don't seem to realize how much is at stake, Lieutenant. I've counted on you to prevent strikes here. I thought you had guts. Back in Washington, Ruthie told me you had guts. I wish Ruthie were alive now to see what a mistake she made. My father had men with guts when he had to deal with troublemakers in his time. You aren't sparking. I expected you to tell me you had planned something drastic for these two maniacs before December first."

"Just a minute," said Buddy again. His voice was liquid cold like the drops of music coming from the wire-tape recorder. "I'd like to know what you mean by asking Park to plan something drastic for Nogusi and Subie, E. P."

There was another short pause.

"Buddy," E. P. cawed, "I don't think you quite understood me."

"I'd like to know," Buddy said.

"I was being technical," E. P. explained. "When you know these boys better you'll learn they express details technically to save time. You understood I was being technical, didn't you, Park?"

"Yes, Colonel," Park said.

"By asking Park to spark on something drastic for me, I was asking him to—Park, I think you can explain these technical terms to Buddy better than I can."

"E. P. expects us to smear Subie and Nogusi in a hurry," Park said. "We can't be too ethical with those boys when they aren't being ethical with us."

"How aren't they being ethical with us?" Buddy asked. "For ten years we've promised to begin the housing program, haven't we?"

It was like a child asking embarrassing questions in front of company. You ignored him and pretended you didn't hear the questions.

E. P. looked around and said briskly, "I think that closes the meeting. While I'm not entirely satisfied, I think we ought to give Park's plan a chance for at least the next fifteen days." He nodded to By. "Glad to have you here, Byron. We ought to see more of each other." He looked toward Buddy. "I'll need a few more days before getting back into the saddle. I'll see you at the cannery Tuesday or Wednesday. Now, if you two don't mind, I'll have a word with Park on his contract." He waited while By nodded silently, glanced once at Park, and departed from the bedroom. Buddy hesitated as if he still had something more to say but didn't know exactly how to put it. E. P. said, "That's all, Buddy. Thank you for dropping in."

Park watched Buddy leave the bedroom. It seemed to him, after all, there was really little difference between Buddy and his wife. When the cards were down, Buddy was very much like his wife. He was ineffectual and he didn't know how to fight back.

E. P. was saying thoughtfully, "When I get back in the saddle next week I'm going to have to start working on that boy, Park.

I'll say this for Dickie Stewart. He was slow on his feet, but he was a good soldier. He tried to carry out orders without arguing. That boy, Buddy, has a good head but he hasn't learned the facts of life. When I get back, I think I'm going to have to break in that boy for his own good. I never had to break in Dickie Stewart. I'll say that for Dickie, too."

E. P. paused. For a second Park thought E. P. was going to admit he had lied and it was he who'd loused up everything by ordering Dick Stewart to bribe Bull Amani last year.

He said, "I made a mistake suggesting you plan something drastic on those two maniacs while Buddy was in the room. That boy, Buddy, needs more breaking in before we go into too many details in front of him."

Park said, "We'll take care of Nogusi and Subie for you."

Park saw the dark eyes become luminous. . . .

"How soon?" E. P. asked.

"Inside twenty days."

"Can I count on that?"

"Yes, Colonel, you can count on that."

E. P. relaxed. He stretched a brown hand chidingly toward Park. "Come, now. No formalities after staff meetings, Park. If I can count on you it's all I ask."

"I won't let you down, E. P."

"Pip," said E. P. with his warming smile.

Park perceived that the trusted lieutenant had received another chance to measure up.

" 'I've looked at that five-year contract," E. P. said. "You had me worried this week. I almost decided not to sign it. Here I was, needing you, and where were you? You ran off with a girl to another island. I felt you had let me down."

Park swallowed. "It won't happen again, Pip."

"But you know how I operate. When I make a promise, I keep it. The contract satisfies me as you wrote it. I'm not going to quibble with you on the details. The day you tell me the two wrong boys are out and Charley Wong's got his way cleared to get in, I'll sign that contract. The sooner you tell me, the more I'll enjoy signing it for you." The brown fingers plucked at the sheet. "But I've got this to say, Park. I want this for the record. You know how I operate. I want it clearly understood I'm telling you no harm's to come to those two maniacs. I want that for the record."

It was a farce, Park thought. By Meaker was frightened and worried, Park knew, but at least By was willing to go along deeper into the slot machine. E. P. was staying outside. Now he was talking for the record just as he had after Dick Stewart got himself caught.

"Just don't worry about it, Pip," said Park gently.

"One thing more, before we call this a day. That—that Stewart woman, Park . . ."

Park waited in the dim bedroom. The wire-tape recorder had switched itself back to the beginning of the suite again.

"That Stewart woman's leaving for the mainland in a week. In respect for Dickie's memory, I've decided to do nothing against her. But I can't pass by the public insult I've received from that scandal-monger, Kimball. I have my integrity to maintain. After we're over this hump, I want you to go after Kimball. I want Kimball hurt. I want him taken down a dark alley and taught a drastic lesson. That's an order, Lieutenant."

"Yes, Pip," said Park.

The brown hand stretched out. Park felt it take his. "It's good to see you. I want to keep in touch with the progress you're making. While I'm resting here for a few days, I think you'd better plan to report here. Suppose you see me Monday, say at nine-thirty in the morning, and we can have breakfast together. We don't ever see enough of each other, do we?"

Park steeled himself against what was more than merely a heaving sensation. His head pulsed. He thought of the five sweet years he had wanted so much; he had never thought until now how costly they might be. The realization came very slowly. He wished he had asked for more than seventy-five thousand a year. He must have miscalculated, although he didn't know how or where. Now that he was close to getting all he had dreamed of, somehow seventy-five thousand dollars a year didn't seem quite enough to be sure every year would be a sweet year.

15

It took much longer than Park had expected to finish with By and it was nearly six o'clock when he drove his Buick from Pua Heights down Hibiscus Road into the four-lane highway which curved into the lovely half-mile curve of Halepule Beach. By and Park had coordinated the emergency blueprint of action over the next few critical weeks. They wanted to give everything else a try before hitting the deadline they had set for themselves, November 21, at which point they would give up everything else and plan to have it look like an accident for two labor jokers.

Park decided the feeling of broken bottles in his stomach came because he had forgotten to eat today. At the fourth intersection in the highway, he turned left. From the massed yellow and orange flowers at the base of the intersection another of the graceful steel towers lifted into the dimming pinkness of a short tropical twilight. The cone-shaped loudspeakers were pouring forth another romantic tune of old Hawaii. Park wondered how it would be if some day all the towers were suddenly silent over the island and once more you had peace.

He had planned to have dinner tonight at "L'On Y Mange Bien" but decided against it because Harry Kimball often ate there. He did not want to encounter Harry tonight and have to explain why Laina hadn't returned with him. He thought it would be safe to leave Harry for later. He drove by Harry's galleries and the new cinema and parked in an empty space near the Grass Shack Drug Store.

He recalled the last time Laina and he had eaten on the strip. He wished she were with him now—he missed her. He had not quite realized until now how much he did miss her; it was like having innumerable fine wires snap. He had finished with By. He could trust By to go ahead over Sunday to retool the big M. O. network for "Operation Anxiety." Park had tonight and tomorrow on his hands with nothing to do.

He dragged himself from the Buick. He felt pooped and sickly hollow after having it happen almost on schedule up there in that house on the Pua cliff. Half an hour ago he had seen By to the door, had forced himself to stay there until By drove away; and then he had run like hell for the bathroom. It was Harry Kimball, he recalled, who told him that nervous spasms were responsible for E. P.'s intimate nickname. Park hoped what he had was also a nervous spasm, although there had been a trace of blood in it. He was quite certain it wasn't ulcers or even the beginning of them because ulcers were caused by worry and Park knew he was not one of the types who worried. He knew the dozen or so responsible physicians of the island were all in the clinic at the Ruth Tothic Memorial Hospital. If he went to one of them to ask why his stomach was failing to adjust itself to the climate it was quite probable that E. P. might hear about it. Park didn't want to risk falling into the hands of a quack.

It was growing darker now. The brilliant neon signs flamed all along the curving strip. Park thought he could let it ride, at least for a few days. He had too much else on his mind to become a hypochondriac. He ought to start eating more than he had these past few months and he'd feel a hell of a lot better. He entered the drug store, sat at the counter, and ordered a double portion of ham and eggs and coffee with cream. He wished he could shut his eyes and when he opened them have Monday morning magically here, with Laina back. All he had to do, he told himself, was hang on a little longer.

As soon as he was over this last hump, he would take at least a month off with Laina, perhaps two months. The trip to the island of Hawaii had not turned out to be time off at all. He would fly her to New York for Christmas. Better yet, it might be fun to go to Mexico. You could be in Mexico and even if you heard people talking you would not know what they were saying. Park thought he would like to go where he did not know what anyone around him, except Laina, was saying.

"Here," said the Korean girl from behind the counter.

"Thanks."

Park looked at his ham and eggs. He should be hungry. He should be very hungry. He drank his coffee. Although Laina was still an awful cook, at least she served her instant coffee piping hot. This coffee was lukewarm.

He noticed the early evening tourist crowd flowing into the drug store. After Laina's contralto with its faint suggestion of a kanaka accent, the voices of the haole women from the mainland all seemed very high and very sharp. He looked to his left where a young woman was saying, "You see what I mean, darling? Aren't you pleased we didn't go to the Riviera this fall? It's something tropical you can feel here, can't you? I really feel terribly happy once more."

"I was talking to that flower girl at the hotel," Park heard the man say to the girl. "Do you know what that little flower girl told me?"

"*What* little flower girl, darling?"

"Now, Grace. That little flower girl in the hotel. She told me everyone was happier on this island because they lived more happily. It was one of those simple thoughts that come from the hearts of simple uncomplicated people."

"Darling, I'll give you a simple thought, too."

"Now, Grace. Not so loud."

Park looked at his unfinished ham and eggs.

On his way to the Pikaki Flower Shop in the next block, his attention was attracted by a display in the brilliantly illuminated windows of a newly established branch of Tennoy and Ganes, one of the big Honolulu jewelry stores specializing in Danish porcelain and silverware. It used to amuse him to halt in front of window displays such as this one and to anticipate the delight it gave Laina when he returned to her with some inexpensive trinket. He had a notion it was not so much the gift in itself which gave Laina such pleasure because he had never really bought her anything worthy of the gratitude she expressed. He thought perhaps it was assurance to her that she was in his mind even when she wasn't there to remind him of herself. It seemed to him peculiarly a woman's way of thinking; by now she ought to know that she had pierced so deeply into his mind and heart that no woman could ever replace her.

In one of the plush cases in the window he saw a display of silver and gold charms. Park entered the store and was approached by a small haole man with a neat moustache and a pleasant relaxed air.

"That little airplane in the window," said Park.

"Yes," said the man. "It's very pretty, isn't it?"

He went to the window and returned with the plush case.

"That one," Park said. "How much, please?"

"One hundred and thirty dollars, sir."

Park must have looked startled.

"It's solid gold, sir. The propeller turns."

"Well," said Park. "It actually turns."

"Like this. See?" With his little finger the man proved that the tiny golden propeller really turned.

"One hundred and thirty dollars?" said Park.

"The propeller hub and the wing and tail lights are real diamonds, sir, not glass. It's imported from Denmark."

"Well, thank you," said Park.

"We have others much cheaper."

Park remembered his and Laina's flight to Hawaii and he remembered that the dead Japanese boy had saved up his money to buy Laina a fifteen-minute ride when Laina had been sixteen. It seemed to him that the Japanese boy had given her a gift which was a true gift and expressed something which the Japanese boy felt for Laina. It seemed to Park that he had failed in everything he gave her because Laina always gave so very much more in return. Anything he bought her would not really be a gift because he gave her little or nothing of himself; he resented that sense of failing her, not trying or wanting to understand it; he was no longer pleased about picking up something inexpensive whose only true value was the trouble it cost him to find the exact charm with its special significance.

Park asked, "I'll look at the others, if you don't mind."

"Not at all, sir. But they're not airplane charms."

Park hesitated. What would Laina say? She would probably return the charm as being much too expensive. If she did not, and wore it, one of these days she would show it to Hattie Subie or to some of the girls she had known at the plant. Park had established himself on the island as an artist. Even though one of his paintings had been bought by a movie star, still, a solid gold charm with real diamonds was not the charm you would expect an artist of no particular affluence to buy for his girl.

"I'd like to think it over," Park said.

"We could hold it for you several days if you cared to give your name."

"I'll drop in again," said Park. "If you've sold it, I've saved a hundred and thirty dollars, haven't I?"

In the flower shop he ordered twenty-five dollars' worth of roses for Mrs. Byron Meaker in the Ruth Tothic Memorial Hospital. He paused to think of what to write on the card.

"Just a simple thought, Millie—please get well quickly," he wrote finally and signed his name. On his way back to the Buick he wondered if he should have written "Mrs. Meaker" instead of "Millie." He scarcely knew her; he just felt as if he did from hearing By worry about her so often.

Instead of getting into the Buick, he stopped, held by a kind of inertia. He was staring thoughtfully at the left front wheel while a segment of his mind was engaged in recalling the demolition training he had received during the war. It was really very simple to goofer an automobile to have it look like an accident.

Someone said, "Mattison! I thought you were on the big island?"

Park jumped and felt foolish for showing he was startled. For a moment he could not recall the name of the man who had stopped. It was Parsons—Phil Parsons, the etcher who sold some of his stuff through Kimball's Galleries.

"Hello."

"When did you get back?"

"I flew in this afternoon."

Phil Parsons glanced toward the Buick, not seeing Laina. "Where's Caroline?"

"She didn't like flying. She's coming by ship."

"I'd like to use her as a model."

"Well," Park said, "we'll discuss it some time."

"Coming to Harry's tonight?"

"No, I'm afraid I'm pooped."

"I've been owing you an apology," said Phil Parsons, his face diffident and gaunt under the flare of neon lights. "I've been looking at that painting of yours that Harry sold to that Hollywood actor. Caroline was right."

"About what?" Park was puzzled.

"That night when she lit into me on the stairs. We were at Harry's."

"Oh." Park remembered.

"You have got something in those paintings and I was wrong not to have seen it."

"Sometimes," said Park, "I don't even see it myself."

"I still say it's not a painting in the accepted sense, though," said Parsons stubbornly. "That's what put me off. You're expressing an emotion through patterns of the damnedest and most unusual combinations of colors I've ever seen and I don't know how you do it."

"I just keep trying," said Park. "I don't think about it."

The gaunt face moved jerkily. "That might be the explanation. If it is, for God's sake, don't ever think about what you're painting while you're painting."

Park didn't know what Parsons was talking about and had a strong notion Parsons didn't, either. After Parsons left, Park wearily slid under the Buick's wheel. He should have driven away as soon as he finished sending the roses instead of standing there on the sidewalk, staring at the Buick's front wheel with his thoughts far away.

He took the long way to the empty house on the top of Pua Cliff. Passing the shadowy grounds of the new Kamehameha

Hotel, he heard the faint and plaintive strumming of ukuleles from the pavilion. They were having another one of their Saturday evening old romantic Hawaiian entertainments for the tourists.

The house was empty without Laina. Because he thought he should have another try at eating before calling it a night, he stepped into the kitchen. But Laina had cleared the refrigerator before leaving and also remembered to stop the milk delivery—there were only several cans of condensed milk. He opened one, filled a glass, half with milk, half with water.

The kitchen was sultry and he walked out onto the back patio made of lava stones. The starlight picked up the line of the lava stone wall in the rear of the garden and from where Park stood, slowly drinking the milk, he had a view of all of the great night. Beyond the wall was the edge of Pua Cliff, with a drop of a thousand feet or so to Ilohana Cove below. Often in the daytime when the wind blew in from the south across the sea and up the face of the cliff you could hear the voices of the Hinoni kids playing along by the rounded shore of coarse lava sand and fragmented coral. Sometimes at night, again when the wind was right, you could hear one of the grown sons of old man Hinoni playing on a real guitar, not a ukelele, while the women sang. Tonight the wind was not right. It was blowing out to sea with a rustling sound like great invisible sheets of silk being swept through the soft darkness.

Park remembered a Sunday, last month, when Laina had tried to persuade him to go down the cliff with her to her boat in the cove instead of driving eight miles around by car. There was a path of sorts down to the cove. From the top of the cliff you could see it winding in a zigzag fashion, down and down. A third of the way from the bottom there was a gap in the pathway where the cliff lifted sheer for thirty or forty feet. The Hinonis had laboriously hauled up a giant koa wood log, notching it with hewn steps, and propped it securely on the lower ledge to connect with the end of the goat's track above. You could not see the log with its hewn steps from the top of the cliff but when Laina told him about it and assured him it was safe, he said,

"No, thanks." He was not in that much of a hurry to descend to the cove. If Laina wanted to go sailing, she could go with him in the Buick around to the narrow shore road. She had laughed at him, he remembered, but had returned with him to his car. He remembered her laughter.

In bed with him sometimes she would laugh softly, but that was another kind of laughter. When something tickled her or caught her fancy she would go off into extravagant peals. He had not known he would miss her so much. He looked up at the stars and went back into the kitchen and wondered if heating the canned milk and water would make it taste any better.

He heard an automobile rolling into the driveway and stood motionless. The automobile stopped. He placed the half-empty glass of milk on the kitchen sink. By Meaker, again? What the hell else had slid loose?

When he opened the front door, it was not By Meaker.

It was the Tolliver woman arriving in one of those rented Cadillacs. She explained that she had been driving along the strip before dinner and had seen Park in his Buick. She had waved. Didn't Park ever see people? She was bored to death with Cyril Brolly drinking like a fish so she had decided to run up here to welcome Laina and Park home.

Before he could say that Laina was not here, the Tolliver woman passed by him into the front room, her wide circular skirt of red cotton flicking his legs. A scent of gardenias trailed behind her.

"Darling, where's Laina?"

He had almost forgotten everyone on Halepule beach soon learned to call everyone else "darling." He explained about Laina. He had returned by air, leaving her to take the Sunday night ship.

"Darling, you haven't forgotten my name, have you?"

"How could I do that?"

"You might at least offer me a drink."

By God, couldn't she see she wasn't wanted? "I'm sorry," Park said. "I've nothing but canned milk."

"Canned milk? How exciting. I'd love some."

· 215 ·

He was in a black rage while he poured a glass of canned milk for the woman. If she refused to drink it, he would stuff it down her throat. She sat back in one of the chairs and drank it and crossed her legs and Park noticed her legs were no longer that scorched pink color.

What she had come here for, actually, was to ask him to do a portrait of her. She had spoken about it yesterday to Harry Kimball. She was willing to pay two thousand dollars for a portrait.

"I'm no good at portraits," Park said.

She crushed another cigarette in the bronze ash tray on the table. There was an appreciable lag before Park could will himself to stand in order to light her next cigarette. She stood, smiling. She said for two thousand dollars what did he care how good he was as long as she thought so? She glanced down at one of her nicely tanned legs and tilted her face to him. She wanted a full-length portrait. All of her. He knew, didn't he? He thought he did know, too. Perhaps being so pooped made him so horribly embarrassed. His mind went dead. He could not think of how to get rid of her in a polite way. Kick her out? No, try again. He wished Laina were here.

"Darling, I don't know why I have to so suddenly, but where's the little boys' room? It couldn't have been your canned milk, could it?"

From her breath he was convinced it could not possibly be the canned milk. Before deserting Cyril Brolly she must have poured herself more than several for the road. Park waited while she finished with the boys' room and nearly fell asleep standing up. He finally heard the bathroom door open.

"Darling," she called from the bedroom, "has somebody gone upsy recently? The bathroom has a funny stink."

"I've been disinfecting against cockroaches."

He heard her moving around in the bedroom. He started into the room to drag her out; she had switched on Laina's radio for the hotel dance music. She met him in that dark warm bedroom where the gardenia scent mingled with the fainter scent of sandalwood.

"Dance with me, please?"

"It's getting on a little, isn't it? Besides, this is a hell of a hot night."

"Darling, just once before I go?"

Presently came a welcome break, a pause for station identification before the next musical number. The Tolliver woman still clung to him; Park saw her face swimming palely below his eyes. He had not meant to be quite so obvious about it when he disengaged himself, though.

He asked quickly, "Why don't we call it a night, Jill—" and the instant he said the name he knew it was not her first name. "Jane—" He was making a botch of it. He did know her name. "Janet," he said apologetically.

"Yes, it's Janet," she said and seemed to waver in the moist warmness about them. "You almost had it on the second try, didn't you?" She turned rapidly and passed through the front room and was having difficulty opening the front door when Park came to her.

"Here—" Park said, opening the door for her. "Take me with a grain of salt tonight, won't you? I've had a rough day, Janet." After he spoke she remained a moment or so where she was, silent, her face rather blurred, her eyes smudged.

With raw self-contempt she told him, "I didn't see you on the strip. Cyril and I went to Harry Kimball's. Harry told me you were alone here and probably would appreciate company. I thought it might be fun if you wanted it to be. It was just one of those thoughts I get sometimes."

Park said nothing because he had nothing to say. Phil Parsons had seen Harry. There it was. Harry loved a hotfoot. If you were Harry's best friend, he would still give you a hotfoot if he had the chance.

After Park helped her into the Cadillac she said politely, "Have sweet dreams, darling—" but she could not sustain it. Her voice broke. "I'm going back to Charles G., in Chicago. Damn! Damn! How I hate this happy, happy, happy island of yours."

He did not have the sweet dreams the Tolliver woman had

so politely wished him, but neither did he have a recurrence of the nightmare from which he had awakened a dozen or so mornings ago when he had dreamed that E. P. refused to sign the contract and that all was finally and completely lost, even Laina. He dreamed of nothing. He slept like a log.

Sunday morning when he realized he was no longer asleep, he was reluctant to open his eyes to look to his left at the electric clock. He wished he could sleep all through Sunday until Monday morning. He heard an automobile roll into the graveled driveway and out again and decided it must be the Hawaiian boy delivering a copy of *The Sunday Sentinel*. From habit he lazily rolled his head to the right to say good morning to Laina. Laina, of course, was not in bed beside him.

He heard the front door open and shut and sat up, instantly alert. At the back of his mind he feared the possibility that some day he would be found out by the men on the other side of the street. Just like that night after the fight when Herby Subie had surprised him in the basement of the Paradise Auditorium. Park thought of Doc Fields' revolver, but it was hidden in his foot locker. He heard footsteps approaching the bedroom, and knew he didn't have time to dive from the bed toward the foot locker in the far closet.

Laina entered the room and stopped and Park's heart also stopped. It stopped a whole beat. He sagged. Immediately he had a rebounding all through him. She was holding the wide and now rather crushed straw hat in her left hand and she was wearing the pale green linen suit which was so becoming. Around her neck was the necklace of carved ivory gardenia buds which he had bought for her that first afternoon at the hotel. She looked trim and fresh and he thought she had never looked so lovely and he stared and could find no words to express his joy. She stooped quickly to kiss him, and stepped back, smiling, obviously pleased by the effect of her entrance on Park.

"I flew in twenty minutes ago. A man at the hotel had a ticket on the seven A.M. plane from Hilo but he gave it to me."

Park spoke. "What man?" As he asked, a picture flashed

through his mind of that girl in the Grass Shack Drug Store and again he seemed to hear her demanding, *"What* little flower girl, darling?" and unexpectedly Park laughed at himself. He swung bare feet and legs to the floor, facing Laina. "Nuts to what man, Caroline."

"It was just a man. He was giving his ticket to the hotel clerk last night because his wife decided to meet him at the hotel instead of waiting in Honolulu for him. So I asked could I have his ticket. He—" She resisted, pulling away, seating herself on the dressing table bench. "Give a girl a minute to be home, won't you?" She eyed herself in the mirror. "Now, look at me! This damn hair! Can't I have some of it cut?"

As she asked, he saw her pick up her hairbrush. She glanced casually at it. She glanced at it a second time and rather slowly removed a small yellow thread of hair from it. His throat tightened.

Although it must have been only an instant, it seemed to Park that Laina had been staring a very long time at that thread of another woman's hair. She wiped her thumb and forefinger on the pale green skirt as if she had picked up something unclean. She turned to Park and her eyes were very wide. They suddenly squeezed shut like a child's in sudden agony.

"Listen. I was going to explain as soon as I had time. The Tolliver woman was here last night because Harry Kimball told her I was alone. He sent her here as his idea of a hotfoot—Caroline!"

Wordlessly, Laina ran into the living room. Park ran after her. She stopped before the table, her lips clenched tight and bloodless. For the first time she was seeing the litter of lipstick-red cigarette stubs in the tray. With a passionate gesture, she struck the tray from the table, the cigarette stubs flying.

"Caroline! At least say something!"

Her face was muted by its despair. She bumped clumsily into the table as she headed for the front door. When Park took her, she struggled silently. He thrust her back into the bedroom, pointing her in the direction of the bed.

"Go on. See for yourself. Tell me if a woman was in it last

night with me. The Tolliver woman asked me to paint her portrait. She drove away before ten by the clock, sore as they come, because I'd forgotten her first name. . . ." He explained to Laina, "It was one of those ideas that sometimes mainlanders have here when they've been too long on Halepule Beach. Cyril has loused her up, and Harry didn't help any."

"Oh, Park—" After the silence it came from Laina in a torrent, once more all of her flowing so warmly. "I was as sore as they come, too. For a minute I wanted to kill you and that haole woman from Chicago! Are you terribly mad at me?"

Perhaps it was half an hour later when the telephone rang loudly and imperatively from the study. In spite of himself, Park jerked up his head.

"Park! *Christ!*"

Finally, it ceased ringing.

But it had rung. It shattered something for Park. The morning was no longer quite the morning it should have been after Laina had so unexpectedly returned.

16

About eleven o'clock the telephone startled him a second
time. In the bathroom, Laina was putting her hair in pincurls. Park was half-dressed, having promised to go sailing off Ilohana Cove with her. He heard the ringing of the telephone and glanced once at the closed bathroom door. Perhaps
Laina didn't hear the phone ringing.

He passed hastily through the front room, closing and locking the study door. He lifted the receiver and said quietly, "Mattison speaking," and from the other end of the line a voice began
counting the numbers. It was E. P. dutifully following procedures. Park felt his skin prickle. He didn't know what new
emergency had caused E. P. to telephone here. In turn, E. P.
was unaware that Laina had unexpectedly arrived this morning
and might, any second, start rapping on the study door to ask
Park why he had locked it and who was calling?

Park whispered, "Don't ring me here—I'll get through to you
as soon as I can," and hung up. Park's skin still prickled.

He was dressed and waiting when Laina came from the bathroom. She had a scarf of bright blue wrapped around her hair
and a large beach towel hiding everything between the wide
shoulders and the long legs. She selected faded blue beach slacks
and a bright blue pullover for today. She did not say anything
as she dressed and Park hoped she had not heard the second
ringing of the phone. He looked at her and liked her very much

in blue. He would be damned, though, if he would ever allow her to pose for Phil Parsons or any other artist. The thought struck him that it would be interesting to try to paint her himself. He wondered if you could set up an easel in that boat she used.

"I think I'll take my easel and paints along with me. About ready?"

"Five minutes," she promised. "The room's a mess. Let me at least do the bed."

"Why rush it? The Japanese woman doesn't come today."

"Park. Was it anyone on the telephone?"

Sometimes Park caught himself wondering if Laina had a special intuition and knew the precise instant when she could most successfully change the subject to throw him off balance. It took him a moment to recover.

"It was—a drunk wanting Kulanini Courts."

"Park," she asked. "Please tell me. Was it Mr. Meaker phoning you?"

He looked at her sharply. "Hey?"

"Is Mr. Meaker still after you for something because Doc Fields made you fall-guy for that fight? I can't help asking. I know you told me you had to return to see Mr. Meaker. And he didn't come through with the painting assignment he'd promised. And, Park—I might as well tell you, I didn't have such a bad cold on the other island; I was hardly sick at all. But I knew Mr. Meaker was worrying you by phoning you so often so I tried not to do anything to increase your worries."

"Meaker didn't phone me, just now. Why should Meaker phone me?"

"Honestly, did Mr. Meaker ask you to get back to the island in a hurry because he promised to have someone buy some of your paintings? I have to ask you. I haven't forgotten that Mr. Meaker did the publicity for Doc Fields. I still keep wondering if you aren't in some kind of trouble from that fight. Herby and Hattie Subie lost money by betting just like you did. If you're in trouble with Mr. Meaker or somebody because of that fight, why don't you go to Herby? He's an important man on this island, more than you might think. Herby's little, but he's a fighter when he thinks someone's being unjustly treated. I'll go to Herby for you, Park, if Mr. Meaker or that betting commissioner wants money from you that you can't pay."

Park laughed. He held her firmly by the arms. "Your imagination."

"I'm scared."

"What for?"

"I don't know what for. I just feel something terrible's going to happen if we don't get away."

"What do you say to this? Give me time to do a few more paintings and finish my work at Dr. Kirsch's office. We could leave by the middle of December. We could go to Mexico. Prices are cheap there. Would you like living in Mexico for a week or a month or until we got tired of it?"

"Oh, Park, I'd never get tired of it. I'd love it there. I'd love anywhere with you away from this rotten island. . . ."

Laina suggested they go down the quick way to the cove by taking the steep path but Park had to telephone E. P. He believed he could safely do so from the Grass Shack Drug Store. He believed Laina would stay in the car because, he knew, she didn't enjoy having haoles stare at her when her hair was in pincurls even if she had a scarf around her head.

When he stopped the Buick in front of the drug store he said, "I won't be more than a minute. I've got to get a tube of shaving cream and razor blades." He was opening the door, certain she would stay where she was.

"I'll come with you. I'd like to see if the new issue of *Vogue* is in."

He sat there a long moment. Next he said curtly, "If it's in, I'll get it for you. Wait here. Why not let those haole women in the drug store see you when you're more of a treat to look at?"

The telephone booths in the rear were beyond the line of sight from Laina in the Buick. Park dialed the Koko Point number. Instead of chopping her down with that crack, he could have hit her in the face, and it would have hurt her less. It was cruel to remind her she was not quite the same as the haole women from the mainland who crowded into the drug store on a Sunday morning.

"Park?" asked E. P. over the line.

"Caroline arrived unexpectedly. I had to hang up on you."

"Sorry I alarmed you."

"I got down here to a pay phone as soon as I could make it."

"Dr. Austen's been having a look at me this morning. He can't understand why that flu bug's holding on so long when I've kept myself in such fit condition. He's decided it might even be a new strain of flu bug. He wants me to go into the hospital Monday for a few days to have some of that bang-up new stuff—what's it called?—better than penicillin—shot into me. While I don't believe a man as fit as I am ought to waste time in a hospital, I think it's probably my duty to give a couple of days to seeing how those boys are taking care of it. After all, Pater and I built it in Ruthie's memory. If I go into the hospital I won't be able to see you until Wednesday or Thursday. I thought you might like to drive here this afternoon for an hour or so?"

"There's nothing to report," said Park. "We're at it. That's all I can say."

"I wasn't suggesting a staff meeting. We never do see enough of each other and I've got time on my hands. I was suggesting you might like to drop in for a drink. I've some bang-up Scotch. . . ."

It was difficult for Park to believe but it came slowly to him that E. P. was lonely. With all he had, E. P. was lonely this Sunday. E. P. was asking for company.

"Not today," Park said.

"I know you're sparking for me as hard as you can. I merely thought if you weren't too occupied . . ." The voice trailed.

"I have a date with you tomorrow morning. We'll have to skip that if you're going into the hospital, won't we? I can see Buddy if anything—"

"No, these next few weeks I'd like to keep in touch. They won't cart me off until around noon, Monday. Suppose you make it ten o'clock for a late breakfast? Is ten o'clock O. K.? I know you're on the firing line. You set the time."

"Ten's fine."

"What do you like for breakfast?"

"Anything, Pip. I never eat much for breakfast."

"That's a mistake. If you take care of your stomach, your stomach will take care of you. I'll have a surprise for you tomorrow. I find I get tired of guavas or mangoes or Kona oranges for breakfast, don't you? I get tired of fresh pineapple, too. How would you like a real surprise for breakfast?"

"Well, fine," said Park, wondering what sort of expensive delicacy E. P. had in mind for breakfast tomorrow.

"We'll have a real surprise for a change, one to tempt you. Goodbye, Park."

"Goodbye, Pip."

Park hung up, mopping his face as he went to the counter to buy shaving cream and blades. It once had given Park a warm pleased feeling to hear E. P. exclaim, "We've got to see more of each other, Lieutenant." It surprised him to find a faint tug still existed. Every man had his faults and E. P. had his share but for all his faults he had one rare gift, Park thought. He could bring himself into whatever you were doing. He could take you up to the top of your hill and show you the magic beyond it. You wanted to do your very best for him even if you realized he might not be there when you turned around to speak to him.

Park thought of Laina waiting for him in the Buick and that ended his brief pang for a man who did not like to be alone with himself. He was in a hurry to return to her. He heard a tourist ahead of him complaining to the Japanese clerk, "What's wrong with the beach today? It seems like a Sunday."

"It is Sunday, sir."

But Park believed he knew what the malahini meant. He had noticed the headlines of the Sunday morning papers: "Sugar Prices Drop!" and "Lay-Offs Expected at Plantations!" Anxiety headlines, they were. Since yesterday evening By Meaker must have pushed along like a house afire with the new plan of action, even with Millie in the hospital. By was hoping that everything else would not fail before they had to make it look like an accident.

Park opened the Buick's left front door, dropping the new *Vogue* on Laina's lap. He shoved the package of shaving cream and razor blades into the glove compartment. "I'm sorry I made that crack, Caroline." She looked straight ahead.

He drove toward the hotel, the Buick passing one intersection after another. He glanced several times at Laina and saw she had that muted expression on her face. He didn't blame her. It was a lousy crack.

"Don't be sore. Please."

She was listening through the open car window to the solemn blare of church hymns being broadcast from the steel towers. Suddenly she turned her head to Park and demanded angrily, "Good night! Can't they play anything better than organ music from those towers?"

"But it's Sunday."

"They never played organ music on other Sundays, did they? It gives me the willies."

Park turned right, going west away from the hotel and the shining white beach on a narrow macadam road which soon frayed into a red sandy dirt road. Sometimes spray from the sea flung upward from the black rocks a few feet to the left of the old road, the whole air sparkling as if from a sudden explosion of diamonds and rubies and emeralds. Now the line of cliffs began to rise higher and higher to the right of the road until, two miles west from the hotel, through a jagged crimson shafting of the cliff, Park saw another steel tower high up in the middle distance.

Park was too far away to hear what was coming from that tower but he knew the plantation hands and their families living in a camp on the gentle slope of land could not escape the ceaseless pounding. Park was deliberately taking a Sunday off; he knew that he had done all that he could do until tomorrow. The invisible M. O. network was solidly at work. All the towers were wired in to a main station on the island, city-side. Last night Howie Wright would have telephoned to the disk jockey in charge to slow the speed of record players to thirty-one revolutions a minute. Two revolutions less than normal playing speed was so insignificant that anyone listening could not say precisely what was wrong.

The music merely dragged slightly. Until the emergency ended, everything was going to drag slightly. A different emotional climate was being prepared for the immediate future, one of anxiety and foreboding. There was to be an increase of anxiety headlines in the newspapers. Plantation stores would cut down on credit. Movie houses would bill more films drawn from real life where people starved and went hungry.

The road ended at Ilohana Cove and you could go no farther. On the west side of the cove were the three shacks where the Hinonis lived and Park saw that the big boat was not tied at the wharf but the smaller one was there. Laina ran down to the wharf and Park followed more slowly. He sighted upward; the path went up and up the cliff to the dark red log with its thick base planted in the wide shallow groove of lava rock. It seemed to be fastened at the top, forty feet up, with vines or, more probably, strong ship's rope. He could not see his white and pink coral cottage; it was set back from the steep thrust of cliff.

He still didn't think he wanted to climb down that cliff with Laina. It was too far to fall and he didn't want Laina to try the descent, either. He continued toward the wharf where old man Hinoni was assisting Laina into the boat.

"Hello, Mr. Hinoni. Where's the rest of your family?"

Park always enjoyed seeing the old giant and somehow he had a feeling the old giant enjoyed seeing him, or perhaps all Hawaiians had the gift of making you feel they enjoyed seeing you each time you appeared. Old man Hinoni said his sons had sailed to the Maui side of the channel for a few days in the new fishing boat. When he spoke his teeth flashed white in the sunlight. The women and children had loaded themselves in the Ford truck to visit relatives at Iki while their men were gone. Towering a good twelve inches above Park, he lugged down two G. I. cans of gasoline to Park's one from the wharf shanty. The gasoline was for the sixty-horsepower engine in the hatchway behind the cabin of the boat. A wind was blowing from the northwest but it was dying and they might need the engine to get home. It was a thirty-six foot boat, sturdy enough, the small cabin well forward, and rigged with a sail which Laina informed Park was called a mutton leg.

Laina took the tiller, her face shiny in the sunlight, eyebrows and lashes almost invisible against the warm richness of her skin. She had something of that look of a Scotch lass about her as she firmly ordered Park to give a hand and take in the slack on the purchase until the sail was set. It made him wonder if she might not imagine herself back in the days of the great four-masters, walking the deck of a ship which her grandfather from Scotland commanded.

Slowly the little horseshoe cove drifted astern, the line of Pua Cliff diminishing in height and extending farther and farther to the west. Park had thought he could set up his easel on top of the little cabin; but he soon gave it up. He went aft to Laina who held the tiller and they had nothing to say to each other. He realized the day was going to hell for them both. Sunday came only once a week and he had wanted this to be a pleasant Sunday. Now, within the hour, the wind was dying. Soon they would be quite becalmed.

He broke the silence.

"Aren't you still my girl, Caroline?"

She nodded absently. She looked up at the white sail and back to Park. "If you can't paint aboard ship, we could head in toward Pohaku Point and tie up there."

"You're the captain."

His question, however, had started her thinking about being Park's girl. "Suppose some day I look like any other kanaka girl who drinks once too often from the mullet pond and swallows a little fish inside her? Park, whose girl am I then?"

He gave her a startled glance. One of the things Park had instinctively refused to think about was the growing passion between Laina and himself. As long as you never worried about anything it never got you down. Park had been satisfied to let everything ride unless Laina became anxious or one night they forgot to be careful and he made her pregnant. However, after being with her on the other island he knew in his heart he would marry her rather than lose her. He asked, "You're not—"

"No, I'm not." She shook her head. "Not that I know of. I was only wondering."

"Why talk of something we don't have to worry about? I'm hungry, for a change. The wind's died on us. Suppose I start the motor. We can tie in at Pohaku and stop at the Pohaku store for milk and bread and cheese to eat on the beach. What do you say?"

"Park—" Laina looked toward the green rise of cliffs from the happy island. "Yes. Yes, if you want to."

They came into Pohaku about two-thirty in the afternoon. From there they walked around the point to the little beach of black sand which they had discovered another Sunday, months ago. After eating, Park tried to paint while Laina pulled off her turban and combed the flaming darkness of her hair in the hot yellow air. Park tried to paint the pointed black rocks and the sea beyond but something interfered. This time he wanted to paint a picture Laina would like and he couldn't lose himself in what he was doing.

Laina walked across to look over his shoulder.

"It's rotten," Park said.

"Park—" She gazed thoughtfully at the wet smears of color. "Did that Tolliver woman really offer you two thousand dollars for a portrait?"

Park put down his brush. He was ill at ease with Laina this afternoon and he wanted more than ever to be completely at ease with her.

"Forget her, Caroline."

"I just can't. I don't know why I got cross at you when we stopped at the drug store. I did look like a mess with my hair done up. Park, I feel so damned proud of myself because you refused that money. I'm not really cross at you. I don't like either that Tolliver woman or Cyril Brolly. I refused an offer he made me, too. I wasn't going to tell you because I didn't want it to spoil our vacation on the other island. But that night after the fights when Mr. Brolly took Mrs. Tolliver and me home, he had her stay in the car while he walked me to the door. He offered to pay my way to Hollywood to have a screen test. I told him, 'Nothing doing, Mr. Brolly' so he'd know I meant it. Park . . . will we go to Mexico? You're not just saying it?"

Park didn't hear all she had said too clearly because something was happening inside him. In his mind he saw Brolly speaking to Laina of her future and of a chance at a really fine career in Hollywood.

"Park, you aren't listening. You never do listen when I'm serious."

"I was listening. I think I'll have a short talk with that son-of-a-bitch. I don't much like having that son-of-a-bitch trying to steal you."

"Park," she said hastily, "I wouldn't have told you if I'd thought you'd think that. Brolly's an old man. He was just trying to do me a favor."

"No strings at all?" said Park. "That son-of-a-bitch!"

She said violently, "There weren't any strings! Besides, I told him 'nothing doing'! Can't you and I go to Mexico now? I have three thousand and you must have something."

"I won't have enough for us to go to Mexico until I finish a few more paintings," Park said. "I'm not taking money from you. Forget your three thousand."

"Why can't you take it?" she asked.

"Because I can't," Park said. "Let's don't talk about it."

"I'll draw my money out of the bank tomorrow and give it to you and you'll have to buy tickets for Mexico," said Laina stubbornly.

He flung an arm around her shoulder, more moved by her loyalty than he wanted to be. "Look," he said gently, "I'll get all the money you and I need to go to Mexico. Keep yours until you need it. Let me finish a few more paintings and we'll sail in December. That isn't too long to wait, is it? Now, suppose for a change I try painting you instead of rocks? I might even be able to hit Harry Kimball for a nice advance if he sees I can do portraits."

"Naked?" asked Laina dubiously. "What if somebody comes?"

Park thought of someone coming while he was painting her. Next, he thought of having to show Harry Kimball a nude portrait of Laina if he could do one. He thought of the possibility of Cyril Brolly and Harry, together, looking at Laina, discussing it and her all so very freely.

"No," he said. "We'll have a try as you are."

He did much better than he had expected to with his first portrait, and he felt slightly better at the end of the afternoon than he had at the beginning. His headache had stopped. They returned home late, and he was taking a bath when Laina knocked.

"Dey ain't nobody here but us chickens, mister," Park said.

She opened the door. Although Park knew it was corny at least he expected her to be smiling. Often when they were with each other they said things much cornier than that about the chickens and usually it seemed very funny. But she was frowning.

"I'd make a terrible housekeeper, Park. I bought everything for our dinner but butter and sugar. Now I've got to run down to the Chinaman's in the Chevy. He'll be open."

"Wait, I'll get dressed."

"Finish your bath. It won't take me twenty minutes."

"No, wait. I don't like having you drive alone."

She gave him an obstinate look. "They're all kanakas at the Chinaman's. They won't even know if I'm giving them a treat when I walk in."

He heard her Chevy as it backed into the driveway. She could not have seen him telephoning this afternoon in the Grass Shack Drug Store. He was convinced of that. It was unreasonable of him to imagine Laina might have quietly slipped out of the Buick and seen him in one of the booths when he was occupied with E. P. He was savage with himself. She did not operate—and he caught himself. But he allowed the thought to continue. Yes, he operated that way. E. P. possibly operated that way. But Laina did not. Tomorrow was Monday. Tomorrow began another week. It was not a chain reaction, one explosion continuing steadily after another. He dried himself. He dressed. He looked at the electric clock. She had been gone no longer than five minutes. Fifteen more minutes. He wanted today to be like any Sunday ought to be.

The telephone rang.

It was ringing very loudly. Park felt one of those sudden spasms of fury which struck him every now and then of late. He had asked E. P. not to ring here again. Tomorrow, he decided, he would have the telephone company discontinue their phone service. A telephone was too dangerous. What did E. P. want now? If E. P. was lonely at Koko Point why didn't he have his latest wife fly to him from New York, or wherever she was, or if she refused to fly to the happy island why couldn't he find a wife who liked living on the island for more than the first couple of months?

"Mattison," said Park into the mouthpiece.

"Maybe you don't remember me, Mr. Mattison, but I took to you when I saw you one night. I'd like to have a talk with you."

It was not E. P.'s voice this time. It was slightly muffled, as if someone were speaking through a handkerchief. Park was wary. He resisted a panicky impulse to hang up.

"What's this, a gag?"

"No, friend, it ain't no gag. We don't have to mention names. I'm at Mama Pikea's. I thought maybe you'd like to drop by and see me. Maybe I can say something to place me in your mind better, Mr. Mattison. Las' week I knocked you down. You got up and called me a son-of-a-bitch. Remember?"

It was unbelievable. It could not be Willi calling, but it was. It was a trick, a snare, someone from the other side of the street finally calling for an accounting. The study, as hot as it was tonight, suddenly had something of that chilled rarefied quality which he remembered from the other island. Park could not hang up now. He had to follow through, he had to know. Sunday came only once a week, but a Sunday night call like this might come only once in Park's lifetime.

17

Park said, "Yes," warily into the telephone, "I remember you."

"I'm at Mama Pikea's. I'm a big shot now, Mr. Mattison. I'm as good as any haole on the island. Danny—" The muffled voice ceased. It began again. "A friend I met, who took some photos of me this morning to send to the mainland press, introduced me here this afternoon. They're treating me right here, Mr. Mattison. I been thinking how to see you. I was thinking a haole like you could walk into Mama Pikea's and nobody would ask you why. What's a better place than here for two fellas to talk over a little proposition?"

"What sort—" said Park, "—of a proposition? Let's have it."

"We can talk better here. I got a room upstairs. You been here before?"

"No."

"That makes it easy. Say you're Bill Bassum. Bill's my partner in a—business I own on the mainland. Just say you're Bill Bassum. What've you got to lose by seeing me, Mr. Mattison? Doc Fields use'a tell me you was a game sport and a smart boy. Can you come right now?"

Park thought rapidly. "Who else is with you?"

"Nobody. We can get us some girls later. But this is a classy house, Mr. Mattison. We can have a private talk firs' in a room I got here, jus' like a hotel. Jus' say you're Bill Bassum to the woman downstairs."

Park reached a decision. Sometimes you had to gamble. "I'll be there at nine o'clock," he said and hung up.

He thought of telephoning By or Lew and decided not to. They could do nothing at their end in this sort of situation. Park remembered how it had been when he was waiting it out with Doc Fields after the wolves had been let loose on Bull Amani. Park had always believed Willi Nogusi would soften more quickly than Bull Amani had. He hadn't believed it would happen as quickly and as unexpectedly as this, though. Either it was a proposition, exactly as Willi said it was, or it was a snare, something ugly and huge shifting across from the other side of the street at last. Whatever it might be, it was top-level; and Park knew it was his job and no one else's to deal with it.

He opened his foot locker, removed Doc's revolver, checked it to make sure the chambers were loaded, and thrust it into his coat pocket with a handkerchief wadded carelessly around it to obscure the hard outline through the coat's fabric. He realized he was sweating profusely, his heart pounding with a labored and uneven pounding which he could feel in his temples and down through the arteries of his wrists; but there was nothing he could do either about the night's heat or his physical tension. He wrote a hasty note to Laina:

> Mr. Meaker's phoned about that painting assignment. Something's evidently turned up again and he wants to see me tonight. Please don't be sore at me. I'll get back as quick as I can.

He coldly read what he had written. He was lying much too frequently to Laina these days. The lies were beginning to pile up but until he got over the hump there was nothing he could do. Nothing at all.

He drove rapidly down the long grade of Hibiscus Road and the fragrance of night-blooming flowers was so heavy in the hot darkness that their cloying scent seemed to thicken in his nose and stick to the roof of his mouth. As Park recalled, Mama Pikea's was located on one of the sandy side lanes at the east end of the beach, near the old town. It was the best choice on the island, he thought, for having a meeting with Nogusi. At least that much was all to the good. Mama Pikea's was secluded. Any man seen entering Mama Pikea's would not have to explain why he was there.

He'd also heard the place had purchased excellent police protection. You would not have much of a chance to beat up a man in one of Mama Pikea's rooms because Mama Pikea's was run to attract the trade of well-heeled mainlanders who expected everything to be done discreetly, quietly, and with the utmost safety for themselves and their reputations. No, Willi could scarcely be planning to suck Park into some sort of row at Mama Pikea's. It could not be that, Park decided. He turned right on the old road, away from the highway, to avoid encountering Laina if she were returning. He drove along the ocean, spume blowing through the Buick's open side window onto his face.

He was relieved to see only a few cars parked in the deep shadows under the huge banyan trees which almost hid the low two-story house set back from Flower Lane. Evidently Sunday night was slow here. He heard a dog bark suddenly as he walked between the high fragrant shrubs toward the house. A man's sharp command in the darkness quieted the dog. No one disturbed Park at all. He hesitated before the door and finally knocked. A tall pleasant-faced woman opened the door and said politely, "Please come in," and waited for him to enter. She must have been one of the rare full-blooded Hawaiian women for she was well over six feet tall, her hair quite white.

Park looked around, not knowing exactly what he had expected to see. At least no girls were here. It was like being in the lobby of a small and second-rate hotel with a gray lounge to one side, a few tables, several chairs, a desk on the other side, and several closed doors. He had expected something more. The windows were all closed with varnished bamboo blinds. It was all very clean, very tidy, and completely undistinguished. It was silent in here, and he wondered if the walls had been soundproofed. He was aware of a slight draft of fresher air, much cooler than the air outside. There must be an air-conditioner operating somewhere. He looked at the tall self-contained Hawaiian woman. He felt self-conscious about calling her "Madam Pikea."

"Mrs. Pikea?"

The Hawaiian woman smiled, still politely.

"I'm Mrs. Kulaohi, the manager. Mrs. Pikea is here very seldom."

Park was even more self-conscious after he said, "I'm Bill Bassum. I was to meet a friend of mine here," because for an instant the kindly dark Hawaiian face altered slightly.

"Yes, of course. This way, please. Upstairs."

It was a long hall like a hall in a clean but second-rate hotel, although the carpet was new and thick and it must have been expensive. The lights were quite dim. She rapped lightly on one of the closed doors, gave him another look under the dim light, and turned and went back toward the stairs. The door opened. There was Willi Nogusi. He was still wearing that worn checked suit which Park remembered seeing him in that night in Doc's office after the fights.

"Come in," said Nogusi and shut the door. "How are you?"

For a moment the two looked at each other. Then Park hastily glanced around to see where he was. The room was also like a neat second-rate living room of a two-room hotel suite, an open door at one end. He stepped to the door. It was a bedroom. No one was in there. He looked back and saw Nogusi grinning.

"Nobody's here," Nogusi said. "Sit down." He pointed to the table upon which was a bottle of good bourbon, ice, water in a pottery pitcher, and two glasses. "I tole the madam I needed some rest before another one of the girls and I was bringing my partner here for a little quiet drinking. It's safe. Go on. Sit down. Make yourself comfortable, Mr. Mattison. You smoke? Here." Willi handed him a cigar. It was not a good cigar but it was not one of the very bad cigars which you bought two for a nickel down in the Makakina district on the other side of the island.

"Well. Thank you."

"Don't mention it, Mr. Mattison. You like a drink?" He motioned to the table. "Help yourself. I'm a big shot here. I'm just like any haole man, here."

Park selected one of the wooden matches from the glass match holder next to the bottle of bourbon and sat down. He said, "Well, thanks. I never drink very much."

Willi sat opposite him, spreading the big scarred hands on the table. "Me neither. I run a bar in Reno but I don't drink much. It don't do you any good, too much drinking. Look at Doc. I figure that was his trouble. You ought to see my bar in Reno."

"I'd like to see it some time, Mr. Nogusi." Park had trouble lighting the cigar. He was afraid his hands were shaking. He did not want Nogusi to notice.

"Just call me Willi, Mr. Mattison. Doc always called me Willi. A fighter like me gets used to people calling him Willi. Like at my bar in Reno, ever'body walks in and says, 'H'are ya, Willi?' It makes you feel good. I got a half-interest in that bar. I name it myself. It's the 'Aloha Bar and Lounge.' How you like that for a classy name? Ain't that classy?"

"It's quite a classy name, Willi." Park helped himself to a second match.

"It's what I think, too. In Reno, ever'body thinks I'm a Hawaiian. Full-blooded Hawaiian. Ain't that a kick for you? Here . . . let me, Mr. Mattison." Solicitously, Willi held a big silver-plated cigarette lighter to Park's cigar. "How's that?"

"Better, thanks."

"So all the Reno haole girls come to my bar. Lookers, Mr. Mattison. In Reno, I'm jus' as good as any white man. Maybe better." Above the pitted ridge of cheekbones the small dull eyes had a reminiscent flicker. "Them Reno girls think I'm ro-man-tic." Willi liked that word. With almost ludicrous gravity he repeated it. "Ro-man-tic." He stared anxiously at Park. Perhaps Willi was afraid of being laughed at.

Park did not laugh. He nodded his head.

"I need three grand to buy my par'ner's half-interest and be fixed for life in Reno. Maybe I marry one of them white girls someday. Why not?" The yellowish pockmarked face thrust forward slightly under the light to regard Park.

Park's cigar seemed to draw unevenly. He said, "Well, why not?"

"Over here, you white boys get the breaks with our girls. In Reno, it's the other way around. I like it better in Reno. You like it here."

"That's one way to put it."

Willi laughed. "Doc Fields offered me three grand to fight Bull. I needed that three grand to buy the other half-interest in my bar but Doc screwed me. He run off and I din't have no manager to look after me. Here. Your cigar's out." Again Willi leaned forward, clicking his big lighter.

"Thanks."

"All the cigars you want. Just tell me. Mr. Mattison, I'm looking for a smart boy who'd like to manage me. Doc Fields use'a say you were a smart boy."

"I only worked at Doc's books."

"But Doc trusted you. He even trusted you enough to leave you dough to pay his bills when he shook off."

"If you've got a beef against me," Park said, "let's have it. I was Doc's bookkeeper. I'm sorry he screwed you up but he did all the managing, not me. I thought we had everything straight with each other that night after the fight?" Park stood up.

"I got no beef, Mr. Mattison. Sit down. I want a frien'ly talk with you. You're sure you don't want no drink?"

Park shook his head.

"Sit down and listen to what I got to say. I'm looking for a manager. I thought maybe you'd like to be my manager."

Park sat down again.

Park said carefully, "I thought Herby Subie was managing you?"

"Him? That little son-of-a-bitch? You din't hear what he did to me? You know what Bull Amani got when he was pres'dunt of this F. I. U. thing? Seven grand. He got seven grand. You know what I get? It was that Herby's idea. He never tole me. After electing me pres'dunt, Herby says we officers of the F. I. U. don't have any more right to more dough than a field hand or plant worker or dock worker. So he's going to propose a motion to the labor council. I won't get no seven grand. I'll get exactly what a punk field hand gets a week, plus five bucks extra a day for expenses, each nickel what I have to account for like I was a thief. Me, back to earning field-hand wages! Mr. Mattison, it's murder if Herby or anybody in the F. I. U. learns I'm hunting myself a smart manager so I got nowhere to turn with anybody I know. I think and think. Then I think of what

Doc Fields tole me about how you was a smart boy. And I think, he played a hunch and trusted you. So why don't I play a hunch and have a little talk with you? So here we are."

"I'm not in the prize-fight game, Willi," Park said.

"I ain't talking about the prize-fight game. I need a manager who's smart enough to have contacts. I took to you that night when you got up on your feet and said I was a son-of-a-bitch. Then you stuck up for me when Herby was at me. I din't forget that night, Mr. Mattison."

"I haven't either," Park said grimly.

"I'll stack it all up for you quick. I come here to get three grand to buy my bar but Doc, he runs off. Then Herby, what does he do? How can I get three grand from seventy-five or eighty-five bucks a week as pres'dunt of any damn union? Herby says, 'Willi, this your chance to help thousands of your people— you're a hero to 'em—' Jesus K. Christ, Mr. Mattison! I want to get back to Reno where I'm treated good as any haole man. That's why I need me a manager because I read how Bull Amani collects ten grand last year for helping to stop a strike. I showed I was a better man than Bull ever was. If Bull could stop a strike, I can stop the one this year if somebody pays me enough and tells me what to do. But how'm I gonna find that somebody? I gotta be careful. I ain't lived here like Bull did to know where to look. So, finally I think of Doc's boy. . . . Mr. Mattison," he asked, "can you find a contact for me so we don't get our feet wet? I figger I'm worth at least what Bull got. I want ten grand for my share. Anything you can get me over ten grand, I'll split half. Say you get fifteen grand. That's two and a half grand for you. What do you say? It ought to be enough so you wouldn't have no cause to give me away to them F. I. U. bastids. If ever you did—"

For an instant that yellowish pockmarked face was not pleasant for Park to contemplate. But the face laughed. Willi explained, "I jus' want to own my bar, that's all. I got away once from this damn island and I'll get away again with dough in my pockets. If Doc trusted you, I figger what's good enough for Doc is good enough for me. What do you say?"

18

He had time this morning, he thought. He had all the time he needed. He stopped to look into the display window of Tennoy and Ganes but he didn't mean to go inside. Then he went inside. He wore the freshly laundered sharkskin coat and trousers and he must have looked very presentable for the clerk said, "Yes, a check will be satisfactory, sir." And then the clerk recognized Park's name. "Mr. Mattison, the painter?" When you had sold a painting to a movie star evidently your name reflected a little of the luster of the purchaser's. "I saw the painting displayed in Kimball's Galleries, sir. It was a very—very—"

Park was afraid the man was going to bog down and spoil it.

"—unusually interesting painting, sir."

"Thank you."

"You'll want this wrapped as a gift?"

Park looked at his watch. "Haven't you a little box to stick it in? I'm in a hurry. Don't trouble to wrap it up."

Because E. P. liked his boys sparking right on the dot, Park timed it to drive into the private Koko Point turnoff at exactly five minutes of ten. It was going to be a nice morning. It was going to be a beautiful day. He was glad he had stopped at the jewelers'. For breakfast this morning, E. P. had promised a surprise as a change from guavas or mangoes or Kona oranges or even fresh pineapple. Park thought he also had a surprise for E. P. as a hell of a change from all the bad news. E. P. was giving him a surprise and he was giving E. P. an extremely pleasant surprise. He smiled to himself because he felt happy this morning; it seemed to him Laina was being left out and she deserved to receive a pleasant surprise today, too.

Park arrived at ten o'clock on the dot. E. P. opened the door for him. "It's good to see you, Lieutenant. We must have breakfast together more often. Come in."

E. P. was wearing a dark purple silk Chinese dressing gown edged with gold threads, with a gold embroidered dragon on the back. There was no doubt it was a sumptuous and expensive dressing gown. Park decided it was not the sort of dressing gown E. P. should be seen wearing for it showed how slight and desiccated he really was. Park noticed E. P. was shaky on his legs. But E. P. said he felt fit, he felt really fit this morning, much more like himself than he had Saturday. He was really going into the hospital for three days to see how those boys were running it. When you built a hospital to perpetuate the memory of your sister, you wanted the hospital run in bang-up order. Dr. Austen planned to shoot some of that new stuff in him—he forgot what it was called—it was better than penicillin—to wipe out the flu bug for good.

He took Park by the arm, rather shakily steering him through the front room to the other lanai at the rear of the house. He pointed to the table laid for breakfast and said, "How's that for a real surprise? Pears."

"Pears?" said Park blankly.

And that was what they were, too. They were big Comice pears from Oregon. They were golden in color, specked with red, and you ate them with a spoon. They had been shipped by air express less than forty hours before from the pear orchards in Oregon. They were good, very good, although one was all Park could manage. It was like dipping into a small melon, he thought. E. P. had special spoons for his pears. They were small solid silver spoons with pointed tips, made for him in Denmark, he said; and instead of the acorn pattern which was so commonplace and seen almost everywhere now, his spoons had a pear pattern. Park remembered E. P. liked perry brandy which came from pears. It struck him as slightly ironic. When you lived on an exotic island, if you wanted to cultivate an exotic taste it was necessary to cultivate a taste for ordinary fruit from a colder climate.

After the butler returned to the house, Park said, "I've a surprise for you. I've seen Nogusi."

"Nogusi?" E. P.'s eyes bulged. "That prize fighter they elected—"

"Last night."

"Not to talk to?"

"Yes, to talk to." Park liked the effect of his surprise.

"How—" asked E. P. and had difficulty asking it, "—did you get to that boy?"

Park enjoyed telling him how it had happened. Park knew Nogusi did not like this island. He had hoped eventually to move through to Nogusi but he never expected Nogusi to move first. Nogusi had no idea Park was any more than Doc Fields' boy. It was one of those things that came unexpectedly out of the sky. Nogusi wanted more than ten thousand dollars if he could get it but he would deal for ten thousand dollars, the same amount paid to Bull Amani last year. He was prepared to resign this week, explaining to the unions that he had no training for such a position and was sorry he had allowed Herby Subie to talk him into accepting the nomination. While he probably could not make a very good speech, at least he was a professional pug and was unafraid of crowds and could get up on his feet and talk. He would damn Herby for not having the true interests of the workers at heart; and he would praise Charley Wong. When Nogusi resigned, to fly back to Reno, Wong automatically became acting president again. That put Wong in immediately. Herby Subie had always been a poor third in popularity. With Nogusi resigning, damning him, Herby became a nobody, having not only lost his man but having lost face. . . .

When Park finished, E. P. sat there for a space of several minutes, absorbed in thought. Finally E. P. said, his face looking very sallow, "I'd better tell you something. This is just between

· 242 ·

us and the gate post. You know the money Stewart used last year to pay off Amani? It came from me. That—bitch, Cecelia Stewart, found proof it came from me because Dickie was stupid and entered the whole transaction in his private account book."

Park pretended to be surprised. He found it difficult but E. P. was too engrossed in his own thoughts to notice.

"Your gang hadn't been here very long and I was hard-pressed last year. I should have waited for your gang to finish driving wedges but that big strike pressed me very hard." His thin fingers plucked nervously at the tablecloth. "I got into deep water with Stewart. I'm not a very popular man on the island as it is, right now. If you paid off another man and ever I got tied to it—" E. P. looked toward the beach. It was beautiful this morning, the sea green as grass and riffled with white from the surf flowing in. It was his private beach. Perhaps he considered that section of ocean out there as his private ocean. "It wouldn't be safe for me to live here any more," he said.

Park remembered going on record with E. P. that it had been a blunder for Dick Stewart to bribe Amani. Park had gone on record before he learned it was E. P. who had ordered Dick Stewart to do the bribing. He remembered also telling Buddy Morton that it was a blunder to bribe a labor leader. But Park meant that it was a blunder for a company man to bribe a labor leader because it made a straight connection. You risked having the company and everyone in the company implicated that way.

The Nogusi deal was not the same thing at all, Park explained to E. P. Park had no connection with the company. Nogusi didn't even know the name of Park's possible contact. It could be anyone wanting Nogusi to resign as president of the F. I. U. It could be old Charley Wong, for that matter. Tonight, when he saw Nogusi to pay him off, Park was prepared to let Nogusi think it might be Charley Wong. Nogusi would ask no embarassing questions; he would do his job and get off the island by the end of the week.

"That takes one wrong boy out," said E. P. thoughtfully.

"It takes Herby out, too."

"Yes, that boy, Herby Subie, loses face as soon as his man turns against him. It's a nice double play. Well done." E. P.'s eyes became misty with sudden emotion. "Well done, Lieutenant."

"It's been a long row, Colonel."

"Will we need that Red smear now we've got something better? I didn't want to say anything to you Saturday, but those employer-association boys in Honolulu have been working that Red smear to death because they have nothing better."

Park had been desperate Saturday, ready to use anything available on Herby Subie. It was Laina who had told him Herby had once been a party member. While the chance of her connecting Park with smears at Herby was small there was a risk. There was no longer any necessity for him to expose himself even to that slight risk. As E. P. said, they had something better. Park wished Lew Kirsch had not been sent to Kauai.

"Let's keep clear of the Honolulu-San Francisco axis against the labor Reds," Park said, smiling. "They're doing well enough. They don't need our help."

"When I get back in the saddle, I might make a speech hitting at those employer-association boys in Honolulu. I might say I'm opposed to labor-baiting employers?"

"Howie could write it for you."

"I don't like feeling I'm a pariah on this island since that bitch ran to Kimball," E. P. said reflectively. "Yes, I think I might make a speech against labor-baiting employers. I think that might show my employees I stand four-square for their true interests."

"There's one more detail about Nogusi—"

"I don't want details. Just pay that boy off tonight."

"Well, I'll need ten thousand to pay him off."

E. P. looked surprised. "Use the money in your budget."

"Because you haven't signed the new contract, we're down to peanuts in our budget. Kirsch's emergency surveys stripped the budget. We've even got October bills coming due which we can't pay. Tomorrow's the end of the month. We're down to five or six hundred dollars. I don't want to dangle Nogusi or stall him after promising to pay him off tonight. He's ready to jump in our pockets and—"

"No, don't dangle him," E. P. said. "Pay him off. I appreciate what you've done. Don't think I don't. It *has* been a long row for both of us. Let's finish hoeing this particular row tonight. What was your estimate for operating expenses in the new contract? One hundred thousand a quarter, wasn't it, to be paid into Lew Kirsch's account?"

Lew Kirsch's offices for conducting the frame-of-mind reports were run in the open so Paradise Products paid all funds directly into the Kirsch account. It was an open transaction and no one in the Paradise Products' accounting department had any reason to be curious about the transfer of such sums every three months. As Lew's bookkeeper, Park controlled the money when it came in. He even had the proper authorization from Lew, allowing him to sign checks. It was simple and open and you could look at the accounts any time you liked, providing you could prove you had a right to stick your nose into the books.

"Four hundred thousand a year," Park said. He only belatedly realized the significance of E. P.'s question. It was like having pushed on a door for a long time and having it slowly open by itself when you had almost given up hope.

"We'll have Buddy handle these financial details. It's why I brought him here. You don't have to tell that boy why you need any specific amount in a hurry. Until I break that boy in more, he doesn't have to know of the Nogusi arrangement. Just tell him I've authorized him to go ahead on your new contract arrangements. I'm not going to sign your contract until you tell me Wong's safely in but to show you how I operate I'm not going to quibble, either. Have Buddy transfer a hundred thousand for the November through January quarter from our general contingency fund. Buddy can use the same procedures Stewart followed to transfer funds into the Kirsch account. Now," said E. P., selecting another pear, "I think we deserve a little cheer for ourselves. What do you think? You might tell Billy to select us something nice and dry in the way of champagne from the cellar. Have you ever had a small glass of champagne with pears for breakfast? I think Dr. Austen won't object if I have a small glass before he comes to cart me off."

Park stood. It hit him in the stomach as he slowly realized E. P. was actually authorizing money to be transferred on the new contract. For a few instants the pain was unbearable. Fine brass wires were knotting in his stomach and drawing upward through his legs.

"Park," said E. P. anxiously. "You're not allergic to pears?"

It passed as suddenly as it had hit him, leaving him with a queer lightheaded feeling.

"No, that pear was fine. I couldn't have had a nicer breakfast."

At fifteen minutes before noon Park entered the Chinese Bazaar still feeling as if hydrogen were filling the cells of his body. If someone gave him a shove, he might go floating away. At least he had steadied himself at Koko Point. When E. P. had told him to authorize Buddy to transfer the funds on the new contract, Park didn't think he had revealed how much it meant to him, although you never really could tell how much or how little was revealed to E. P. Sometimes he surprised you.

In one of the Bazaar's phone booths, Park dialed the number of the private telephone in E. P.'s office at the cannery. Buddy answered, forgetting to count the numbers slowly. Instead he promptly gave his name. But it was a beautiful day. Park still had that feeling of floating gently and he did not care to have anyone push him too hard nor did he have a desire to push at anyone else. He didn't feel like chiding Buddy for failing to count the numbers. Park merely asked where he could meet Buddy for a few minutes. It wouldn't take long but it was important and he was in something of a rush.

Buddy answered and those odd dry tones were back in his voice. Buddy said his wife was driving to this side of the island to have lunch with him at the Commercial Club before going back to be with the two boys for their daily afternoon swim at Halepule Beach. Ellen was expecting him to tell her whether she should sign a year's lease on the Stewart house. Buddy said he was sorry if he was being difficult about meeting Park but everything was piling up on him while E. P. was not feeling well.

The new shipment of cans had not arrived from Honolulu as promised. The morning's run of pineapple juice had too much cellulose sediment in it to be packed for mainland markets. Something had gone haywire with the Kleber filters. Ellen and the two boys were tired of living at the hotel on the other side of the island and wanted to find a house. Frankly, Buddy said, he was getting tired of the elaborate procedures necessary every time Park and he had to see each other, unless they met at Koko Point. Today he lacked the time to waste an hour to an hour and a half driving where it would be safe to meet Park. He was not going to break his luncheon date with his wife. It was too late to break it; she'd be halfway across the island by now. He did not see how he could see Park at all today. Would tomorrow do?

Park wished for God's sake Ellen and Buddy could have attended to their private business at night and not during noon hours. Buddy had to transfer the new funds into the Kirsch account today before the banks closed.

Park said, "Tomorrow won't do," and was shorter and crisper with Buddy than he usually was. "It won't take long—"

"Can't you explain over the phone, then?"

Park didn't like having to try to explain over a telephone the details of transferring a hundred thousand dollars for the next quarter into Kirsch's account. He had never thought he could find himself missing Dick Stewart. He did now. Dick might not have had the head on him that E. P. thought Buddy had, but at least Dick knew the procedures at the plant. Regularly every three months Dick had transferred funds into the Kirsch account without a hitch. Resentment welled up in Park because Buddy was feeling harassed and being difficult about it.

Park said, "If you're so jammed I'll see you at the cannery."

"Is it safe?"

No, it wasn't safe. Nothing was really safe. It entailed a small risk when he had purchased that little golden airplane for Laina's bracelet. Having to see Nogusi tonight was not safe—it was taking another calculated risk. You got paid for calculating your risks and being right. Going to the cannery where he had never gone before was a small one-time risk, probably much safer than crossing John Oliver Street at noontime.

"I'll be there in ten minutes," Park promised and hung up. He had ample time before the banks closed at four but not enough to dawdle.

Exactly as E. P. had once told him, everything at the cannery was completely systematized. A guard in a neat pineapple-green uniform stepped forward to ask Park politely whom he wished to see. Park said whom he wished to see. The guard asked who was asking, sir, to see Mr. Morton? Park said who it was. When you took pains to establish a secure cover for yourself, it was a mistake to yield to anxiety and hide your identity with a false name.

Park waited in the garage reserved for cars of the high brass echelon, the guard entered a glass booth which was part of the complete system. It permitted the guard to watch you politely as he telephoned upstairs. Park saw the guard's lips move silently while he spoke into the mouthpiece. It was absurd to think of being held and searched and detained as a suspicious person by these guards in their neat pineapple-green uniforms. But they made him uneasy. He wished he had not given in to the impulse to see Buddy here.

Park saw the guard nod on the other side of the glass and hang up the receiver. The guard stepped forth and removed his smartly visored cap before addressing Park. The guard's whole demeanor subtly changed after the telephoned orders from the third floor. The system was not only complete but thorough. Instead of a polite but suspicious guard there was now a suggestion of the old family retainer, pleased to welcome one of the young master's guests. Mr. Mattison was all cleared. He could go to the president's private office, sir. Just push the green button in the elevator, sir. It took you there directly.

Park was relieved to know he was all cleared, although it had been ridiculous to think the guards might detain him. Buddy had cleared him. If anyone had asked what he wished of Mr. Morton, Park had been prepared to say he hoped to sell Mr. Morton paintings of the island to be used in Paradise Products' advertising. It would have been an open and frank statement. Mrs. Morton was interested in his paintings, having offered him an art fellowship. There was no reason why her husband couldn't be equally interested. But no one asked.

The elevator was noiseless. It lifted so gently that Park scarcely knew he was being carried upwards. It stopped effortlessly, the automatic doors opening so silently that Park stood for a minute before realizing he was in what must be E. P.'s private sanctum. It looked completely systematized. You even bypassed the outer offices filled with secretaries and the inner-outer office containing the special private secretary.

Park stepped into a long sunny room and saw Buddy sitting in what must have been E. P.'s chair. He was sitting behind a highly polished executive-model koa wood glass-topped desk.

"Hello," said Buddy, standing. "Don't mind this desk. It looks like a kidney, I'll admit. Sit down, if you can find a chair that fits you. Frankly, I haven't found anything in this office that fits me."

Park glanced at the red leather chairs, Hawaiian modern, and decided he would rather stand. Buddy grinned wryly at him and said, "If E. P. stays away much longer I'm going to have the desk and a couple of chairs from my own office down the hall dragged in here. I hope I didn't sound too difficult over the phone?"

"No. You sounded as if trying to run the plant without E. P. was starting to grind a little."

"It's what's happening outside the plant."

"Well, don't let it get you down. We may have a lucky break sooner than we think."

Buddy studied Park for a moment. "Frankly, I just don't like the situation. I know what I should do and I find I haven't the courage to do it."

"All we have to do is hang on," Park said. "That doesn't take too much courage. If it'll cheer you any, I saw E. P. this morning before Dr. Austen drove him to the hospital. E. P.'s much more hopeful. We haven't lost too much time since Saturday in establishing an anxiety climate for the island."

"These newspapers . . ." Buddy stepped to the window.

"The two dailies are cooperating very well," Park said.

"Do they always do what you tell them to do?"

"I don't tell them to do anything," Park said. "Howie gives suggestions. Sometimes By Meaker has to have a talk with one or the other of the publishers."

"I've never been anywhere before where all news and information is controlled. It's a new experience for me."

"We aren't quite that good yet," Park said. "We missed badly on Kimball's scandal sheet. We'll have to do something about that next year, when we have more time." He glanced at his watch. It was six minutes after twelve. He expected Buddy was in a hurry to cut it short if he had to meet Ellen. "This morning E. P. decided to go ahead with the financial terms in our new contract. He asked me to have you transfer a hundred thousand into Kirsch's account for the next three months. Dick Stewart's office used to handle it through your accounting department."

Buddy came away from the window, the sunlight on his thin sensitive face. "I don't think I can do that, Park."

Park said patiently, "E. P. seemed to think you knew the procedures."

"I know the procedures but I don't think I can do it."

Park didn't get it. If Buddy knew the procedures Dick used, there was no reason for delay. "Howie Wright can handle the details for you. We put Howie in with Stewart to give him a hand."

Buddy went behind the desk and sat in the red leather chair. "I can't do it. I'll need a written authorization from E. P."

Park frowned, then remembering Buddy had been a banker, he said patiently, "If you won't take my word, you'd better phone E. P. at the hospital."

"After you called me," Buddy said, "I did try to get through to E. P. I wanted to tell him I'd try to run the plant while he was away but I wouldn't have anything to do with his M. O. policies. They didn't let me talk to him. Dr. Austen's given him two shots and put him to sleep."

"You aren't trying to put me on a spot, are you?" asked Park.

"Perhaps I'm trying to keep off one, myself," Buddy answered. "I don't doubt your word. I'll grant E. P. may have told you to come to me, but I want a written statement from E. P. For a year and a half Stewart made transfers to Kirsch's account on his own authority as far as the record goes. I can't find any authorization from E. P. in the file. Suppose there's an investigation someday?"

"Well, look," said Park, not wanting to get sore at Buddy.

"There isn't going to be an investigation. If I can't get through to E. P. today, you're putting me in a hole. I have bills to pay."

"I'm sorry. I don't mean to put you in a hole but I think E. P. should have thought of it when he sent you to me without a written authorization."

"Stewart didn't ask for written authorizations."

"Frankly, I think Stewart had more faith in E. P. than I find I have. E. P. told Stewart to bribe Amani, too. I'm not Stewart, Park. I'm a businessman. I'm sorry this came up like this. I haven't been able to sleep nights, trying to decide what I should do. I don't think I'd even accept a written authorization from E. P. unless it were given after a meeting of the board of directors. This is a company. It's an organization. Although E. P. controls the company and the board of directors through his control of the Tothic Estate, through my family I'm still representing the second largest group of stockholders. Before your group receives any more money from Paradise Products I'm afraid you'll have to wait until E. P.'s out of the hospital and at least until I have a talk with him."

Park saw Buddy very clearly in the sunlight streaming through the window. He noticed Buddy was back to wearing the herringbone business suit from the mainland. He gazed at Buddy speculatively. He had not realized Buddy had it in him to balk when E. P. was temporarily out of the picture.

"We're trying to do a job right now for E. P. Our budget's down to nothing. You're not trying to stop us short?"

"Frankly, after that meeting Saturday, I think I do want to stop it short." Buddy slowly rose from the chair. "Yes," he repeated, "I think that's exactly what I do want to do. I've lacked the moral strength to face it."

It made Park want to spit on the floor to hear Buddy talk about moralities. He stuck his hands in his pockets, straddled his legs, and said, "Well, look, Buddy. I'm not trying to argue with you but we both have the same end in mind. We want to prevent a strike. You may disagree as to the means we're using—"

"Park, I don't believe any means justify an end. Means are all we have to go by. We never can attain an end any more than men can attain the stars they look at. Stopping a strike isn't an end.

Last year we stopped a strike, but it wasn't a solution. If the unions won't listen to reason and truth, we ought to face the consequences. Why can't we give the unions the truth for once? Why not say we spent too much money building Halepule Beach and tunneling for water? Why not say we can't go ahead with a decent housing program for field hands and their families until after we pay off the bond issue next year?"

As Park listened to Buddy, he became aware of another sensation. It felt like a stomach cramp from swimming in very cold water, the agony spreading to his legs and drawing them up. Park felt his legs bending and he could do nothing about it. The pain in his stomach seemed to end, leaving nothing but a numbness; his legs were all rubber. Sweat sprang out on his forehead. He had to choose between plunking on the floor or into one of the red leather chairs. He managed to guide himself into the chair and his chagrin changed to rage, but primarily at himself, not Buddy. It frightened him to have such a thing happening to his legs. Everything else was all right. His mind was functioning with an almost abnormal clarity. It was not his task to deal with Buddy's unexpected rebellion. It was E. P.'s. It was important to have ten thousand dollars tonight but Park had no real anxiety about getting the sum together quickly. He had eight thousand of his own in the bank, if it were necessary to draw on it, and By Meaker and Lew Kirsch should each have much more than eight thousand stored away in their personal accounts. It was frustration that he could do nothing with Buddy. Because the top man was away for a few days, Buddy was trying to step into his shoes. Park had seen the same thing happen several times during the war. Your colonel departed for a duty tour and the major took over and laid down the law and all you could do was wait it out. Then when your colonel returned, usually the major was unexpectedly transferred.

"If that's how you see it," Park said. His legs slowly responded. He thought it would be safe to stand in another minute, to leave, and drive to By's office.

Buddy said earnestly it was how he saw it. He believed the workers would see it, too, if given the truth instead of lies. It was time all of them on the island realized sugar and pineapple were in a marginal state of production because of rising costs. He had been here long enough to think about what should be done. Instead of expanding production, year by year draining more water from the island, production ought to be gradually reduced to approximately half of what it was. The rest of the land could be sold off for small truck farms. Halepule Beach could be extended several more miles, with two or three smaller hotels built to attract tourists of moderate means. It was time this island found a middle road before it was too late. Buddy had decided if he were a worker he would rather starve to death, and know what was being done to him, than to have someone make a docile robot of him by tinkering with his mind through unceasing M. O. pressures. He was tired of so much secrecy. Every time he saw his wife he felt like a criminal because formerly he used to discuss everything with her. Now he had to evade Ellen's questions. He had not signed a lease for the Stewart house because he was trying to decide whether to stay on or to throw up the job here and return with his family to the mainland.

Park leaned forward, testing his legs. As soon as E. P. got back Buddy would not have to decide anything. E. P. would decide it for him. Sweat streamed down Park's face as he rocked forward and carefully stood up, balancing himself on his legs. They were holding. Now he had to walk to the elevator without falling, get to his car, and to By's office and the bank.

"We'd have a strike," Park said. "Your policies won't work."

"If it's too late for reason and decency, then let's face a strike. Shut down the cannery. Sell the mainland sales and distributing company. At least we'll have clear consciences."

With terrifying clarity, Park saw he had far more to lose by a strike than E. P. had, or even Buddy. If there were a strike, and the mainland sales company was sold off to meet the bond issue, the Tothic Estate would remain solvent. E. P. would have all the money still coming in even if the island stopped growing sugar cane and pineapples and was run primarily for tourists as a new Nassau in the Pacific. E. P.'s father, old Pater Tothic, had wanted the island to become a new Nassau. But you did not require an expensive M. O. task force to police tourists.

"Park," asked Buddy, "help me prove to E. P. that we can find

· 253 ·

a middle road. You can't like what E. P.'s ordering you to do. Don't forget—I was in E. P.'s bedroom Saturday with you and By Meaker. I heard him tell you he wanted more drastic action on those two men running the unions than even you had planned. It's bad enough to plan to smear one man with false Red charges and the other—Good Lord, Park! I can't believe you're the man I thought I knew, deliberately planning to drag someone into a filthy scandal with a wretched woman. But even that wasn't enough for E. P. He was asking you to have Nogusi and Subie murdered. Isn't that true?"

"No, it wasn't true." Park turned to go toward the elevator. It was like walking on stilts. He had never had this happen to his legs before.

"Don't go yet. Please." Buddy followed after him. "I'll telephone the club and tell Ellen I'll be late. You and I've got to settle this before you go. You can't like these dirty M. O. tactics any more than I do. Make this your chance to get free. I'd stand by you."

Park stopped. "What the hell are you trying to say?"

"Get off this island. You're a C. P. A. I've friends in Seattle. Besides, I'd be willing to advance you enough to establish your own accounting office. You could get back into a decent business. I have a few resources, you know."

Park said harshly, "Are you trying to bribe me to get out?"

"That's not a fair statement. I'm trying to help you. I'm trying to help all of us," Buddy said earnestly. "Unless the war made you indifferent to hurting human minds and lives, I can't believe you approve of these dirty M. O. tactics E. P.'s asking you to carry through."

Park's professional pride was stung. He had nothing more to say to Buddy. The new boy had failed completely to get in line, and Park knew E. P. would make short work of packing the new boy off the island. Park's voice lost its brisk pleasant quality.

"*You've* got a few resources? Where do you think your resources come from? Ask By Meaker to show you the newspaper files for the twenties and thirties on this island. Read the record of strikes and strike-busting when your great-uncle Enders was

Mr. Big. How many years has your family been getting its cut from the melon out here? Look back over 1921, 1922, 1924, 1925—to name a few vintage years when you had plantation workers killed in labor fights and riots. You had even better years later on. In 1931 machine guns were used to stop the Iki plantation riots. Sixteen men were shot to death that year, Buddy. Or take the year—"

"I don't believe you."

"*You* don't believe me?" Park was sorry for the little man's ignorance. "Read the facts. I had to read the facts because it was my job to know what happened. Your family merely got its cut from the island. You didn't want to know what was happening. And you tell me my M. O.'s too dirty for you? There's a laugh. Don't you even know our record for the time we've been here? It's clean. No men killed. Two took a clubbing, but we didn't kill them. Bull Amani—we shipped him to Australia to save him from being killed by the Flips. That's how dirty our record is. Yes, and a movie house burned down at Iki after everyone had gone home. I've always opposed drastic pressures except as a last resort. The trouble with boys like you, born into money, you're born with guilty consciences. You'll live on the dirty money you inherited, but you'll shy away from the job to be done on this island, now, to prevent a strike and save jobs for everyone."

Park jabbed at the elevator button. He saw how white and pinched-looking Buddy's face had become. He said savagely, "Goddamn it, you can't have a middle road. If there's a strike and everything closes down, you'll have exactly what your great-uncle Enders hoped to have before E. P. took control. Most of the Oriental population will be driven off the island by economic pressures. Well, is that so moral and righteous? Your family will still get its cut from the tourist business. Why don't you," Park asked, contempt entering his voice, "give all your money and your wife's, too, to the workers if you're so honest and filled with good works? Try starting even on the ladder with the rest of us who weren't born with gold spoons in our mouths. Then see how much you like it. Then see if it's the war that changed you. Then see if you're still so red-hot on moral dilemmas."

The elevator doors opened noiselessly. As Park entered the elevator he heard Buddy say, "Fair enough." The way Buddy said it made Park look back. Buddy was clenching his hands together tightly. "I think I told you before if anyone stuck out his neck, I ought to. I've been avoiding the dilemma long enough. You're quite right. I was wrong to make an issue of it with you. I've got to go farther than I have. I'll go to E. P. If necessary I can go even farther than him. Thank you for reminding me. Goodbye, Park."

"Wait a minute," said Park. His voice sounded far away because he had a bursting and crashing in his head. He thought if he did not hurry and say what had to be said, his whole skull would shatter. "For your own good, don't go too far."

Buddy appeared very small and frail when he looked at Park. "I can't take threats from you or anyone."

"I'm not threatening you," Park said. "I'm telling you this time. I told you at that first meeting, I'll tell you again. Anyone on this island's out of luck who doesn't get in line with thinking the way E. P. decides the line's going to be. You're no better to me than Amani or those boys we beat up, or that tough little Jap whose movie house we burned down. You've got a wife. You've got two kids on this island."

"Just what—" asked Buddy as if he had chunks of ice in his mouth, "—do you mean by that?"

"If E. P. decides you're going too far, by God, I'll have you stopped," said Park. "That's what I mean."

It was almost a pleasure to see what was happening to Buddy's thin face; it seemed to be breaking into small pieces. Park pressed the "down" button.

He was in a hurry. It was nearly one o'clock. He had taken longer than he'd planned with Buddy. He should not have allowed himself to blow his top with the new boy. It was E. P.'s job to deal with Buddy, but it was time Buddy learned a few of the facts of life. Park drove rapidly from the cannery. He still had time to get to By's office and afterward to the bank before it closed, but he'd have to hurry.

19

It was ten minutes after one by the time he had parked his Buick on a side street, walked to the John Oliver building through one of the early afternoon showers, and arrived at By Meaker's offices. His legs were still not quite right; he couldn't understand what had happened to him to make his legs feel that way. He remembered not having eaten much for breakfast at E. P.'s and he had not had time for lunch; that was the trouble, he told himself. As soon as he saw By and had By's personal check for two thousand dollars—better make it twenty-five hundred to be on the safe side—he would pack some food into himself and feel all there again.

Elsie Flavola was back from lunch but my gracious, she said, she didn't know how soon Mr. Meaker would return. He ought to be here very soon. He had been with Mr. Branner and a whole crowd of men from station BYQ at the Makakina airfield since eleven o'clock. Mr. Branner, Park recalled vaguely, was program manager of station BYQ.

Elsie asked Mr. Mattison if he had heard the new program from the Makakina airfield. It was station BYQ's new "Aloha Program" broadcast directly from the field, interviewing important tourists before they departed on the afternoon flight to Honolulu. The broadcast yesterday was terribly interesting. They had a ceremony of giving those cute malahini buttons to the tourists who had been here just this once and Mr. Branner was awfully funny, too. For this afternoon they had lined up

General Holloway Burton who had been here before as a captain early in the war and Mr. Branner had written a wonderful speech for General Burton to give, all about how happy he was to receive a genuine coconut ring because he was now a real kamaaina who had been here more than once. Mr. Meaker had gone to the field to arrange everything for this afternoon, but Mr. Meaker ought to have finished by now. Wasn't it wonderful of Mr. Meaker to have thought of such a wonderful program?"

Park didn't care how wonderful she thought By was. He looked at his watch. It was sixteen minutes after one. What was keeping the guy? Elsie was sympathetic. Goodness gracious! She didn't know what was keeping Mr. Meaker. She telephoned Mr. Branner's office at station BYQ. Mr. Branner had been in but he was out again. No one had seen Mr. Meaker since the broadcast. Park was beginning to feel apprehensive. He remembered Lew Kirsch was still in Kauai. Park had not had a chance to tell By to send a wireless to Lew for him to return. If Lew were here Park could get the money from Lew, but Lew was not here. Park sat there in the office and felt as if time were picking up speed and rushing very fast. He told Elsie he'd be back in a half-hour. Have Mr. Meaker wait for him, please. It was quite important.

It was still raining when he walked the six blocks east on John Oliver Street to the old First National Bank. It was nearly two by the time he had drawn out his savings. It was not quite as much as he had thought it was, either. It came to exactly seventy-four hundred dollars. Tonight Nogusi expected to be paid at least ten thousand dollars. When you asked a man to deliver for you, you had to deliver, yourself.

Park's anxiety tightened. It was absurd to find himself needing twenty-six hundred dollars when only this morning he had been assured of having a hundred thousand established to his credit. He asked the bank guard where the phones were and was told the pay booths were down in the basement. It was hot and humid in the basement and Park could feel his shirt sticking to his skin. It took thirty cents to phone the Ruth Tothic Memorial Hospital and although Park had seventy-four hundred dollars in crisp bills and several fifty-cent pieces, he did not have the right change for thirty cents. It took him three or four more minutes of waiting to get to the girl at the bank vault desk for the right change.

When Park got through to the hospital he was informed that Mr. Tothic was asleep. Dr. Austen had given orders that his patient was not to be disturbed. Who was asking for Mr. Tothic, please? The hospital would take any messages for Mr. Tothic to give to him some time tomorrow. Park hung up.

The thought of Buddy lousing up what should have been a small detail angered him. Kirsch was in Kauai; Park could not get money from Kirsch. Suppose By was off somewhere on the island on business and failed to return to his office before the banks closed? Park remembered Laina had three thousand dollars of her savings in the bank here. Sunday, she had offered to withdraw it for him to purchase tickets for them to get off this rotten island. He could get the money from her. It was a half-hour's drive to the Halepule side of the island, and a half-hour to bring her back. He had time. They could be here by three. For that matter, there was a branch bank on the Halepule side. But he disliked going to her. He was involving her in his business affairs more than he had ever wished to do. Damn Buddy. It was infuriating to need twenty-four hundred dollars so desperately.

Buddy was filthy with money. So was his wife. Park recalled Ellen's offer of a four-thousand-dollar fellowship. He thought of going to Ellen and telling her he had reconsidered. He toyed with the idea, not really meaning to go. It revolted him. At the same time he felt a tingling in his veins. He thought of how quickly she had acceded to his wishes the last time he had seen her. He noticed that the girl at the bank vault desk was eying him as if he might be a suspicious person.

"Hot, isn't it?" he said.

"I wish it'd rain good," she said.

She had not been eying him suspiciously. She was bored. She was ready to talk to anybody. He stepped inside the booth again, dialing By's office. Elsie answered. Yes, she had telephoned station BYQ again and had talked this time to Mr. Branner. Mr. Meaker had left for the Memorial Hospital at Pohaku fifteen minutes before she got Mr. Branner. He was bringing Mrs. Meaker home today.

An unreasoning blind fury came over Park; he could not speak. Elsie was terribly terribly sorry. She had just forgotten, she guessed, to leave word the first time she had telephoned the radio station to have someone there ask Mr. Meaker to call back.

Park hung up, resting weakly inside the booth. The hot thick air choked into his lungs. If he hurried he still had time to get to his house at the top of Pua cliff and drive Laina to the branch bank at the beach and then he realized Laina could not withdraw her savings from the branch bank. He would have to drive her here. He got out of the booth, mopping his face.

"What we need is a real good rain," the girl said. "It's time we ought to have some real good rain."

It was ten minutes after two when Park reached the street. It was not raining very hard but at least it was still raining. The air was fresher than in the bank's basement. His resentment against Buddy increased. He had hoped to keep Laina apart from his business affairs. Despite himself, she was becoming more and more involved. He hated having to ask Laina for her savings.

On the way to his car, he seriously considered going to Ellen Morton. He would not tell her he had reconsidered her offer because he had refused it once in good faith and he did not wish to do anything to renew her alarm. However, he didn't see why he couldn't go to her and ask for a loan of twenty-six hundred dollars, with interest at six per cent, and a promise to repay within a month. She knew him only as an artist. It would not surprise her that an artist was hard-pressed. And it was not, he thought, as if Ellen and he were entirely strangers. She had a generous heart. Yes, he could go to her. Damn her husband. Damn Buddy. It seemed to him that Buddy and Ellen had obscurely been against him ever since they had arrived. First Ellen had tried to louse him up and now here was Buddy lousing him up wonderfully this afternoon.

After taking the wheel of the Buick, he glanced at his watch. It was surprising how fast the time went. It was twenty-one minutes after two. He could still make it with Laina. As he drove rapidly toward Hibiscus Road and thought of having to ask Laina for the money, he felt a hardening against Buddy. All Park had to do was to go a little faster and by tonight the fix would be secured, but it was Buddy who now was forcing Park to go just a little faster.

He had no doubt of Laina's giving him the money. It was not that. She had offered to give it to him Sunday when he painted her portrait. Her portrait! He had a sort of inner convulsion. It was frightening for his mind to fail to connect when so little time remained. He had Laina's portrait. And Harry Kimball had urged him to accept a lump sum of three thousand dollars to continue doing nothing else but paint. Laina's portrait was the best thing he had done, too. Park had painted it for Laina to like and she liked it, very much. He could take the portrait to Harry as proof he was seriously determined to devote his time henceforth to painting. He even stopped five minutes at a wayside stand near the Hono plantation for a sandwich and a glass of fresh pineapple juice.

He lost more time than he had anticipated because Laina was not at the house to help him wrap the portrait. Her Chevy was gone, but he did not have time to think of her or of where she might have gone. It was fortunate he had remembered Harry's promise. Why was it when you needed something which ordinarily was comparatively trivial, suddenly it became so hard to get? He thought again of Buddy turning him down this morning. He felt something hard and solid with a raw taste to it of pineapple with too much fresh bromelin in it pushing through his throat and mouth from his stomach.

By his watch it was ten minutes after three when he stopped a half-block away from Kimball's Galleries.

He turned left to the receptionist's desk tucked discreetly to one side of the large room. It startled him to see the girl at the desk. She looked as Laina might have looked had Laina cropped her hair. It required an instant for him to realize this was still the same pretty Chinese-Hawaiian girl whom he had seen before; but since last seeing her, she had cut her long tawny hair in the new clipped sleek fashion. Her head looked rather nude and, to Park's surprise, more attractive than he would have thought.

She recognized Mr. Mattison and rang through to Mr. Kimball

at once. She said Mr. Kimball would be free to see Mr. Mattison in five minutes. Five minutes? Park decided he still had all the time he needed. He wished he had stopped to eat more than a sandwich and pineapple juice at a wayside stand. If he was not careful he was going to have a hell of a headache by tonight, a sick one, with his stomach squirming. He tried to make himself very easy, while waiting. He even managed to smile at the girl and ask her why she had decided to cut her hair. She said, in her soft kanaka accents, that all the girls were cutting their hair. It was too hot to have such long hair. Didn't Mr. Mattison like her hair this way? Even Mr. Kimball liked it. Mr. Brolly had been in this morning. He'd liked her hair cut short, too. Mr. Brolly had come in to pick up Mr. Mattison's painting. The painting had been on display in the front window over the week end, with a card saying it was painted by Mr. Mattison and had been purchased by Mr. Cyril Brolly, of Hollywood. Mr. Kimball never missed any bets, did he? But Mr. Brolly was leaving in a day or so for Hollywood and wanted his painting to take with him.

Park had almost forgotten Cyril Brolly was still here. He thought it was time that little son-of-a-bitch did leave. He looked at his watch; six minutes had passed. Then the telephone buzzed discreetly. The girl answered, listened, and nodded to Mr. Mattison. He could go upstairs now. He knew where Mr. Kimball's office was, didn't he? Yes, Park knew.

Harry flung open the door, filling all the space; and he was as big as ever.

The little eyes twinkled. Park was pulled into the office, placed in one of the chairs, and Harry was saying this indeed was a happy surprise. Why hadn't Park seen him sooner after flying home so unexpectedly last Saturday from the other island? Park placed the portrait between his legs, preparing to unwrap it, but Harry was in a jovial mood this afternoon and clearly not quite ready to look at a portrait.

Harry expected Park to return blooming and here, indeed, was Park, but not blooming. Harry did not wish Park to misunderstand, but how was Laina? He expected Laina must be blooming more enticingly than ever after that little excursion last week to the island of Hawaii? A wave of helpless fury came over Park. He was more tender about Laina and himself than he had suspected. In the past he had heard most of the jokes your friends liked to repeat when you returned from a week-end romp with a girl. It was banter. You shrugged it off. This time Park was unable to shrug it off when Harry bantered him jovially. That great obese swine! Harry should know Laina was no week-end girl for anyone.

"She had a lousy cold, Harry."

Park realized he sounded as if he had his back up to Harry and he had not walked in this afternoon to get his back up the first cast from the box. He forced himself to sit deeper in the chair. He told Harry he had flown back to finish a portrait of Laina because he could work better on this island where it was warmer. Laina had been supposed to take the Sunday night ship but she had fooled him by taking an early Sunday plane, instead.

"My boy," Harry said, "I haven't lost sight of your interests even if I have been very busy while you were away. I expect you've seen last Thursday's issue of my little weekly? It sold nineteen thousand copies. It was a great sensation, my boy. I hear it started Pip Tothic to puking and he still can't control himself. I hear they've had to take him to the hospital until he can begin to control himself again."

"It was quite a sensation, Harry," Park said, and he knew he still sounded as if he had his back up.

"But I've made progress with that little brochure I'm going to issue on you when we have a show of your paintings next year," Harry said. "I haven't forgotten you, my boy, but I do wish you were a little less difficult."

Park looked up. His fingers were all thumbs as he attempted to unwrap the portrait. "How's that?"

"That Tolliver woman wanted a portrait by you. I sent her to you Saturday night, my boy, when Phil Parsons told me you were in town. I haven't seen her since. Brolly was in this morning and said she was leaving. She was very angry at us both. You couldn't have been very tactful with her, my boy, could you? Did you try to rush her a little too fast?"

Park looked at Harry. For a moment he forgot why he was

here and thought simply of the pleasure it would give him to hit Harry in his huge stomach. Then he remembered why he was here and sweat started on his forehead. The splitting sensation in his head increased. But he said very mildly, "I don't quite get you, Harry."

Harry chuckled. "All right, my boy. I wish I were your age and had half my weight. I won't ask you what you did to that Tolliver woman. But don't let Caroline hear of it. Sometimes those hapa-haole girls can be extremely jealous of mainland women. What have you got for me today? I don't wish to rush you, but I have to see my printer and get my little weekly to bed for this week, you know."

Again Park had to control himself. He said, "I had a chance to do some thinking on the other island. I decided to take you up on that offer you made me."

"Offer, my boy? *What* offer?"

"To give me a lump sum while I paint."

"Oh, yes. *That* offer. Yes, my boy. Have you decided?"

"Yes, I think I'll take it. I finished a portrait of Laina and it doesn't look too bad to me."

"You mustn't depreciate yourself, my boy."

"Well, I think you're right. I think I can do more by sticking to painting and not doing part-time jobs, Harry. I told Lew Kirsch today I was through working for him."

"You told Lew Kirsch?" Harry said. "I heard Dr. Kirsch had flown to Kauai, Sunday. I don't know who told me. Did Kirsch get back?"

Park had a prickling. You could go along and forget to be careful and of a sudden, when it was least expected, find you had accidentally lifted a corner from your cover. Even with two years, the odds were mounting. Even though it was no longer necessary for him to chop off two labor jokers by goofering an ash-can model Oldsmobile, Park wondered uneasily if the five more years were going to be quite as sweet as he'd thought they would be.

"I left a note for Lew," Park said. "I'm through working for him." He pulled off the paper wrappings, lifted the portrait, standing between it and Harry as he placed the portrait in its rough wooden stretchers on the two arms of the chair. "I'm ready to go to work for you, Harry." Park stepped away from the portrait.

Instead of looking at the portrait of Laina, Harry was gazing at Park. The gaze made Park realize how he must look this afternoon. The rain had soaked his gray sharkskins. A puddle of water was collecting around his shoes. "My boy, I wouldn't want you to put it that you're working for me. I have faith in you. We'll call it an advance. How much did I promise?"

"Three thousand dollars," said Park. "I could get by on twenty-six hundred if I had to."

"Three thousand dollars won't break me," said Harry. He lifted his bulk from the chair, taking his eyes off Park. Harry regarded the portrait. Park heard the big man's heavy breathing in the silence of the room. He heard the faint whine of the small electric clock on the desk and through the window Park could hear the rain still falling with a soft wind clashing the wet leaves of the palm trees in the courtyard. Harry squeezed from behind his desk, stepping closer to the portrait on the chair.

"My boy . . ." As Harry's head swung around Park saw the thick fleshy creasings fold in Harry's neck. "I'm very serious about painting. I don't like jokes of this sort."

"Jokes?" asked Park, startled.

"Who did that thing, there? Caroline?"

"Look here—" Park laughed. This was another hotfoot. "Don't do that to me, Harry. I really worked on this one. How do you like it?"

Harry gave no answer, stooping and wheezing a little to have a closer view of the portrait. Park looked at it and saw it clearly, as if he had not done it, himself, at all. It was a big canvas. The sky was there and you knew it was a sky. You saw rocks. You saw a girl, too, at least it might have been a girl. When Park looked at it now, detached and critical, he had to admit it was not very good but still it was not much worse than those Gauguin reproductions hanging in his bedroom. It was not good but it was not too bad.

Harry said, "I'm sorry, my boy."

"You're—*sorry*?" asked Park, not understanding.

Harry got himself back into his chair. He appeared to be searching for words. It was strange, too, but this time Park did not have the impression Harry was delivering a hotfoot. It was as if Harry were trying to explain something which he did not enjoy having to explain.

For a short time, Harry tried to explain, Park had done a few paintings which were almost unique because they were painted as a primitive might paint. Yet they had a degree of symbolism which was extremely rare in paintings by primitives such as Rousseau or, to push it further, by Gauguin who actually was never a true primitive.

All along Harry had been holding his breath for fear Park might become aware of his painting and attempt to do consciously what he had been doing—Harry did not know exactly how to put it. Harry thought it had been something like automatic writing, but Park somehow had done it in painting, not in writing. Now, it wasn't there. It was gone in this portrait. For Harry, it was a very great shock. Perhaps Park could recapture what he had once had by returning to landscapes. Harry didn't know. He was really very shocked. It was very unpleasant. He hoped Park would understand. Harry was not an affluent man by any means. While he had been prepared to lay out a small sum to subsidize Park during the next year, it was impossible for Harry to consider doing it unless Park could recapture himself. He could not give Park any money. He could not attempt to advise Park what Park should do. Perhaps if it were not too late, Park ought to hurry to the city to retrieve his note to Dr. Kirsch. He ought to plan staying on with Dr. Kirsch until he recaptured himself. Harry was sorry, my boy.

"Are you short of cash?" he asked.

"What do you think, after that trip to the other island?"

"I owe you ninety dollars from those two other landscapes. I owe you four hundred fifty from the painting of yours I sold to Brolly." Harry paused, staring with small hostile eyes at the portrait of Laina. "Yes, I'm sorry for you, my boy. I'll give you an additional fifty for that frightful mess on the chair and you can watch me destroy it. I'll do that much for you, my boy. I'll write you a check for five hundred ninety dollars but I'll destroy that painting. No one will know you've lost your grip. We'll keep it between ourselves and give you time to try to recapture yourself." He pulled open his desk drawer, reaching for his checkbook.

Park stepped to the table, bending forward. "Harry, I need more than six hundred dollars."

"Don't misunderstand me, but I'm not a charitable institution. I can give you five hundred ninety dollars, not a cent more. If you can recapture what you used to have, come in with a new landscape and we'll have another little talk. We—"

"Goddamn you, Harry—"

Harry looked up. The big moon face seemed to sag. He thrust back in the chair, a thick arm lifting hastily to shield his face.

"Wait, my boy—"

Park came back on his heels. My God, how he wanted to smash at that enormous face. If only once he could let himself go and have the ecstatic delight of not having to calculate in advance the effects of everything he did. He had to remember that there were five sweet years for him on the island, five more years to go, five more years of seeing Harry, of hiding from Harry while he was here on the island. There was so much he must remember.

"Goddamn you, Harry," he said, this time not at all as he had said it the first time. "You knocked me off my feet. I'd hoped you would like it. O. K. Write the check."

"I'm more sorry than you know, my boy."

"Well, I can still keep trying."

Park saw Harry's fleshy hands go into the drawer for the checkbook and he noticed a framed photograph in the drawer. It was the red leather of the frame that first attracted his eye. He leaned farther over the desk, twisting his head a little, for it seemed to him he had seen the face in that photograph before. It was of a girl, very dark-eyed, with dark curly hair.

Park savagely wondered if Harry were as good at taking a hotfoot as he was at giving one.

He pointed to the photograph in the open drawer. "I thought

you liked Chinese girls, Harry? That one looks almost like a haole girl."

You never could tell about Harry and if Park had not known he could not have told now, for Harry rumbled, "My boy, that's a niece of mine. Ugly little brat, isn't she?" He did not even glance into the drawer. Without haste, he pushed the drawer shut, pulled his big chair forward, and wrote the check with a steady hand. "Here, my boy." He flicked the check across the desk. He rose, he went around the desk, and placed himself before Park's portrait. Park could smell the fresh sweet smell of pikaki growing in the little garden below the windows. Harry shoved his fist through the canvas. Park felt as if the fist had gone into his stomach. The photograph in Harry's drawer was of Ruth Tothic. It was of Ruth Tothic and it must have been taken when she was twenty or twenty-one, long before the war. Park heard the sound of canvas ripping and looked away from what Harry was doing to the portrait of Laina. Even if you gave Harry a hotfoot, Park thought, Harry was right back at you, trying to top you. He felt raw hatred. But he could not afford to have hatred.

"So long, Harry."

"Try to recapture yourself, my boy."

He shut Harry's office door behind him. Laina had liked the portrait he had done of her. Park walked down the black marble stairs. He had five more years, he was thinking. It would be necessary for him to recapture himself for Harry; and at the thought came a pang followed by a feeling of emptiness. He was not very certain he could recapture whatever Harry had seen in the landscapes because he had never really known what it was anyone had seen in them. He had not cared at all whether anyone liked them when he did them and now he cared because some-where and somehow he had lost something which he had never been aware of having.

But he had no time to think of how Harry felt or of why Harry hid an old photograph of Ruth Tothic in his desk drawer. He had to think of going on, just a little faster. He had to think of where to go. Buddy loused him this morning. Ellen Morton ought to have returned to the hotel from her lunch with Buddy. Outside Kimball's Galleries, Park paused. It was another interval between afternoon showers, the sun very hot, and it gave his skin a steamy sensation when the warmth passed through the wet gray sharkskin cloth. Ellen had fifty million dollars in her own name. He would not be the first artist who had asked her for a loan. He walked to the new Kamehameha Hotel to allow the brilliant flood of yellowness a chance to dry him off. Later, he was thinking, later, when he had time, when he had all the time he needed, he could plan to recapture himself with Harry.

When he entered the garden-like lobby of the new Kamehameha Hotel, it was seventeen minutes of four by the big clock above the reception desk. It was the lazy hour of the afternoon. It was almost time to come in from the sun for cocktails, but not quite. Park passed the cigar counter without checking his stride, turning left into the arcade to the hotel phone booths. At his right were the many glass doors of the empty dining room. The far double-doors at the end of the arcade were open as though framing another colored postcard view of the beach, the ocean, and the mountains. As Park glanced down the arcade, a small boy came from the beach. He looked like a black cardboard figure against the dazzling light and colors of the background.

Park opened the door of a booth to step inside, intending to ring Ellen's room. The explosion of sunlight into the arcade hurt his eyes and he closed them tightly. The retinas still held an image of that very small boy framed against all the brightness. Park opened his eyes, forgetting his intention of ringing Ellen Morton's room. The boy stopped before entering the lobby. He had been carrying beach sandals in one hand. He was carefully slipping the sandals on his bare feet. Park felt his heart beat violently.

"Well, hello there," he said, approaching the boy. "Don't I know you?"

The boy looked and said, "I'm Freddy Morton."

"Yes, I thought you were. I know your father." Park's mouth was dry and it was unexpectedly difficult to articulate when he asked, "Where's your mother?"

"She's upstairs."

"On—a fine afternoon like this?"

"She has a headache."

Park got breath into his lungs. "That's tough. You aren't leaving her all alone?"

"She sent us to the beach with Nana." The boy clutched a fifty-cent piece in his hand. He had very good manners because he said politely, "I have to go now. Nana sent me in to buy a bottle of sun lotion at the counter. She gets an awful burn if she isn't careful."

Ellen was alone, upstairs! He went hot from thinking of her and went cold again. He seemed to see her up there as something white and soft and frail. It was curious because he seemed to see both her and Buddy as one and the same and Buddy and Ellen were not one and the same.

He gave the boy an engaging smile. "Well, Freddy. Don't let me keep you then."

At the desk he learned the Mortons had the northwest corner suite on the top floor. Instead of riding the elevator he climbed the stairs. He felt very strong. He could feel the blood pounding through him vigorously. He could not understand what had hit him this morning. All he needed was one final spurt and the fix would be in by tonight. . . .

She was wearing one of those long Hawaiian holokus of a papaya yellow color which Park had seen displayed in the window of the fashionable dress shop just off the lobby of the hotel. Park had the impression of seeing a very young girl who had dressed herself in something old-fashioned and flowing in order to look very grown-up. Evidently Ellen had been lying down because the crinkly hair was tousled. One freckled cheek was still slightly crumpled from the pillow.

She asked sleepily, "Yes?" not really seeing who it was. The banjo eyes grew large. Instinctively she tried to shut the door.

He had been planning to keep everything on a polite and formal level, as a hard-pressed artist might when he found he had to ask a loan from someone of wealth who had previously shown an interest in his work. But as she acted instinctively to shut the door in his face, Park said, "Ellen—" urgently, and placed his foot against the door. She stepped back. He entered, shutting the door behind him.

She had a hand to her mouth as if to stop a cry of alarm. This was not beginning as he had hoped it would begin and he said, "I'm not going to bite you." She dropped her hand from her mouth. Instead of saying anything she stared at him from the immense blue eyes as if something unimaginable and frightful had intruded itself upon her. He had not conceived of entering as an intruder. Now he was in here he had gone too far to withdraw. He could not retreat. She was his last resource. What would a loan of twenty-six hundred dollars be to her? She had fifty-three millions.

"I wanted to see you, Mrs. Morton."

It sounded false and wrong in his ears. He waited to give her a chance to pick it up from there. But she did not pick it up from there. He cast a wary look around. Although her son had indicated that she was alone, Park had a quickening anxiety as if he had become an intruder whose visit might be discovered by a third person. He saw he was in the large living room of the suite, the glass doors open to the sun deck. Outside it was trying to shower, the light glittering from the descent of a few raindrops. In that single wary survey he saw two doors on one side of the room which were partially open into empty bedrooms. On the other side of the room was a closed door, most probably to the bath.

Well, she was alone. Because his mind had been rigorously trained to consider all security measures, the realization instantly followed that the cannery did not close until five and Buddy would not be here until between five-thirty and six. His eyes returned to her. He had not expected to have it start out like this. He felt awkward and uneasy which made it difficult for him to explain his intrusion.

He tried to say it pleasantly and lightly. "Won't you invite me to sit down?" but all the wrong notes were still there.

Well, thank you, he thought when she failed to acknowledge his appeal. She was evidently determined to make it rough for them both when he wanted to have it easy for Ellen to be gracious, the lady bountiful, the patroness of the arts.

"To tell the truth, Mrs. Morton, something's come up for me and I hoped you might give me a minute or so. I wouldn't have intruded but because you were kind enough to be interested in my paintings I thought you wouldn't mind too much if I asked for a minute or so of your time."

That, he believed, was a little better. But she still made no reply. Goddamn it! Did she expect him to get on his knees?

"The truth is, I find myself caught in a slight hole. I'll need more cash than I've got. I've all sorts of chances. I'm beginning to sell my paintings. I shouldn't like to have to quit painting to take a full-time job and I'm not even certain I could find a full-time job on the island. I've been promised a show of my paintings in February, if I can finish enough in time. With a show promised, I ought to be certain of having enough of my paintings sold to pay back any money it was necessary to borrow. If I had twenty-six hundred dollars loaned to me, I ought to be certain of paying it back by February and probably before February. With a loan to go on, I ought to be certain . . ." He was repeating himself, he realized. "It would be a very great favor to me," he said. "I'd sign a note. I'm certain I could repay you before February. Say, within thirty days. I'd make that a firm promise."

She gave him a look of loathing. "Like the firm promise you gave me last week?"

It checked him. He remembered he had told her that he would leave her alone. He said apologetically, "This is something I couldn't foresee. I'm in a hole. You must have helped other artists who've been in holes, haven't you?"

"I'm sorry I ever was so weak as to offer you an art fellowship."

He knew why she had offered him an art fellowship and so did she. Something ironic came into his voice. "If you've finally come to the conclusion I'm no great shakes as an artist remember, at least, I turned down your offer."

"Because you thought you could get more from me by refusing to leave the island. You can't extort money from me, Mr. Mattison. I'm not that weak."

He advanced toward her and stopped. By God! If she had been a man he would have hit her. All he was asking for was a loan of twenty-six hundred dollars because this morning her husband had loused him up.

"Don't be a little fool," he said roughly.

"I'm through being one, Mr. Mattison!"

She had moved so naturally to the door, even beginning to open it, that he was caught unaware. He had a frightful vision of her running along the hall, crying for help. It would ruin them both. Neither she nor he ever could satisfactorily explain to Buddy. All on the instant, he gathered himself, giving a great leap to the door. After the door slammed shut there was still an echoing silence in the room.

In a final attempt to maintain the fiction that they were two old acquaintances, if not old friends, he said, "Ellen, can't we be sensible about this? If I've frightened you by busting in like this, I'm sorry. But you don't know the hole I'm in. I'll never ask you for more than twenty-six hundred dollars and I'll pay that back as soon as I can."

Wordlessly, she shook her head. He knew he should go now because he had failed. It was finished. But he realized he had no one else to turn to in time today. He was irrevocably caught and she was caught with him. For God's sake, couldn't she understand?

"I tell you I'm in a hell of a bad way. You don't think I came to you because I liked doing it, do you? I even tried seeing Harry Kimball this afternoon before coming here."

He saw her head jerk up. "You talked with Harry Kimball?"

"Yes. But he refused to lend me money on a portrait I did. He wanted me to come back with something better. Ellen, I was stuck. I had to see you."

"You wouldn't. Oh, my God," she said faintly.

He was astonished. "I wouldn't what?"

"I know about Harry Kimball."

"Who doesn't?" he said. "Listen, let's keep Harry Kimball out of this—" and stopped because he had the impression she was crumpling before him even though she was still upon her feet.

"Last Friday I talked with Cecelia Stewart because I thought she'd been unfair to Buddy by saying Mr. Tothic had put Buddy in over her husband. Cecelia told me she went to Kimball because she was afraid the other island newspapers would try to suppress what she wanted printed."

"I suppose that's right. Harry'll print anything sensational or nasty you give—" Something briefly disconnected in Park's mind. His thoughts rocked. He saw Ellen sway, blindly placing a hand on the wall to support herself. "Ellen. Ellen—" he repeated helplessly.

His mind was back on track but it seemed to him the track came to an abrupt stop with a tearing shock. That was what she thought of him now? He looked very hard at her, groping for words to explain. She had misunderstood. He was not that much of a swine.

She spoke as if she were being suffocated. "I'll telephone the hotel manager to send up the money."

He did not move to stop her from going to the telephone. Ever since she had been old enough to know she would inherit a great fortune, he thought savagely, the people around her must have constantly warned her against the predacious creatures who might at any time spring at her for her money. He had refused money from her once when she had thought him dangerous and had tried to pay him to leave the island. Now he had no choice. Well, let her telephone. Hadn't he, Park thought with increased bitterness, come here for twenty-six hundred dollars?

He listened to her speak to the hotel manager, marveling at how much better at it a woman always would be than a man. He heard her take a gasping breath. Her voice was very low but it remained steady. She was explaining that she wished to make several large cash purchases from one of the big shops on the strip. Yes, she did know. But she preferred not to charge her purchases. It saved trouble when you paid cash. Yes, she'd wait, thank you. She hung up and did not look at Park but remained huddled against the wall, hands pressed tightly to her cheeks. It was that easy to get twenty-six hundred dollars; it was that easy when the hotel knew you had inherited fifty-three million dollars. When he paid her back next week he would write her a short thank-you note, very brief and very polite. After he had repaid her she might realize that sometimes people who asked you for a loan were not trying to blackmail you.

As he waited for the money to arrive, he heard her whisper to herself, "I don't want to stay on this island any longer," and he knew that she had forgotten he was in the room.

20

On his way to the lobby, he tried not to think of Ellen. It was done with. Although he knew he should feel relieved, he didn't feel much of anything. He decided it was because the fix still remained to be clinched with Nogusi tonight before he could draw a long breath.

Driving up Hibiscus Road, he decided what he really needed was to go with Laina for a month to Mexico where he could get used to the idea of not being loused up again. A month in Mexico would give Buddy and Ellen time to depart with their two kids. He might even recapture what Harry had said was gone from his painting. Although it was unreasonable to be irked by what Harry had said about his portrait, still, there was that obscure gnawing.

Laina must have heard him enter the house for she called cheerfully from the kitchen, "Hey, Park? I'll be with you in a minute. What do you think? I've made real yeast rolls for dinner tonight. Boy, am I getting to be the cook around here!"

Park went as far as the living-room table and thought he could go no farther. He felt drugged. It was like slowly awakening from a bad dream and realizing you still had a hell of a head on from last night. He inched the chair closer to the table, rested his arms on the table, his head on his arms.

It was tough when you had to get it through a woman. It was Buddy's fault. No, he blamed both Ellen and Buddy. He wished he had never seen either one of them. They were both filled with righteousness and good works because their consciences would not give them rest, but they could not carry through. Each was a tortoise inside a golden shell. If you prodded hard enough they withdrew their heads. Park recalled Buddy's pinched face from this morning. He remembered how Ellen's face had turned a dead white with a faint bluish tinge to it.

He had not known it would gnaw at him like this. He had liked them but they had always been his enemies. Until now he had not thought of them in that light, but it was true. The real wrong boy was not Nogusi nor Subie, or even Bull Amani. Ever since arriving, Buddy Morton had been the wrong boy and Park had to get him out if Park were to remain and be the right boy for five sweet years. Park had given too much attention to E. P.'s interests and failed to look after his own. He had failed until almost too late to appreciate that it was Buddy Morton, no one else, who was really the wrong boy. By going to Ellen and deliberately holding back when she believed he was black-mailing her, he had got through to Buddy. Now, Ellen would go. She would pack up with her two kids and Buddy would go with her. But Park felt no satisfaction in his success.

He lifted his head. He realized that Laina had forgotten to turn off her bedroom radio. She was always forgetting. What was that song?

> *He made them laugh and he made them cry;*
> *Oh, he was the cockeyed mayor of Kaunakakai . . .*

Park remembered how not so very long ago that tune had run so cheerfully through his head. Perhaps, he thought, he could find a place remote and secluded enough in Mexico not to hear the radio for a whole month. As he listened, he heard all the familiar sounds of the house. A wet fresh wind was blowing up from the ocean beyond the cliff. He heard Laina busy in the kitchen. A smell of baking was wafted to him when the kitchen door opened. Laina entered, pausing to look rather anxiously at him. He realized he needed a bath and a change to fresh clothes.

He tried to straighten up in the chair. Laina's dark red hair was pulled back tightly from her smooth forehead, knotted with a ribbon into a hard hunter's loop to keep it out of her way while she was cooking dinner. She quickly stripped off her apron, dropping it on the nearest chair. She was wearing a dress he liked, the one with the blue circus prints which always gave her something of the air of a girl returning from a high time at a party. Her eyes glowed. A smudge of white flour on one curving cheek heightened the colors of her skin.

He made an effort. "You look slicked up, Caroline."

"I wanted to look slicked up for you," said Laina, and put her hand on his shoulder. "You look kinda pooped."

"I feel pooped."

When she leaned over to kiss his cheek, she smelled fresh and scrubbed and beautiful. "You wait here while I fix your bath." She smiled at him. "You haven't heard the news, I'll bet."

"What news?"

Park had to push on the table to get to his feet. That talk with Ellen had taken a great deal out of him.

"On the radio," Laina said. "I was listening to station BYQ on the Chevy's radio this afternoon when I drove back from the city."

Park recalled that when he had been here this afternoon for the portrait of Laina she had not been home. If Laina had been here, it came to him, and he had been willing to ask her for her savings, at least he could have spared himself that bitter scene with Ellen at the hotel. But perhaps it was better the way it was; it was inevitable for him to have to settle with Ellen and Buddy at some point, and this had done it.

"Where were you this afternoon?"

"I'll tell you in a minute. First, I've got something really maikailoa to tell you!"

That meant something wonderful or very special. Ordinarily Laina tried to model herself after her conception of mainland girls. She was careful not to speak as you heard the kanaka girls speak, using a Hawaiian word when a Hawaiian word was more expressive. He glanced at Laina and envied her freshness and vitality. He was feeling very old when he should be feeling very young and very happy.

"Suppose," Park asked, "I get a bath and you give it to me after I'm not so pooped?"

"That Tolliver woman was on the radio this afternoon!"

Park got as far as the bedroom door. "Look. I don't give a damn what she gets on."

"Park, you dope. You don't understand. It was some sort of 'Aloha Program' for all the tourists taking the afternoon flight to Honolulu. They had her saying how sorry she was to leave this happy island, with an army general and somebody from a soap company in New York. And," Laina said, taking a quick breath, "if you want to know, I think the Tolliver woman was a little stinko. But anyway—she's gone. She's flown for home. She's pau. I'm *so* damned happy!"

"Well, fine." Park was glad somebody on this island was so damned happy. "If you're happy, I'll pick it up from you."

His voice sounded all right to him, too. He could pick it up from her once he got away for a month to Mexico. He continued into the bedroom, Laina chattering cheerfully along with him— and he felt himself foundering. It hit him harder than it had this morning. He plunged to his knees.

He heard Laina's startled cry, "Park! Park!"

He struggled silently, pulling himself onto the bed with his hands. He felt Laina's strong arms supporting him. He got himself seated on the edge of the bed, his legs dangling numbly to the floor. His stomach was writhing and he had the taste of raw pineapple and bromelin in his mouth. Laina kneeled, tightly grasping his hands.

"Park! Are you all right?"

He asked, muffled, "Leave me alone a minute."

She jumped up. "I'll telephone Dr. Raisho."

"Goddamn it, don't. I'll be fine in a minute."

"What's wrong? Tell me."

What could he tell her? He had to think, and he could not think very well. What was wrong with him? He could not tell Laina it felt as if small foxes were biting through the walls of his stomach because he was still feeling the effects of that scene with Ellen. He had to think of something.

"I lost my job at Kirsch's, if you want to know."

It was not very good. He should have thought of something better but it hurt his head when he tried to think of anything. He looked up at her. He heard her quick intake of breath.

She said, "Don't give me a scare like that again. Good night! You lost a job. Is *that* all?"

Now he had to get on with it. . . .

"We'll be on short rations, I'm afraid."

"Don't you think," she asked explosively, "I've been on short rations before?"

She swung toward her dressing table. The thin print skirt lifted and fell lightly around the long bare legs. She jerked impatiently at the drawer of the table, taking something from it with both hands. She returned to Park. She thrust her hands to him, palms up. Each hand contained a neat packet of bank notes.

She said rebelliously, "I told you Sunday I was going to draw out my money. I drove my heap into the city today. It's three thousand and twenty-two dollars. Here, take it!"

Park did not move. He had all the money he needed tonight. In a day or so, E. P. would have transferred a hundred thousand dollars into Kirsch's account. There would not be a strike. Nogusi would resign and leave for the mainland. Buddy and Ellen and the two boys would be going. All the wrong people would be going. The Tolliver woman had already gone.

"I'm tired of this rotten island," she said. "I'm not afraid of short rations. That money and whatever you've got is enough to buy us steamship tickets to Mexico and to keep us while I find a job and you begin painting." She looked down at him and said very seriously, "I won't stay on this rotten island any longer. I'll go with you anywhere you say, but I won't stay here any longer. I'll go alone if you won't go."

He tried to rise and could not. If he didn't go with her she would take the money and go for good. How could he hope for five sweet years on the island if Laina were not here with him? How could there be any sweet years for him, anywhere, if Laina were not there? His expression of agony must have struck a pang through her. She sat beside him, thrusting the two packets of bank notes into his coat pocket.

"There!" She smiled, wanting him to smile back.

He felt loaded. He could feel the heavy wad of money in his wallet pressing against his hip. All day he had run desperately trying to get together a few thousand dollars. Now it was being showered on him when he no longer needed it. His first impulse was to return Laina's savings, then he thought, keep it. Without her savings she would go nowhere without him. By God, even Laina was horsing him without realizing it. In a month he would be free to take her to Mexico. When they were in Mexico, he would have another month to talk her around. He put his arm over her shoulder.

"If you want the truth, we just can't pack and go off to Mexico tomorrow."

"Why can't we?"

"Because I can't leave yet. That's why."

"Tell me why you can't."

He had been lying so much to her that one more should have been easy. But his brain was aching. There were no more lanes for him to go down.

"It's that fight, isn't it?" demanded Laina. "You told me you bet on that fight."

"Yes. It's something like that."

"Park, I don't care what it is but just tell me. How much did you lose? How much have you got to pay?"

He had a sense of falling into one hole as fast as he pulled himself from another. His head was splitting.

"Five thousand dollars," he said.

"To the betting commissioner?" Laina cried. "Park, Jake Kutu might kill you if you don't pay up. You don't know Jake. You're worse than my old man on Kauai. He used to get himself in jams and lie to my mother to keep her from worrying. But she always knew when he was lying and it made it even worse for her. Are you dead broke? How much have you got?"

Ellen had given him two thousand-dollar bills and six hundred-dollar bills. It had surprised him a little when the hotel desk had sent up the two thousand-dollar bills.

"Twenty-six hundred dollars."

"That was why you had to see Mr. Meaker last night? You didn't have enough? Oh, damn it, Park, why did you ever get mixed up with those men? You're an artist." Then she said, "Well, good night! With my three thousand and your money, we've got more than enough. What are we worrying for? How much time have you got to pay up?"

Park did not reply at first. It was slowly coming to him. If only you hung on long enough and refused to despair you still could be very happy. He realized suddenly that he could stop running so fast because it was right there before him. All that remained was to clinch it tonight with Nogusi.

"Tonight," he said. "I'm supposed to pay up tonight."

She gave a great sigh. "Why are we worrying?" she repeated. "Pay up and we'll start fresh. Anyway, that three thousand is mostly money you've put into my account. Now I'm giving it back. I can feel happier about myself again because I won't have been living here because you paid me to. And I'm awfully tired of sitting around, Park. . . . I can get a job here to help us earn money for tickets off this rotten island. So can you. Haven't you ever lost a job before? Just because Kirsch doesn't need you any more doesn't mean you can't find another bookkeeping job, does it? You can sell more paintings, too. Have you showed Mr. Kimball that painting you did of me? It wasn't here when I got back."

It was as if Laina had inadvertently touched a raw spot which Park had not known he had. He turned his face from her too late.

"Oh, Park!" he looked back. He saw her face squeeze up. Then she said furiously, "I told you he'd give you a hotfoot someday. Did he say why he didn't like it?"

"I never was a painter," Park protested. "Hell. You knew I wasn't."

"I like that!" she said angrily. "Mr. Kimball's a damn fool! I liked that portrait you did of me, didn't I? Are you going to quit because a stupid old man gave you a hotfoot? You can paint when we get to Mexico. In a month or two months we'll both earn enough to buy tickets to Mexico. I'm a good secretary— you watch me," she promised. "I'll find someone in Mexico who needs a good secretary even if I can't speak Spanish. I'll help carry us until you begin selling your paintings."

She was like a strong fresh wind blowing in from the sea. He turned, wanting to take her into his arms.

"Hey, no," she protested, again anxious about him. "Go easy. I'm a big girl, Park. Don't you know you nearly passed out on me?"

"Don't worry," said Park. "I won't drop you. I won't ever drop you."

She stretched out her legs, pulled the blue print to cover the rounded knees, and cautiously yielded herself into his arms. He did not drop her. He felt her slowly relax. As evening's darkness filled the bedroom he saw the clear outline of the face below his gradually blur and become mysterious and shadowy.

Presently, she stirred comfortably and tipped up her face to whisper, "I nearly died when I saw you stumble and go down on your knees."

"It was a stomach cramp. It caught me unexpectedly."

"You don't eat enough. Suppose you had something wrong with your stomach?"

"Anybody can have a stomach cramp. Let's don't talk about my stomach."

"Park, you never like to talk about anything that bothers you. Suppose you had ulcers?"

"I haven't got ulcers. You have to worry to have ulcers."

"Park, you worry all the time. . . .

"You worry the worst way, too," she was saying seriously from the darkness. "You don't explode like I do and get rid of it. Sometimes at night I wake up and it makes me want to cry because I can feel you twitching and jerking in your sleep and there's nothing I can do to help because you never talk to me or tell me. It's not good for you to hold your worries inside. Why don't you tell me? Don't you trust me enough?"

"Hell, yes. I trust you."

"What's the use of being like this if we don't share things? I don't like to think you only like to be in bed with me. I wish you'd promise you'll tell me the next time you're in trouble. I can stand short rations with you. I can stand anything with you except not having you share things with me. Just tell me next time so I'll know I'm really your girl."

"You are my girl," Park told her, his voice rough. "As long

as I live there'll never be another like you for me. But I want you to know something. I want you to know I don't like having to take your money tonight."

"You're not taking it," said Laina from the darkness. "I'm giving it to you."

"Caroline . . ."

"Don't say anything more for a minute. Just hold me as hard as you can."

Park did not understand what it was that gave him a feeling that unexpectedly Laina and he had come together over all the hurdles and were at last in that long delicious cool space. He did not want the moment ever to cease. "Mrs. Mattison," he was thinking. "Caroline McKenzie Mattison." He would be proud of her, too. If he had married her sooner, he would not have had to take her savings tonight because he was afraid she might pack up and leave without him. When you married, and worked at making a good marriage, you began having something solid which could weather even very tough storms. He thought Laina would be hard to beat at making a go at a marriage. . . .

"My rolls!" wailed Laina, sitting up in the warm darkness. He heard her sniffing. "They're burning!"

While she set the table, he took a quick shower. When he returned to the bedroom she was putting out fresh linen for him. She picked up his crumpled suit and scowled at it.

"What's wrong?"

"Park, I guess I was just dumb but I sent all your suits to the cleaners' today. We still aren't caught up after that trip to the other island. Some of your white ducks were starting to mildew." She placed the coat on a hanger in the closet, and folded his trousers carefully on a second hanger. "Have you been trying to swim in this suit? It looks awful."

"I got caught in the rain."

She said dubiously, "I could try pressing your pants tonight."

He thought of the last time she had tried to press his pants.

He said, "It's not worth the trouble. They're all right if you can stand seeing me in them."

"The Chinaman ought to have one of your suits ready by tomorrow noon."

"Well, that's fine. Are we about ready to eat?"

He felt more refreshed than he would have believed possible. He did not know how to describe it when he thought about himself and the agony which had struck him, doubling him up. He was aware of no aftereffects except possibly a small shaky feeling of relief. It was strange, but he felt fine. In the bathroom mirror he thought that he looked pale and he had been sweating but he always sweated after a warm shower and a hard rubdown. He didn't feel very hungry but he never did feel very hungry, anyway. When he sat at the table, Laina's rolls tasted good. She had washed her face and brushed the shining hair and altogether it seemed to Park he had been a fool for delaying so long. Before he could speak, she asked him what time it was by his watch and there came a slight tension between them. She knew he had to leave the house tonight. It was only seven-thirty, he said. They had all of another hour.

Laina said, "I'll go with you and stay in the car when you pay off Jake Kutu. Park, he's dangerous."

"No, let me handle it my way tonight, alone. I want to keep you out of it."

"I'm tired of you keeping me out of it. I want to be with you."

"If that's how you feel," he said, trying to make it light and casual as if it were something they both knew was inevitable, "why don't we get married? Then we'd be certain of being with each other for the rest of—"

He got up quickly from the chair, going around the table to her. . . .

He had never suspected she wanted so much to be married to him. He could be very happy married to her. He wondered why he had not thought sooner of such a simple solution for making certain he would be very happy for much longer than just the next five years.

He found it very much like the first time he had visited Mama Pikea's except that everything flowed more easily this time because both Willi Nogusi and Park knew their way around with each other. Nogusi gave Park a cigar and it was better than the cigar he had given Park on the first visit. There was one moment of slight difficulty when Park counted the ten thousand dollars. Evidently Willi had expected to receive more than ten thousand. It was not that Willi was greedy but he had beaten Bull Amani. Willi considered himself a better man than Bull Amani and worth more than him.

But it seemed to Park that he knew exactly what to say even when there was a slight strain. He said the ten thousand was merely a first installment. The second came after Nogusi did his job this week. When Nogusi repudiated Herby Subie tomorrow, spoke in favor of the right boy, resigned for Wong to succeed him, and sailed for the mainland, a second installment would be mailed to his Reno bar. There it was.

Nogusi began smiling again.

Actually, Park continued, the second installment amounted to five thousand. But Park was taking his cut from the five thousand, one-half of it. Still, twelve and a half grand was a tidy sum to receive for resigning from a union and going back to the mainland. Park believed it made everything flow easier to emphasize that he was taking his cut; and he was right. Nogusi nodded, agreeing.

"Yes, sir. You make a fine manager. That gives me jus' what I wanted."

Park thought that made them both happy for it gave him just what he wanted, too. He thought E. P. would also be very happy. If E. P. was in the hospital, not because of flu bugs but because he had started puking and needed injections to stop, knowing the fix was finally clinched would be better than any injections Dr. Austen might have ordered.

Park let all of it come to him slowly, to relish it all the more. Although he was in a hurry to return to Laina, he waited to have one more drink with Willi. He almost said, "Willi, I'm being married tomorrow," but he couldn't let Willi intrude on anything having to do with Laina.

Willi put down his glass. "I can get you a girl?"

"No, thanks. I'm pooped." Park stood. Willi didn't know it but Park had a girl. Tomorrow at five o'clock in the afternoon,

Park and his girl were being married by a Mormon minister. Park did not know what a Mormon marriage ceremony would be like, but he was certain it would be all in the book and you could ask for nothing better than to have it regularized, clinched tight, for all your life. Laina wanted to be married by a minister and Park had decided he wanted it to be by a minister, too. He had known the Mormons were strong in Hawaii, but he hadn't known Laina was a Mormon until she told him after dinner, her eyes crinkling with amusement.

At the door, Park said, "We're all set?"

"I'm gonna go in there swinging. I'm gonna work close with Mr. Wong."

Willi believed a Chinese *hui*, an association, on the island had paid for the prestige of having Charley Wong in as head of the unions. It was not particularly stupid of Willi to have such a notion. There was a great deal of talk on all the islands of how the *huis* were rising since the war, becoming more powerful as the domination of the old haole kamaaina families rapidly disintegrated. It was just as well that Willi had such a notion, Park thought. It made everything more secure.

"That's the way to look at it," Park told Willi. "You go in there swinging for Wong, tomorrow. Good luck, Willi."

He could not drive back to Laina quickly enough.

In the house, she put her arms around him. Although she had put her arms around him many times before somehow it was different tonight. He had not known she had still more of herself to give to him.

"It's all right," Park said.

"You're paid up?"

"We're fixed. It's all right. Just don't worry."

"I couldn't help worrying."

"Well, you don't have to any more."

After they had turned off the lights in the bedroom she said, "Park, I telephoned Hattie and Herby Subie. You don't know how excited they were. They're coming tomorrow."

They were her best friends on the island. He had not been able to refuse that much when Laina asked him if she could invite them to the ceremony. He knew how sensitive she was.

He did not want her to think he was ashamed of her friends. He wasn't. His feeling of wariness about Herby Subie was not because Herby was of Japanese descent. He didn't believe Herby Subie would be here tomorrow for the wedding, but he could not tell Laina. At the labor hall tomorrow, Nogusi would cut loose. Herby Subie would be much too occupied to come to a wedding on the other side of the island.

Her voice asked, "Haven't you any friends you want to ask for tomorrow?"

It came to Park how alone he was on this island after a year and a half. All he really had was Laina. By Meaker was a friend, a good friend, but they could not see each other freely. He wondered what By would think of his marriage. Probably By would not have much time to think of it once the news of Nogusi's surprise resignation was out. Lew Kirsch was a business associate. E. P. was not a friend in the sense of what a friend meant. A gap always existed between you and a client even if you pretended none existed and even if the client always wanted to see more of you.

"The reason I haven't asked anyone is that I've been too busy with you and painting and earning a living to make any friends on the island. I hope your friends will be my friends."

"Oh, Park. I want it that way."

"Well, it'll be that way."

Presently her voice broke the silence. "Would it be awfully extravagant if I bought a new dress tomorrow to be married in? I know Mabel Ena at the Kamehameha dress shop. Mabel used to work with me at the cannery. She promised to give me a discount if ever I bought any clothes from her. As soon as I get a job—"

"Listen. We're not that broke. Get the prettiest dress in the shop for tomorrow afternoon."

He thought of Laina and himself sailing away from this island to some far shore to be by themselves for a month. It was difficult for him to realize how very happy he was.

21

L aina must have awakened at least a half-hour before he had.
When he opened his eyes she was dressed as if she were
going somewhere. He sat up in bed, smiling at her.

"I thought we were being married today? If you're going
somewhere, I'll go with you."

He couldn't go anywhere with her, she informed him, because
he didn't have anything respectable to wear until she returned
and brought his white ducks from the Chinaman's. She was going to buy the new dress for herself at the Kamehameha shop
and afterward have her hair washed and waved at the hairdressers' in the hotel to save time. She was in a terrible rush
because she had overslept. It was fifteen minutes of eleven, now.
She had made coffee for Park but he would have to boil his own
eggs this morning. She would try to be back by two o'clock,
perhaps sooner. She kissed him hastily.

"Hey—"

She paused in the bedroom door. "I do have to hurry."

"Watch that damned hairdresser!"

"Not a snip. I want it like you want it for my wedding day,"
she promised.

After Laina drove off in her Chevy, he tried to sleep but he
was too wide awake. He looked at his watch. It was four minutes
after eleven. In five hours and fifty-six minutes he would be a
married man. He wished he had thought of asking Laina to

marry him five months ago, but five months ago she might not have been ready to want to marry him.

While he was shaving, the pleasant fancy struck Park of holding the wedding in the garden, providing it didn't rain. The garden was flowery and fragrant, the gardenias waxy and white from last night's showers. And there was the immense view of the sea beyond, all across the horizon. It was sentimental, perhaps, but this morning Park liked the feeling. He could relax with the secure knowledge that at last everything was flowing very smoothly because he had got over the hump. Years from now Laina and Park would have the memory of their wedding in that tiny Hawaiian garden on top of the cliff. It would be a memory to cherish.

He took a bath and he did not feel pooped. He pulled on the shorts, the socks, the clean shirt, and the white shoes which Laina had remembered to put out for him but he did not use the silk bathrobe she expected him to wear because he did not like going around the house with no pants on. He pulled down his crumpled gray sharkskin trousers and knocked the hanger holding the coat to the floor. When he picked up the coat he felt a small hard object in the breast pocket.

So much had happened yesterday that he had completely forgotten! The little airplane charm was in a box the size of a pill box. Park opened it. The tiny propeller still turned. The diamond chips gleamed brightly. Well, it would be even more of a surprise for Laina today. He would give it to her as a wedding gift.

He whistled to himself. By God, and what about a ring for Laina? You couldn't have a wedding without a ring. He had almost forgotten. He pulled on his coat and was on his way from the front room to the kitchen. He stopped. He heard a car roll into the gravel driveway. Perhaps Laina had forgotten something and was returning. He hurried to open the front door for her. He knew it was foolish to have such a feeling for Laina, as if she were his first love. But he was glad he had it. He felt very young.

It was not Laina's Chevy in the drive, though. It was By Meaker in his Plymouth and Millie was there with him. He stopped in the doorway, astonished. Why had By picked today to pay a social call with Millie. What was By thinking of? By was having trouble getting out of the car. In his haste, he caught his coat pocket on the door handle and instead of taking the time to disengage his pocket he jerked savagely. Park heard the sound of fabric ripping. He wondered if By was drunk. He must be drunk. He came toward Park, staggering a little as he ran. He was holding a rolled newspaper in one hand and at any other time Park might have laughed because By looked as if he had hung one on himself this morning. His thin face was white and when he got to Park he stopped and could not seem to speak; his mouth worked spasmodically. Park started with alarm. By was not at all drunk.

"What's wrong?"

"We're blown up."

Park glanced toward the car and began pulling By inside. "O. K. We've had trouble before. But you shouldn't have brought Millie along if we've got more—"

"Trouble?" By's voice pitched high. His legs and arms were jerking. "Papa, I brought Millie with me because we're getting out. We're leaving. It's over. It's finished. It's not just trouble. We've been blown up."

Park felt as if the whole house had momentarily lifted, dropping back on its foundations with a jar which he could feel up through his feet to his spine and head. It had been fixed last night. He could not imagine how Nogusi had rolled out the wrong numbers at the labor hall today. Everything had been loaded. It was all secured.

"What happened?" he asked sharply.

When By tried to take a breath he choked. His eyes bulged. He hit frantically at his pants leg with the rolled newspaper. "That Morton woman has blown us up."

"Ellen Morton blew us up? What the hell are you talking about?"

"Mrs. Morton blew us up. Her husband spilled on us to her but she set off the dynamite. For some goddamned reason we'll never know she went to Harry Kimball some time late yesterday and blew the works. You know that job press in the city that gets out Harry's paper?"

By's face was still like old parchment but he was talking more coherently. Park nodded. It seemed to Park that his heart had stopped a full beat and was still not beating with any regularity.

"Somehow Harry must have got the owner and printers rounded up because they started putting a special edition together around midnight last night, working for triple rates. Because Howie had done one of the printers a few favors, the printer sneaked a rough copy and got it to Howie when the shop took a break this morning for late breakfast. On his way to find a ship to get off the island, Howie had the guts to come first to my office. There you are. I rushed for Millie and drove off. Let's get going. I've got an airplane standing by for us. By two o'clock Harry will have twenty-five thousand copies spread over the island and I don't want to be here when a pack of Flips start hunting for me."

By started for the front door but Park grabbed his arm. "No. Let's see what Harry's got against us first."

"You can read it in the car."

"No, goddamn it. Let me see it now before I start running."

"I tell you, he's got everything. He's got your picture. He's got you from the time you used to work in Hertz and Finnhaven. He's got me with almost as much space as you've got. He's listed Danny, the whorehouses, the towers, the radio, the newspaper tie-ins—Oh, my God! Millie passed out when I was fool enough to let her grab it. He's split Kirsch down the seams. He's exposed Howie. He tells of the movie house we burned, about the jokers we had beat up. Papa, I want to get out of here. Kimball's even printed that you were planning to smear Herby as a Red."

That took Park in the pit of the stomach. What would Laina have to say when she learned he had not hesitated to betray a confidence received from her? He said harshly to By, "I want to see what he's got printed," and took the rolled paper, unfolding it on the table. "Beat it, if you can't wait a minute."

Park heard By's breath rasp his throat. "Just make it fast then."

It was an eight-page issue, hastily printed, the ink still wet.

Park didn't know where Harry found the photograph of him printed under the front-page banner heading:

NEW DISCLOSURES: TOTHIC'S THOUGHT-CONTROL THUGS EXPOSED!

He went through it hastily. He saw it was all there, exactly as By had said. He recalled that Harry had tried to pump him on his background. Harry had been planning to write a little brochure of Parker Mattison for a show of Park's paintings in February. Here was far more than a little brochure on Park. It made him wince to see what Harry had written. He let his eyes go rapidly down the columns as he turned one page after another.

Harry had missed nothing. He had written that the fight between Amani and Nogusi was rigged so thousands of islanders would lose their entire savings by betting on a man certain to lose. Yes, here it was in a boxed editorial on page four where Harry had given space to Herby Subie. Park scanned a few lines: "The problem of communistic infiltration is serious enough in Hawaii without complicating and confusing issues by smearing innocent labor leaders. We can state that Mattison was planning to launch an attack upon Mr. Herbert Subie, recently reelected secretary of the federated unions. Mr. Subie was to be slandered as a Red. If that slander failed to drive him off the island, more determined measures were to be taken which might end in Mr. Subie's death. . . ."

Park could feel something gnawing in his stomach. He had been confident that he had brought everything to a successful conclusion yesterday with Buddy and Ellen. After giving him the twenty-six hundred dollars yesterday afternoon, instead of considering it a termination and an ending, Ellen must have told Buddy everything. It had never crossed Park's mind that she would do such a thing. She had made too much of it. She must have thought after striking at her once that he would continue to strike at her. Because she believed he was threatening to go to Kimball to have a nasty piece of scandal printed about her, she had gone to Kimball first, Park saw vaguely, to forestall him. It had never occurred to him that she would stick her neck out or that Buddy would stick out his neck by attacking him.

In that high-pitched tone, By was saying for God's sake, hurry. But Park turned to the last page and saw something he wanted to read:

"This island cannot express its gratitude too strongly to Mr. and Mrs. Wilfred Morton. Although Mr. Morton's family has long been connected with the island's growth and development through the Tothics, he has never been responsible for the policies of Paradise Products while under the regime of Mr. E. P. Tothic, Sr., or Junior Tothic. Without the larger resources of his wife's assets, Mrs. Morton having inherited the estate of her father, a lumber magnate and financier, it is doubtful if Mr. Morton could purchase control of the company; but as was exclusively reported to your editor, he plans to do so as quickly as it can be effected, and also meet the bond issue due early next year. Mrs. Morton has informed your editor, 'I think everyone on the island should know the truth of what has been attempted against them. I have learned the truth and have been appalled by it. I shall not hesitate in any way to assist my husband to restore a working relationship based on truth and common decency and fair dealing between the working population of this island and the company in which Mr. Morton's family for so many years has held an interest. . . .' "

Park suddenly crumpled the eight pages in his fist. He had seen enough. He was not interested in reading more of Ellen's statement. It was as if suddenly, between one minute and another, the world had gone on by and had left him standing where he was. He was still the same as ever. But he knew it was all over—it was irrevocably finished. All his worries were ended. He had an odd feeling of relief. He would not have to go just a little faster because the need to go just a little faster and just a little faster had ended. He saw By sag against the wall, holding his hands tightly to his face. By mumbled distractedly, "Why did she do it to us? She's got fifty million dollars. Did she want to blow us out to get that goddamn Buddy in as big man?"

"I pushed her too hard," Park said. He could be almost detached, thinking back to yesterday afternoon.

By's face looked ravaged. There was a constant jerking of his body which he could not control. "You did *what* to that bitch?"

Ellen wasn't a bitch, Park thought. By God, for all of that Sunday School air about her, she had stuck out her neck. Park felt as if he were in the dead center of a storm, neither By nor he moving. In a minute they would have to move very rapidly because when your hand was tipped your only hope was to move rapidly.

Park said and was surprised how his voice had lost its normal pitch, "I had Nogusi taped. I couldn't tell you but he was going to resign. Buddy loused it for me yesterday morning and I couldn't locate you for money so I went to Ellen Morton. I knew something unimportant about her a long time ago and I thought I could scare her into thinking—" He broke off because of By's wild stare.

"That's a laugh for you. Holy Mother! You had Nogusi taped? I caught a special radio flash on the radio coming up here. It reported a fight in the labor council meeting this morning. It said Nogusi had been attacked by two of the labor delegates and in trying to get away had busted Subie's arm and was nearly beaten to death before the police got there." By took several unsteady steps toward the hall. "I didn't connect it. I expect Subie got word from Harry. Everything's gone to pieces. Millie," he said, as if his thoughts were going off at a tangent, "wants to divorce me. You should have heard what she called me. Oh, Christ, papa!" He clinched his hands to his head.

"You can't tell about a woman," Park said, thinking how Ellen had revealed more strength than he had known she possessed. "Give Millie time," and his voice had a bitter-iron quality in it. "What's this airplane you've got? I don't want a pack of Flips on me, either." By moved jerkily to the door and paused. Both of them were going past dead center now.

By said, "I told you last week I was going to have to think of Millie if our hands got tipped and I saw Ken Ludwig, Sunday—" his eyes bulged, trying to get breath. His words came pelting faster. "Ken's got a Stinson at Iki airport. I phoned Ken. He's waiting for us. I'm hoping you're right and those Flips won't think of trying to hunt us at one of the smaller airports. Ken will get us to Honolulu. Come on. We've got thirty miles to drive. . . ." By went through the door. He stopped. He returned, roughly grabbing Park as if he thought Park to be in a state of shock, too dazed to save himself. "Let's shove, papa. We've still got a margin but it isn't too big a margin. That job press can't get newspapers out like a big newspaper press but Howie warned me by two o'clock the damned sheets would be on their way all over the island."

Park resisted. As he got away from dead center, he thought of Laina, this time much more urgently. "Hold it. I'll have to get Laina. She's at the dress shop or hairdressers'."

"Have her meet us later in Honolulu. That Stinson only carries four people. It's a hundred and seventy-five mile flight. Ken can't crowd in more than the three of us and himself."

"Listen. You go on with Millie," Park said. "I'll get Laina."

"You can't stay on this island. By the middle of the afternoon those Flips'll start hunting for you and the police won't be able—"

"No, here's how we'll do it. There's a fair-sized sailing boat down at the cove. Laina's rented it before. Look—" Park said, with a feeling of picking up a few of the pieces. "It's a night's sail. I'll meet you at the Pan-Pacific flight offices in Honolulu at, say, noon tomorrow."

By hesitated. "I hate leaving you."

"Nuts. We'll manage. . . . Look. When I get Laina I'll wireless Lew from the hotel. We can't leave him holding any bag."

"I had Elsie Flavola wireless him we were out of business . . ." By's face became convulsed with agony. He looked searchingly at Park and said hastily, "I'd like you to know something. I'd like you to know it was good while it lasted, papa."

"We'll still be in there pitching together when we get back to the mainland, won't we?"

"Sure, sure. 'Mattison and Meaker'—"

Then By turned and ran with great awkward strides toward the Plymouth.

It was raining but it was not raining very hard when Park drove the Buick down Hibiscus Road. He hoped By had a good pilot. A rain squall would not trouble a big transport, but Park knew that a four-passenger Stinson was not in the same category with a big transport and a hundred and seventy-five miles over the ocean was something to think about. He preferred trying to make it in a sailboat.

He was concentrating on driving, but his thoughts did not continue along any one line. They were like flashes against a darkness. He was anxious about Laina and impatient to get to her. It was like finding yourself in an earthquake and continuing to live. You saw one house totter and smash, and another, a chimney crumple, the whole side of a building go falling with a roar into the street. Nogusi had walked into it this morning. Evidently he had swung but he had not swung hard enough to get out of what he had walked into. But Herby Subie's arm had been broken. Well, that would help enrage the Flips. Everything would help to enrage the Flips. The labor delegates had beaten Nogusi nearly to death. Park had seen a few men nearly beaten to death.

After picking up Laina at the dress shop or hairdressers' it would be folly to return to the house to pack; he would drive straight to Ilohana Cove with her. Then—there seemed to be another flashing in the darkness of his mind. Yesterday, he had pressed too hard on Ellen Morton. It had made her believe he was the wrong boy. It had sent her to her husband when it never had crossed Park's mind that she would go to her husband. It was too late now for hindsight. But it occurred to Park that he had been secure only so long as neither Ellen nor Buddy told each other everything. He wondered about them. He had a feeling there was something about Ellen and Buddy, or something about what they had made of their marriage, which he had missed. Instead of having their marriage shatter, evidently they had joined even more firmly with Ellen helping Buddy buy a controlling interest in Paradise Products. It would be a risk, too. Buddy might not be able to save Paradise Products. It had never crossed Park's mind that Ellen and Buddy were prepared to stick out their necks.

Although something began shaping in his mind about Ellen and Buddy, his anxiety over Laina intruded. He was driving very fast down the grade and the pavement was slippery from the light rains. He was watching closely for Laina's Chevy after he turned right into the four-lane highway. There was always the chance she might have finished early and might be on her way back. He did not want to miss her. He did not want Hattie Subie telephoning to Laina at the house and it was possible Hattie might do exactly that.

By had said Harry's special edition would not be distributed until around two o'clock. Even if any early copies were distributed by now along the strip, at least Laina would not have seen one if she were at the hairdressers' or trying on dresses in a shop. He would pick her up and take the beach road west from the hotel to Ilohana Cove. It might be safer to hire old man Hinoni to make the trip with them and help Laina sail the boat.

Park did not care how much he had to pay. He had all of Laina's savings in his pocket. Her money was not the big money he had expected from E. P. But now that everything else seemed to be shrinking and reducing into new proportions, a wad of three thousand dollars was a good-sized sum. And he still had Kimball's check. He had that to cash. A random thought passed through his brain: He wondered how E. P. was taking the news. Perhaps no one had yet informed E. P. Again, he was thinking of Laina. She came first. He could phone E. P. from the hotel.

It took him a few extra minutes to find parking space for his Buick. He made his way to the dress shop which was tucked off on one side of the hotel lobby. It had a small salon, the fitting rooms hidden in the rear. Park felt very large and out of place in the completely feminine little salon. A tall languid woman behind a gilt desk remembered Miss McKenzie very well. She was the tall girl with the beautiful red hair? Yes, Miss Ena had attended to Miss McKenzie. But Miss Ena was in a fitting room with another customer. She thought Miss McKenzie had gone toward the hairdressers' fifteen or twenty minutes ago. But she hadn't really noticed. The hairdressers' was just beyond, to the left, she said, three doors.

Park had a sensation of running although he was still walking.

He must have missed Laina by only a few minutes. When Park asked at the hairdressers', no one really seemed to know for whom Park was looking. He had always had a fear in the back of his mind that some day he might lose her. Suppose she was now gone for good? He turned, going back to the dress shop. She could not have gone very far. She had no money to go anywhere. He stopped, seeing a girl across the lobby. But the girl was not Laina. He thought of how Laina would smile at him when she saw him after an interval. He remembered how her face was when it was without makeup, her lashes and eyebrows almost invisible against the curving rich warmness of her skin. He would not leave the island until he found her.

When Park returned to the dress shop he lost several more minutes before the languid woman agreed to bring Miss Ena in for a minute. Miss Ena was chubby and she probably had Japanese in her. When Park asked about Laina it seemed to him that Miss Ena regarded him in a manner that was rather odd and personal.

Yes, Caroline had been here. She had selected a dress. The dress was waiting for her, wrapped. But a customer had entered while Caroline was waiting for Miss Ena to finish wrapping the dress. Miss Ena paused. It seemed to Park that Miss Ena's slanted eyes held something malicious in them.

"The woman was carrying a newspaper," said Miss Ena, "and Caroline noticed the picture on the front page. Caroline asked the woman to see the newspaper. Then Caroline asked to use our telephone and she telephoned to Mrs. Morton. I heard her—"

"*Mrs. Morton?*" Park had trouble speaking.

"Yes, Caroline had trouble getting through. If you're looking for Caroline you'll probably find her in the lanai dining room. That's where she went because Mrs. Morton was in the dining room eating lunch. . . . You *are* Mr. Mattison, aren't you?"

He had never seen eyes quite so shining with malice.

He still was not running but he was walking very rapidly through the lobby. By had been certain that Harry's newspaper would not be distributed before two o'clock. It was another blow to Park to know that Laina had seen one of the early copies. If he lost her, all the rest of his life he would think of her and remember her, her vivid lips, her direct eyes, and the dark red hair which he had refused to allow her to cut. *Oh, God! Oh, God!* Why had she gone to see Ellen?

He passed through the lobby, around by the arcade, and through the glass doors; he felt himself rock forward on his toes as he came to a dead stop. He saw Ellen and Harry Kimball at a far table, near the gray lava stone wall. The two of them were there, silhouetted against the white beach, the awning overhead shielding them from the warm rain. But Laina was not there.

He saw Ellen stand as she caught sight of him and he wanted to turn and go but he could not. He must ask her if she knew where Laina was. He must have lost more time than he had realized while searching for Laina for the dining room was almost empty. The chairs and tables seemed to spring up in front of him and stretch endlessly before him; he had not thought it would take so long to go from the arcade to the end of the dining room, Ellen and Harry watching him approach.

Harry spoke first. "Well, my boy?"

"Where's Caroline?" Park did not look at Ellen.

"I'm afraid Caroline's very angry with you, my boy. She was here a few minutes ago asking Mrs. Morton if all I printed in my little paper today was true. I have to think. . . . Now, where did Caroline say she was going?"

Park looked to his left and saw that Ellen had taken a few steps toward the arcade. She stopped between one of the tables and the retaining wall when he came to her. She was wearing a white dress and her crinkly hair looked as if it needed brushing. The banjo-eyes were swollen from lack of sleep but they were clear and very steady when she lifted up her face to him.

"Why did you tell him about me?" Park asked because it was still inconceivable to think of her going to Harry Kimball.

"I told my husband long ago about the marine captain I met in Washington," she said. "Yesterday afternoon I decided I had been wrong not to give him the captain's name."

She had misunderstood his question. But she had told Buddy long ago of meeting a captain one evening in Washington.

"Why did you tell Harry Kimball?"

She answered, "My husband said I must." Then she turned and walked rapidly toward the lobby.

Park remained there a moment longer before turning to ask Harry where Laina had gone. He heard the rain on the canvas over his head. When it rained, all the flowers smelled sweeter. It was the one thing Park had never considered Buddy and Ellen would do, tell each other everything. He had thought they were soft because they had everything but actually, he realized, they did not count what they had except each other. It had never crossed his mind that the two of them together could defeat him.

P ark became aware of someone chuckling behind him and he returned to Harry.

"Sit down. I was nearly through with lunch, anyway, when Caroline came charging in to ask Mrs. Morton such furious questions. If you care to stay for a cup of coffee we ought to have Buddy Morton here in another half-hour. He's promised me a statement as soon as he finishes the preliminaries of a stock transfer. But for your own safety, I wonder if you should delay? Shouldn't you think of departing from the island? I hear a mob of Flips is growing very ugly in the city. You know Pip flew off to the mainland in the big Tothic transport, don't you? I dare say that's not news to you. It was announced on both radio stations a half-hour ago. Yes, he's gone. *He* won't be back. You tried to do your best for him but I fear it wasn't quite good—"

"Harry—"

"My boy . . ." The little eyes were black as pitch and very old as they gazed up at Park. "No, you *must* give me a minute. I must compose my mind if you expect me to remember what Caroline said. . . . Mrs. Morton was very kind to her. She was very kind to me, too. I owe Mrs. Morton a debt of gratitude I never can fully repay for assisting me in my little campaign against Pip. Did Pip ever tell you how he once convinced Ruthie it was ridiculous of her to be seen so frequently in the company of a man of my grotesque size and Bohemian tendencies? Perhaps Pip has forgotten the incident. It was so long ago. His sister was very young then, not any older than Caroline would be at present—"

"Where's Caroline?"

Harry heaved himself up from the chair and said hastily, "The truth is, I can't tell you where she is. I don't believe, after all, she said. I presume she must have gone home to pack. But you must think of yourself now, my boy, not Caroline. If you remain too long on the island . . ."

Harry's rumble went fading away as Park turned on his heel; it was all in the past, irrevocably in the past. Park did not care what became of Harry Kimball any more. And he did not care that E. P. had gone. It was no surprise to learn E. P. had hauled tail, it was what you expected. All Park now thought of was finding Laina and sailing with her to Honolulu before a pack of Flips thought of piling into their cars and driving up Hibiscus Road.

After he started toward Hibiscus Road, at first he could not understand why it seemed so quiet. He heard the rain, the motor running, and now and then the soft booming rush of a car going by; but that was all. Presently he realized why it was so unnaturally quiet. All the loudspeaker towers were silent. It was uncanny. No voices came from the towers to tell you how happy everyone was to be living on the happy island. No old romantic Hawaiian music sprayed into the air. It was simply very very quiet this afternoon.

He had lost all account of time when his Buick came to the top of Hibiscus grade. He saw Laina's old Chevy in the drive and was almost sick from the sudden feeling of relief. At a shambling gait he ran from the Buick to the house. He flung open the door and called, "Hey, Caroline?" and received no answer. She was not in the front room.

He tried to open the bedroom door and found she had locked it. "Caroline!" he called urgently. She made no reply. He listened. He thought he heard her in there. He could not imagine what she might be doing. He was seized by a paroxysm of anxiety. He slammed his shoulder against the door; the third time he broke a middle panel. He thrust arm and hand through to turn the lock and came on into the bedroom.

He saw Laina seated at her dressing table silently and savagely hacking at her hair with a pair of nail scissors.

"Caroline, don't!"

He must have jerked her harder than he knew, for she tumbled backward in a heap between the bench and the bed. Before he could lift her, she jumped up and darted around him, the dark red hair flying. She shut the bathroom door, locking it before he could collect his senses. He called. She did not reply.

"Listen, Caroline. Please! I can explain—"

How could he explain? What could he say to her? He heard the water from the shower which she had turned on to drown the sound of his voice; he heard nothing more. He was shaking. It was difficult for him to breathe. He ripped open his collar and flung off his coat and went to the south window, thrusting it up, standing there for the rain to wash against his face.

He heard a rustling of cloth and looked around and saw the wet wind was blowing the dresses which Laina had neatly piled on the bed. He shut the window. In a daze he picked a frilly blouse from the floor and returned it to the pile on the bed. Her suitcase was open. She must have gathered her things to pack and get away and, in a sudden access of emotion, begun cutting her hair. He tried again. "Caroline," he called through the door. "Listen! I took your money last night because I didn't want you to leave me. I've still got it. . . ."

He heard only the dull rushing of water from the shower. He was terrified at what she might be doing to herself. He could imagine her lying on the bathroom floor or in the tub with her wrists and her throat slashed with one of his razor blades. He pounded on the door. He drew back to smash it down, heard the lock click, and she came into the bedroom.

He saw what she had done. Beyond her he could see a section of the white enamel basin with one of his single-edge razor blades there, great tufts of the silky hair on the edge of the basin and scattered over the tile floor. She passed by him without a word, her hair ragged and short. She began packing her clothes, with not a glance at him.

"Caroline. I won't stop you from going. I know enough to know I can't keep you by forcing you to stay. But I'll die if you leave me."

She was folding the green suit. She placed it in the suitcase. She had to select and choose because she did not have room in the single suitcase for all her clothes. He remembered how mute and sullen she had been that time when she thought he had betrayed her with the Tolliver woman. Eventually, she had listened to him, but nothing he could say now could persuade her to heed him again.

He couldn't bear to watch her shorn red head bend over the suitcase. He stepped into the front room to wait for her. He heard the rattling of the windows, becoming aware of the dark wet wind. He saw that the rain had become fierce, the air had a dark liquid redness, and he wondered dully why four or five automobiles had gathered there on Hibiscus Road before his house. He stiffened. Through the darkening afternoon light he saw the heads of men beyond the bushes and trees lining the road.

He went to the study to telephone the police but the telephone was dead. He tried to pull himself together to think. Through the study's back window he had a glimpse of the sea, now redly dark, the view of it almost obscured by the sheets of rain. A big transport would fly safely over weather of this sort, but Park had a passing thought for By and Millie Meaker sitting huddled in a small plane attempting to beat its way to safety through a dark blowing of wind and rain.

Then he thought of the men gathering out there in Hibiscus Road, silently waiting until it was dark enough for them to move in closer and closer. He pulled down the shades in the study and front room; as he took a final glance, he thought that among the shapes out there was one which was a little smaller. Perhaps it was Herby Subie, with his broken arm, waiting among the other jokers. Well, they had come across from the other side of the street at last.

He pulled down the blinds of the front windows in the bed-room. Laina had closed her suitcase; she had not noticed the jokers out there. She was incapable of noticing very much of anything. It hurt Park to see the agony in her face as she looked about the room as if he were not there. She was seeing it for the last time. Those jokers, he thought, would let her go. He wanted to get her out and to see that she departed safely. It was all he asked. He waited. He saw her touch the bed, smoothing it. She carefully closed the doors to the closets. She had always liked to have the bedroom neat before she left the house.

"Caroline—"

He spoke without meaning to speak. She was still mute. If only she would say one word to him. He had better get Doc's revolver in the foot-locker. He would make certain those jokers would pass her and the Chevy.

He saw her take the coat he had flung to the floor. As a sleep-walker might, she was going toward the closet to hang it up when a small round pasteboard box dropped from the breast pocket and fell open on the floor, a small golden airplane gleam-ing and sparkling between the two halves of the box. She stooped, picking up his gift.

Park felt his throat close. "It was for our trip to Hawaii. I bought it yesterday when I thought I'd have all the money we'd ever need in a week or so. I forgot to give it to you."

In a burst of passion, she threw his gift to the floor. She snatched her suitcase and was out of the bedroom. He caught her arm.

"Here's the money you gave me."

She turned. She dropped the suitcase. She hit him across his face with her hand.

He said steadily, "Take your money, Caroline."

She was crying. She ran back into the bedroom and knelt and took up the little golden airplane.

"Park, I broke its wing."

Park did not know what to say.

"Can you have it fixed?"

"Yes."

She placed it in the box and gave it to him. He stuck the box in his pocket and said, "You'd better wipe your eyes and take your money, Caroline."

"Oh, Park! I love you so damned much. I don't care what you are or what anybody says you are!"

She flung her arms around his neck. He held her tightly. He did not want to let her go, but it would be dark very soon and those jokers would not wait very much longer before trying to take him.

"Caroline," he said very gently. "They're out there—"

"Who's out there?" She was startled.

He told her who was out there, waiting until it became darker.

She said, "Park, I don't care whether they'll let me go away or not. I'm not going to drive off and leave you. Mr. Hinoni will let me take his boat. We can get down to the cove easy enough."

"I'd thought of the boat."

"You can't stay here. It's partly my fault about Herby Subie, too. I don't want him to kill you if he's out there or for you to try to kill him. I can sail the boat easily to Maui or even to Honolulu. I don't care where we go just so we get off this rotten island. Let's go quickly before it's too dark to go down the cliff."

"All right," he said after a pause. "But you'll go with me farther than Honolulu? You won't leave me?"

She shook her head. "No, I'll never go anywhere without you. But I get so goddamn mad at you sometimes. What are you doing now?"

He was getting Doc's revolver from his foot-locker.

"Park!"

"I won't use it," he promised. "Not unless those Flips make me."

As he was opening the back door of the kitchen, he realized Laina and he were now leaving the house for the last time. There was a moment, with the wind blowing into the house, stirring the shades, clattering the dishes, shutting a bedroom door, when it seemed to Park as if Laina and he might still be somewhere among those rooms at the front, living over all the days and nights they had lived here. This had been their first house. He wished Laina and he were not leaving like this. He wished he could take the time to get one of his cigars from the box in the study. He would have liked to leave with a big cigar in his mouth and his head up but it would be a gesture, a piece of false bravado. No. Shut the kitchen door. Get the hell going.

"Hurry," said Laina anxiously.

They climbed swiftly across the garden wall, water sluicing down upon them; and he followed Laina to the edge. At first it was not as difficult as he had imagined it would be. It was no more than going down a very steep pathway. Then he stumbled and he was falling, he thought; and Laina's voice came to him, "Park!"

He felt her hands grasp at his arm. He was lying face downward on the steep path. He inched himself to his feet, his teeth tightly clamped together. He didn't want Laina to guess that the fall seemed to detach something in his stomach. His weakness, he thought, would pass in a second or so. He could still breathe. His heart was merely pounding very hard. It was only a cramp catching at him again.

He had no clear memory of Laina leading him downward until they came to the ledge with nothing below it but a sheer drop of rock for thirty or thirty-five feet and the huge log by which you had to descend.

Laina asked, "You can do it, can't you?"

"Yes. Go on first."

He waited, watching her. The light was rapidly dimming. He heard the sound of the rain and from somewhere below him the distant thunder of the sea. The log was something like a ladder. All he had to do was squirm and ease himself upon it as Laina had done, holding the log with his arms, feeling down with his feet for the notches.

He heard Laina anxiously calling to him from below but he could not understand what she said. He was doing all right. His legs felt weak but as long as he was careful they would get him down and to the boat.

A stone hurled through the rain. Another dropped past his head and shoulders. Those jokers up there must have discovered that Laina and he were escaping. Well, there was still time if only he hurried a little faster. Now he was down to the second ledge. He saw Laina was below him, nearly to the base of the cliff. It was going to be all right. He could see the wharf from here and the boat tied to the wharf.

He saw Laina stop and point and he heard her thin scream. He looked up and he saw three or four of those jokers slashing away at the ropes holding the top of the log. He tried to steady himself on the steep descent, taking the revolver from his pocket. He aimed and fired. He fired twice. He saw the log slowly tilt outward on its base above him. Then he huddled flat against the rock. There was a noise of all the world splintering and crashing apart.

He had not been touched. He could still feel the blood roaring through his head. If you didn't worry about it and didn't let it get you down, you'd always be all right. All you had to do was to go on a little faster and a little farther until you found yourself deep in clover, the sugar plums dangling over your head.

He tried to sight downward. He saw the big log where it had fallen at an angle on the coral beach but at first he did not see Laina. Then he saw a small black blotch of darkness lying very still near the log and it took him several minutes more to get down to where Laina was.

He kneeled on the wet coral sand, taking her hands in his. He bent lower. She was trying to tell him something. He wanted to ask her not to speak, for her to do nothing, to hold herself while he picked her up and got her to a hospital. He felt her hands tighten with a terrible urgency.

"Oh, Park," she whispered. "I loved you so much. I so wanted us to get off this rotten island. Don't leave me to be alone when you go . . ."

She never finished.

When finally he stood it was too dark to see very much of the cliff or if any of those men might still be up there. He fired uselessly at the cliff. For a little time afterward he continued pulling the trigger of the empty revolver. He threw the revolver at the cliff. He heard the rain and the ceaseless washing of the waves. Suddenly, he lifted her in his arms and went staggering toward the wharf. He could not think very coherently but he was glad she had died quickly.

He brought her into the boat, laying her upon the wooden after-seat behind the engine hatch. He had the engine going within a couple of turns. He cast off, steadying himself because the waves, even within the protected cove, were running strong. Through the darkness he saw a giant shape come running down to the wharf. Old man Hinoni's voice called, "Where you go, Laina?"

Park did not call back because he did not know the answer to old man Hinoni's question. Where had Laina gone when she had promised never to go anywhere without Park?

As the boat moved farther out from the island the red darkness changed into purple, the rain falling heavily. There was a small light you turned on to sight the compass. But Park did not trouble to switch it on because even if he had a small light to see the compass he would not have known what course to set.